ALSO BY TESSA FONTAINE

The Electric Woman

The RED GROVE

TESSA FONTAINE

The
RED
GROVE

FARRAR, STRAUS AND GIROUX NEW YORK

Farrar, Straus and Giroux
120 Broadway, New York 10271

Printed in the United States of America
First edition, 2024

Hand-lettering on title page and half-title pages by Sara Wood.
Title-page art by YIK2007 / Shutterstock.com.

Library of Congress Cataloging-in-Publication Data
Names: Fontaine, Tessa, author.
Title: The red grove : a novel / Tessa Fontaine.
Description: First edition. | New York : Farrar, Straus and Giroux, 2024.
Identifiers: LCCN 2023050753 | ISBN 9780374605810 (hardcover)
Subjects: LCGFT: Novels.
Classification: LCC PS3606.O586 R43 2024 | DDC 813/.6—dc23/eng/20231106
LC record available at https://lccn.loc.gov/2023050753

Designed by Abby Kagan

Our books may be purchased in bulk for promotional, educational, or business use. Please
contact your local bookseller or the Macmillan Corporate and Premium Sales Department at
1-800-221-7945, extension 5442, or by email at MacmillanSpecialMarkets@macmillan.com.

www.fsgbooks.com
Follow us on social media at @fsgbooks

10 9 8 7 6 5 4 3 2 1

For baby Leela:
may you stay safe
and wild

And for imperfect mothers

The trees soon revealed startling secrets. I discovered that they are in a web of interdependence, linked by a system of underground channels, where they perceive and connect and relate with an ancient intricacy and wisdom that can no longer be denied . . . They pass their wisdom to their kin, generation after generation, sharing the knowledge of what helps and what harms.

—SUZANNE SIMARD, *Finding the Mother Tree*

The RED GROVE

The women asked: Who is safe?

And Tamsen Nightingale said: The women who shelter in this red grove are safe.

The women asked: How are they safe?

And Tamsen Nightingale said: In this red grove, no woman can be harmed. No violence may come upon her. No injury to her flesh from the flesh of another.

The women asked: Who is welcome?

And Tamsen Nightingale said: Those who can walk in darkness are welcome and those who affix to the deeply woven roots are free.

—*The Story of the Sisters*, Welcoming Incantation

1

June 18, 1997

THE TREES COULD FEEL IT COMING. Even the dead snags still standing on the forest floor, the decaying nurse logs sprouting redwood shoots, even they knew.

There had been nothing unusual about the man when he'd shown up half an hour earlier. Luce had already begun the preparations, which, by now, she could do while reading a book, chewing gum, and instructing her brother to hide his weird animal projects. She went through the motions: clicked off the lamps, lit a few candles, all the while listening.

It was midafternoon, stippled light filtered through the windows. There was never a full bright wash of sun inside because of the surrounding spires of redwoods, their tops two and three hundred feet in the air. When she was outside, Luce was careful not to break off saplings as she passed. Each of them might live to be three thousand years old, as long as no idiot human killed them.

Luce Shelley, Luce the goose, Luce, meaning light, with a preference for the dark. Olive-skinned, chestnut-haired, in her uniform of cutoff jean shorts and a T-shirt, this one gray-and-blue striped with the neckline stretched into a lopsided oval, but who cared, that was the whole point, to show how little she cared. Low-top purple Converse, which did the most to minimize her giant feet. Up her wrist, coils of friendship bracelets she'd made herself. Luce, preparing for the seeker.

And then, ah-ha, the old wooden steps groaned, the house signaling the man's arrival. She slid her book under an armchair, the glossy face of the man who kept severed heads as trophies pressed against the rug.

"Hello," she said, opening the front door. She wore a mask of solemnity that she'd never had to practice. "We're so glad you've made it to the Red Grove."

"Not as creepy as I thought it'd be here," the seeker said, gesturing vaguely back toward the road he'd taken. He was breathing hard, had gray wisps of hair combed over a bald patch and a face like half-kneaded bread dough. "My son swore this whole valley would be guarded by chicks with machine guns." When she didn't laugh, he stopped smiling.

She said, "There's no need."

He followed her inside, started to tell her his name, but she held up her hand to stop him. Not her place to know any of his particulars. Her mother didn't want even a sliver of doubt that something someone said in passing was used later on; seekers should come to her as fresh as a fiddlehead.

"Sit," Luce said. He was still breathing heavily, his mouth hanging open to show his plump tongue. "You okay?" she asked. He nodded, said he was fine, just out of shape, and thudded onto the futon. "It'll be a minute. She's preparing."

He was taking it all in, she knew, glancing around at the batiks and piles of stone cairns and dried grasses, the piano missing a few keys, the worn, overlapping oriental rugs. She'd been embarrassed about their house for a long time. When she was thirteen and fourteen, realizing that they had no matching dinner plates or co-

ordinated side tables, she had started ordering home furnishing catalogs to get a glimpse of life on the outside. The four of them in this
house did not match the families in those pictures, with oafish men
whose arms corralled their brood while eating popcorn on plush
leather sofas, who flashed their straight white teeth while they
laughed around the foosball table.

She was not embarrassed anymore. Sixteen years old, burning with
purpose.

From the kitchen Roo appeared—so small for eight, most people
thought he was five—and gave a low bow. So theatrical, like their
mom, a little much really. But they fell easily into their familiar roles.
Roo asked the man if he wanted tea, ginger to ground himself or
chamomile to elevate. Moose, the mutt—blond with orange speckled legs and a purple tongue that hung perpetually out the right side
of his mouth—strolled over to lean against the man's shins.

Down the hallway, the office door opened and shut, and then
there she was, floral kimono billowing behind her like dry grass in
the wind. Beautiful Gloria Shelley, their mother. Luce watched the
man take her in, lick his lips, pupils widening, typical, though he did
not stand up to go to her.

"I don't usually do this kind of thing," the seeker said, jiggling
one knee and sounding nervous as he blinked up at Gloria with a raw
hopefulness so many of the seekers radiated; no matter how bored
Luce grew of this routine—day after day, year after year—she had to
give her mother credit for offering that gift of hope.

Gloria bent her elbow, looking at him expectantly until he fumbled to standing. She hooked the man's elbow with her own and led
him into the office. Luce heard the lock catch. As if they didn't know
they weren't allowed inside.

It would be an hour or two with them in the office, nothing else
required of Luce. Roo trotted back into the kitchen, pulled maple
syrup from the fridge, and squirted a trail along the counter, to attract ants, he explained when Luce told him to cut it out. But quickly,

the office door clicked open, and Luce heard her mother's loud voice saying, "My most powerful tool."

Oh no, Luce thought, tearing out of the kitchen and down the hallway. She passed the open crack of the office door and hustled, freezing in the doorway of her aunt Gem's room. She was supposed to clean in here and hadn't. One last big breath of fresh hallway air, and then she plunged in. The dresser top and table were covered in prescription bottles, orange and translucent like goldfish, and half-empty jars of ointment, silicone feeding tubes snake-coiled in plastic, empty worms of catheter, a plate with crusted peanut butter, and scattered between it all, crumbled tissues with smears of yellowed, dried liquid and blood. The evidence of struggle killed any magic.

Quick quick quick, Luce thought, gathering trash, breathing through her mouth as she kept an ear toward her mother's office. A tapestry thrown over the dresser top, a spritz of lavender water for the smell, the room transformed into a portal.

She scanned to see what she missed, realizing she had not actually looked at Gem. Thin, dry lines around Gem's mouth like parentheses. Her dreamy, half-lidded eyes rested somewhere by her feet. Luce rubbed a crust of dried skin from the corner of Gem's mouth, this mouth that, she knew, had pre-chewed food and fed it to her when she was a baby, mama-birding you, she explained to Luce later, laughing. The face Luce couldn't look at longer than a few seconds before the stinging in her chest grew too sharp.

"She will help me find the answers you seek," Gloria said over her shoulder, striding into the room. She gestured at the bed like she was unveiling a prize. "My twin sister, Gem."

The seeker stared. They always did. Luce stepped back against the wall, willing herself invisible. "Sit," Gloria said, pointing to a chair beside Gem's bed. Bare summer branches peeked into the window frame behind Gem, poison oak clinging to the lattice up the side of the house. Gem's pinky twitched, but otherwise, she was still.

Gloria bent close to her sister's face, then made a series of clicks with her tongue against the roof of her mouth. Gem did nothing. Gloria made the sound again, clicking, stroking the side of her sister's face with the back of her hand. The gesture brought a little stab of jealousy to Luce's gut.

"I'd like you to concentrate on the reason you came to see me today," Gloria said to the seeker.

"What happened to her?" he said.

Gloria kept her face over her sister's. "In Delphi, in Ancient Greece, an oracle spoke for the god Apollo. People traveled hundreds of miles to ask her questions and seek her wisdom, wars were fought or peace was declared based on the few sentences she spoke. The oracle was always a woman. A direct channel to another world."

There were hidden dimensions, Luce knew. Outside, in the canopy of the redwood trees, an entire hidden world: dense mats of soil atop the branches; from the soil, fuzzy grass-green moss, whips of lichen, small sprouts of hemlock, huckleberry, a flowering rhododendron bush. Hanging forests of ferns. Salamanders who live their whole lives in the sky. Worlds that existed beyond what anyone could see.

Gloria brought her face low, right up against Gem's ear, and whispered something. She tilted her head toward Gem's mouth, listening. Luce held her breath. She wasn't usually allowed to stay in the room during the sessions, but Gloria must be distracted, thrown off by Luce's blunder. "You're here about your wife," Gloria said, not looking at the man. She didn't check for confirmation but, after a moment, said she was sorry his wife had experienced a difficult transition.

He wanted to know if she was still in any pain, and Gloria told him, quickly, that she was not. She felt, in fact, and wasn't this beautiful to think about, the kind of allover peace and warmth they'd felt together that winter day when they were newly married and went to the beach for sunset and lay back in their jackets, holding hands, and let the last wash of sun warm their skin. "She feels like that all the time now," Gloria explained. The man made a faint gasping sound, a sort of sob.

"She's worried about your health," Gloria said. Luce was standing back against the wall, and why was her mother starting out with that, why not be a little gentler. "She's funny, your wife, she's telling me—" but the man made the gasping sound again, and god, Gloria was giving him too much too fast. Luce would go get him a glass of water. But when she looked over at his face, she was surprised to see that he wasn't looking at Gem in bed. And he wasn't looking at Gloria either. Instead, he faced the window, sweating, his cheeks pinking, like that salmon Luce had once seen throw itself onto the bank of the creek that ran through the Red Grove. It had been part of the mass fighting upstream that year to lay eggs and then die, and Luce had been shocked by how gnarled the fish was, flaps of thin gray flesh peeling away, scales no longer shimmery but dull, milky-eyed, which was also what the man's eyes suddenly looked like.

"She's telling me the joke about the whale," Gloria said. Luce looked over at her mother, still bent low near her twin. Gloria had no idea what was happening.

"Okay, okay, so a whale walks into a bar," Gloria said, chuckling, but Luce cut her off, repeating Gloria's name low and urgently, pointing to the man.

"Oh shit," Gloria said. She took a few fast steps toward him, and Luce did the same. He'd staggered to his feet, was bent over the table of Gem's supplies, one arm grabbing at his neck while the other flailed for purchase, knocking empty pill bottles and boxes of tissues off the table. His arms went rigid, pushing something away, and then his legs buckled and he fell to the ground.

"Luce, call 911," Gloria said. Luce stood up fast, spun toward the door to run to the kitchen phone, but then froze. Gloria said, Go, go,

911 wasn't only for the police, it was for the paramedics too, Jesus, go. But Luce had never called that number before. Never needed to, but more importantly, knew she never should. He wasn't one of them. Was this a dire enough emergency? Did they know what was even happening with him really?

"Go," Gloria yelled, looking up at Luce. The man's head was in her lap, his eyes flashing wildly around. Roo's small head peeked into the doorway. Luce told him to get out, shooing him, but he darted into a corner of the room.

"Go, someone, now," Gloria said, trying to loosen the buttons on the man's shirt and then shouting, "And don't call Una."

In the kitchen, Luce's fingers froze over the numbers. Trembling. Take a breath, she told herself. You are fine. She heard her mother's voice down the hall asking the man if he could hear her, telling him to take some deep breaths. A wasp flew up and down the length of the cupboards in front of her, its elegant legs dangling. This is life, which is also always death, you've known that forever. Handle it.

"Una?" Luce said into the phone. "Come right away."

And then, once she'd explained what was happening and heard the rustling pages of Una's folk medicine handbook still, Una told her to call the paramedics.

It would not be fast. It was twenty-seven minutes to the closest hospital. Down the big hill, through the redwoods, along the single road that ran through the Red Grove, out of the valley and up over the next hills that closed their borders, then into the bigger town past that for the hospital. The wait for the ambulance was long.

Una was there in six minutes.

Gloria was cradling the man's head, murmuring for him to hold on. His breathing was fast, thick with strain. Roo was sucking his thumb in the corner, Luce pressed back against the wall, looking out to the hallway every few seconds, when the front door crashed open and Una came barreling into the room. She held still for a moment in the doorframe, surveying the scene, like a backlit angel in her white linen shift, a tangle of necklaces—silver amulets, turquoise, amber beads—clinking together from her hustle.

"You're shitting me," Gloria said, but Una moved swiftly, kneeling beside the man.

"He can't die here," Una said, sliding her lean fingers around his wrist to check the pulse. "Ambulance is on its way. Is he breathing?" She didn't wait for an answer, brought her face down to the man's to check for breath, a movement so closely parallel to what Luce's mother had been doing just minutes before with Gem, the warmth of shared inhales and exhales, and it was so strange, Luce thought, how much could be learned from pressing your face against another's.

Una turned to Roo. "You know 'Stayin' Alive'?" He nodded, obviously he did. "I need you to sing it, baby. Sing it loud. And Luce, you count." Gloria started to protest but Roo didn't hesitate. *"Ah, ha, ha, ha, stayin' alive, stayin' alive."*

"For the beat," Luce said to her mother, who'd started to tell them to be fucking serious. "It's the right rhythm for CPR." It was the only thing she remembered from their medical unit in school that year. She started to count.

"I'll breathe, you compress," Una said to Gloria, and Luce, still pressed against the wall, let a little air out of her lungs, grateful for the way Una took charge.

Una put her mouth over the man's, breathing into him, and when she took a break, Gloria started chest compressions. *"Ah, ha, ha, ha, stayin' alive, stayin' alive,"* Roo sang, fluttering his fingers during the chorus even though his little worried face seemed to know it was not appropriate. Ten chest pumps and then blow, Luce counted. It was hard to look at the man. The rest of him started looking like the salmon, too, gray in the face, eyes clouded. She could already imagine the flesh that would peel off his body. Floppy, reeking, enveloped by flies.

Under her breath Gloria said, "I was handling it." Luce wasn't sure if it was meant for her or Una.

"More hands are better than fewer," Una said, stroking the man's forehead with surprising tenderness given that she was touching an outsider, a man, but Luce tried to open her heart wider—he was a human too, he didn't need to suffer alone, he had done no wrong to them, to women, as far as they knew, but then again, statistically, it was very possible that he had—but he gasped again. Luce pressed herself further against the wall. Her fingers twitched, what should she be doing to help, what could she do? The wall pressed into her bare shoulder blades. Think. *"Ah, ha, ha, ha, stayin' alive, stayin' alive."* The room got cold. Luce was not helping. She chewed the inside of her cheek. Una and Gloria kept breathing, pumping. Roo, tired, stopped singing. He curled into a little ball in the corner. Scared, probably. They'd never had someone—well, what was this—have a medical emergency? Die? Sisters, she hoped not, but that's what it seemed like was happening. She should comfort Roo, reassure him. This was a traumatic thing for a little kid to witness. She bit her nail, leaning back against the wall in the shadow, but didn't go to him.

Instead she slipped across the hall into her bedroom and ripped off a scrap of paper. On her bedside table was eyeliner. She would help. Back in Gem's room, her mother compressed and Una breathed and her brother started up his song again from the floor, and they waited for outsiders to come barreling in, for the fact that they had to be called at all to ripple out however it would.

Luce knelt nearer to Una when the sirens came close. She needed the note to get to his family. The front door slammed open, and everyone looked up, waiting to be saved. Heavy shoes stomping through the house, her mother's voice calling the outsiders right to them, all focus on this next thing. Luce slipped the note into his pocket without anyone seeing.

Just below them, beneath the old wooden floorboards and dirt and crumbs and droppings and webs and hairs and spit and blood, under the foundation, in the dirt alongside the worms were the roots of redwood trees reaching as wide as the trees were tall, passing sugars and water back and forth, feeding the weak, holding the tallest of them upright, flashing memories to one another along the mycorrhizal network of a time before this time, when something had been set in motion. Gathering what was needed because it seemed it was beginning again.

2

June 21, 1997

THERE WERE NINE NEWCOMERS following Luce down the dirt path. Behind them, Heartwood Community Center's deck flickered with lantern glow, the twilight insects bombing toward the light. The women had half a mile to go along the path that wound through the redwoods. Dusk fading to black. Luce reminded herself to walk slowly, letting the newcomers' eyes adjust to the darkness, their hearts to the increased pulse that walking at night brought for most.

Is he gonna die, Roo had asked that first night and then the next morning, and over again. They didn't know, Luce said. He better not, their neighbor Juan had said when he'd stopped by for the story once the ambulance had gone. The last thing you need is another ghost in here. And Una had called just after Juan left, checking to see whether they'd heard how he was doing. Let's just hope he lives, she told Roo when he picked up, then Gloria when she took over, then Luce when she wanted to say hello. Let's hope he lives, or we might get some unwanted attention out here, she'd said. Cops always had to investigate a death. Luce shuddered, said, fuck the police. And Una said, exactly.

But three days had passed and the man was holding on, and there were so many other lives that needed tending. Luce let her fingertips graze the thick, soft redwood bark, tannic acid rendering it fire-resistant, insect repellent, and she said this to the woman directly behind her, "Amazing, right?" This redwood grove was a mile long, but there were others in clusters along the valley, which was four miles long and one mile wide, and the redwoods rose up on the slopes of the hills and then eventually, far enough up, grew less dense and gave way to the dry, dead-grass hills, the valley's own crown of gold. The redwoods kept the valley air damp, crisp, and chilly at night, but above on the hills, the air was dry and the sun beat down so strong it cracked open the earth in small fissures, like broken blood vessels. Five miles of open, undeveloped space on all sides, a border of wildness.

Luce let her mind visit the private suspicion that had been growing the last three days—maybe the man's heart gave out on purpose. Maybe the Red Grove was doing its wild, unknowable work, keeping them safe. She'd never say that to anyone, of course; she was not glad that he suffered, but, absently rolling a piece of dried moss between her fingers, she wondered. She wondered, and then imagined the man's family unfolding her note, their eyes misty with gratitude that he'd been enveloped by their care.

But what if he does die? Roo had asked that morning, not eating his oats, and worn out by this question, Gloria and Luce had said, in unison, He won't.

"See that?" Luce said to the newcomer behind her, trying again. She pointed to a massive dark opening in the tree, spanning a third of its circumference. "It's a wound. Redwoods get them from fires, mostly. But they don't kill the tree, just create these giant holes in the base. The tree survives. It can have a huge wound, big enough to climb around inside, and be fine."

"Makes some creepy hiding places," the newcomer said with a shiver, stepping over a branch. Luce knew her a little bit—Sam; she'd arrived in the Red Grove for the last few days of school, but Luce hadn't seen her much since then. Sam was short, uneven in her gait, guarded. "Like, anyone could be hiding in there."

Of course she was still afraid. Luce dug her fingernails into her palms; she could do better. "I used the wounds all the time in hide-and-seek when I was a kid," Luce said, trying to keep her voice gentle. "They were our playground. Listen." She cocked her ear toward the sky. There were the sounds of the animals going home as twilight pinched closed, and the nighttime hunters winging toward prey. Crickets chirping beneath everything. "No bad guys out here."

They didn't use to have a ritual. The women were allowed to take their time and adapt to the Red Grove slowly, gently. But Una had changed that. It was detrimental for newcomers to dwell in this period of adjustment riddled with fear, she'd said. What they needed was a clear demarcation. Before the Red Grove, your life was one way. After, something else entirely. Four times a year, the solstices and equinoxes, if a woman had arrived within the three previous months, she would take part in the ritual.

They walked on, a small animal rustling the ferns nearby. "Putting in a pool?" a woman behind Luce asked, pointing to a big hole at the edge of a grove.

"Used to be a Japanese peace garden here, but it got overrun with bamboo," Luce said. She scanned for rattlesnakes before crouching under a fallen trunk, the earth soft beneath her feet. "It's invasive, had to be dug out wide and deep to clear the margins." They were sprouting new redwood saplings to plant here instead, Luce explained. You had to wait for them to become a foot high before they could go in the ground. "Something as strong and giant as a redwood, and it takes a whole year before it can survive on its own," Luce said, trying to impart some wisdom about vulnerability and strength, but she turned and saw that nobody was listening. They were in the extra dark of the forest canopy, which people said was instinctually frightening, but Luce always pushed back—babies aren't afraid of the dark. Fear of the dark is learned.

They were mostly quiet as they walked, a few women whispering to one another in the back of the line, the occasional thud of someone tripping over a root. Luce stopped one last time, a fern brushing her bare leg, and gathered the group before the final bend in the path. There was a faraway scream. Luce said "Barn owl" as quickly as she could, but not before a few women had reached out for one another. And one of the women, her arms crossed over her chest, was shivering even though it wasn't cold.

"You okay?" Luce asked, keeping her voice low.

The woman nodded vigorously. Faker, Luce thought. She reached out her hand to the woman's arm. "What if Ron can find me here?" the woman said, and at that a few of the other women put their hands on her. Luce didn't recognize this woman. Likely she had just arrived.

"We're almost there," Luce said. They would feel better after what came next. "Remind yourself of what you know about being here."

The woman sniffed, wiped her nose. "*In this red grove, no woman can be harmed.*"

"Exactly," Luce said, squeezing her hand.

They rounded the last bend, coming into an opening in the trees where the moon cast its last slashes of light before the needles become too thick. There, a dozen Red Grove women standing in a semicircle faced the newcomers. Una in the center. Lantern light in golden pools on their faces, watching the newcomers with calm, with knowingness. With serene we-are-not-fucking-around-ness. A yellow-breasted chat cackled, but its gleaming eyes, watching the women from somewhere deep in the forest, shone unseen.

Luce arranged the newcomers into the other half of the circle, her mind growing sharper, focused. Standing in the center of the women, scanning the newcomers, she thought, yes, they are all looking at me, there is no other moment where I want to be the focal point of all these eyes except for right here, these women and the brown salamanders and red-bellied newts under the wet needles and bark, wood warblers on the branches above. She could swallow any shyness because she told herself this crystalline truth: you are helping the women save themselves. She was the guide through the darkness.

Luce asked for a volunteer to go first, and Sam said she would, she wanted it over with. Sam's hand was clammy as Luce squeezed it, pulling her into the center of the circle and angling her body toward the dark forest. Luce tried to still the fingers of her other hand drumming against her leg, excitement lifting in her like summer dust. Gramms caught her eye and winked, good old Gramms, whose sweatshirt bore three wolves howling up to a cloudy moon, and who was, she could smell, chewing watermelon gum.

Luce steadied her nerves and began speaking, the other women of the Red Grove joining her:

"*The women asked: Who is safe?*

"*And Tamsen Nightingale said: The women who shelter in this red grove are safe.*"

Goose bumps on Luce's arms, the back of her neck.

"*The women asked: How are they safe?*

"*And Tamsen Nightingale said: In this red grove, no woman can be harmed. No violence may come upon her. No injury to her flesh from the flesh of another.*

"*The women asked: Who is welcome?*

"*And Tamsen Nightingale said: Those who can walk in darkness are welcome and those who affix to the deeply woven roots are free.*"

Luce spoke loud enough for all the newcomers to hear: ahead of them was one mile of pitch-black, dense, old-growth redwood forest. The women would walk into the dark forest one by one and keep walking until they saw a candle burning on the other side. They would be completely alone. It is their chance to walk through the darkness and let go of fear.

Sam didn't move. Her arms quivered against her stilled body. Luce knew the cause of this stillness. All her years living in the outside world had taught her that going out in the dark by herself was the exact kind of thing she was never supposed to do, and now, one month living in the Red Grove, and it's exactly what she must do, so yes, Luce understood how profoundly difficult this was. Gently, she placed her arm around Sam's shoulders and squeezed. She whispered, "You will be fine. I promise." Sam was blinking fast, tears building.

"We're with you," said the women in the circle. "We will see you on the other side."

"What if I can't do it?" Sam asked, looking panicked. She wasn't the first to ask. "Will you kick me out?"

"No," Luce assured her. "You will simply try again. You are here, and you may remain as long as you wish. And also—" Luce tilted her chin to look Sam right in the eye, steadying her voice as a reminder that kidnapping lunatics weren't here, couldn't be. "You will make it," she said.

Sam took a step forward. One step and then another, into the dark, where even the moonlight didn't seep past the thickness of branches overhead, trees towering three hundred feet high, tallest in the world. There was just the dark below.

Luce would hold the candle at the other side, she told them, looking each in the eyes before she left. The call of a spotted owl far away. A giant fallen branch, under which she'd once seen a nest of writhing garter snakes, the mama's jaw wide, with a mouse halfway down her throat. The rest of the newcomers stayed with the Red Grove women—hugged for reassurance, murmured to, hyped up, whatever they needed—until they too were sent out, one by one, into the dark.

As soon as Luce rounded the bend in the path, she stepped off into the trees. She slid between the shadows where no moonlight broke through, silent. This was where she became all animal. Her senses were taut, tuned to the frequency of the forest. Her quiet foot stepped on layers of forest debris, a faint waft of musk. Sight reduced, she could hear more, frog croak and the distant echo of one of the newcomers' loud voices; she smelled sharper, tasted the night air. Because Sam was not accustomed to the darkness, she was noisy. Luce stepped quickly, quietly toward her, palms pressing against the soft red bark of the trees as she pushed past them, this giant and now this, past this wound and toward the sound, with nothing to slow her down. She was powerful in her invisibility. She kept moving toward the sound of the newcomer, feeling her muscles flex and contract, trusting her haunches, smelling the damp bark and decaying logs and waft of bay leaves, the trace of skunk or sweat, the damp slime of witch's butter or banana slug—all her senses wildly awake. As guide, she must stay close, a helpful ghost should the newcomer twist an ankle or step on a snake, but still far enough, silent enough, that the newcomer never has any idea she is there.

She cannot see the fog, but feels it, wet and thick, on the back of her neck. She is going deeper, feels a gust of air from a bat swooping low, the yellow flash of eyes close to the ground. Beneath her feet, there are tender green shoots of redwood sorrel and ferns and thick layers of all the dead things that have come before, and she thinks, power coursing through her, I have never been this strong. The women are scared now, but they will not be forever. I will help them feel this strong.

Sam stumbled through. Luce heard her swear a few times, steady herself against a tree. But Luce didn't go to her. This is the journey. To make it through the darkness, to trust it. To let all that Sam has been clenching to keep herself safe finally unclench. That's the work. That's freedom.

Once Sam was close enough to the far edge of the grove, Luce gave her a wide berth and hustled around to the forest's break, lighting the candle. Sam stepped out, cheeks flushed but eyes clear.

"You okay?" Luce said. Sam was breathing hard, wiping her forehead with the back of her arm. "You did it. The darkness is yours."

Sam showed no pleasure. Blinked in the candlelight, looked back to the forest. "Well, damn," she said, shivering, pulling a stick from her hair. "I guess I survived."

The women can do anything. They do not need to be afraid ever again.

3

June 21, 1997

THE WHOLE OF THE RED GROVE was on Heartwood's back deck to welcome them. Una stood up on a bench, clapping her hands way up above her head. She caught Luce's eye, and without even meaning to, like squinting her eyes in bright sun, Luce smiled. She saw other people do the same to Una all the time, delight in the intensity with which she looked at them, as if they were the night-blooming cereus flower, unfurling once a year, rare and majestic. All around them, in the low grasses of the clearing and the forest beyond, the crickets joined together in song, and then so did the hands of all the good people of the Red Grove, nearly two hundred of them, clapping and whooping for the women as they emerged from the darkness back into the light.

As the applause thinned, chattering voices quieted and the community turned to Una, her white dress aglow in the candlelight. She slid on her moon mask—white and round, papier-mâché, black holes for eyes and a mouth. Everyone followed.

"To those of you who've just found your way through the darkness, my dears: welcome to freedom." Cheers rose up again, Luce clapping and hooting and grinning beneath her mask. Una continued: "We gather each solstice and equinox, days that mark the shifting between darkness and light, to be reminded of the balance that allows for our lives here. Together we will bear witness to the reenactment of horror that led to the creation of our sanctuary."

Luce glanced around, checking to make sure her mom had come, but she couldn't find her. Great. If only Gem could be here, of course she would be. Luce squinted her into ghost form sometimes, imagining for a split second that a tree's blur was Gem at the edge of the crowd, translucent, beaming.

Her eyes landed on a cluster of her friends, leaning close to one another and whispering, Aya touching Tangerine's hair. They were so easy with themselves, with one another, and a little ache made Luce long to be there, between them, but she tamped it out. They hadn't even glanced over at her. She brought her attention back to Una, who was still talking.

"It is from nature that we model our reenactments, the way our animal friends experience trauma from start to finish, allowing them to discharge the fright. To regain a balance of light and dark. We follow their lead so that the darkness may no longer infect or inhabit us." Though it was a solemn moment, Luce knew it was coming: *yip-yips* and ululation from some of the old-timers among the crowd who would not pass up any moment to celebrate the miracle of their lives here. Una, ever graceful, acknowledged them with a nod, twisting a bead on her necklace, and completed her part. "And so, let us be reminded. Friends, the story of Tamsen Nightingale," she said, stepping aside. Luce steadied her nerves and guided the six children wearing their small moon masks up to the front, a few *awwws* from the crowd, one *woop*, and all the little bodies, none taller than Luce's shoulders, faced the community.

Luce stepped up to Una's place on the bench, cleared her throat, and began. "Three sisters once married three brothers and began the journey to California to claim their fortune in gold." The children began marching back and forth in front of her. People knew the story, its cadence, its dramatic rise. They settled in for it, adjusting their masks and shifting their weight to get a good view of the children, and they nodded in the right places, shook their head in disappointment at others. It was a story they knew well, of the perilous journey through the mountains and the wicked winter storm that trapped them all.

"Amidst the blizzard, the brothers made a decision—they would help one another survive no matter what it took, as their lives were more valuable than those of their wives." In tandem, the boys walked around the girls, who had fallen to the ground, and began to bob their moon faces up and down. Luce continued, simply, "The husbands began to eat their wives."

But, the story went on, one of the sisters—Tamsen—escaped. At that, one of the little girls, Rosa, a coiled spring, popped up from the ground and began running wild circles around the brothers, creating larger arcs until she was dodging in and out of the trees. "Tamsen fled, walking for days without knowing where she was going and finally, exhausted, collapsed right here in the Red Grove." The two girls who'd played the eaten sisters stood up tall, reached their arms into the air, and swayed gently. One of the girls looked back at Luce with panic, forgetting whether this was right, but Luce nodded her on. This was a new addition; when Luce had done the performance as a kid, once you were eaten, you were gone.

"Tamsen Nightingale feared that the men would try to finish her off." Rosa crouched between the two other girls, whose tree-branch arms swayed. "But something special was happening in this valley of the Red Grove. And one day, one of the brothers found her." Rosa was seated beneath a tree, pretend-stitching something on her lap, when a boy ran at her, fast and mean. Rosa shielded her face with her hands, but, like a mime in a box, the boy seemed to be hitting the invisible edge of something. "He was unable to do her harm," Luce said. He kicked and hit again and again, but could not reach her. Rosa, playing Tamsen, stood up slowly to face him. He tried and tried, but could not get to her. Finally, standing tall, she waved good-bye to him, and like a seed in a gust of wind, he spun away.

"Here, in the Red Grove, she built a sanctuary for other women, understanding that the hills, the mountain lions, the golden grasses, and the giant red groves would keep them safe." Rosa extended her arms to all the other children, who clasped their hands together, forming a circle. "And they lived peacefully ever after," Luce said. The kids spread out in a line, their moon masks glowing in the flickering light, little stars, tousled hair, and skinned knees. They looked at Luce, who mouthed *one, two, three*, and then they all took a bow.

Heartwood's railing held small candles in paper bags. Looked nicer than in the sunlight, Luce thought, weaving through the crowd, where you could see the black widows nesting between the beams, dark, wet rings of mold, and layers of dirt in the grooves between boards. Luce liked the grime, though, a reminder of how old and important this space was, a gathering place for the people of the Red Grove for almost a century, she loved to explain as she showed them the newer arms snaking off in all directions—a few bedrooms used as transitional housing before newcomers were oriented and placed else-where in the Red Grove, a meditation nook, a community kitchen, a makeshift sauna, a library, and the connected trailers that made up the school. The throbbing heart of the community, she'd say, where you could always find a pot of soup on the stove and a listening ear to walk with through the woods, a pack of diapers, a ziplock bag of mini-toiletries, a set of sheets or rain boots or a frying pan, a case of dented cans of pinto beans, a Tibetan prayer flag, a crucifix, a half-full bottle of lube, one of Gramms's red knitted beanies, of which she made so many that in the winter, from above, a gathering in the Red Grove would look like a bowl of cranberries.

A few people were congratulating Luce as she wove through the crowd—this was only her third time leading the reenactment on her own—when a voice called her from behind. She turned, and there was Boog, breathing heavy, her white-blond hair frizzing out of its bun. "You're getting better every time, Goose," she said, her Alabama upbringing still a twang behind her words. Boog had made the news when she was eleven for punching a shark between the eyes; the shark had flung itself aboard her family's boat—that was the story Luce introduced her with every time, because how could you not? "I think you just about could take over here one day, don't you?"

Luce's face went red. "No. I could never do all that Una does."

"Beg to differ, cupcake."

Without realizing it, Luce straightened her spine. "I dunno," she said, feeling the tingle that would run up her arms and legs when she let herself think about this exact future, all that would come and all that had happened, and she wanted to ask Boog a question about the early days—she'd been here a long time, was an encyclopedia of Red Grove history, as mean as a cornered possum, she liked to tell people, though Luce had never seen that side—but Boog spoke again.

"I think you should know—a young man, not anyone I recognize, knocked on my door yesterday. He was asking about your family. I saw him knocking on other doors, too. He wanted to know where you live."

A shiver ran up the back of Luce's neck. There were no gates around the Red Grove, and they occasionally had an unknowing outsider come to their doors to try to sell them life insurance or Mormonism, but their distance from other towns made it rare. And it wouldn't be a seeker; Gloria always told them what they needed to know to find their house.

"I couldn't find your mom to tell her. So pass the word along. And keep your ear out."

Luce nodded, wandering into the woods, but something was off: first the seeker's heart collapsing, and now another man looking for them—never anything like this before, and then two strange things in a row. Wind shivered the trees. Things could build so easily: weather over the Pacific—eight miles away as the crow flies, but a forty-minute twisty drive—growing until it was right here, on top of them. Or an outsider wanting to know about them, and then what?

She'd often wondered what would happen if someone like the Sunday Slasher came into the Red Grove. Out there, all you had to do was climb into a woman's window at night or take a rock to her head while she was on a jog, and boom, dead meat. The going theory was that each person unknowingly interacted with five serial killers in their lifetime. Five! They were everywhere.

But here? She'd played out so many scenarios. Would he raise his arm to strike a blow and be physically unable? Or was it more like a force field on the women's bodies that acted like armor, repelling his harm like rain sliding off a duck's feathers? How did it work? As a kid, new to the Red Grove, Luce had insisted on the other kids testing it out on her. Hit me, she said, I dare you. They wouldn't, they didn't, it wasn't the thing they did here, the kids said. Punch me, you have to, she said, unwilling to be the bearer of violence but desperate to receive it, to see if she could. Bet you can't make my eye purple, she taunted. Until she finally met a kid who would. Marty Kahn. Chipmunk cheeks and allergies that kept his nose running; he'd do it 'cause he liked her, she knew. So, after school, they slid into a nearby grove, ducking into the open center in a circle of trees where the mother tree had died—fairy ring, it was called, which she loved—as a privacy shield. Do it, Luce said. Marty smiled, licked the snot from his upper lip, but didn't move. Hit me, Luce said, louder. He raised his hands. Come on, quick, Luce said, please. She needed to feel it— either the pain or the impossibility of it. He stood with arms raised, stilled. I can't, he said. Like you *can't* can't, she'd asked, or like you won't? I don't know, he said, I just can't. If you do it, I'll kiss you, she said, and that had done it, that had been enough—he'd flung one arm out in a kind of loose punch, but it did not, in fact, hit her. He missed.

Or it missed. Was forced to miss. Luce was astonished. But there wasn't time to try again, because an adult was stepping into the circle of trees.

I'd wondered what you two were doing, Una said. It's okay, Marty, she said, and Luce could see that he was holding his arms tight around himself, rocking, more upset than she'd ever seen him, and though she knew this could be deep trouble, she did not feel ashamed. Una looked at her. It's a natural curiosity, Luce, she said. And what did you learn? Luce twisted her toe in the dirt. She wasn't sure what she'd learned, she needed more time. Una tried again: Was Marty able to hurt you? Well, no, Luce said, and wanted to say more, but Una carried on. That's right, Una said. He did not hurt you. He cannot hurt you. Marty, you understand how awful and unforgivable that impulse to hit is, don't you? He had tears streaming down his face, still clenching his stomach. Good boy. Go away. She turned all her attention to Luce. I am going on a night walk tonight, Luce, in the darkness—would you come with me? Oh boy, would she. And she'd gone, her first walk through the night, and had begun to learn that invisibility could be power.

How did it work? She'd heard others ask it too—how was it possible? It works, Una had said, in the same way our earth spins slowly on its axis without careening off into space, and a migratory bird flies to the same spot each winter, halfway around the world. With the unknowable forces of Mother Earth.

Luce had once heard one of the newcomers, a science teacher, say that we know why the earth spins on its axis, inertia for one, and—but Una had cut her off. You're right, she'd told the woman, we know *some* of the pieces to the puzzle, a few. But there is still so much that is unknown, and unknowable. To claim full understanding would be hubris, don't you think?

And so Luce didn't know, exactly, and to probe the question would suggest doubt she did not feel. Instead she imagined a killer entering the Red Grove, sneaking up on a woman slumbering out under the stars, bringing his knife down upon her chest, and just before it hits, the metal blade shattering into ten thousand slivers. She'd recounted this fantasy to her mom one day, overcome with excitement as she imagined the look on his face when he realized he was impotent, and Gloria had snapped at Luce: This is so creepy, you have got to let it go.

It's real-life stuff, Luce had said, and would say to anyone who asked her how she knew so much about the worst of the violence out there. She had an obligation to know the truth, which does not discriminate between easy and difficult facts.

Lives change in an instant. Are completely destroyed. Her mother, of all people, should understand that. Luce wasn't choosing this reality, she was just paying attention.

And it was because she was paying attention that she felt such devotion to the Red Grove, to the way Una had told her its histories. The people of the Red Grove came and went, some seeking refuge only for a short while, months, a few years, while others decided to stay forever. The community had grown by word of mouth, women passing information on to cousins who told them of a friend in need, midwives who were called to deliver Red Grove babies, then mentioning the place to other women when it seemed there was a need. A number of newspapers had written about the Red Grove over the years, including a slanderous article written by an undercover reporter in 1977 who'd posed as a woman seeking asylum and then described them as a lesbian cult, blaming them for America's skyrocketing divorce rates. There was often speculation about whether they were a coven of witches. Because the women themselves wouldn't pose for photographs by outsiders, the stories included pictures of someone's old woven camp chair left outside their trailer, strings and metal bones overrun by wildflowers, and once of a long, smoothed stick lying in the dirt, which the reporter speculated was some kind of wand. MODERN DAY WITCHES, the story said again, and nobody in the Red Grove reached out to correct the record.

There were tenuous connections to women's shelters that were spread around Northern California, but the Red Grove preferred to take in those who would stay. It wasn't temporary respite before people flung themselves back into the fanged world. The Red Grove was a way of life that required communal acceptance and sacrifice. Habitation required participation; as an unincorporated town, they had to maintain many of their own roads, and though there were technically lower taxes, the agreement was that a small tithe was given to the community. Plenty of folks worked jobs in the neighboring cities, a few arrived with money, and so had some to share, though it was always a mystery to Luce how there was enough to cover so much of what was freely given, food and shelter to those who needed it, a small stipend to help new arrivals get on their feet.

When Una moved here, she'd explained to Luce a while back, the community was smaller, run communally by a few women who were already old and looking for fresh energy. They'd cautioned her against the pitfalls of their shared governance—nobody could agree, so nothing could ever really get done—and suggested instead that Una, with her charisma and wisdom, return to the foundational design and keep this sacred space protected through singular leadership, as Tamsen Nightingale had done.

And so Una did. In those days, there were thirty-five or forty women living there, some with children, others without, but there was plenty of space for more. And wasn't that Una's role, her responsibility, to allow as many people to flourish here as possible? She'd been thinking about this the night she met a man, gentle and thoughtful and all for women's liberation, he said, and she knew then what she needed to do. She would allow men—some men, carefully vetted—into the community as well and, in doing so, expand the boundaries of who could reap the bounty of their community. The men weren't protected, but they were harmless here, couldn't hurt a woman even if somehow, Tamsen forbid, they tried.

And men came. They were choosing to live somewhere outside

the pervasive chest-pounding company of other men they'd been around most of their lives, and the world created by and for those men. It wasn't a woman's world out there, everyone knew that, but it also wasn't a man's world if you were a certain kind of man, soft or small or maybe didn't think of yourself as a man at all, or one of a million other things that made a man's world not yours. They were vetted; female leadership wasn't for everyone. But there were men who had been harmed themselves or were committed to collaboration or would happily hand over whatever was needed to live among so many women. Peace was most sacred.

This was very unpopular with the older generation. Una knew it would be. Some of the old guard moved out of the community altogether, one tried to stage an intervention, but it became clear pretty quickly that Una's hunch had been right. More people heard about the community, more people moved there, some women with female partners, some male, most without partners at all, and even a few men on their own, and with the new burst of energy and life and, yes, resources in the community, Una'd set out what she'd intended to do: share this gift as wide as the land would allow. And no wider. Their population was restricted by the boundaries of the community and the edict to preserve the groves of redwood forest and open space in which they lived. The population reached 170ish by the late 1980s. Things got to be how Una liked them.

Back on Heartwood's deck, shrieks of laughter punched through the music, people dancing or gathered in clusters or clasping beloveds, a couple Luce couldn't quite identify holding hands as they disappeared into the trees together. If all the world's experiences were lined up from most horrific to the sublime, this would be shoulder to shoulder with the very best things life could invent.

The voices of little kids carried from the creek, past the trees. She followed the sound, as she liked to keep an ear out to know what the kids talked about, an idea from Una she was happy to oblige since yes, she was exceptionally good at remaining unseen in the dark. Also, though she'd never tell him, she kept an ear on Roo from time to time, making sure he wasn't getting picked on because he was so small.

"Did you know Tamsen Nightingale was a witch?" It was Roo, his voice echoing over the banks.

"Duh," another kid said. The littler kids had obstacle courses set up out there, and bike jumps and fairy traps and hiding places in the wounds of redwood trees. She knew from the way their voices carried that they were tucked in under the bank of the creek, where water had hollowed away dirt, and tree branches had kept the surface strong, and she stepped farther into the woods, toward them.

"And that in the beginning there were no boys allowed here at all? So if a boy came here by accident, he would get turned into a girl." Another kid's voice then, hard to tell how many were down there.

"I wish I would get turned into a girl. Then I would wear beautiful dresses." That one was Roo.

"You already do wear beautiful dresses."

"I know. But I'd wear even more."

"I heard that Tamsen Nightingale was an outlaw and collected gold and jewels and bought up all this land before she cast a spell on it." The small voices layered on top of one another. Luce loved hearing what the kids were wondering about, what mythologies they created.

"There's not a spell cast on it, idiot."

"It's the mountain lions. They guard us."

"It's the trees that make it magic."

"Magic isn't real, my mom said."

"Well then, if you're so smart, how does it work?"

"Duh, you don't know?"

"Nobody knows."

Luce had also crouched in this creek with friends and speculated about the Red Grove, about Tamsen Nightingale. It had not been a quick adjustment from the apartment she'd lived in before they came, where she wasn't allowed to be alone at all, never, especially not outside, especially especially not in the dark. But once she was rooted here, it was like opening her eyes underwater for the first time.

"Roo," she heard a kid say, "why did your mom kill a man?"

Luce held her breath.

Roo's tiny voice rose an octave. He said the man wasn't dead, and they should just shut up.

"My dad said that if he dies, we're gonna have a big old problem," another kid said. "Someone came to my house, looking for you, and he was so mad because—"

Another voice chimed in, but Luce lurched out from where she was hiding and called for Roo to come, said she needed his help cleaning up at Heartwood right away. "A little hustle please, let's go." She would not let him be dragged into the muck of worry. She found, as they walked back through the trees, that for the first time since she could remember, she was watching for a stranger.

4

June 22, 1997

THEY WERE EATING DINNER when Gloria got the call. Black bean tacos. Roo recounting his newt's dream from the night before to Gem. Luce, Gloria, and Roo surrounded her, their plates on the small table in Gem's room, Moose lying beneath the table, patiently waiting for a scrap to fall. They liked to keep Gem company, so they did whatever they could in her room. Most people in her state couldn't be left alone at all, but Gem was always fine, like the fakirs Gloria had read about who existed for years without food or water, or buried in a tomb underground. Gem had a feeding tube, and they bathed her in love, but something else seemed to be the real source of her nourishment. Luce thought it was the Red Grove.

Others fed Gem love too. Mei came Thursdays to play the harp. Sharon and Dee showed up once a month to trim her hair, massage floral oils into her legs and arms. Bob performed Reiki. Juan came by sporadically to read aloud to her, mostly deep space stuff and the occasional biography—Tina Turner's most recently. Of all the things

Gloria questioned about the Red Grove, there was no getting around the generosity of this network.

And then the kitchen phone rang. It was a seeker Gloria regularly helped who worked as a nurse at the closest hospital, and she'd promised to keep Gloria informed. So here it was. The man was dead. Gloria wondered, for a moment, whether she could keep his death a secret from her kids and the community. She didn't want to add any fuel to the frenzy. She hated the reenactments. Retelling the stories of violence against women normalizes it, even glorifies it, she argued, or tried to argue, but nobody wanted to hear it. At the reenactment the night before, she'd tucked far into the back, present because she'd known that Luce was nervous, but determined not to participate.

But no—too many people already knew about the seeker. There could be no silencing of the news. So what Gloria needed was a cigarette and a fuck, in that order, and not to be reprimanded once they heard he was dead, for bringing this man to the Red Grove in the first place.

As Gloria told the kids, Roo climbed off his chair and knelt down on the rug, clasping his hands together. Where had he learned this? Roo said he thought they should have a funeral for the man, that they should bury him in their yard, that he was feeling very sad because he was a nice man, wasn't he, hadn't he been especially nice?

"Not especially," Gloria said, but seeing the wrinkle in her little boy's forehead, she caught herself. "You're right, Roo. We can have our own little funeral." Roo wanted to know if it could be now, always in a rush toward feeling things, her Roo, reminded her of that line from e. e. cummings, "since feeling is first." That was her boy. That was not her girl. She could not wait, *could not wait*, for Luce to no longer be a teenager.

Gloria said they needed a few days to plan the funeral and think about it, and would Roo mind being in charge? He nodded gravely. And then she tried to put the whole thing out of her mind.

But later that night, Boog swung by to deliver hand salve she'd just jarred, and oh, also, had they heard anything about the man? "How extremely terrible," she said, rubbing salve into Gem's hands, and did Gloria think it might possibly have something to do with her sister's abilities? No, Gloria did not. And so Boog ran home and returned with a ham casserole she'd frozen for just such an occasion, she said, the way they did it down in Alabama, and there would be no fussing about it, and when Gloria protested that there really was no need, that they weren't in mourning, Boog had pulled her into a hug and, patting her back, said, "I know, I know."

And then Juan was there to help set a trap for the rat that had been sneaking around their kitchen at night and he said that he knew Gloria sometimes developed, uh, intimate relations with the seekers, a question with a hint of jealousy, Gloria thought, and was the man who died one of them? "Juan, sweetie," she'd said, "it's none of your fucking business," and he blushed, nodded in agreement. A couple days of these blame-laced questions, and she was desperate to close the door on everyone and go back to the thing she was burning with lately, the thing she had been hearing from her sister.

But the phone rang the next day and the voice identified herself to Gloria as the journalist Ruby Wells. Gloria knew the name; Ruby had one of those faces you see on the sides of buses with a stern half smile, arms crossed, all business. Luce was a devoted fan, always following Ruby's stories with rapt attention, like the one on sexual abuse inside the girls' school a few towns over, or the man let out on bail after his third wife in a row was hospitalized for head injuries, or the woman who killed her abusive boyfriend. It had been a story reported by Ruby Wells years back that first introduced Gloria to the Red Grove.

Ruby was calling, she said, because she'd been contacted by the son of the man who'd died in their house. Gloria's neck went cold. "He thinks there's something more going on," Ruby said. "Something else that caused his father's heart to fail. Do you have a comment on that?"

Did she have a comment? She would like to comment that it was hard every single day to wake up and make breakfast for her children and change her sister's diaper, make dinner, engage in small talk with visitors, bathe the dog, and not get in her car and never return, that's what she thought, a fucking miracle she wasn't waving her scarf over her head in a farewell tribute as she drove for the final time over the Golden Gate Bridge. Instead, she swallowed, explaining that there was no story here. Nothing strange, just pure bad luck. She had been very sorry that the man died, he seemed nice, clearly in pain over the death of his wife. End of story.

"You should know that his son, Bobby, is really angry," Ruby said.

"Angry at what?" Gloria wanted to know. "And don't start telling me it's one of the stages of grief, because first of all, the lady who came up with those five stages actually wrote them about the five stages a dying person goes through, not a grieving person. And second, the poor man had heart disease, and—"

"No, not that," Ruby said, exhaling into the phone. A smoker. "It's more about you, actually. Not really your psychic, uh, stuff. It's your community. He thinks the Red Grove is the problem."

Gloria looked at her children in the living room. Roo was crouched low over his ant farm, and Luce was sprawled across the futon, reading, filling her head with shotguns and pantyhose used for strangulation and the discarded bodies of prostitutes. When Gloria had tried to have a respectful, reasonable conversation with her— treating her like an adult, as she requested—to express that obsessively reading about murderers might be making her more afraid than she needed to be, this stuff was pretty dark, her daughter had said that as soon as the news stopped filling with stories of women murdered and beaten by men, she'd stop needing to know about it. Gloria thought Luce's obsession was really a way for her daughter to feel she knew enough about the very worst, so that what had happened to Gem wasn't singular, so she wasn't the only person who had to carry on with this particular kind of a broken heart. It wasn't enough that Gloria and Roo were here with her, living on. Luce wanted to believe that the whole world was barely surviving.

The man thought the Red Grove was the problem? So did Gloria. Because the longer they lived here, the more Gloria realized that any isolated community, no matter how noble its intentions, restricted you. It made the world too small. That was the truth, though she could not, would not, say it.

"Thinking the Red Grove is the problem is stupid," Gloria said. She wasn't dumb enough to stoke the fire.

"Maybe," Ruby said. She took a long inhale. "But I've been wondering about that place for a long time myself. One of my first stories was about the Red Grove, and even back then I knew something was different about it. A childhood friend of mine moved out there, and I never heard from her again. But I want to understand it. Let me interview you, Gloria. Nobody wants their story told by someone else, someone who gets it wrong."

"I know this tactic—try to become my friend, pretend you're empowering me. It's not going to work."

"You could tell me, in your own words, why this is where you've chosen to raise your daughter."

"See? You're very good."

"Is it a place," Ruby said, as if they were two old friends, "where I should move with my own daughter?"

Gloria tried to imagine hard-hitting Ruby Wells wrestling a toddler into socks, soothing a baby whose temperature wouldn't go down in the middle of the night. What would it be like to go home to your daughter after spending your days reporting on the worst things that happened? She looked again at her children. She thought about Roo, back when he was as big as a cat, how floppy, how smiley. She tried to conjure up Luce when she was a baby, but she couldn't hold on to any image.

"What's his son saying exactly?" Gloria asked. People said

nonsense about the Red Grove, but because they tried to stay out of the spotlight and didn't usually correct the record, the stories built up, then dissipated.

"It's the note," Ruby said. "He's convinced it shows willful intent to let him die, a kind of revenge-on-men plot. I am interested in whether that was your intention, or if not, why you wrote it?"

There was not a single thing she could come up with to make sense of what Ruby was saying. "I don't know about any note," Gloria said.

"I already have a copy, so there's no use pleading ignorance."

"Would you mind reading me what it says?"

Ruby took a drag, quiet a moment, considering. "Who was the note intended for?"

"Forget it," Gloria said, anger flaring. "There was no note. Nothing to tell, no story. Goodbye." She hung up.

She kept her eyes on Luce, sprawled on the couch. There were these small yellow birds called palila, with black stripes on their faces, as cute as can be, who lived on one slope of volcanic soil on one side of a mountain on one island in Hawaii, and they were almost extinct. Eaten by cats, mostly. There were millions of feral cats on the island. But the problem wasn't the cats per se; the problem was the birds themselves. Palila had evolved and lived for millions of years on the island without cats, and, moreover, without any land predators at all. They did not have instinctual fear. No flight response. They just hopped around on the ground as a cat approached, thinking themselves impervious to harm.

She looked over at her children one more time, trying to convince herself not to be rattled by the call. But she was. A man, thinking they had let his father die? Or worse, somehow hastened it, so sure of his anger that he'd invented a note as fake proof. She did not like any of it. They were not prepared for something like that. Her daughter's head was so full of serial killers that she might not know when to use common sense to stay safe. Her daughter, the little yellow bird.

Gloria fell into the chair beside Gem's bed, laid her head down on her sister's stomach. Soft lavender scent on the sheet. She closed her eyes. Clicked her tongue up against the roof of her mouth. Waited, listened. Clicked. Scooped one dry, limp hand into her palm, felt a sudden seasickness. What was her sister telling her? But there was nothing else. "You got me into this mess," Gloria whispered. "You tell me how to get us out."

Outside the window, a redwood groaned, scaring a squirrel off. Needles quivered even without wind. Long before Gloria and her family were in the Red Grove, before Una arrived, before Tamsen Nightingale, before any Europeans arrived on the continent, a thousand years before the beginning of the Christian calendar, around the time of the Parthenon's construction in Greece, this particular redwood tree on the hill outside the window had begun to grow. Its bark was deep red, fibrous, flame-retardant, though fires sometimes did catch a part of the tree and open up hollow caves in the trunk, wounds so large that herders used them as livestock pens. This big, this ancient, and their pine cones, filled with seeds that can unfurl into new redwoods, were no bigger than Gloria's thumb.

"How worried should I be about this guy?" Gloria asked her sister. She brushed the hair away that had been stuck to Gem's forehead, leaned in close. Every piece of her life was in the Red Grove because of her sister. How deeply she was entwined. How stuck.

She clicked again. Waited for a message, her face hovering above her sister's. Gloria would never forget the night they arrived in the Red Grove. She was at the helm of a vehicle full of people she was responsible for: a kid, a baby, her twin sister, propped up carefully, with pillows, in the back. They'd gotten permission to move right into a house, none of the transitional apartment in Heartwood nonsense, though the instructions she'd been given on the phone were as vague as she worried they might be in a place like this: drop down into the valley and take your first left as the trees get dense, another left at the boulder with quartz striations, right at the buckeye tree to the top of the hill, past the cluster of yurts, up the narrow winding road, and yours is the last house at the top, as deep within the community—as protected—as can be.

And then, like in some artsy, horny horror flick, all these half-naked women were walking around at night. The moonlight cast their faces blue-silver, and the massive trees hid yowling animals. Gloria rolled down her window. These were not the women of the fashion magazines she'd grown up reading. One woman right alongside the road waved. Gloria looked at her: saggy-titted with no bra, letting her gray hairs run frizzy, her legs grow long, dark hair like a dog. Don't be so judgy, Gloria thought. God, but she couldn't stop looking at the woman's stretch marks and scars, and then another woman coming up beside the first, completely naked, what in the hell, her big bush erupting from her crotch and growing down the insides of her thighs, the cellulite on her legs bared for anyone to notice, jiggly as the sea and cratered as the moon.

Well, not everyone was like that. She spotted a few women with lean, tight bodies and buoyant breasts and cascades of perfect hair, Renaissance goddesses.

Gem had been talking to people in the community on and off for years, since they first saw Ruby Wells's news story about the Red Grove, but she had never actually made the move. Gloria kept telling her sister that a place like the Red Grove was ridiculous. Unnecessary. It washed her in shame to think about how she'd berated her sister for even considering a place whose currency was the fear of men. No, Gem would say, you're missing the point. It's not fear of men, it's absolute strength of women, of nature. And in response, Gloria, fool that she was back then, had told Gem that she just needed to meet the right guy and had signed her up for speed dating.

But once Gem was unable to make the final choice to come live here, Gloria called the phone number scrawled in her sister's slanted

THE RED GROVE   43

cursive. She had so many questions for Una. Did all the rumors—satanic cult, lesbian commune, witches, freaks, lunatics—bother them?

They were very happy with what they were, how they had become that way, Una told Gloria. They were no drain on local services—they took care of their own. Food pantry in Heartwood, big room of goods people could leave and take and trade. Some people had jobs outside and some didn't, they could do what they wanted. Had no police or jail—no need—and no criminals, none of the kind that mattered, were allowed in, not that they could do their bad deeds here, anyway. That was the thing about this place. A woman could step out onto her front porch wearing whatever she wanted, no bra, short dress, who cared, and have no worry that someone might mistake her body for something they could take or touch without permission. A woman could drink a neighbor's home-brew beer all day and night—cup after cup, until she was tripping over and didn't know her own name—pass out drunk on his bed in her skivvies, and wake in the morning worried only about the hangover. She would not find herself plagued by flashbacks of what he'd done in the night. She would not have to check her panties for goop. There was no wasted time wondering if something bad had happened. So the women had time for other things, daydreaming and growing roses and playing fiddle and sleeping and smoking and a relationship with darkness and solitude that was not rooted in potential danger.

And your sister, Una had said. I'm so sorry about what has happened to her. I can't promise anything, of course, but miraculous recoveries have taken place in the Red Grove. It is a very special place.

Gloria squeezed her eyes shut, leaning against the hospital wall, sticky, citrus-scented disinfectant, holding on to that dimmest of hopes. And she said that she had a baby and a girl, a daughter, who was eight, and what was it like to raise a girl there.

A girl could rise from her sleepless bed in the darkest hour of night, Una said, and walk into the forest, no flashlight, no fear. She could hear the snap of a twig and not startle. And if her nighttime walk took her climbing up into the golden hills, all the way to the community's boundary, well then that's when she might double back.

But a woman would not have to waste the glorious, twinkling starlight on planning an escape route or keeping watch for a potential weapon. And if, on those rare occasions where a man in the community said something rude, something she didn't like, she could tell him he was full of shit. She could yell at him. She could ignore him. She could have a pleasant, rational conversation with him. She was not afraid of his anger. There was no need to smile or fake laugh at his jokes if they were not funny. If he was boring, she could be bored. There was no need to feign interest.

There was no need to navigate his potential violence as she moved through the world, and so she moved through it as her whole, singular, unflinching self.

This is what we're offering, Una had explained to Gloria. A place where a girl was not protected or coddled, was not taught to be afraid. Where a girl could just be a human.

But now, eyes closed, creases of skin across her forehead damp from the June day, Gloria looked at her sister, listening, waiting, and yes, there it was. A click. Yes, she could hear her. It was happening again.

Gloria moved quickly, grabbing the notebook and pen hidden beneath the bed, and opened to a fresh page, scribbling immediately, not wanting to miss anything. "How did you learn this story?" she asked when Gem paused her clicks for a moment, but Gem kept on. She leaned in toward her sister. "Okay, okay, go on," Gloria said. And she wrote.

She had been writing for an hour when a sound pulled her out: in the kitchen, the ringing phone. As familiar as a jay's song, yet this time it startled her. Maybe it would be Una, she told herself, or a seeker. Hiding the notebook as quickly as she could, she hollered for her children not to pick up, but when she got to the kitchen, Luce was already on the phone.

"Last house at the top of Buckeye Drive," she said just as her mother called out "Wait." Luce squinted at Gloria, mouthed *what?* God, Luce was ignorant. Gloria pulled at a cuticle on one of her fingers. Maybe her hunch was wrong and this was someone new, someone regular. Maybe whatever worry she was picking up from her sister wasn't about this at all.

"Sure," Luce said into the phone. Then: "It's for you," to her mom, passing the receiver, raised eyebrows, this face her daughter gave her so often, like she was looking at something disgusting, roadkill, rotten fish.

Gloria held the phone to her chest and waited for Luce to leave the kitchen. "Hello?"

"Listen," the voice said. A man. Youngish. "I've been suspicious of your man-hating commune bullshit for years," he said, and Gloria started to speak, but he barreled on. It was exactly who she feared it would be. "And I found the note, which proved me right," but she had no idea what he meant by that—a note? Maybe something his father wrote before he came to them, she wondered, but he was still yammering on. "If I'd had any idea my dad was coming there, I'd have kicked his ass, some feminist revenge bullshit, but I guess I'm gonna have to come there myself—"

Gloria heard nothing else. She slammed down the phone.

5

June 23, 1997

W<small>E NEED TO TALK</small>, Goosey." Gloria pushed open the batiks that hung as curtains on Luce's bedroom windows. The morning fog had already burned off, the sun illuminating flecks of dust that swirled like underwater debris. Gloria had not slept, sitting beside her sister all night, writing. Thinking. Cocking her ear toward the window, the front door, past that to the road below, listening for him.

"Stop," Luce said, mumbling, turning toward the wall. "I'm sleeping."

Gloria let out a quick laugh, addressing the window as if she had an audience. "Folks, she is, indeed, a living, breathing teenager." Moose, at the foot of Luce's bed, yawned wide and lifted his head, considering, but thumped it back down on the covers, nuzzling Luce's foot.

"Giddyap, baby," Gloria said.

Luce's eyes were still closed. On the wall surrounding her bed, fat stalks of sunflowers hung upside down to dry. Luce's clothes were mostly folded, tucked into plastic shelves in the small closet. At least she wasn't a slovenly teenager. Three old deck boards had been made into shelves with cinder blocks between them, stuffed with notebooks, books, the biographies of men who had done horrible things; and tucked into the back, spine uncreased, *Chicken Soup for the Teenage Soul*, given to her by Mei the harpist for her birthday last year, Gloria and Luce rolling their eyes together when Mei's back was turned.

Gloria bent over her daughter, twisting a piece of her hair in her fingers. Luce batted her away. "This is serious," Gloria said, not taking it personally. That was rule number one with teenagers: it's not you, it's them. She walked to Luce's closet, rubbed a crocheted dress between her thumb and pointer, cocked her head to consider it.

"Oh my god, fine," Luce said, opening an eye, not trying to hide her annoyance. "Let's talk." She sat up.

Gloria thumbed past a few other items of clothing, stopped on a huge, stained bowling shirt with the name Louise embroidered on the breast. "Where'd this heinous thing come from?"

"I like it."

"God, why is there such an insistence here that ugliness means freedom?"

"Mom—"

"I don't see Aya or Tangerine wearing this kind of stuff."

Luce tilted her head back, banged it against the wall behind her, and closed her eyes. "This is really what you woke me up to talk about?"

Gloria stopped rummaging through Luce's closet and, arms crossed, turned to look at her. "I'm worried for you. All this time creeping in the shadows, all this time by yourself, filling your head with stories of serial killers and tortured women. Honey, it's not what you should be doing at your age."

Luce explained, slowly, like she was talking to a child, that she was doing something very, very important. She was helping the women save their own lives. "To save themselves," she said again, slowly, "which is essentially the plot of all those cheesy musicals you love—"

But there were so many other versions of who Luce could become and what she could do in her life, Gloria said, knowing that she was, once again, not getting through. How to get through? She scraped at a crusty piece of food on a sweatshirt hanging in the closet.

Luce pinched her brow. "I cannot believe we're having this conversation again."

Gloria sighed. What she wanted to tell her daughter, was trying to somehow say, was that she was worried in a new way about this guy, this asshole, who seemed to be blaming his father's death on the Red Grove. She wanted to say, *You're a little bird who has never learned to watch out for predators*, or, really, *You're entirely focused on the apex predators, not the real threat of quotidian anger.* "I'm afraid, honey," Gloria said, keeping it in familiar territory, "that your devotion to the Red Grove has limited the options you see for yourself." Luce raised her eyebrows at her mother, annoyed. Gloria recognized that expression, had given it to her own mother. "This," Gloria said, something catching her eye as she turned and reached deeper into Luce's closet. She pulled out a sequined spandex minidress that had been hers when she was younger. "This is exactly what I'm talking about. Most sixteen-year-olds are dying to wear stuff like this. Their lives are full of reasons. Prom. Parties. Dates. Sneaking out to go dancing. It's fun. You could be having fun."

"So to be clear, you woke me up to tell me I should be wearing some cheesy disco dress and sneaking out to share milkshakes with guys named Chad," she said, flopping back down on the bed. She pulled the sheet over her face.

"Luce," Gloria said, softly this time, sitting down at the bottom of the bed. She reached her arm out, hovered it above her daughter's knee. She needed to be more careful, gentle with this daughter of hers. She should lay her hand down on Luce's knee, remind her that her mother was solid, unruffled by teenage angst. It was time for Luce to find her own path, and she could help. "I really think college would be good for you. Give you a fresh start. Strong women don't exist only in the Red Grove. Look at Ruby Wells. I know you love it here, but you don't know anywhere else."

"If you think things are better somewhere else, then you should move, not me."

"Luce—"

"Just go. I'll stay with Gem—"

"Stop," Gloria said, louder than she meant. Now was the time for her to move her hand down, to grasp her daughter, make contact, a good, solid thing in the world, but she left it hovering above a moment longer, and in that space, remembered what it was like to slide into Luce's room years ago, her sister watching from the doorframe as she reached her arm down into the crib, just above Luce's round stomach. How beautiful, that little face, long, dark eyelashes, how vulnerable to be so new in the world. She wouldn't have seen Luce in a month, or a few; how much bigger she'd look, how different. She wouldn't touch that little stomach, didn't want to wake the baby, plus, how hard *were* you supposed to pat a baby? What would hurt them, what would be comforting? It was a horrible myth that these things come naturally. Instead, she looked at the baby's pursed wet lips, listened to her grunt in her sleep, and kept her hand hovering above the hot little stomach.

"Are we done?" Luce asked, staring at the wall.

It would break her heart, walking out of that room without having touched her daughter. "Why don't we go thrifting together? We can make a day of it. I remember some great spots over in Fairfax." She would show her girl that things were okay out there, not perfect, of course not, nowhere was, but she would draw her girl out of this valley. And this time, she brought her hand down. Not too hard, not too soft.

Luce sat up straighter. Maybe this would work. "I have plans," Luce said, sliding past her mom and out of bed and then out of her sight.

Luce climbed the trail back behind their house up into the open hills, legs strong beneath her and breath barely short even though she was climbing up and up. She was above the coast redwoods, among the low wild oats, filaree, star thistle, a clump of wild hyacinths whose cluster of purple stars gathered at the top of the stalk like a scepter. Earlier in the spring there'd been a patch of ground iris here and, for the brief green of April, clover, which she'd sat amidst and searched, unsuccessfully, for a four-leaf.

She turned up a dirt path that climbed higher, up onto the next big hill. Manzanita and low chaparral bushes by her shins as she climbed, small rocks hitting her toes. She was exhausted by these conversations with her mom. Gloria barging in to her room, acting like she really knew her, knew what was best for her, as if she didn't spend all her concern on Gem, or Roo, or moaning in her bedroom with some guy or another.

A jackrabbit sprinted across the trail ahead. She was above the tree line, where it was hot and dry. All the houses were lower down, on the south, shadier hills rising from the valley, closer to the two-lane road that connected them to the towns beyond. There was no Red Grove town sign to mark when you arrived. She'd been part of the nighttime missions to take down the signs every time the county put one up. Most of her friends had them on their walls.

She kept climbing, feeling the burn in her legs, the sun wicking sweat right off her skin, until she made it to the low stone wall on the crest of the ridge surrounding the valley. She pressed her hand against one of the large rocks in the stone wall. It wasn't that it actually kept anyone in or, more importantly, anyone out, but it felt solid beneath her hand, and it marked the boundary.

There was a game she'd played as a kid. They'd line up beside the trees that marked the boundary, giant trunks that were, by way of warning, wrapped in red yarn. The kids would wrap red string around their throats until they looked like slit-necked corpses and then inch their toes past the boundary. This was no fairy tale; they knew that creeping over the line wouldn't beckon a monster, but deep in their hearts they also had all the stories the women told at the reenactments, and up there, necks ringed in red, they'd repeat the stories to one another, about men with knives hiding behind rocks, about beatings, about fear, about what the teeth of Tamsen's husband's brothers did to the bodies of Tamsen's sisters and the evil that stretched its tendrils across every inch of this earth, except for right here in this one place.

Luce turned, staying on the inside of the wall, down a short gulley and up the next rise. Sticking up out of the earth were massive rock formations, blue sandstone and limestone, rough and ragged and sharp at the edges where it had been chipped away.

A little farther along the boundary, she could see remnants of the original smash shack, so named because once upon a time there had been an actual shack and, inside that shack, giant boulders and small hammers with which to pound at the rocks. Now, though the shack was gone, there were plenty of other rock outcroppings and faces, and always a pile of hammers or chisels. If it was deemed that you needed to "burn off some energy," that was the code, you were sent to the smash shack for a certain amount of time, an hour, a day, and could smash at those rocks as you pleased, then, grunting, sweaty, and covered in dust, carry them to the stone wall bordering the Red Grove. The wall was in constant need of repair, with patches that were never completed, so on any day you might see a few people up there, teenagers often, boys most especially, burning off some of their energy. Sometimes a striation of quartz was revealed, a frozen waterfall inside the rock that, when struck, burst into the air, glittering like sun-pierced falling snow. And sometimes nobody else thought it was time for you to go to the smash shack. People sent themselves.

Nobody else up here at the moment. A little unusual. Luce picked up the closest hammer, kicked aside the smudged safety goggles, and swung. She hit the edge of a rock, but nothing broke, so she swung again, harder, more precise, still nothing, and again, and then a few small pieces chipped off and fell nearby. She thought about her mom's conversation this morning and swung. Bang. The rock chipped away. She thought about Tamsen Nightingale, carrying her own sister's bones on her back, how terrified she'd been, how sure she was going to die, and she swung. Little rocks flew, a bigger chunk, one that hit her shin. No matter.

Birds hid in high branches. Blue-bellied lizards held still in the crevices between stones. She thought about the time she was four or five, not yet asleep, when suddenly there was a shadow over her bed, how she'd peeked one eye open oh so carefully and seen it was her mother, whom she hadn't seen in months, and how she knew she should open both eyes and throw her arms around her mother, how she wanted to, kind of, because she did feel joyful, kind of, but how she also felt mad. And the mad feeling won. She stayed pretend asleep. The shadow did not touch her. And in the morning the person to get her out of bed and brush her tangled hair and make her pancakes and hold her hand while they walked to the bus was not her mother, who was long gone. That person was Gem. She would not let herself think about Gem's face in the hospital, mauve and cracked open and swollen shut.

She swung. Little Luce, good, quiet girl, sitting on the couch, hands folded on her lap, waiting for days, for weeks, for her Gem to get better and come home. She swung harder. Because of course she would. Big chunk of rock cracking off. Little Luce, falling to the tile floor in the school bathroom, weeping and wailing, the school nurse rushing in and Luce saying she was so sick, her brain was bashed, take her to the hospital, and the school nurse pulling her onto her lap. Sweetie, she said, stroking Luce's hair. Oh, sweetie.

Her arms ached and her breath was heavy, and she stopped.

Wiped her eyes with the back of her hand. She would not allow these thoughts anywhere but here, where they could be useful. Gem had taught her to take care of other living things beyond all else, and that was exactly, exactly what she spent all her time here doing.

She grabbed one of the nearby baskets and began loading up the smaller rocks she'd broken off. Being here didn't always rid violence from a body, Luce knew, it didn't evaporate out of the brain or the muscles. And it wasn't just men. Women carried violence too. They talked about it in school, how it wasn't only male violence that was harmful out in the world. Luce remembered the slap hard and sharp across the face that she herself had loosed on Roo a few years back. And there were whispers of the violence that sometimes took place in relationships between women. The Red Grove didn't protect against that, which was pretty messed up. Luce kept her ears open for these stories, ready to help devise a plan, shelter a survivor, whatever.

She lumbered with the basket of rocks halfway up a small rise, then dumped it on a part of the wall that could use some shoring up. Back and forth a few times, till she'd cleared the rocks she smashed, till she'd put in the work to draw the line around her home.

It was time to go back. But the sun stung her shoulders with its perfect heat, and rattlesnake grass swished nearby and she thought, What's the harm, just a little bit longer. She stretched, sore already from the hammering, then tightened one of her friendship bracelets that had come loose. She'd made bracelets for Aya and Tangerine, had passed them along after school almost a year ago, something they'd done when they were nine and ten, and since she didn't see them nearly as much these days, she thought it'd be a sweet reminder of the past. But they'd never worn them. They weren't ten anymore.

Up higher, to the barer patches of hill, where she saw a clod of dirt beside a tuft of dried grass, disturbed soil nearby. She crouched. It looked fresh. Mountain lion tracks. She lifted her head and spun quickly, surveying the wildness. Mountain lions attack from behind. They travel long distances, track their prey, bite at the base of its skull. And then they bury it and leave, coming back to feed when they're hungry. Every year, a couple of people in Northern California were killed by mountain lions. Hikers and runners, the occasional small child playing alone at the edge of his yard. The eyes of unseen things tracked people all the time.

Something did catch Luce's eye then—an odd flash of white in the dirt. A surge of cold crept up her hand and arm the closer she came to touching what was in the dirt, the faint sensation that something was pushing her hand, how?

And then there was a sound. A click. No animal makes that sound, though of course, what else could it be? Fingernail in the dirt, scraping dry dirt clods from the buried thing, loosing an edge enough to pry it out. A tingle along her ribs. The thing did not come out easily—she had to use two hands to pull it, as if it were bound to the earth by thick roots. There was a sound, too—a distant buzzing. Or perhaps not so distant. The buzzing of an animal, hunting. Something was happening here. She thought, I'm not afraid. Something is happening, but I am not afraid. Again she looked around her for a lion, but she was alone, except for the click and the buzz and the thing in her hand that felt somehow the smallest bit familiar, like a toy she'd lost when she was a child. It was a bone. She was not afraid, well, a little afraid, yes, and it was a bone, intricately carved, with the figure of a mountain lion carved into the center.

She was overcome with the sense that the trees and hills were watching her carefully, but something else too, something deeper, and she looked down to the hole from which she'd pulled the bone. There were tiny threads in the soil, broken filaments laced through the dirt, white and brown and pink and green, not worms, yet moving, faintly, like a whole network had come together to pulse the bone up to her. Impossible, of course. She laughed to herself, but she could not look away. There was something down there. Something showing her what it wanted her to see.

6

June 23, 1997

WHEN LUCE ARRIVED HOME a few hours later, she climbed the long, rickety steps—mold swirled like storm clouds on the old wood—crossed the deck, and reached for the front door, but it didn't open.

She tried again. No. It was locked. Warm pulse of blood in her neck. Their houses weren't even supposed to have locks, but Gloria had insisted on one, just in case, she said. They'd never used it before. Luce was silent, listening. There was a creak from inside, somewhere close, wasn't there? Like a foot shifting weight on an old wooden floor.

She remembered that a key was hidden beneath a planter on the deck, an emergency key Gloria had called it, reminding them of the location from time to time—it fit into the dead-bolt lock, though she had to jam it to make it turn. She was quiet. Listening. Unlocked the door, turned the handle. The trees swayed behind her, the old dry deck sprung a splinter, thin and sharp. Her palms were cold but sweating. Slowly, slowly, the door opened.

Her eyes were as wide as she could hold them, forcing her pupils to expand and see more in the dim interior. She recognized something happening, something strange, as she took one more step inside—she felt fearful. Well, no. Enough of that. There was nothing to be afraid of, there was nothing that could happen, and where the hell was Moose, not running up to greet her, not barking, but then Luce heard a loud snap and there was something flying at her face. She shrieked, bringing an arm up to block her head. The thing hit her forearm and fell to the ground. She looked down, and lying by her feet was a stuffed dog.

On all fours, his head sticking out from behind the couch, was Roo, laughing hysterically. He fell flat on the ground on his back, clutching his stomach.

"You shit," Luce said, slamming the door behind her.

"Your. Face," Roo managed to say between bouts of laughter. Luce lunged toward him, all that blood still pumping, but Roo, quick-legged, practiced in fleeing, was scrambling up and back in one motion, dashing around the far side of the living room, laugh-screaming, glancing back over his shoulder as Luce followed.

"Okay, okay, okay, okay. Sorry!" Roo yelled, still laughing as he reached the bathroom and slammed the door.

"Open," Luce called to the closed door.

"You're lucky," Roo said. "If I'd had more time, I was gonna hitch a bucket of flour up over the bathroom door."

"Roo." She pounded on the door.

"Imagine you all covered in white. Like a ghost!"

"You've got to cut this shit out," Luce said. It was then that her mother walked into the hallway and locked the dead bolt on the front door. "Wait, you locked the door? Not Roo?" This was an alarming detail.

"He was making it into a bit of fun," Gloria said. She was scrunching her wet hair in her palms.

"We never lock the door."

"Well," Gloria said, and Luce watched the beautiful, controlled mask rise over her face. She smiled. "We're locking it. Starting immediately."

"A mad guy keeps calling," Roo hollered from behind the bathroom door.

"He was aggravated, yes. It happens from time to time, you know that."

"And you're locking the door because you think he's coming here?" Luce asked. She thought about what Boog told her at the reenactments, a man asking about where they lived. Gloria continued scrunching her hair, as if they were talking about any old thing.

"He's been calling," Roo yelled. "He won't stop calling."

"Why? What does he want?"

"What does anyone want?" Gloria asked, moving to a new task. She began rearranging candles on the hallway table. "Peace. Love. Forgiveness."

"He said we killed his daddy," Roo called, and Gloria spun toward the bathroom door.

"Enough, Roo. Get out of there," she said. And then, as if on cue, the phone rang. "Don't answer it," Gloria said quickly. She ran her fingertips over Luce's hair, brushing it back, and then hustled to the kitchen. The fridge door banged open. Roo followed the sounds, and so did Luce. There was more to what was going on.

Gloria was standing over a bowl of green beans picked that morning from the garden, snapping off stem and tail. Roo climbed onto a chair, and Luce pulled the bowl to the center of the table so they could reach. She pulled one out and pinched off its head. For a moment, the only sounds were the snapping and plopping, their hands reaching in from different sides of their small round table. Luce knew this game well. She could always wait out her mother's silence.

"It doesn't make any sense," Gloria said, biting into a bean she'd just cleaned. "He thinks his father dying here means it was our fault. He's invented something about a note that he claims proves him right."

The note. That's not what it said. Luce kept her eyes on the bean in her hand, hoped her mother would not notice the redness spreading across her neck, her chest.

"What if he never stops calling?" Roo asked. He was arranging the nipped ends into a circle.

"He will," Gloria said.

"But what if he doesn't?"

"Well, my kangaroo, here's the deal. We don't have to keep the Red Grove so wrapped up in magic and secrecy," Gloria said. She stopped her busywork and sat down so she was closer to eye level with Roo.

"Mom—" Luce started, but her mother carried on.

"The man is mad because he thinks we willed his father's death somehow, like we are enacting revenge on men or something. He was prowling around town, asking questions about us, and about the Red Grove. And then he claims he found a note I wrote that proves we knew his dad was going to die. So he's clearly delusional. There was no note, of course—"

"Mom," Luce said, louder this time, but Gloria was in her rhythm, grabbing and snapping and tossing, and she kept on.

"If he believed that this is just a place like any other place and we are normal people like any other people, I don't think we'd have this problem."

"But it isn't a place like any other place, is it, Goose?" Roo said, looking over at Luce.

"I wrote the note," Luce blurted. Gloria stilled her frantic motion, looked up at Luce as if she had spotted a lion on the trail. "I meant it to be helpful," she said, quieter.

Gloria set the half-cleaned green bean down on the table and, keeping her voice eerily calm, asked Luce what exactly the note had said.

"Nothing bad," Luce said quickly, feeling the ache in her stomach that came when she knew she'd done something wrong. "It was the same kind of thing you would have said."

"Tell me what you wrote," Gloria said. Luce could see her mother taking controlled breaths, nostrils flaring. She remembered exactly what she'd written. It was part of her responsibility to the business to keep things running smoothly, and she'd done that, reaching out to the family of this seeker, following Una's cues and doing what she could to make sure no blame or attention was put onto the Red Grove.

"It said that we were sorry for their loss." Luce picked up another green bean, hoping the task would keep her hands from trembling. "That's a thoughtful and normal thing to say," she clarified.

"What else, Luce?" Gloria said, her voice losing its patience.

"I told them that if someone wanted to come use our services to communicate with him later, you know, if he died, their first session would be free. That's, like, customer service," Luce said, and Gloria's head swiveled up so she was looking at the ceiling, her eyelids fluttering.

"And I wanted them to know that his sickness didn't come out of the blue. He already looked kind of sick when he got here, he was out of breath and sweating a lot, so I think something had been going on for a while."

"Why didn't you tell me that? Oh my god, maybe we could have gotten him help earlier—"

"I mean not *sick* sick, just—"

"Okay, okay, okay, give me a second." Gloria rubbed her temples, eyes closed. Luce and Roo watched her closely, not moving. Anything could happen next—Gloria storming from the room, remaining silent, yelling at Luce for her thoughtlessness—and, Luce, muscles tensed, tried to run through every option.

Gloria opened her eyes, reached into the bowl, and pulled out another green bean. She clicked the ends off, set it into the cleaned pile, and started on another. Not knowing what else to do, Luce fol-lowed suit. Roo did too. Then Gloria said, with a cool, clear voice, that it was okay. Luce had been trying to help, she understood that. Gloria would sort it out with the man himself. She finished the last green bean, wiped her hands on a towel, and kissed Luce and Roo on the tops of their heads. "I'm turning off the phone's ringer so I can hear myself think. Don't pick up the phone. Don't open the door to anyone you don't know. Okay, kids?" They nodded, listening to the clack of her heels retreating down the hall.

Roo was rolling a bean between his fingers, his chin resting on the table, eyebrows heavy.

"Hey, it's okay. He can't hurt us," Luce said.

"He can't hurt you. Or Mom," Roo said. It wasn't something any of them had said out loud before, although of course, he was right. Luce and Gloria could not be hurt. But Roo—

"He's confused," Luce said, "but he's not mad at you."

"You think he's going to hurt me," Roo said. "Because he hates us for living here." Not a question. Luce put a hand on his skinny little shoulder blades, but he shrugged it off.

"Nobody is going to hurt you," she said, putting her hand on his back again. He allowed it this time, and she could feel his little-boy body shivering. His blond bowl cut swung with each jerk of his head. She crouched down so her face was directly in front of his. "I will not allow it."

7

THE CABINET where they kept Gem's supplies stood in the corner of her room, well-stocked by one of Gloria's seekers who
worked at the hospital and came regularly for appointments. The
seeker, a nurse, had a son who had died at seven of leukemia, and
she talked to him often, via Gloria, via Gem, in exchange for the
supplies to keep Gem going. Luce riffled through, making sure they
had what they needed for the coming week. Moose, the good boy, lay
beneath Gem's bed, and Luce stooped down every few minutes to
rub his belly or scratch behind his ear. She liked to give him extra
attention in this room so he'd sleep in here when Gem was the only
one home, her own little guard. Gloria was out somewhere, Luce
didn't know where. She was happy for the space after admitting to
the note. Maybe, possibly, it wouldn't be that big of a deal. Her mom
had been weirdly calm—forgiving even. And then in the hours since,
so distracted, thumbing through pages and pages in a notebook,
muttering to herself like a crone, *hello stereotype,* as she stomped

through the house, barely acknowledging Roo when he said he was hungry. Always hungry, that kid.

The phone was no longer ringing incessantly, but the silence was even more eerie.

Wind rattled a branch against the window, and Gem twitched her arm at the same moment, as if the wind had rustled her, too. So many strange moments with Gem where she seemed to be almost responding to nature, her skin plump and relaxed in the wet spring, brittle during the summers of drought, as this was. Luce worked lotion into her arms.

Part of their agreement with the nurse was that she couldn't talk about Gem back at work—they didn't want bullshit agencies coming to their house and telling them what they were doing wrong, as if they hadn't kept Gem alive all on their own for these years. Gem was an amazing case, people in the community always said so, but it was especially true when the nurse said it. Gem had progressed from a coma to something called unresponsive wakefulness syndrome, though Gloria referred to this state as everdream. An everlasting waking dream. It was surprising that there wasn't a greater trail of concern following such a violent case, but there hadn't been. Gem's story was quickly washed away by a woman killed by her estranged boyfriend the next day, then two kids stabbed on a playground, a shooting in the post office, and on and on. They'd taken her out of the hospital eventually, and that was that. Nobody needed their new address. Nobody asked about her.

At first they'd been told that Gem had at most a few months to live, but as soon as she arrived in the Red Grove, her blood pressure stabilized, her oxygen levels increased, and her skin shifted back to its olive hue. As if she were pulling vitality from something on the land. Gem wouldn't die. That was the thing nobody said out loud, but everyone thought. She *should* die, but she just kept on not dying.

Luce rubbed a warm washcloth along the underside of Gem's arm, the skin loose and fragile, like tissue paper. She scrubbed at the pit, not too hard, and circled the bicep, elbow, forearm, ignoring the pink trail that was left because of how little it got rubbed. Poor skin. Sure that she was alone with Gem, she leaned in close and, with her tongue against the roof of her mouth, made a clicking sound. It wasn't her thing, she knew, but it was worth a try from time to time to see if it would grant her, like her mom, access to that in-between space where Gem lived. She clicked again. But Gem's eyes never shifted from the wall.

Luce took small sips of air, breathing through her mouth when she could, always a little queasy from the smell, not just the urine but also the body smells of sweat and yeast and decay, the stagnant air of a body held still for too long. But this was her person, her Gem, and so she never complained, not to Gem, of course, but never to her mother, never to a friend. She kept it private, smiling at Gem even when Gem wasn't looking at her, trying to say, all the time, *You are loved*. And then sometimes, still smiling as she backed out of Gem's room, blowing her a kiss, she locked herself in the bathroom, both hands clasped over her mouth, and wept. It's okay, sweetie, she would say to herself. Or if it was really bad, and she could not break out of her own grief, she would go to her room, pull a book off the shelf, and begin reading. The one about the guy who dismembered the women. Or the one where he ate them. The one where he never disclosed the hidden bodies of dozens of women, so they remain out in the world somewhere, lost. They are lost, and Gem is not. Remember how much worse it could be. Gem is here, and a ray of sun is warming her arm, and she has lavender by the bed, and she is safe.

Once, Luce had told her mother that she didn't think it was right using Gem like this. Gem wouldn't like it. You don't know what she would or wouldn't like, her mother had said. Bullshit, Luce said, I know her more than I know you. Gloria had not disputed this, but told her daughter that Gem's participation separated her from the ho-hum two-bit charlatans using tarot cards or crystal balls or palm readings or other predictable channels. And when Luce rolled her eyes, Gloria had asked her daughter whether she liked having their lights turned on and food on the table? Yes? Then let it go.

Luce used the washcloth to massage the thin bones of Gem's hand, to scrub in the crevices between digits. She kneaded the muscles, bent and flexed the joints, and then she heard the unmistakable low thumps as a heavy body climbed the steps up to the deck. The house was announcing the arrival of an outsider, and she felt, with hair raising on the back of her neck, watching Gem's arm grow goose bumps at that same moment, that they were not welcome.

She moved fast. Dropped the washcloth, leapt up, and closed Gem's door. She hollered for Roo to stay in his room. She would handle this alone. But instead of pounding wildly, like she'd expected, he knocked politely. She imagined throwing open the door, standing tall and straight, and telling this man to fuck off. That he couldn't come into the Red Grove whenever he pleased, but she thought about the note. Yes, she'd intended to be helpful, but as she well knew from the testimonies of people convicted for involuntary manslaughter, intentions weren't what mattered. If she had a tail, she'd tuck it between her legs, feeling foolish, and sorry. Luce opened the door a few inches, offered a smile. She considered him, tried to decide if he looked like his father, and he did, something about the pinched eyes, his big frame. The fact of his size and presence insisted that she evaluate his strength, and even the smallness of that shift, the power he claimed by being huge and mad and not leaving them alone, opened a sliver of rage in her. She had to resist it.

"I don't want to be here," the man said through the crack. In his left fist he held a blue umbrella with dinosaurs printed on the fabric. A child's, Luce thought. How strange to have an umbrella on this hot day. The knuckles gripping his umbrella were sharp against the skin, angry bone taut inside. Breathe, Luce told herself. Breathe. "But your mother isn't answering the phone. I don't know how else to reach her. I need to talk to her."

Luce agreed—it did seem like maybe her mother could talk to him, sort it out, calm him down, let them all move on. "She's not here, but I'll tell her to call you," Luce said, and remembering that he had just lost his father, added "Sorry about your dad." She began shutting the front door, but he stuck out a toe before the door clicked closed, blocking it. She felt the blood pump a little faster in her chest, her throat. There was the sound of a board creaking beneath his weight on the deck. A bird outside loosing its call. Her own heartbeat thrumming in her ears.

"You listen, then," he said, and kept his foot in place. It was so close to her, the dirty tread on his boot's sole. This foot that should not, *should not*, be here. And why didn't he know that? "You pass this on to her, that Gloria, thinking she's all special tucked away and hidden up here. Well, she's not. None of you are. This whole man-hating commune thing is bullshit. You tell her she better straighten this shit out." He ran his hand through his hair, thin, sweat-streaked. "I know you did something to my dad. I'm going to expose you so everyone knows, and you'll never be able to brainwash anyone again."

There were three clear crystals hanging by fishing line in the door's glass panels, swaying from when she'd tried to close the door. As they spun, blades of rainbow light traveled Luce's face, caught in the center of her eye, and blinded her. She gritted her teeth, blinked each time the light came, but she didn't want to hold her hand up against her eyes for fear it would show the brand-new, soft, quivering feeling she felt, which she wished was not so easy to identify, but like a song she'd once known and was played again, she recognized it— fear. She felt fearful. Of a man. In her own home. It was new, this feeling, sending a hot wash across her whole body. Well, hell no. She would not let that stand. Her hand wished for the sharp, carved bone she'd found up on the ridge to wield at him like a knife, but she'd left it in her room.

She had learned about the mindful techniques of de-escalation in school, and peaceful conflict resolution and negotiation, and the power of vulnerability, the strength of softness, and also about women warriors who used tact and skill to outwit their foes. But she had not learned much about when to choose which tactic, or why. She thought fast.

"Come inside, let's talk," she said, stepping back a half step, gripping the inside of the door handle tightly. The man hesitated a moment but began stepping inside. He placed his hand—the empty one—on the inside of the doorframe, and that's when she gathered all her might and slammed the front door closed. The edge of the door crushed his fingers. He called out, pulling his hand up to his chest, staggering back from the door, and she slammed it all the way then, leaning hard into the wood and latching the dead bolt.

A crystal bounced against the door and hit her cheekbone, but she didn't retreat and pressed her face to the small glass panel, watching. The man cursed, cradling his hand, pacing up and down the old bleached wood of the deck, in and out of the shadows of the giant redwood trees all around, his body going purple in the darkness and then almost crackling with brightness when he emerged into the light.

Her muscles were tensed. She was ready for him to charge the door, punch the glass, kick the wood, something. But he stopped moving. Held still. He was standing at the top of the deck's steps, looking down, his body in one of the pillars of light escaping the tree's canopy. Cradling gnarled fingers in his other hand. Slowly, he turned his head so he was looking at Luce through the door. He spoke.

"'And if a man cause a blemish in his neighbour; as he hath done, so shall it be done to him; breach for breach, eye for eye, tooth for tooth.'"

Heat in her throat, her chest. Luce looked at him through the small glass pane on the door, trying to come up with an explanation, reaching desperately for something to say to lessen his anger, her mind spinning, lurching, but he looked at her one last time, bit his upper lip in a way that looked, horribly, like a snarl, and was gone.

In the center of the deck, the dinosaur umbrella, stilled and forgotten in a bruise of shadow.

8

June 26, 1997

SOMEONE HAD SPOTTED SOMETHING UNUSUAL moving in the Red Grove's cliffs. High up in an alcove, a mountain lion had made a den for her three kittens. Nobody in the community remembered seeing a whole mountain lion family before, as they are secretive, stealthy, and rare. Evidence appeared sometimes—a dried paw print in the mud, a deer carcass, a missing cat—but their presence was mostly theoretical, mythical, the ghost of something lethal that was somehow tied to what made the Red Grove safe, always just out of sight.

A news anchor from one of the nearby towns had arrived first thing that morning. Within the Red Grove, the rules were clear: no reporters. A cult in California had committed mass suicide a few months earlier, leaving thirty-nine people dead, and though the Red Grove was nothing like that, the people in the community all knew how damaging media spotlights could be, *especially* for the people who lived here in order to disappear.

By midday after the early-morning news report, there were thirty or so spectators, including a dozen outsiders who set up camp chairs along the road, everyone squinting through binoculars across the fields and up onto the rock outcropping, where the fat kits wrestled in the sun. Yes, the lions in and of themselves were spectacular, but beyond that, for the people of the Red Grove, they raised spiritual questions, supernatural questions. What might it *mean*? An indication of Tamsen Nightingale's reincarnation? These wild animals wanting their land back, another person said. That's not it, Luce thought, seeing in their brute strength a reminder to the world: nobody can fuck with us here.

Gloria spotted Ruby Wells talking to one of the outsiders, gesturing toward the lions and also back toward the red groves that dotted the valley. Yes, sure, Gloria wanted her kids to see the miracle of lion cubs, but mostly she'd hoped Ruby would be here. That fucker would not stop calling and had the nerve to show up on their goddamned doorstep. Well, no more.

Luce scanned the crowd, lingering on the outsiders. Not all serial killers fit the young-crazy-white-guy-listening-to-possessed-dogs type. There were the suave bankers you'd never suspect, or that meek baker who set women free in the Alaskan wilderness and then hunted them. You just never knew when someone was going to try to carve you out of your life. Right here in this crowd, someone had on a suspiciously thick jacket for the warm day, and that was the kind of thing someone would later remember, tearfully— I knew something was off about him. Why didn't I follow my instincts? But it's more than instinct. It's common sense. Every sixty seconds a woman in the United States is sexually assaulted, perhaps by someone who seems perfectly nice at a speed-dating event, who tells you how pretty you look when he comes to pick you up, who even pulls a quarter from behind your niece's ear.

Luce leaned over to her mother and pointed at the man in the oversize coat, saying, "There are laws on the books that say if you steal a bundle of hay, it's a felony. But you can stab a woman with a knife or shoot her with a gun and get charged with assault, which is a misdemeanor."

"Not now, Luce—why don't you pay attention to these lions? This is amazing."

"Gloria, these are the foundational belief systems of the world they live in," Luce said, nodding toward the outsiders.

Gloria stiffened, embarrassed by the possibility of anyone hearing her paranoid daughter, but something in her softened, and she put a hand across Luce's back, her daughter's sweet skin smell and baby powder–scented deodorant up close, turned her so they were face-to-face. "Listen, baby," Gloria said. "Do you hear yourself? You're sixteen. When I was your age, I was playing volleyball and making out in cars and going to prom and—"

"Prom is basically the Cinderella fantasy—" Luce started, but her mother cut her off.

"Just hush for a second. Please? I made a lot of mistakes in the past. You know that. I know that. I'm sorry. But I am going to make things better. For you." Gloria put both arms behind Luce's neck, leaned down, and pulled her in so their foreheads touched.

Luce opened her eyes and was ready to hate it, but there was her mother, wild animal, softest animal, looking right at her. It took her breath. Something older than she could remember wanted it to never, ever end. "You're mine," Gloria said, so softly Luce could barely hear the words over the chattering crowd. Gloria lifted her hand from Luce's neck and brushed a thumb against her cheek. "Stay here, soak in the gloriousness of these kittens, and hey, maybe even go talk to a cute stranger?" Luce rolled her eyes. "I'll be home a little later. Walk Roo home when you guys are done." She winked and disappeared into the crowd.

The presence of the mountain lions was weird, surprising in ways Gloria didn't even yet understand. Something she couldn't quite put her finger on—how, in this supposedly safe place, what they were celebrating was the proximal presence of a goddamned lion, as if that were safe, as if nature itself weren't brutal and violent. She knew the way a mother lion could rip open the throat of anyone, anything at all, trying to harm her babies.

She slipped back through the crowd. What is a mother? She asked herself this question not infrequently, trying to articulate what she was supposed to be doing. What is a mother if not a protector? If not a person who must provide the information and guidance to help a child make the best choices. There were a lot of things Gloria had not done as a mother. Hell, she was a human, her own human first and foremost. She would not sacrifice all of herself. Why should she? The sacrificial mother was a bullshit narrative. But she could do this one thing.

When Luce was one or two years old, Gloria had brought her a plastic clown mask. Here, she'd said, handing it to the baby, who still looked a little drunk in her new wobbling walk. Luce looked at her mother, not smiling, not reaching out to take it. Gloria tried again—here, shaking it closer to Luce's hand, making it easy, but Luce stared, maybe didn't even blink. It's silly, don't you see, honey, it's so funny, she said, booping the nose. She said, Hi, Luce, in a high-pitched drawl, a clown voice, it was funny—but Luce didn't budge. Didn't crack a smile. Luce held in her hand a wooden mixing spoon, which Gem told Gloria she brought everywhere. This child so small and already so stubborn, so skeptical, so sure of what she liked and what she did not. But this is a clown, Gloria had tried once more, sticking out her tongue. Nothing.

Luce was not a baby who would pander. She did not pretend to be moved by something that did not move her. Not as a baby, not as a child. Not now, as a young woman. Gloria had brought the wrong toy. The only way to reach Luce was on Luce's own terms.

She breathed in again, shakily, the mountain lions behind her. Got into the car, started the ignition. She had thought her children would never be as vulnerable as they were back when they were small. How foolish she'd been.

She could do this one thing, and even if her daughter didn't understand yet, she would come to understand it.

The tall golden grass covering the hillside ahead bowed with a gust of wind that sent a pair of birds up out of hiding. One circled the other once before they flew away, not far off the ground, ducking and weaving between each other until they both shot up toward the sun.

Luce and Roo took the long route home, Luce pointing out the redwood wound where she'd recently seen a skunk family, the little one no bigger than her fist, Roo flinching at the creaking trees for the first time in his life, asking if Luce was worried about the calling man. "Nah," she told him. "Do you know what seeing a family of lions means?" she asked. He didn't. "It means fierce mother warrior protection for all those around," she said. "It's some of the old knowledge, Tamsen Nightingale stuff," and though she'd made it up, it felt true.

They walked, stretching into the sun when the dense trees broke, snacking on a packet of beef jerky Roo had gotten from an outsider kid in exchange for a blue-bellied lizard he'd caught under a rock. The afternoon heat blurred the air off the road, but they weren't in a hurry.

When they climbed up the long deck's steps and into their house, they found only their aunt Gem, asleep in the same place she always was. Luce read, and Roo designed clothes for his dinosaurs, but Gloria hadn't come home by later that afternoon or that evening. Luce warmed up tortillas with beans and cheese, let Roo tell her about the diet of Brachiosaurus, and cleaned the packed dirt from the carved bone she'd found, carefully scraping in its chiseled pockets, rinsing it under warm water to reveal the fine detail. Still, Gloria wasn't there.

Their mother wasn't there when the sun finally went down on one of the longest days of the year, wasn't there when the near-full moon rose, when fog rolled halfway in but dissipated before it took hold, when a coyote yelled once the sky was full of stars.

She wasn't there when everyone in the house was dreaming, except for Luce, who walked to the deck and peered down at the empty driveway once again. Gloria still wasn't home.

For years, Luce had worked to convince herself that her mother would not up and disappear now that she had Roo and Gem to care for, but as she waited and waited she couldn't help it—the idea growing as the hours ticked by and her mother was still gone. She'd never left for more than a few hours, and even then would have Gramms or Juan or someone check on them. But nobody called. No one came by.

What had her mother said as she left? She was going to make things better for Luce—better how? She told herself to stop worrying. Worry is a misuse of the imagination, Gramms liked to say. There was no point in worrying about Gloria running into someone like that monster in the Andes, murderer of some three hundred and fifty girls, their bodies revealed when a flood unearthed them.

About Gem, and her purple, swollen face. A berry, squeezed to bursting.

About this man who'd shown up at their house because she'd brought him here, yes, admit it—she was the one who'd made this all worse. She'd written the note, and then, instead of patching things over as she'd intended, she'd let her anger take hold and she'd hurt him, and now what? Now she'd given herself a reason to worry.

Luce looked out into the night and told herself to cut it out. Gloria would be home any minute. The stars held steady, pinpricks of light on a dark cloth, all up there in the sky even though the trees blocked much of the view. The star is there, she thought, even if I can't see it. Though you could see a star's light long after it was dead.

From *The Red Grove: The Story of the Sisters*

There was a day when the summer greens were going brown twice as fast as they ever had. The tundra swans were leaving in great clouds of white, and a green darner dragonfly, as long as a lily, landed on Tamsen Nightingale's palm and then died before it could take off again. That was the thing—everyone and everything they knew were starving.

Tamsen and her two sisters, Margaret and Minnie, were newly married to three brothers, Arthur, Albert, and August. The state of Wisconsin—five years young—was looking bleak. The brothers, with no jobs or land, sat by the fire and spun tales of a better life. There was a place they heard of where the snow never fell. Where swans didn't leave. There, it was easy to find a little plot of land where they could march out into golden sunshine that lasted all year. They could go to California. Land of warm creeks where your hands dig into the cool mud. And do you know what ends up in your palms? Gold.

There had been whispers of gold on the lips of every passing traveler, rumors of creeks so full of glitter you were likely to find golden nuggets stuck between your toes when you waded in.

The oldest brother, Arthur, had married the oldest sister, Tamsen, after a short courtship conducted in her family's cabbage field. He was polite, he loved his brothers fiercely, and he mostly left her alone in the garden when she wanted to be alone. They smiled shyly at each other, and she imagined them old, in chairs by a fire, reading and sewing and smelling the night. The other sisters married the other brothers shortly thereafter so that they could stay knitted to their kin, so that where one string of yarn was tugged, the others would follow. The brothers' father gave them his horse, and the sisters' mother wrapped all her fine things in a chest and everyone wept with the knowledge that there was nothing for them to do if they stayed, no work and no food. The only direction was west.

And the morning they left, a warm spring day, Tamsen's mother clutched her face and told her, tearfully, pleading, that she must keep her sisters safe. That no harm may come upon them, no injury, no violence. Tamsen looked over to where her sisters, elbows hooked, blew kisses to the donkey at the far end of the field. She promised.

The journey was full of perils. The nights were cold and the plains never ended and the bears were hungry and the snakes were angry. On they went.

They passed people friendly and willing to trade; they passed people unfriendly and unwilling to trade. The sisters sketched tulips and primrose and creeping hollyhock, chipmunks and beavers and eagles. Having spent their lives running the family farm, the sisters were skilled in identifying edible plants, and they kept the party fed even on nights when no hunting or trapping or fishing was possible, when the wind snuck right through their coats and scraped at them to turn around.

On day 129, weeks later than they'd expected, the brothers and sisters reached the base of the Sierra Nevada mountains. Fall was falling fast toward winter, and they started up.

Though Tamsen, as the oldest, was usually first among her sisters to climb trees back home or to plunge into the cold lake in the summertime, she was not first as they began climbing the mountain. Her sisters thought it was her homesickness.

"I think we should wait until spring," Tamsen whispered to Arthur one night as they lay side by side under the stars. Though they shared private smiles, their intimacy, in bed and conversation, was still so new that it had taken her a few days to find the right words. They were halfway up the mountain. But Arthur knew at least a dozen other men from his hometown who were headed in the same direction, and he had promised his brothers that they would be first, already swimming in gold by the time the others arrived. They must press on, he said. Besides, they were a hearty winter people, thick-boned, callus-skinned, no dainty dragonflies.

She watched the back of her husband's legs the next morning as he stepped onto rocks and dirt slick with frost; she watched his sure-footedness and the way her sisters helped each other up difficult passages, thinking about how they'd always done that, even when they were young, grabbing for one another like an instinct.

When they were still two days from the peak, a storm came in. The needled trees shook as the wind picked up, the air piercingly cold and pregnant with snow. But they were winter people, the brothers said again, "Snow-bred," they chanted, pounding their fists against their chests, and they were heading into the golden promise of California. They pressed on.

Tamsen knew how to read the weather. She knew that they were nearly out of food, that the storm would bury plants and send the animals into their burrows. She also knew that none of the brothers would heed her warning; they thought it ungodly and strange when she read the wind or listened to the dirt. She tried a different approach. She told them she was having woman problems of the worst order, and she would not move another step off that canyon trail or the blood coming from her body would call the bears. Because of their histories with bears, she thought it would work. They'd huddle and wait out the storm. She'd keep her sisters safe, which she'd always done.

The brothers considered her predicament, shoulder to shoulder in a tight circle. Several times she approached the brothers, but they batted her away. By the time they came back to announce to the wives what they would do, Tamsen knew.

When she refused to go on, sure of their fate, the brothers decided they had to forge ahead without her lest they miss the gold that should be rightfully theirs. But Arthur knew he could not. A man was not supposed to leave his bride.

Arthur said they would catch up to his brothers on the other side of the summit. As they were packing, Tamsen whispered with her sisters, pointing out the cave she'd spotted nearby, instructing them to double back once the brothers were asleep that night. In that cave they'd stay safe together with Arthur, who was the most decent of the brothers. She whispered a curse on anyone who would hurt her sisters, kissed them, and promised to see them soon.

Tamsen brought Arthur into the cave and began cutting wood from fallen branches she'd dragged inside. "Don't work, Tamsen, your body is leaking away," Arthur said. He was smoking his pipe, leaning back against a rock.

"A bad storm is coming," Tamsen said, nodding toward the mouth of the cave where the snow was already fat and heavy.

"What about my brothers? You didn't even warn them," he said.

"I tried."

"You didn't try. If you'd told me, really told me, I could of told them."

Arthur stood and began collecting their things. "We must go immediately," he said. "Pack up."

"Don't be a fool," she said, the shyness of their early months fading and anger building. "We'd die out there." Arthur ignored her, pacing the cave, looking out at the weather, which was thickening by the minute. Tamsen said, "I told my sisters to shelter in a cave up the mountain. If your brothers have the sense to listen to their wives, they will be fine too."

"What will they think of me?" he said to her, and she saw the soft boy shape of his eyebrows from when he was with his brothers, the three of them talking about the animals they caught and loved when they were small and how they would sit together beneath the stairs to hide from their own raging daddy.

He told her to pack up again, but she did not, readying the cave instead for shelter. She tried once more to explain that her sisters knew of another cave, and so all his brothers needed was to listen and follow as the storm slammed harder. But Arthur knew the stubborn pride of his brothers, doubted that they would listen to these new women over each other, and his heart froze right to pieces at the thought of losing them. He grabbed his pack and lurched toward the cave entrance, determined to find them, but Tamsen, sure of his fate were he to head into the storm alone, and fond of him despite herself, grabbed at his legs from her crouch on the ground, a movement practiced from days of catching goats, and brought him down with a thud. From there, he would have to take a breath and reconsider, and she patted him on the shoulder, told him that first they needed a fire, pointing to the pile of logs, readied for his help, and turned away to prepare more wood.

She did not see the log come up over his head. She had no warning before it smashed down against the back of her skull.

Tamsen woke to blackness. She could see nothing. She slept. When she woke the next time, she could see with one eye, though it was difficult to open. She could not feel her hands or feet from cold. She sat up and looked around the cave, but Arthur was gone. Her sisters had not come back. She dragged herself to the edge of the cave. The tracks in the snow outside were faint, so it had been at least a day since Arthur had left, maybe more. Though the snow had stopped falling, it was piled high outside. She stood up and, retching, followed the tracks, bleeding, dragging herself along until, unable to see almost anything, she fell into the snow.

She'd die there, she knew. She closed her eyes, accepting her fate. But something stepped on her foot—once, then again, something heavy, and she feared a mountain lion, which she'd heard stalked these mountains. She used all her energy to kick the animal away, but her leg met only air. She opened her eyes and sat up. No animal was around. The snow was deep, the air was freezing, and she knew she'd die quickly there, much too quickly for her to find her sisters, already too far ahead.

She began crawling back toward the cave. She crawled for a hundred years. She imagined the future, when some mother would be walking with her daughter and point to a mountain range in the shape of a crawling figure's silhouette and tell her daughter the fable of Tamsen Nightingale, but how would anyone know that fable, she realized, if she weren't alive to tell it.

When she dragged herself back into the cave, she was startled by a faint hissing and cluck. Without thinking, she pulled out the knife she kept tucked into her skirt, and as the family of jackrabbits that had entered the cave was fleeing, she crushed two baby rabbits under her body and caught an adult with her hands. She slit their throats with her knife and passed out, exhausted. The snow fell.

She woke, her hands covered in blood, and she slept.

On the second day, she woke, feeling a dryness in her throat and a cracking on her lips, as if she were made of the roads she grew up running down, dust flying behind her, rocks tripping her up. She melted snow in her hands and licked it. The cold was so deep in her body that even when she slipped back into sleep, she dreamed she was trapped in ice. In a small miracle, Arthur had left behind a pack—probably too much for him to carry—and once she could keep her eyes open long enough to riffle through, she found the tinderbox and started a fire. She cooked one rabbit and smoked the others. She dragged herself farther back into the cave, where there was a nest of pink, hairless rabbits from when she'd scared the parents out, dead from the cold. She ate them too.

She waited in the cave while the back of her head, gashed open, healed enough to allow her to walk. Daylight dimmed into darkness, darkness bled into daylight. She wasn't sure how much time had passed—ten days, two weeks perhaps—but when she went outside, there were no footprints for her to follow.

There were some animal tracks, though, the tiny forks of bird prints and rounded paws of something catlike. She walked on and found no trail. She walked and walked, eating the last of the smoked rabbit, drinking melted snow, and she made it to the summit and started walking down, sure she'd find her sisters and also sure she wouldn't.

It had snowed and snowed. She would find her sisters and run, and they'd start again.

Down the mountain she walked, snaking back and forth, hunting for her sisters, finding comfort in nothing. For days she walked, a week. She didn't know how long they'd been separated—was it two weeks or three? She'd found food, but had they? They would have been out of their reserves a long time by now. She thought about Margaret, who would whisper out the window in the darkness of their childhood bedroom, telling her sisters she was soothing ghosts. She thought about Minnie, who'd steal their mother's dresses and their father's hats as costume pieces and jump out of closets to sing for them. Where were they? She grew weak, meat gone, body weary and freezing, and to stay warm, she imagined her sisters in a cave somewhere, warming themselves by the fire, for certainly they'd taken shelter in the last big storm, and that was when she came upon one big lump in the snow.

It was about six feet long, two feet across. She leaned down, knowing, just as she knew with the litter of kittens she'd found after they'd been accidentally shut out of the barn one night in a late spring frost. She brushed away the snow. There, beneath a thin layer of ice, was one of her husband's brother's faces. He looked like the ice on a shallow pond, bluish, fragile, with dusted snow in the eyelashes. The snow atop his body wasn't thick; he'd died recently. There was no reason to shake his shoulder. She felt a pang of sadness for this man, who had gathered violets for Minnie, who could perfectly imitate the song of a sparrow.

But a sliver of yellow fabric on his neck caught her eye. She brushed the snow away and saw, wound around his throat like a scarf, Minnie's dress. She had helped Minnie sew it the year before. Minnie had been wearing the dress the last time Tamsen had seen her, though she told herself not to worry, that likely she'd changed out of it and they'd all bundled in whatever clothes they could find for warmth. But her ribs ached—where were her sisters? Searching around, she found no smaller bodies, no sister-size shapes. Perhaps they'd made it? Run from their husbands or found animals to help them live, as she had?

She searched the snow, walking wide circles as hope buoyed her. She would do one more pass through the deep snow, and as she walked, she scanned the horizon for shelter—caves, a den, something to keep them warm. And then, up ahead, against the trunk of a large pine tree, she saw a length of canvas strung into a shelter. She hurried through the snow, anticipating her sisters inside.

And there was one huddled figure in the shelter. But it was not one of her sisters. It was Arthur's other brother, leaning against the base of the tree, wrapped in many clothes.

"Brother," she called, ducking in under the canvas. He didn't respond. "Are you all right? Where are my sisters?" His eyes were open, though glazed, staring out into the snow. She tried again. "Where are Margaret and Minnie?" It would do no good to panic, though their absence caused greater alarm as the seconds passed. Still he said nothing. She crouched down so she was level with his face. Finally, then, she caught his eye. His mouth barely moved as he spoke.

"Help me," he said.

"Where are they?" she asked, and the panic she had been tamping down began to swell.

"There was no food. The cold was too great," he said, one hand clutching at her elbow; she moved quickly. She ducked out of the shelter and searched around, desperate, creating wide concentric circles in the snow, like the wake of a stone slipping into a pond. Blue, clear sky overhead, sparkling snow rounding everything beneath it into smoothed lumps. She searched, walking, stumbling, plunging her arms down to feel what was beneath her, big rocks, fallen trees. But then she tripped. Something else buried. It felt different, something in the air, inside her, knew. She did not want to dig. She had to dig. She dropped to her knees, not breathing, and began pulling out armfuls of snow. In her hand, something thin and hard.

She pulled it to the surface. Gripped in her fist was her sister's arm. Frozen, skin tinged cornflower blue, rubbery.

There was movement in her peripheral vision. The brother was dragging himself out of the shelter, through the snow, coming toward her. Tamsen did not turn to him. She pushed more snow off her sister's body, cradled not just this familiar arm and hand she knew so well, no sleeves covering it, but also the elbow, this shoulder she loved, with no clothes to keep it warm under all this snow, digging until she found the chest and then the neck and finally her beloved sister's face. Tamsen opened her mouth wide. The sound that came out screamed the moon in half.

Arthur's brother was crawling toward her. Too weak to stand. He stopped a few feet away, dropped to his stomach, and clasped his palms in prayer. "We did not save them," he said.

"Say what you did," Tamsen said. He shook his head. Shame's infection deep in him, too. Tamsen turned from her sister and stood above him, her foot very close to his face.

"Say it," she said. All around, the dark, wet earth peeked through the shimmering snow where she'd dug, shadow craters of the moon.

"We took their rations."

"And?"

"And their clothes."

"You took their food and their warmth."

"We would have frozen to death," he said, and she heard his sorrow, but it did not move her.

"You let them die," she said, amazed by the calm in her voice. "Where is my husband?"

"Three days gone. Searching for help. May God forgive us."

"I see no God here to forgive you," she said. "Only me." A flurry of snow built in the air and stung the inside of her nose, her lungs, and she felt as strong as she ever had, swollen with purpose. She told her brother-in-law that she understood, that he should pray for forgiveness and she would pray with him for the souls of her sisters. He closed his eyes again, thanking her, so grateful for her understanding, he said, and clasped his palms. She leaned over, picking up one of the rocks she had uncovered during her search. She did not hesitate. Brought it up above her head and then down on his skull.

She turned back to her sister then, knelt in the snow, and howled. When she could catch her breath, she uncovered the rest of Minnie's body and the body of Margaret beside her. She howled, holding the naked, emaciated bodies, and the evergreens overhead swayed in a small gust of wind and the sky above glittered blue and there was nothing she could do but hold the bodies, and so she held them.

There would come a moment when her husband would return and find his brother bleeding out into the snow and find Tamsen crouched over the bodies of her sisters, not helping him, having harmed him, and he would explode with rage at her, she knew, but she could not bring herself to do anything about it. She stayed with her sisters' bodies. She held them for one whole day and one whole night.

On the second day, under a clear blue sky, the freeze began to thaw. The exhaustion set into her body, the cold, the dark ache in her belly so far past hunger, but she carried on. She took her sister's faces in her hands and closed their eyes. She filled their mouths with spruce. Limbs quivering, she worked. There was almost nothing left of her. The words she spoke and then sang came from somewhere deep in her bones, cells spinning themselves into harmony. She took her knife and cut off their hair. She dragged them farther, so they could be gifted to the animals for food, so the animals could do the work of cleaning their bones.

There was a version of her who might have ended things there, lay in the snow and slept beside her sisters. Maybe a mountain range would be named for all three sisters. But that version was gone.

The snow was too deep and hard to traverse for much travel, what with the weakness of her body, so she would have to wait a little while, find food nearby. She searched, though she knew it was pointless. Too much snow, winter laid down upon everything. She could die or she could live. She looked over at her dead brother-in-law, face down in the snow. The brothers had taken something from her sisters.

She crawled over to him and did not ask for forgiveness before she began pulling the stiff clothing off his body. Her sister's dress, socks, coat, the fur-lined mittens, all of it went onto her body. With the extra warmth, in the protection of the shelter, she had to wait for the animals to do their work on her sisters, and she had to survive. She rested, but any strength in her body was leaving her hour by hour. She needed food. There was no other option. In the dawn light of the next morning she crawled back to the brother, held her knife in her shivering palm, and squinted against the bright orange rays shimmering on the snow. She wanted to live, and in order to live, she plunged the knife into his thigh.

Many times she had seen her mama butcher a deer or an elk or a moose, she had helped clean the meat, she knew how to separate the sinew. She loosened skin, cut all the way around the joints. Peeled the skin off, slit clean what meat she could. It wasn't fast, but she didn't need to be fast. She retched, swallowed, breathed. She would live.

She wanted to live, and she did. She ate the meat off her sister's husband's body. She ate and grew strength, and ate and removed more meat, shoulders and rump, preparing some for her journey, and then she was ready. She wiped the blood into the snow. Two pine cones over his eyes in thanks, in horror.

By then her sisters had been mostly cleaned. She collected what bones remained. As many as she could carry, she packed.

Down she walked, from mountain snow to rock, from rock to mud, from mud down the foothills to where the grasslands stopped holding snow. Into the long grasses. She walked and walked right into spring, the bones of her sisters on her back, the hair wound round her wrists, and found, finally, a valley. It was empty of people. It was filled with red-bark trees that reached almost to the sky. There, she set down the bones and, from them, began to build.

9

1981

PEOPLE TOLD GLORIA that the day her first child was born would be the most magical of her life. You'll fall madly in love, everyone said. You'll witness a miracle. You'll meet your little soulmate.

Nobody had told her that to give birth was to be smashed up against death, pressed all the way against a quickly cracking window to the other side. And the pain—holy goddamned motherfucking shit. No, there was no language for it. Nothing to compare it to. She remembered believing that her pelvis would shatter. She remembered thinking that the pressure would actually shoot her eyeballs out of their sockets. And then, after forty hours, at midnight exactly, this weirdly pink creature came out of her with a shrieking cry and wide, dark eyes that stayed open for a strangely long time, the doctor said, so alert for a newborn, so awake. And her hands, as small as a walnut, flexing open and closed on Gloria's breast like a tiny cat. She named her Luce, *light*, an aspirational name for what she thought the baby might bring to her life. And then she waited for the love that everyone said would flood her.

She waited, and stared, and waited. She fed the baby. She changed diapers. She waited. But it wasn't love that rushed in. It was something darker.

Throughout her pregnancy this darkness had grown as another creature inside her. It was about her sister. Gem, who made nests in shoeboxes for the abandoned baby possum they found in the yard. Gem, who would wander a forest alone for hours and turn flailing beetles on their feet again and recount the walk with the intricacy of a movie plot. She knew how to help things grow, to save them. Gloria didn't. She knew something about herself, that she was a person who needed to be seen. To be onstage, to be the center of light, and that in the spotlight, there was only ever room for one person. This realization was what seeped in: Gem would do better. Gloria would fuck it up.

Gloria remembered crouching in front of her sister's face when they were nine, just after the paramedics had left, telling her that she was sorry, so sorry, and that she would never allow anyone to hurt her. Gloria and Gem were identical in every way except for the oblong patch of puckered skin on Gem's neck from a pot of boiling water Gloria had thrown at her in an argument. They had been alone in their apartment, making spaghetti to surprise their father. The police report was amended several times because of a discrepancy over how many people were injured. Upon entering the home, two young females were found screaming and rolling on the floor, but once the medics were able to calm the girls and examine both carefully, injuries were found on only Gem. It didn't make any sense to the medics. Gem had the wound, but they both seemed to feel the pain.

Their father used to bring the girls to the bar where he hung out after work, showing off their ability to finish each other's sentences and dances, invent song lyrics. Their father drank for free on those days, always said he was going to take them on the road with a traveling circus. The girls clapped, and said yes, Daddy, yes please, Gloria especially. She sparkled under the eyes of strangers. There was no other time she felt that her body was wholly hers, untwinned.

Gem didn't like it. But she went along with it because Gloria loved it—that was exactly the kind of person her sister was, as if they had a full deck of personality traits divvied out between them, no overlap.

"Here's how it works, fellas," their daddy said to the work friends who would listen. He put on his teacherly voice, gestured exuberantly; an excellent talker, their daddy. "When an embryo splits early, within the first few days, the twins form independently from each other, so they have a relationship more like siblings. If, however, the zygote is late to split—sometimes it can be as long as two weeks after fertilization—the resulting twins almost always exhibit telepathy and ESP. They started their life as one, and so share more than only identical genes. My girls were actually the *same person* at the beginning. These two girls right here! That's why their minds meld. To the circus, my peanuts," he'd say, sloshing back a whiskey and smiling at Gloria and Gem as if they were made of sunshine itself.

Once, they had been the very same person. Though most people thought that would preclude you from loneliness, what it meant for Gloria was an eternal missing half.

The idea became a refrain: Gloria was going to fuck this up.

She kept this dark secret inside her the first week with her new baby at home, tucking it deep in the hope that nature would kick on some new, capable, more generous part of herself, the innate love she saw stretched across the faces of all the other mothers she encountered who calmed writhing toddlers in grocery stores. But the nights started blurring into days, and her nipples were bleeding, had actual scabs on them, and Luce only slept for thirty minutes at a time, ever, at all—certainly nobody told Gloria that might happen—and she cried continuously when she was awake, and the secret started to rise.

You can't imagine it until you're inside it, what the screaming does. The small mouth right up by your ear no matter how you hold her. The absolute shock that lungs that small can make such a sound. The face bright pink and so pinched, and you try and try and nothing you do makes it stop. You can't imagine the heat it brings into your own body.

And one day, when Luce was three weeks old and Gem was at work and Gloria was more tired than she'd ever been, more delirious, more full of rage, with a body so tender that even kindnesses felt torturous, she couldn't take it. She set the baby on the floor—nowhere she could fall, not that she could roll anyway, still such a grub of a human—put a blanket over her to keep her warm, and walked outside. She needed a minute. There was a commercial being filmed a few blocks away. She wanted to catch a glimpse. Just a peek at the magic. She hustled, she wasn't going to leave the baby for long, she wasn't a monster, the baby would probably go to sleep anyway, and she had been fed recently, really, she was completely fine. Gloria needed a few goddamned minutes to herself, to be refreshed by all the lights illuminating the street, and maybe they'd have one of those big hoses that shot water onto the road to make it look clean and fresh, maybe even a rain machine, those were so fun to watch. When it came down to it, how could she be a good mother if she lost herself? Didn't every child, especially every girl child, deserve a strong woman to guide her through this life? So she would start to reclaim that for herself, not at this moment of course, ha, she looked like shit, greasy hair and sour milk all over her shirt, but just to breathe it in. And she did. It was beautiful.

And, feeling a little better, she headed home. She hadn't been gone long. Fifteen minutes maybe, twenty, it really was such a short time and there was nothing the baby could have done to hurt herself, it was no big deal.

She could hear Luce from down the hallway of the apartment. The screaming. And then the silence.

This tiny, dark-eyed girl with a dimple in one cheek.

The baby was on the floor, legs kicking madly. The blanket was covering her face. She must've somehow grasped it and pulled it there. The baby was screaming again, and so still breathing, thank god, though the sound was choking, desperate. Gloria yanked the blanket away. Underneath, the baby's face was as red as a fire hydrant, purple in some places too, near blue. She was suffocating.

And so this was the truth that nobody, not her sister, not her daughter, would ever fully understand. It wasn't that Gloria didn't want Luce. Head smell of strawberry jam. It was that she knew, with a lance through her heart, that if it were left to her, the kid wouldn't even survive.

10

June 27, 1997 • Gone Nineteen Hours

Luce was in the dark. Deep dark, like a cave, like the inside of a closed mouth, that's what she imagined. Teeth clamped shut. There was a sound floating in from somewhere far off—her own voice, as a child. Whispering something into the phone. Whispering to Gem, whose ear was unbloodied on the other side, but it would only remain that way if she said the right words, if she told her—

Luce woke with a gasp. She was here, in her bedroom, with light coming in through the window—bright sun having already heated the plants limp. The madrone out the window still had the very last of their red berries, shriveled, puckered wounds.

She got up quickly, sure that her mother had come home. She had been here every other morning since they'd moved to the Red Grove—asleep or cooking or working or angry or harvesting or humming, but here. Quietly she slipped out of her bedroom and began a careful walk through the house. Into the kitchen, where the coffeepot dripped no liquid. She checked the living room, walking slowly past the table and futon and piano, rubbing her fingers along the dusty ears of the snake plant.

She checked the bathroom. Knocked gently on her mother's office, no reply, and then tried the door handle. Locked. No surprise. Her mother had a key, and she locked the office from the hallway whenever she left the house. She must've locked it when they left for the lions.

Luce peeked into Roo's room, but he was alone and still asleep, and then into Gem's, where no twin filled the empty space. Just Gem. Half of the whole. Luce shut the door and then leaned back against the wall.

There was one room left to check. There had never been much in her mother's bedroom, small and dark, the one window shadowed by a clump of trees. Nobody here. She stood above the makeup table and opened each lipstick, French Kiss and Firecracker and Coral Sea, and stabbed them down onto a crumpled tissue. Blunted the tip. A yellowed bra strewn over the back of a chair, a clay mug with a broken handle holding dried lavender from last year's garden, a few photographs stuck together and half tucked beneath a carved stone hand. She pulled them out, cycled through quickly: Gem and Gloria when they were young, in matching sombreros. Gloria with Luce and Roo, before they'd moved here to the Red Grove, looking happy and light in a way they probably hadn't since. She set them down. Nothing to indicate where she'd gone. Something was wrong. She swallowed it down.

She wanted to hear the sound of her mother's car pulling up the steep driveway. To the deck, then, with Moose trotting alongside her, tensed. She sat on the top step of the deck stairs, listening. "Where's Gloria?" she asked Moose, who scanned the trees in response. "Don't think she's up there, bud," Luce said, untangling foxtails from his fur as he leaned into her, trying to listen down the road, over the redwood and bay and madrone, for that certain pitch of her mother's hum. It was a hum she could hear from her bedroom when she was younger, in the early years in this house, when business was good and Gem was improving and Gloria said she'd found her calling—finally, fully herself, she said. Luce would hear the hum coming from the kitchen, waking her in the morning in her little cold bed, redwood-shadowed, damp. Pulling on her sweatpants and T-shirt, she'd rush into the kitchen, and there Gloria would be, smiling that shark grin when she came in, winking like they were in on something together. Gloria brewing herbs on the stove for tea and tinctures, frying eggs, humming her hum, and Luce would cut slices of bread for toast, hoist herself onto the counter, legs dangling, and begin the careful toasting and buttering—her best job. Sometimes Gloria had the radio on and would drum on Luce's legs in rhythm when she passed. Sometimes she'd be humming her own song, and then she'd pick Luce up—too big for this, but still—hoist her onto her hip, hold their arms out straight, clasping their hands and sticking a sprig of rosemary in Luce's mouth like a rose, and then they'd tango back and forth across the kitchen floor and Luce would laugh and laugh, and Gloria would too, and it lit something new in Luce, this woman directing all her attention, all her love, the vastness of her starbright universe, onto Luce.

Now, out on the deck, she listened for her mother's hum, made a pile of freed foxtails, Moose's nose twitching in the breeze, handsomely deweeded. They willed Gloria's car to approach. Come on. The poison oak growing up the edges of the deck and through the slatted boards turned over in the wind, green leaves that would go red in the fall, turn to sticks in the winter. They willed it, but there was nothing.

Luce jimmied a bobby pin into the lock on her mother's office door. This felt like the best place to start.

"What're you doing?" Roo asked, marching out of his bedroom in his pajamas. He licked his hands to smooth his cowlicks. "Mom'll be mad."

"Let her come scold me then," Luce said.

Roo considered this, a little startled frown on his face. "She'll kill you if you go in there."

She would, Luce knew. It was about the only thing she might get in real trouble for. They were encouraged to explore their desires, to learn their own boundaries. She'd heard that some teenagers outside the Red Grove, even as close as the next town fifteen miles away, weren't allowed to swear or cut their hair as they liked or have sex when they wanted to. Occasionally one of those teenagers would take a liking to someone in the Red Grove, and for a short time Luce and her friends would get an influx of information about life outside the community, but it never took long before the adults squashed it or, more often, the Red Grove teenagers called it off themselves—it was pretty easy to imagine how a relationship might play out with some-one from outside.

The bobby pin wasn't working. She rattled and angled, but no luck. And beneath the shaking of her hand, trying to jam the bobby pin in—her pulse, growing faster. Where was her mom?

Una lived down the road from Heartwood in one of the newer cot-tages, with morning glory vines climbing the shingles and six-foot sunflowers along the driveway. A twenty-minute bike ride down the big hill and then along the main flat road through the valley's center brought Luce to Una, who, when Luce wound around back, was sub-merged up to her mouth in her wooden hot tub.

Roo had gone down the hill to play with a friend, and Luce thought to see for herself if her mom was here and, if not, to ask Una a question she somehow couldn't fathom asking over the phone. Una would know. Seeing Luce, Una sat up on the edge of the tub, her skin steam-ing. Over the years, Una had urged Luce to confide in her about her disagreements with her mom, about the canyon she felt was ever-present between them. Oh, Goose, Una would say, chin low and nodding as Luce recounted those early years. She wanted to see Una's face when she told her that Gloria hadn't come home, before Una had a chance to reason and rationalize and say everything was fine. She wanted to see if Una thought that Gloria had decided to move on.

"Have you seen my mom?" Her voice cracked on the first word.

"Your mama? Of course—I see her all the time. Gorgeous, wild creature that she is," Una said, sliding out of the water and fanning her red face with her hand.

"Is she here?"

Una stopped smiling, looked at Luce. "What do you mean?" she asked. "Has she not been home this morning?"

Luce shook her head. Said her mother had been gone since yesterday afternoon, and that no, she didn't know where she'd gone, that's what she was hoping Una would know. Luce watched her face—sweaty, red, and yes, there it was, some alarm. Una reached her arm out for Luce to come close, wrapped it around Luce's waist, hot and steaming. They stared at each other for a moment, silent.

"Luce," Una said, squeezing the top of Luce's arm tightly. "Do you think—"

"What?"

"Well, I'm sure there's no connection, but that man who keeps calling?"

A drop deep down in Luce's stomach. "How do you know about him?" she asked.

"Oh honey, there are no secrets here," Una said, squeezing Luce's bicep. "I've been worried that your mama would decide to go meet him somewhere outside the Grove."

Luce swallowed a glob of spit that almost choked her. She hadn't even considered this yet. Idiot. All she'd been thinking about was her own potential abandonment. "He hasn't called since yesterday, just before we left for the lions," Luce said, and as she said it, she heard the terrible matchup of timing—no call from him since Gloria had been gone.

There was something strange happening in Una's face, a tightening of the brows. She was worried. The worry dropped deeper into Luce, too. The first seventy-two hours are the most crucial in any missing person case. Was her mother a missing person? Technically yes, but—*missing* missing? She didn't know. After twenty-four hours, clues get harder to find: witnesses forget, physical evidence deteriorates. Time is a bully, hell-bent on keeping information buried. She knew the things men did to women's bodies, and a hazy slideshow began looping in the back of her mind: hairy knuckles around her mother's throat. A kick to the kneecaps.

She told Una about the note. How much she was trying to help. How much worse it made everything.

"We'll figure out where she is," Una said, tucking her chin before kissing Luce quickly on the forehead. She needed to take a breath, a step back. "Follow me inside. I'm sending you home with banana bread, but go see the kids down the hall first."

Most of Luce's friends had been born in the Red Grove, and it gave them a kind of ease with one another that Luce always felt she was watching from another planet.

When Gloria moved them here, she had baby Roo and a newly everdreaming twinnie to care for, plus she was setting up her business, and so sent Luce out into the woods most days. Despite her shyness, Luce's life quickly became enmeshed in those of the other kids, a ragtag crew who roamed the woods. Some days, one or many of the kids' moms stayed in bed with their heads beneath pillows, remembering what had come before the Red Grove. The kids played outside while the mothers burrowed. Some of the moms were quick to trust their new home, and some kept their eyes scanning the horizon until the day they moved away. Some days the moms went into the paint store, where many of them worked, a business outside the Red Grove but very close to the boundary and therefore deemed safe-ish, where they rang up gallons for customers to transform their lives—cerulean, mauve, taupe—nodding yes, magenta reorients the energies, and sometimes one or a few of the kids would be taken to the paint store with the moms so they could be kept under a watchful eye. Luce went a few times with the paint store kids. They would strut the aisles pretending not to be the kids of their skittish moms but instead of Hulk Hogan—best wrestler—and they blew air into the tips of their thumbs like they were inflating themselves. They walked around all puffed up. They were never afraid.

But the kids who had been born and raised in the Red Grove had something that Luce didn't, never would—they'd never lived in a world where terrible things could happen to them. When she was twelve or so, lounging in the massive stump of a redwood tree that had been smoothed over time into seats and benches, her friends had decided to play truth or dare, and suddenly people were kissing one another, were being dared to enter a tree's wound in the dark with a boy for thirty seconds to get felt up, and she left.

She knew what happened next. Getting a boyfriend was what had happened to Gem.

Luce had been told plenty of times since then that there were good men, that not all relationships ended with violence, especially not in the Red Grove. But the idea of a boy's hand sliding up her shirt summoned bile.

She'd wandered out of the woods, saying she had to go home, but she didn't walk home. She wove between the trees until she was suddenly behind Heartwood. Reached into a redwood wound where she stored the first book she'd found about the killer who stalked women for weeks, broke into their homes at night. The sentences were hard to read, but she could not help how much she needed to read them.

And Una, somehow spotting her out there, had come to meet her and had not been horrified by the book, as her mother had been.

They'd taken a few walks together by that point. And for reasons Luce had never been able to get totally clear on, she spoke the truth to Una then, about her mother having left her, about what had happened to her aunt Gem. Una sat beside her on a log in the woods, nodding, listening with a pure concentration Luce had never experienced. It felt like stepping out of the shadows into the sunshine. Una, she knew, was very busy. Running this place. But Una, chin down and nodding, made it clear there was nothing more important than what Luce was saying at that very moment.

A few days later, Luce found herself back again, having wandered off from a game of soccer, and again Una left whatever important task she was completing in Heartwood to come outside and talk. And again. Luce did not tell her mother about it, because she knew her mother would ruin it. You're a special girl, Una told her. Luce did not say, I will do anything, forever, to hear someone say that to me.

It set her apart from her friends, this tightness with Una that grew into more time at Heartwood, into helping Una chop carrots for community dinners, into watering the saplings, into having someone to whom Luce could recount the chapter she'd just finished about the murderer who hid the bodies of his female victims through-out his London home, or Ruby Wells's latest news story of the serial rapist. Una would listen, nodding, and squeeze Luce's hand.

A brownnoser, Forrest said when they were younger and Luce was so often with his mother, but she had pretended not to hear. She could be both. She could have her role with Una and also, still, have friends. Of course she could.

Forrest was slumped on his bed with a half-pint of vodka in his hand. Aya, Tangerine, and Sam lay in various states of recline on his futon and the floor, nymphs sunbathing after a dip in a cold, clear pool, like Luce had seen in Renaissance paintings, entirely at home inside their own flopped bodies. Aya threw a peace sign in the air when Luce walked in, Tangerine's hands were busy tying her T-shirt into a knot just below her breasts, and Sam, the new girl, gave her a quick smile—Luce hadn't seen her since her walk through the dark.

"Hey," Luce said, trying hard to look casual as she made her way inside, to press the violence out of her head and be a little normal—*See, Mom, look how normal, you can come back.* Forrest swigged his bottle and blinked hard to try to keep his eyes from watering. "Breakfast of champions," he said, gulping from a carton of orange juice. Luce reached for the vodka. She plopped onto the futon beside Sam, who was spreading aluminum foil across her fingernails. "I thought your parents didn't want you drinking this hard stuff," Luce said to Forrest. "Where'd you find it?"

"In the closet where my dad hides his tax returns," Forrest said.

"Ew, he pays taxes?" Aya said, sitting straight up from the floor. "Traitor."

"He doesn't want anyone to know," Forrest said.

"Capitalist," Tangerine said with disgust. It sparked a moment of curiosity for Luce, this idea—she'd always wondered how Una and her partner had money. Running Heartwood wasn't cheap—Luce had seen bills in the office, and the money collected from tithes couldn't come close to funding it. But Una had never taken Luce up on her offer to help manage the books, as she did for her mother's business, so she didn't know how it all worked.

"So how's it going so far, Sam?" Luce asked, passing the vodka to Tangerine and trying to catch a glimpse of Sam's face.

"Okay I guess," Sam said, brushing back her hair. "My mom said we were moving to protected space, and I thought that meant, like, a national park or something."

"There *is* a shitload of open land all around," Forrest said. "Sick mountain biking."

"Yeah, but that's not what she means, dufus," Aya said, smearing her finger into a tub of lip gloss. There was a tiny star sticker perfectly spaced beside the outside of each of her eyes, and her T-shirt, worn and web-thin in some places, had been cut into a tank top that hung low in the front and showed off a dark crease of her perfect grapefruit boobs. Luce tried not to stare, wasn't even sure why she was staring—if she wanted them herself or wanted to touch them. To Luce, her friends sometimes looked like the girls in glossy magazines like *Seventeen* or *Allure* that they were able to sneak into the Red Grove occasionally and illicitly pass around, sliding them into and out of math textbooks or keeping them rolled tight and shoved inside a small tree hole. When they were sure no adults were around, they'd look at them together, talking about who looked anorexic and how fucked up the advice inside was—nineteen ways to pleasure your man; quiz: are you overreacting; Madonna's workout routine—toxic, all of it, they said, so stupid, all the while trying on the faces they saw the girls in there making, altering their clothes to match, telling each other who was a tomboy, Luce, who was a pixie, Tangerine, who was a vixen, Aya. They ran toward what they should look like with ferocity even though they mostly tried to hide it. They knew they shouldn't chase it. That it was bullshit. Capitalistic. Meant to destroy burgeoning female self-confidence. They knew it and couldn't help themselves, because they wanted to be beautiful, who didn't, and things were different from the way they'd been when their mothers were teenagers, it was 1997, almost the millennium—they could be badass feminist bitch goddesses and also wear bras.

The vodka had smoothed over some of Luce's worries, enough to loose her tongue and tell them that her mom hadn't come home since yesterday afternoon, when they'd gone to see the lions, and then, because it was so much easier to keep talking than to start, and her hand was clasped by Tangerine, and Sam was looking at her with concern, she told them too that there was an angry man who wouldn't stop calling them, and the terrible way the timing of it all lined up.

"So call the guy and demand to talk to your mom," Forrest said. Luce nodded. He made it sound so simple. There was no way she'd tell them about the note, or what she'd done when he came by. She did what she had to do to keep herself safe, she repeated to herself. She didn't have a choice.

"I don't have his number. I don't even know his name," Luce said.

"If there's one bad bitch out of anyone I know, it's your auntie Gem," Aya said. "Shouldn't she be able to tell you where your mom is, like, psychically?"

"I'm not like that," Luce said, knowing she sounded defensive as soon as it came out of her mouth, but it was true, she hadn't been able to communicate with Gem. But—and here the pillow of vodka spread a little further around her head—Aya was right. Why hadn't she already been thinking this? She needed to go home. The only person who would actually know where her mother was right now was Gem.

11

June 27, 1997 • Gone Twenty-Two Hours

G EM HAD BEEN IN HER STATE OF EVERDREAM since Luce was
eight, just before they moved to the Red Grove, and it had, in
the way loss does, locked an oversimplified, glorified, and therefore
treacherous version of who Gem was into all of their lives. Gem
never raised her voice, Luce would say when Gloria got mad. Gem
loved history documentaries, Roo was fond of saying, and though
nobody knew this to be true of Gem, nobody corrected him.

She became a kind of collective story they told together about
someone more interesting, funnier, smarter than the rest of them,
and her unchanging preferences—french fries dipped in vinegar,
bright wrist bangles from India—gave them a fixed point against
which their own fickle, changing selves were always measured. But
their storytelling had its own waves, and every few months their collective adoration would reach a breaking point for Gloria, and after
one of her children made a claim about something—Gem's favorite
ice-cream flavor being mint chip or the unrivaled elegance of her
hands—Gloria would snap. You didn't know her at all, she would

hiss, you were a little kid, and besides, she wasn't so perfect. And there would be silence for a few weeks, after which they all grew independently lonely from the missing presence of their shared, perfect fourth unit, and slowly, carefully, the collective mythmaking would begin again.

As Luce got older, she began to understand these moments of outburst from her mother as something quite simple: jealousy. Here was a near-exact replica of herself, but one unable to make mistakes, adored and looked after by her children and community, kissed, tucked in, whispered to, sighed over, while she, Gloria, had to trudge through the muck of actually raising these children and caring for her sister and aging and paying the bills, all the while living in the Red Grove for, and because of, her sister.

Luce had gone quickly home after leaving Una's house, but her mother still was not there.

She leaned in close to Gem and wondered, not for the first time, whether it was possible that she had a sliver of her mom's abilities. Nothing had ever worked when she'd tried in the past, but she'd always given up so fast, frustrated, telling herself she didn't want to be like that anyway. But this was different. She focused all her energy on Gem, thinking, Please, can you help me? Was there anything Gem could tell her about where her mother had gone? She leaned in closer, straining. And then Gem made a tiny sound. She didn't make sounds. It came from the far back of her throat, very faint, not a hum exactly, but something more like a buzz. Yes, yes, Luce thought, where is my mom, and also, please—where are you? She felt like a little lost child in a storybook. But she was not the one who was lost.

Gem was silent. But there was the buzz again, though it was not coming from her. It was louder, a buzz out in the hallway. Luce followed the buzz into her bedroom. Something in there had changed. Something about the window at the far side of the room. It was the same size, same rectangular shape, a single rattly pane of glass be-hind the blue sarong hanging as a curtain, so she couldn't see the window, not exactly. What was different? It seemed farther away, somehow. And then there it was, that dim buzzing. It wasn't a chainsaw in the hands of a madman. She bit her lip. This was the Red Grove. No need to be scared.

But something was happening. On either side, the walls relin-quished their pale, stained plaster hues, darkening into a shadowed tunnel to the window. The floor was shadow, her own hands just a trace of blackness, and she was walking closer to the buzzing. She was on some sort of conveyer belt toward the window, a few steps away even though she didn't feel like she was walking toward it, no, she wasn't, yet she kept getting closer. It had changed, was changing. She shouldn't look. She would not like to know what was on the other side of the blue sarong. The buzzing was in her head.

Or, no—the buzzing was an actual sound. She was nearly at the window, but the buzzing—yes, some toy Roo had left in here, its wheels spinning on and on. She was scaring herself. She spun around and scanned the room. There were no toys. No bees. The buzzing carried on, and yes, she was afraid, yes.

Back to the window. She didn't take a step, yet there she was, right in front of it, there was her arm, its skin and little hairs all standing straight up as her arm moved away from her body, as it reached for the fabric. She pulled it aside.

Outside the window, at eye level, was a black mass of flies. They hovered together in a loose hoard, though not like the clump she'd seen once around a dead deer up on the ridge. Then, the deer had been partially eaten by some animal, and the flies landed on the carcass, crawled across the pink and gray rotting flesh, flew, landed again.

Not these flies. These flies—a hundred or more, hundreds?—hovered, wings beating too fast to see, in one massive clump, all fac-ing the window. Like they were looking at her. Spying. The buzz of their collective hovering was a constant, and that's when the first sharp sound came. A plunk, like hail falling on metal. One of the flies flew straight into the window. It was against nature—a kind of suicide. But then another followed. And another. They flew straight, hard, wild, right into the window.

Thwack. Straight into the glass.

Thwack.

Luce's hand was holding the fabric open. She could feel her pulse in that hand, her mad heart trying to make sense of what she was seeing. *Thwack*. She closed her eyes a moment. *Thwack*, like rain dripping into a bucket of water. Her eyes snapped open again. What was she doing? She watched a single black fly careen its body, fast, unambiguously, straight into the window.

Stunned or dead, she couldn't tell which, it fell to the windowsill below, onto what Luce first thought was a patch of dark mold on the painted wood but realized it was, instead, a heap of flies. What could cause this? Think. Think.

Flies were magnetized by waste, a pile of excretion, an animal deteriorating. They were creatures bent toward death. She became more aware of the hair standing straight up on her neck and down her arms; they were seeking something dead. Very slowly, she turned around and faced the room behind her. Pressure on her chest. Was there something rotting inside the house that the flies could sense? She could not help it—her brain flashed to her mother's corpse, hidden, rotting, inside their house. But no. Her car was gone. She had left. There was no chance, not even a sliver, that it was her mother. There was no way she was in here somewhere, calling the flies as some sort of flourish on a performance they couldn't understand, no, and what a thought, what a terrible thought.

And anyway, how could flies smell something through the window? What, then? Be rational. Most likely, an animal had died under the house, a raccoon or rat or possum. Probably that was drawing the flies.

She repeated it again. No reason to be afraid.

They wouldn't bore through the glass, hurting her as she might have led to her own mother's hurt. Her heart inside her mouth, pulsing her tongue. What she needed to do was let go of the blue fabric in her hand, let it fall across the window so that she could turn away, so that she could decide what she believed in and what she didn't, but her hand held tight, *thunk, thwack,* and she watched her arm, the free one dangling to her side, move toward the window latch. Was she moving it? Its fingers were taut and shaking and moving closer to the latch, crab-clawed. She shouldn't open the window. Her fingers were on the brass then, pulling up against the window's hardware.

With a rush, the flies flew inside. Dozens, hundreds, rushing past her in a buzzing mass. From outside, a draft of cooler air, the waft of roses, *Where is my mother?* And then, the buzzing gone, there she was—her mother's voice.

Low and forceful, her mother's voice, a laugh breaking through and emanating from the trees, her mother's voice as clear as cool spring water but seeming to come from the trunk of each tree, from the wounds, the ferns below, from the cascading needles above—her voice the forest's very air.

Luce had to follow the voice, quickly—no time to run through and around the house. She climbed out the window, dropping to the ground among the thick poison oak and ferns. Yes, it was her mother's voice, but not her voice right now, a younger voice, as if time had taken her backward and she was stuck in the trees. Luce closed her eyes and breathed in. Was this a thing that was really happening? When she turned to face the house, her mother's voice got louder. That's what it was. The window to her mother's office was open.

"Mom?" she said, peering inside. She was certain the office's door was locked. She'd tested. But here was the office, off-limits, forbidden, and yet. She listened for the office itself to clatter, for alarms to sound or books to fall off their shelves. Stillness. Her mother's voice, singing.

Something moved past her—a breeze? Or the warm air escaping from the house into the evening? She was close to the white-gray fuzz of the house's shingles. She pressed one hand against them, steadying herself. A hornet floated in front of her a moment, then dove away. She leaned closer still to the window, her face inches from the opening, to feel that wind, to see inside, and then she jumped straight into the air when she heard the sound of her name.

"What are you doing?" Roo yelled, leaning out of her bedroom window.

"Nothing," Luce said quickly. She spun toward him, dropping her arms. "I heard—"

"You're breaking in."

"I'm not."

"I'm telling."

"Roo. She's been gone two days." They looked at each other, not speaking the specifics of worry. The most she'd ever left for was a few hours. "She left the window open. It's weird. She's so careful to lock it."

"Mamma?" Roo was looking around, his eyes flashing between trees and sky and dirt. "I hear her."

"It's coming from the office. I'm going in," Luce said.

Roo was chewing on his lip, his hair nearly covering his eyes. "Don't do it, Luce," he said without conviction. Their mother's voice floated around them like golden pollen from the trees, moving and also everywhere.

"Stay inside," Luce said. "I'll be right there." He nodded, unsure, but retreated into the room.

She climbed into the office. Inside was an ordinary room. And then, Gloria's voice. She was singing—"*Who's afraid of the big bad wolf, big bad wolf, big bad wolf?*" The sound was coming from a table filled with electronic equipment—radios, a VCR, a small TV covered with fabric, a tape recorder, a microphone, headsets, and a few big black boxes with switches and outputs and flashing lights. Luce flipped a few switches, twisted a dial, readied for everything to turn on, spark, call out, but only one sound carried on. *"Who's afraid of the big bad wolf, Tra la la la la."* Through the orange fabric, light glowed from the TV. She yanked off the cover, and on the screen, close up, was her mother, elbows locked in unison with Gem. *"Who's afraid of the big bad wolf,"* they sang together, their faces, nearly identical, filling up the screen. Luce couldn't tell who was who. They were laughing as they sang, though their faces weren't clear. The footage was black-and-white, grainy, but something in the way they moved together, little gestures of their chins, fingers coming into the frame, the ticktock of their heads back and forth as they sang, all of it was completely and absolutely in unison.

It was possible, Luce thought, that this video had been playing in a loop since their mother was last in the office. Or it was also possible, she thought, not knowing from where this thought arrived, that something had just turned it on.

Their song ended. The two small faces, smiling into the camera, turned to each other then and, though it was hard to tell in the blurred old video, something passed between them, a movement of the eyebrows and edges of the lips. And then, faces still turned toward each other in their own private universe, one made a buzzing sound with her lips. The other buzzed back. The camera jostled then, swinging away from their faces, and as it did, the strangest thing—surely a trick of the angle—it appeared as if the two of them rose, slightly, into the air.

The screen flicked to black. Luce had never seen footage of the twins when they were young, and it sent an arrowed ache into the soft gunk of her heart, how much she missed Gem, how much her mother must miss her too. She'd never felt zipped to another person in the way the girls were in this video. What a thing, Luce thought: to never, ever be lonely.

She took a breath, flicked on the radio, but no sound came out. No spinning of knobs or pressing of buttons yielded any other sounds, any other movement. She turned away from the electronics. There was more of the office to explore, and maybe, somewhere, the calling man's number. Had her mother really gone somewhere to meet him? Somewhere outside the grove? Could she really and truly be that foolish?

Move faster, then. Behind her was a chipped wooden bookshelf on which stood a row of old books, small statues of various deities— the Buddha, Ganesh, Jesus, a Princess Diana bobblehead. A few candles and incense clusters, dried sage wrapped in twine. A bag of M&M's. A plastic panda. "Hello?" she said to the room, just to see. Nothing.

A deep purple velvet armchair sat beside the table of electronic equipment. On the other side, a small table held a telephone. It was an old rotary, with holes for your fingers, scuffed and plugged into nothing. No cords ran out from the back of the phone. She grasped the receiver in her hand, placed it to her ear, sure she would hear nothing, because there was nothing to hear, but some sliver of her thought—*hoped*—there would be a voice on the line. Whose? Her mother's. Gem's. Because—nerves firing—could the gift finally reveal itself here, in this room where her mother spent so much time? Was it perhaps the room itself that held the gift? She listened to the phone. But it was silent.

A bang somewhere deep in the house. She flinched. Luce knew these sounds, the continual stretching and breathing of the house around them, but she still held her breath, listened for her mother. But there were no other sounds. There was nobody here. She was alone. She thought about Roo, pouting, working his meaty little freckled fingers on whatever his current project was. Roo was not alone. He had a big sister to care for him. But Luce? She was nine, standing at the bedside of someone who had already traveled away from her, completely and forever after alone. "*Who's afraid of the big bad wolf, the big bad wolf, the big bad wolf,*" the girls sang again, the video having started over, though louder this time, turned all the way up, how did it get so loud, faces smooshed into the camera, dark eyes and their conspiratorial laugh, louder and louder until Luce fumbled at the base of the TV to turn down the volume, and in doing so, her hand hit against the corner of something and knocked it down.

It was a folder. It had been tucked between the TV and VCR, and it fell to the ground, papers spilling out. Old newspaper articles folded in halves and quarters. Handwritten notes. She picked one up, scanning it quickly for a man's name and phone number, but it was a list of names of people in the Red Grove. Twelve names. Scanning down, she saw it: *Luce Shelley.*

There was no obvious connection between her and the other names on the list; some younger kids, a few, like Luce, in high school, some older who'd moved out of the Red Grove, some who'd stayed. At the bottom of the list, a few spaces after the last name, was a question mark, all of it in her mother's unmistakable handwriting, and then a few words messily scrawled and circled. *Ask Juan.*

Juan was their closest neighbor. Ask Juan what? There was a loud bang on the office door, Roo's voice from the hallway telling her to open up. She stuffed the list of names into her pocket and put everything else in the folder, slid it back where it had been tucked, and unlocked the door. There was Roo, arms crossed over his chest, his face a small storm.

He took a big breath, ready to scold her, but his eye caught something behind her and he stopped. He pushed past her then, worming inside. In front of the table of electronics, his chin barely taller than the tabletop, he reached his arm up into the air, spun a dial until it clicked, pressed a button, flipped two levers, and out of the speakers burst the sound of radio static.

"How did you know how to do that?" Luce asked. He didn't answer her, but spun on to the next thing, the microphone, small and rectangular and suddenly crackling alive in his hands, and Luce saw, from the side of his face, a wild, wet-eyed thrill that echoed the look the twins had on their faces in the video, something that was hooking him right into whatever was happening here. She felt a chill, something off about the air, "Enough, Roo," she said, but he didn't pay any attention. She raised her voice: "Stop it. Let's go."

He startled then, and spun to her. "I know how to do it."

"Out," she said, grabbing for his shoulder and pointing toward the door, back out of this strange room, into the ordinary hallway, the familiar kitchen, under the enormous shadows of their regular trees. She pushed him out the door. He stumbled, fell onto the floor, but she didn't say sorry.

Luce looked at her brother, whose indignant face had already transformed into something else as his eye caught an ant on the ground. Rapt, he was looking at the tiny creature carrying a crumb of something. He looked the same, didn't he? Or was there something of the faintest kind of glimmer around him? She squinted her eyes. No, of course not.

At least she had a place to start—*Ask Juan.* "I'll be right back," Luce said, Roo's cheek pressed to the floor as he reached out a finger to block the ant's path. "Don't light the house on fire." Just faintly, coming from inside the office, she heard two voices singing in unison: *"Who's afraid of the big bad wolf?"*

From *The Red Grove: The Story of the Sisters*

Beneath the giant towering red trees, the valley floor had one wide creek that ran cold and fast with big, silvery fish, and Tamsen Nightingale dipped her toes into the water and thought of her sisters. The way they'd whisper and hug one another on winter nights, clinging to each other's heat. And then, their frozen naked bodies in the snow. Imagining their husbands, her husband, jamming any remaining food down their own throats, peeling the lovingly stitched dresses right off their bodies as they shook, flesh going blue. And her own teeth pulling apart her sister's husband's skin. She was surprised to feel no remorse. Didn't feel sick thinking of it. Just a burning in her chest that she hadn't been able to do anything to save her sisters. She had the bones. She kept them close. She let herself imagine her sisters' end as often as she needed to, because it filled her with a torrent of anger that nearly combusted, and the anger gave her energy. There was a lot to be done.

Along the banks, dense ferns and low, spindly bushes thrived in the shade of the giant trees overhead, and from one of the bushes she cut thin branches to bend and weave into a basket. The plants were different from those in her Wisconsin home, and one early day she grabbed at a leafless plant that, a few days later, blossomed boils and a red rash across her arms and hands that itched like summer mosquito bites and then bubbled into small blisters that wept clear, warm liquid when she scratched at them in her sleep.

Still, she twisted branches. The land was new, but the tasks were old, and so she wove pliable grasses into the baskets and dipped them into the water for fish. She gathered plants she could recognize from her years on the farm, testing others by first rubbing them along her skin—no reaction and she'd press them against her lips or nibble and spit—poisonous plants stung or tingled, were often bitter, or had shinier leaves; she knew to avoid yellow and white berries, and plants with sap those same colors.

Under her tasks there was always another hum, a tightness in her stomach, a flinch when a tree rustled and she could not identify the source. A shadowed movement over her shoulder, and she would spin, sure that her husband had finally found her. After what he had done to her in the cave, she no longer had any idea about whether he was the kind of man who would come find her to kill her, or whether he would let her be. It felt like a sickness, this unknowing, this fear. Festering.

Traders and travelers moved through the valley, but none stayed for long—it was far from gold country, far from the city on the bay, and the terrain of mountains and hills surrounding the valley made access difficult. She was staying in a cave between rocks, and she needed a more permanent shelter. For that, she'd need an axe, but she had nothing of enough value to trade, and she knew that sometimes someone took something whether or not you wanted to give it.

Back home, her mother's most precious object had been an ivory comb, its teeth thick and its handle carved into leaves and flowers and vines and orbs that wove and wound around one another. When Tamsen was small, she'd slowly run the teeth along her neck until goose bumps rose beneath each tooth and tingles shivered down the rest of her body. The sisters would sprawl across the grass and into one another's laps, letting the white clouds overhead fill their eyes while their skin pricked beneath the comb, and in this way, as in so many ways, they enchanted one another.

Here, she had no ivory. But she had bone.

One night, by the fire, she opened the bundle that held the bones and told her sisters what she was going to do. She knew not to be silly enough to ask permission and expect an answer, but she felt, clenching the thickest bone in one hand, a hastening as she lay the tip of her blade into her sister's femur. The bone did not give beneath the metal. She sharpened the knife then, using rocks she'd found on the hills and built into her fire ring, and tried again. The knife nicked the bone, one divot and then the next. She worked and worked, remembering the small summer wildflowers no bigger than her sisters' fingertips when they were babies, the knife digging out hollows to make vines, carving her memories right onto the bones.

And then, because nobody could resist the kind of beauty these combs radiated, she traded the bone-carved combs for goods from passing travelers. She acquired an axe. With the axe, she felled logs. She was amazed by the packs of turkeys and vultures and hares everywhere, coyotes who yipped, gophers who burrowed, and the occasional scat of something much bigger, though it didn't look like bear.

Tamsen climbed a short way up the most beautiful hill, which also had a creek running down its slope, and found a flat spot tucked beside red trees that were too big to put her arms around, and there, beside a spray of blue-berried bushes that were reaching their round heads into the sunshine, she built a wooden shelter. She felled small trees and, remembering shelters she'd passed on her way down the mountain, built this in their likeness. The work was hard and the days were long, but she felt her muscles growing stronger, loving the feeling that she could ask her body to do new things and it would respond, swinging the axe or rolling a log or hefting a basket of mud to fill in the cracks in the walls.

One night, she woke to the crunching of leaves and snapping of twigs outside her shelter. She heard snorting and sniffing up against the edges of the logs, a pawing at the door. The pine branches she'd tucked between the logs for insulation shook as whatever was outside exhaled, and she shivered in her cabin although she wasn't cold. She listened. A fly buzzed nearby and, oh no, she remembered a strip of rabbit she'd smoked, hanging from a high pole—so stupid to keep it in here, not to hang it out somewhere away from her structure. The animal scratched at the door; Tamsen tensed, bared her teeth.

There was a scream, then, just outside the shelter. It was high, a woman's yell, a yowl, and suddenly Tamsen could hear nothing but the sounds each sister must have made as she watched the other die, naked and shivering in the snow. Margaret and Minnie, her heartstrings, her loves. She thought that her grief would stop the pumping of her heart right then, all dried up, shriveled, and it might've, except a fly landed on the tip of her nose and returned her here. There was an animal outside.

The fly buzzing around the meat, the scream. Tamsen was on her knees. The night was dark, no moonlight inside the shelter, just the sound of her hammering heart, her breath, the animal. The flies. Knife always sheathed to her side, even in slumber, she waited.

Waited. She waited, fingers taut around the knife, breath heavy, but no animal burst inside. It was quiet. At some point, hours later, or maybe minutes, long, panting minutes, she dropped back down to the ground, and eventually to sleep.

In the morning, the rabbit meat was gone.

For three nights, this sniffing and scratching and yowling continued, and so for three days, after having been up all night, terrified, she completed her tasks—mending the shelter and chopping firewood and gathering food and checking her traps and fishing in the creek—with a mind half gone, eyes half closed. And even though she kept no more meat inside her shelter, the same sounds kept on each night, and in the morning, a scramble of prints on the floor inside her cabin. They were smaller than her own handprints, though not by much, with a nail track up front—wolf maybe, coyote, small bear—they stepped over each other, impossible to make out, and yet, there was no sign that an animal had broken into the cabin. Like it had just appeared, inside, circling her.

On the morning of the fourth day, Tamsen was hunting up-creek, higher into the rock outcroppings on the highest hill she'd ever climbed, and there, she heard another strange sound. There were mewls coming from beneath an overhanging rock. She crept closer. Bending low, she saw that inside the den were small creatures. Mountain lion cubs. Their coats were covered with dark brown spots, their eyes half-open and their tails ringed with black. They were tiny, off-balance, could fit on her forearm. There was no mother inside. One of them let out a little scream—not unlike the sounds she'd been hearing at night.

Tamsen could see evidence of previous kills scattered around, big tufts of fur and a dried skull, its backbone still attached. She backed away, not wanting to surprise the returning mother but, also, with these little yowling cubs, wanting to be sure their mother returned and not some other predator first.

Not far from the den, Tamsen found a sturdy tree that had a view of the kittens. She climbed. Waited. She waited and watched and fell asleep, all those sleepless nights weighing like stones on her eyes, her head against the bark of the tree.

Suddenly, branches were swooshing nearby. She heard a wild hiss and growl and knew she was in trouble. Stuck in a tree, ready to be devoured by the angry mountain lion that had almost devoured her nightly, but this time she'd come to perch right above this mother's babies.

When Tamsen opened her eyes, she saw that though the mother mountain lion had returned, she wasn't growling at Tamsen. Not far from the mountain lion were two coyotes, black eyes shining, tails black-tipped. They were open-mouthed, panting. Breathing in the scent of babies. The lion's ears were pressed down tight, and she half-crouched, her body in front of the little den, growling, and the coyotes took a few steps forward.

The coyotes weren't as big as the mountain lion—maybe two-thirds her size—but they started moving quickly, darting a few steps toward her and then away, some kind of complicated dance. The mountain lion bared her teeth and screamed, a high-pitched full-throated human scream, and then lunged as the coyotes came close, swiping. They retreated, light-footed and weaving between each other. The mother lion swiped at one as it came close on one side, and as she did, the other snuck in behind her, closer to the den. She hissed, swung to the other coyote, and the one behind her lunged again, grabbing the back of the lion's leg in its mouth.

Tamsen clung tighter and tighter to her tree, afraid for the lion, afraid of the lion, afraid of the consequence of nature's violence. The lion kicked backward, twisting to release the coyote from her leg, and as she did, the second coyote lunged toward the lion's neck. The coyote clamped down hard. There was a scream, again, from the mountain lion. She swiped at the coyote in front and missed, but it unclamped and backed away, and then she whirled around and dug in her claws, and the coyote attached to her leg let out a high-pitched yelp and let go. She had a new fury coiled in her movements, then, and she charged at the one she hadn't yet struck, and one coyote fled, followed by the other.

Tamsen clung to the branches of the tree, afraid to move, afraid to breathe, and thought about how she would tell the story of the fight to her sisters. *You would not believe how brave*, she'd say. Or, *Once, there was a mother in trouble*.

Finally, the mountain lion was alone. The tip of her black tail flicked back and forth against the gray rock opening of her den, her mouth still open, breathing hard to pull in any trace scents of approaching coyote or, Tamsen realized, startled, maybe even Tamsen herself. She held still in the tree, her muscles aching. Still, she could not look away from the mother. And that's when she noticed, on the rock at the lip of the den, small, dark pools. The lion was bleeding. There was nothing so dangerous as an injured, threatened mother. She'd stay where she was, up in the tree, for a while. She wedged herself more firmly between branches.

From her waistband she pulled out her knife, and from the bag on her back she pulled another of her sisters' bones. She went to work. Under the tip of the blade, the bone lost mass and gained curves, nicks, transforming itself into the muscled haunch of a back leg. She used the tip of her knife to carve notches, the side of the blade to smooth a rough cut, and there, under her fingers, her sister transformed into teeth and blood and a mountain lion.

It had been two days since the fight. After many hours, the mother had finally gone inside her den with the cubs and Tamsen had scrambled down from the tree, fled. She worried about the cubs, whether they had food, whether the mother's injuries were bad enough to keep her from hunting, or to invite the coyotes back.

She thought about them as she trapped squirrel and rabbit, as she pulled the silvery fish from the river. She thought about them and then decided that there was no reason nature had to take its course. With a freshly killed rabbit in her bag, Tamsen snuck back up the hill to the gulley between two high rises. Without getting too close, she lassoed the rabbit over her head and flung them toward the den. Quickly, she left.

Two days later, she did the same thing, hucking a salmon.

Three days after that, she was ready to hurl two squirrels but stopped when she heard a soft, persistent mewl. She held still, listening, waiting to see if the mother was nearby, but the mewl continued. A single voice echoing out of the cave, a note played across the strings. Going in closer was too dangerous—the injured mother would fight for her life, and Tamsen was fighting for her own life—better to keep safe. She began hiking back down the hill.

In her head, though, played the birdsong of her sisters' voices, laughing, fat babies with warm bellies. Her sisters, soft girlchicks, pulling in a bundle of baby mice from the barn on a night it was going to freeze, hiding them against their own warm bellies inside their shirts even though discovery would have earned them lashings.

Her sisters would go back and check on the kittens.

Tamsen turned around. She tried not to think about the sound of the yowling outside her shelter's door or the fight she'd seen in the mother lion, her teeth, her claws. Once she was within sight of the cave, she noticed, again, the dark bloodstains on the rock, the bones of the animals she'd thrown, and was glad to know they'd been eaten. The den was dark, but she took a few steps closer, and then closer still. The mewling had stopped.

When she was twenty feet away, she noticed the gleam of eyes. They were moving, coming out toward her. Tamsen tensed, ready to flee, but a cub tottered out. It was a few months old at best, with stubby legs and spots across most of its body, a little rounded head, eyes more open than they'd been last time, somehow so much like the barn kittens she and her sisters had played with. It didn't yet have any of the sleek movement she'd seen in the mother mountain lion—still a little, rounded squish of a baby, though it wasn't as fat as it'd been when she'd seen it before. The cub mewled again and walked cautiously toward her.

Tamsen took a step closer, reached a hand down toward the cub, and as she did, she noticed something else in the mouth of the den behind the little cub. It wasn't moving. She took another step forward, and then she could see: it was another cub on the ground, emaciated, with flies circling its face. The living cub mewled again, three feet away, and its eyes were as big and blue and bright as the clear sky outside, and where was its mother, how would she know if the mother was all right, and if she left this one little living cub here, would it survive? Probably the coyotes would be back tonight to kill and eat the little cat. And maybe that was right— nature taking its course, the world falling into order.

But then Tamsen imagined scooping up the soft cub into her arms and running. She'd bring the cub back to her cabin, make it a soft bed of rabbit furs and a deer pelt, let it warm itself by her fire. She would hunt for the both of them, trapping an extra squirrel and tossing it to the baby, whose teeth would grow sharp gnawing the bones and ripping through the ligaments she'd feed him.

She imagined passing travelers who would assume that she lived alone, how they'd approach the door believing they could take what they wanted from a woman by herself, then hear a growl and not even see as the lion pounced. That kind of safety. She imagined how the journey over the mountains might have gone if she and her sisters had had a lion— how the lion would have ripped open the flesh and slurped the spouting arteries of their husbands. Whose blood they would have fed to the lion cubs as the cubs turned their snouts to the sky and, like baby birds looking for the worm, drank in droplets of the warmth.

The kitten sat down, still looking at her, and yawned. Tamsen reached into her bag for another scrap of food to toss, wondering the best way to scoop up the cat, when suddenly, all the hair rose on the back of her neck as, from behind, she heard a deep, wild growl.

12

June 27, 1997 • Gone Twenty-Four Hours

THOUGH THERE WAS ONE CENTRAL ROAD through the valley, side roads—paved, dirt, animal—bloomed off the main artery in ever-changing pathways impossible to map. There were trails carved by machete, twisting deer paths through the woods, creek crossings made of signposts that had been knocked down and wired together, and Luce's bike dug into whatever was beneath it, nearly swerving into a tree to avoid a black rat snake crossing the trail because she hadn't been paying attention—too focused on squinting toward the road. On any sound that might be her mother returning.

She didn't have to pedal far to reach Juan. Face pocked and head wild with gray shag, he waved when he saw her. "La Goose, mi corazoncita," he called. In front of him lay a huge metal trap.

"What're you doing?" she asked, laying her bike against a tree. She loved Juan, and at least here, for a moment, the world felt normal.

"Improving my traps," he said, tilting his head at the enclosure in front of him to get a different view. A few small animal carcasses lay on a nearby tarp. Juan had once worked as head of a prominent evolutionary biology research lab and had given it up to move out here, not to study the women, he promised, but to be in the presence of this kind of evolution. He lived a few thousand feet down from her house, through the trees and over downed logs, and had always seemed old to Luce even though he was not much older than her mother, but he'd been damaged in Vietnam, something to his back and maybe also his head, though Luce thought he was one of the smartest people she'd ever met. "I'm hoping to gain strength," he said, "by having some blood on my hands."

"What a creep you are," she said, feigning disgust. She could hear the sound of a motor climbing the hill, though she could already tell it didn't have the rattle of her mother's car. Juan didn't pay it any attention.

"We're a violent species," he said, unfolding a knife and, as if to prove his point, slitting a rabbit across the neck. He reached his fingers into the cut and began to tug the skin apart. Luce shrugged at him—*Now, really?*—but he kept going. "We evolved with violence. Make your hand into a fist," he said, his own hands still inside the rabbit, and fine, what would it hurt to indulge him? Besides, his points often helped her understand the outside world. Its violence. She held her fists up as if she were ready to spar. "Okay, Rocky," he said. "See how your thumb isn't tucked? We're the only species with hand proportions that allow us to use the buttress of that giant thumb muscle to protect our hands when we punch. Our fingers don't break. We hurt each other badly. It's a perfect weapon."

"What bullshit are you going on about?" came a voice from the road. It was Gramms, wearing her wolf sweatshirt again despite the June sun. She ambled slowly side to side, widening her arms toward both Luce and Juan and they took turns folding into her hug, Juan with the half-skinned rabbit still dangling from one hand. Luce could see Gramms's golf cart parked on the side of the road—she'd stopped being able to drive a car a while back, so she got herself a golf cart and glued every fuzzy, sparkly, shimmery piece of trash that came her way to its roof—to scare away the vultures thinking she was a dead cow, she said. Luce felt the tightness in her shoulders unclench. Finally, someone who would have heard from Gloria, who would have instructions on what to do next. "Saw you from the road as I was coming to check on you and Roo, Goose—has your mama come home?"

"No," Luce said, asking what her mother had told Gramms exactly about when she'd be back.

"Honey, I haven't spoken to her in many days, I'm sorry to say," Gramms said, fishing something out of a molar with her fingernail. Luce didn't realize how much she'd been relying on Gramms or Juan to have seen her, to have an answer. She shifted her weight to the other foot, trying to recalibrate—the adults who should know where Gloria was didn't know. But there might be some way they could help; she explained the situation, telling them about the calling man. "Did you see him come up to the house?"

With his free hand, Juan sipped his tin cup, peppermint schnapps wafting toward Luce. "Nobody came to your house."

Luce crossed her arms over her chest. "Maybe you were gone for a while, or missed it—"

But Juan cut her off. "Kiddo, I'm not good for much these days, but you know as well as I do that I don't often leave my homestead here." In one tug he pulled the skin off the rabbit's legs, the final tufts like shoes still attached. "There's no way for someone to pass by on the road without me noticing. I was paying extra attention because I knew a bunch of outsiders were in the valley. Nobody came up here. And, come to think of it, I didn't see your mom go by either. She must not have come home." Well, that was something—she'd not come back to the house. So where did that leave Luce? She imagined the whole of the Red Grove, every trail and nook where her mother might have gone.

"Don't look so sullen, girl," Gramms said. "No creep up here by your house. That's good news." Luce nodded, wiggling the tip of her toe into the dirt. She needed to widen her idea of where her mother might have gone. She could do that. "I'm going up the road to check on your brother and auntie," Gramms said. "You wanna come?" Luce shook her head. She had more to do. Gramms blew them a kiss, and then they heard the thrum of her engine fade away.

Juan was slitting the belly, beginning to gut the rabbit. It was good for her to watch this, Luce thought, her stomach churning. This was a body turned inside out; this was real life, and the strongest among them would not be repulsed by nature. She had waited to ask Juan the question about this list of names, because part of her felt like she'd done wrong, breaking into the office, gathering what wasn't hers. Juan was stretching the rabbit skin out on a drying rack. A fly landed on the hairless pink body.

She handed him the list of names she'd found in her mother's office. "Does this mean anything to you?" He wiped his hands on his pants and pulled a pair of scratched, warped readers from his pocket.

Juan mumbled the names aloud to himself, scratched at his cheeks. "I don't really know, kiddo. Didn't you have some troubles, early on, with your mom?" Luce wanted to laugh. As if it had only been early on. "And didn't you stay for a little while in the guest room at Heartwood?" Luce hadn't thought about that in so long, but it was true. A few years back, when she was eleven or twelve and first started her role as guide through the darkness. Her mother had been furious. Didn't understand, couldn't, how she could be trusted with something so important. So dangerous. She's never trusted me, Luce told Una on one of their walks. She doesn't believe in me, she'd said, and it felt so true, it burned her chest. And so Una had offered for Luce to spend a few days in the guest room at Heartwood while it was open between new families coming in. Una stayed in another room, and other people were always coming and going, so Luce was never lonely. She was, for the first time since Gem's everdream, unlonely. She helped prepare group meals, looked after the little kids after preschool, practiced her nighttime guiding. She went with Una outside the community, to run errands in the next town over, grocery shopping, pharmacy pickups, the thrill of the DMV, all the things she'd have been terrified to do on her own, scared even to go with her own mother, but with Una? To be with her was to wear armor. She told this to Juan, who nodded his head, took another sip from his cup.

"Thought so," he said. "Tangerine stayed at Heartwood alone too. She's on the list. And Bryce. I don't know about the other kids on this list, but the ones I recognize have that in common. You all had some family issue."

Luce knew plenty of stories about kids in the community who'd been put into the guest rooms at Heartwood alone as a kind of rehab, somewhere in the center of many sets of eyes. She and her friends tossed them into the middle of conversations with alternating pity and reverence, Icarus cases, they called them, for the kids who had tried to fly too close to the sun. The crash was terrible, but that journey up toward the light—who could resist that kind of beauty? Bryce, one of the other kids who'd stayed at Heartwood alone, was an Icarus, a kid who took acid at eleven and got stuck. He was a couple of years older than she was, and she felt a little warmth remembering her crush on him from years back, his dark, buzzed hair, skateboarding after school like any normal kid, and then he was living inside a world that was different from the one he'd been in. You could see it in his eyes, how wide they were, how the balls didn't seem to roll around smoothly anymore, but were jagged with stops and starts, like a bad animation. Rumor was he'd hated it in the Red Grove, all the rules and ceremonies. He used to scare girls on the way home from school. They'd be riding their bikes and he'd be crouched inside a bush on the edge of the road. The kids would always say he jumped out and spooked them, but Luce was there once, riding not far behind a group of kids, and he didn't jump out. He stayed right in that bush. Someone said the drugs unlocked a mental illness that was already inside his head. But they were free here to explore their desires, and this was the necessary risk of absolute freedom.

"Tell you what, Goose," Juan said, knife tip opening the chest cavity. "As soon as I'm done here, I'll hop in my car and drive all the Red Grove's roads until I see her car. You head home, stay with Roo, and we'll tell each other what we find out. Only a fool would mess with Gloria. She'll be back soon. I'm sure of it."

Her bike tires gripped small rocks, humped over sticks as she pedaled faster and faster down the back paths, keeping her eyes open to everything she passed, anything that might have witnessed her mother, any flash of a clue. Light through the dense trees above left only the occasional dollop of light on the dirt, and the damp fern earth smell was thick and hot.

Gordon Prince was outside on his deck, his eyes closed, practicing tai chi, so he didn't wave as she passed. She rode on. There was Mariposa, in her cottage, smoking a cigarette and staring out the window—she didn't come out much, a newer arrival and one of the few who'd had to repeat the walk through the darkness a few times before she could make the whole walk alone. Through an open front door Luce saw Kelly Able napping on a couch, her huge Rhodesian ridgeback coiled into the crook of her knees. And then Nancy Able outside, weeding. Outside the Red Grove, Nancy Able had been Nick Able, and only since coming somewhere she'd be safe was she able to be who she really was—she'd told the story many times at community gatherings. The Red Grove kept women safe, Una would say, and when someone in the group had a technical question about womanhood, Una responded with what she'd learned had always been true in the Red Grove: the only person who could decide you were a woman was your own damned self.

Nancy caught Luce's eye as she rode past and waved her over. This wasn't what Luce wanted right now, not at all, and for a split second she pretended not to notice, but changed her mind. Una would stop to talk to anyone who wanted to talk to her. Luce had to practice the same.

Nancy pulled her tight in a hug, all warm soil smell. "I'm worried about you," she whispered into Luce's hair, New Jersey still thick in her voice. Pillowy body. "I'm worried about your mama. And your brother. I know other folks here are saying she's fine, of course she'll be back soon, but I'm a worrier." Luce felt a release of worry rise into her chest, her throat warm. Nancy kept her face close to Luce's. "I'm going to drop off a casserole tonight. And," her voice got quieter and she glanced around quickly before continuing to speak, "if you want to call the police or the FBI or whoever, you tell me. I'll back you up."

Luce was shaking her head before she even realized—of course she wouldn't call any authorities. Cops blundered evidence, didn't solve seventy percent of the violent crimes against women, let the world outside the Red Grove spin on in its chaotic, dark, violent tilt. Luce said they'd be fine.

"Of course you will," Nancy said, putting a little more distance between them. "I'd never call without you telling me to, of course, honey. Just—hold on one sec," she said, and darted inside, then reappeared with a plate. "Piggies in a blanket," she said, beelining one into Luce's mouth and then another into her own. She chewed twice, and then, mouth full, said, "I'm not one of the people who moved here because they'd been physically hurt in the past, and thank god for that. But I believe in the Red Grove so damned much . . . pardon my French." She pushed some escaping puff pastry back into her mouth. "And I think being here without, you know, the damage that can happen to people who have been hurt gives me a unique perspective. So if you need help, I'm right here." She licked her fingers then and gestured toward the plate, which still held a dozen pigs. "I'll only ask this one last time," Nancy whispered hurriedly as Luce packed her pockets full of food. "You don't have to be the bad guy. I can call the police for you. Okay?"

Luce stopped, her hands jammed deep in her pocket. "No. I said no." She took a fistful of pigs in a blanket out from her pocket and dumped it back on the plate.

The stilted summer air was cooler on her face once she was moving again, bumping over sticks and pebbles. It felt good to have Gramms and Juan know what was going on, help figure it out. Even Nancy Able's misguided questions were the tiniest bit comforting, even if Nancy was obviously overstepping what was necessary or helpful, and even if Luce had reacted more childishly than she would have liked.

She had no real destination in mind, looping through the Red Grove and starting back toward home. She was hoping someone would know something, would flag her down and explain everything, and even though they didn't, other people were looking too. She passed a few people at a distance, Boog, recognizable by her white-blond hair glowing like a mirage, who was waving from a distance, doing something with her arms. "What?" Luce called out, unsure what faraway sign language Boog was trying on, and Boog waved her arms again, using one hand to cut across her throat, then another to thrust out a spear. "We'll gut the bastard!" she screamed. Luce gave her a thumbs-up—was that the right response?—but pedaled on, not sure how to take Boog's charade.

She passed Naftali and Lee, inseparable, and then a few freshmen lying out on a patch of brittle grass at the edge of the grove. Their bellies were bared, cutout paper shapes laid across their skin to tan hearts and stars right onto their bodies. She remembered the summer her own friends had done that, a few years back. What Luce had wanted, but would never admit, was to be invited when they'd tanned shapes into their skin. She had been too busy with Red Grove duties.

And so later, alone, she cut out hearts and stuck them to her forearm, angling it out her window into a beam of sun.

She cut onto a trail that wove through old-growth redwoods. The trees never had to worry about anything—redwoods didn't even age. Time had no effect, caused no browning, no withering, no growing apart from nearby trees. A redwood had no known killing diseases, no predators to eat away at its heart. Its exterior layer of bark is fire-retardant and mold-repellant, a careful shield. These trees, in the right circumstances, might never die.

13

1981

GLORIA AND GEM HAD BEEN IN SACRAMENTO for eight years
when they learned about the Red Grove. Luce was growing
inside Gloria, the size of a kiwi. The newscasters started with a picture that had grabbed a lot of attention, a black-and-white shot of
seven women, all of them bald, overlooking an estuary where the
ocean's waters enter the bay.

"Now, I've seen a lot of creative ways to soak up an oil spill, but
this is a new one to me," a newscaster said. Below the women, in the
water, were giant ropes. The rope, the newscaster explained, was woven out of human hair. After the oil spill from one of the tankers off
the coast failed to be contained, women from the community fifteen
miles inland, the Red Grove, gathered all the hair they could from
barbershops and hairstylists all over the county, and from their own
heads too, and began weaving them together into giant ropes stuffed
into pantyhose.

REDWOOD WITCHES PERFORM WATER CEREMONY, one article

read. CAN A SECLUDED WOMEN'S COMMUNE SAVE THE PLANET? read another.

"Can you tell us your name, and how you knew human hair would be effective?" the reporter asked one of the women standing out on the estuary bank. The woman, who wore a tangle of turquoise necklaces, looked at the reporter holding the microphone with the steadiest gaze either of the sisters had ever seen. There was no flinching. No smiling. No nodding. Just her arm, tanned, muscular, coming up into the camera shot as her hand wrapped around the microphone, bringing it closer to her mouth.

"Think about how much oil our scalp produces, and what a great job our hair does soaking it up. It's nature's sponge," the woman said. She was bald too, with moles speckled across her face. "We recommend that scientists look into this for other spills."

"You're from the Red Grove," the reporter stated. "Which is a, uh—"

"Community," the woman cut in.

"A community," the reporter echoed. She was young, and clearly excited to be talking to the bald woman. "But you live inland a ways, so why sacrifice your hair for something miles from you?"

"The ocean connects to the bay, and the bay to the streams and rivers that flow through our whole county," the woman said. "Poison spreads. It would damage the soil and root systems that maintain the redwood ecosystem, and without that interconnected strength, we'd all be toast."

A breeze picked up right then, and the bald woman, following the sound of rustling wind, shifted her focus into the distance and said, "Look there! A heron has landed on our hair barrier."

Obligingly, the camera followed and zoomed in on a heron, gracefully standing on spindly legs, blue-feathered body facing the ocean. When the camera panned back to the reporter, all the women had turned their backs. The reporter, clearly surprised, fumbled with her microphone and then looked into the camera. "I guess some things will remain a mystery," she said, eyes smoldering. "For ABC news, I'm Ruby Wells."

"Oh!" Gem said, her eyes glued to the TV. "That's the most beautiful thing I've ever seen." She clutched at her heart.

"The gross hair logs?" Gloria asked, but Gem didn't answer. She was transfixed by the screen.

The following night, the news had another segment on the oil spill, though it didn't mention the women of the Red Grove, but the next night, they interviewed a scientist from a nearby college who attested to a surprising finding—the hair barriers were, in fact, soaking up large quantities of oil. They were more effective than any other known measure. "We could be part of that," Gem said softly, not looking at Gloria. "It's so perfect. The human body finally helping nature instead of destroying her."

Gem and Gloria together again on the couch, a few nights later. The news showed the image of the bald women once again, and the reporter Ruby Wells explained that other people had started to collect hair to make into these barriers. Gem jumped up from the couch, marched into the kitchen, and came back with a pair of scissors.

"No way," Gloria said, staring at her.

"I'm sending it to the women," Gem said, holding the scissors out in front of her. "We've got to take care of the weakest among us."

"You'll never do it—" Gloria started to say, but Gem brought the scissors to her shoulder-length hair and snipped. Gloria gaped.

"They turned their back on the camera like they didn't even care," Gem said. "They banded together to do something amazing." Voice lowered, like it was a secret, Gem said she'd heard it was the only place in the United States that had absolutely no record of violence against women. None. Zip.

Gloria waggled her fingers toward the TV. "I don't believe in all that hocus-pocus shit," she said.

"Might be real," Gem said, sawing through a clump of hair. "They couldn't make up the fact about the police records." But Gloria said that's just not how the world works. There aren't some chosen special people who are protected while the rest of us have to swim through the shit. She lit a cigarette and lay back against the couch, her belly already a small mound against her shirt.

"You're supposed to quit," Gem said, gentler than before.

"I'm supposed to not be pregnant," Gloria said. "Screw this baby. I'm not keeping it."

Gem collected the hair she was cutting into a pile. "There's plenty of stuff in the world that can't be explained. I mean, us?"

A commercial blared for a kitchen mop, sure to cut any woman's work in half. Gloria said that with them, it was different. They had shared a womb. And a childhood, alone together. She exhaled smoke in a foamy white stream, said that there would be too many scared people crouching in the shadows in a place like the Red Grove.

"They don't look like they're crouching in the shadows," Gem said, picking at her beer label, peeling off the paper in long strips.

"They're clearly overreacting. Think about what it was like to be a woman in the Middle Ages, a bar wench or a concubine. We have it so damned good now."

Gem shrugged and changed the channel. Said it didn't feel all that good.

Gloria sighed. "I'm not going to ruin my life and change what I'm doing because of men. I won't give them that," she said.

Gem looked at Gloria's belly, didn't say how her life was already changed by men, whether she'd wanted it to be or not. The news story had moved on. A serial burglar in the city, who'd been targeting elderly women who lived alone; he liked them to wake up while he was masturbating above them in their beds. They were interviewing the most recent victim, who clutched two small white dogs to her chest while she told the story, using their fur to dab away tears that reached her chin.

"Imagine if you grew up there," Gem said. "Imagine if we had gotten to grow all the way up surrounded by Dad and all his bar friends. Except imagine it's all women, and we're out by the ocean or in the forest. Not locked away in our bedroom. Without people like—" She fished around for the name she'd heard once and once only, after a terrible date Gloria said she'd never speak of again, from which Gloria's belly had swollen. "Without Steve. If you just knew you would be safe. Who would you be?"

"Probably less tough," Gloria said, opening her eyes and meeting Gem's.

"Maybe," Gem said. She let her eyes drift back to the TV, thought a moment. "But also, probably a lot of other things, good things that we can't even imagine." The next commercial featured a chorus of singing dogs. "I'll keep it," Gem said, her gaze on the TV, too afraid of what she was saying to make it serious with eye contact. "The baby, I mean. If you don't want it. I'll raise her."

"Her?" Gloria said, annoyed. "I don't know what it is. Feels like a monster."

"I'd take her to the Red Grove, with the bald women. I'd raise her there," Gem said. "She would get to have exactly whatever life she wanted. She'd never have to be afraid."

They were both quiet a moment, weighing how seriously to take this thing Gem had launched into their lives, whether to let it float away as if it were a joke, whether to feed it.

Finally, Gloria stood up and turned off the TV. She turned to face her sister. "Answer me honestly. Has anything so bad ever happened to you that you'd need to hide away in a place like that?"

Gem looked down at her hands, pulled at a cuticle. No, she conceded to her sister. Nothing so bad had happened.

14

June 27, 1997 • Gone One Day

L UCE BALANCED ON ONE LEG, her foot tucked into her thigh like a crane, staring out the living room window at the driveway. Empty. Dead grass wilted in the asphalt's cracks. Gloria would be one of those women who left trails of breadcrumbs for clues, who outsmarted her torturer—if only Luce could take the first step toward finding her. Forehead pressed against the cool glass, she just needed to think.

"Earth to Luce," Roo said. "You said you'd help." He'd pulled an armload of Gloria's dresses from her closet and dumped them on the rug.

The hours continued to click by. The angry man not calling. Gloria not returning. Luce winding in and out of moments of pure panic that she then talked herself out of, reciting Tamsen Nightingale's incantation or thinking about all the other people of the community looking for her mother, Una and Boog and Juan and Gramms and Nancy and more.

"This is it," Roo said to himself, holding a dress up. It was brown, long, with ties for the straps and repeating batik patterns. Without speaking, they wadded up discarded pieces of clothes from the corner pile and stuffed them inside the dress.

"So what's next?" Luce asked.

"They keep the body at home for a few weeks, sometimes even months. They let the corpse like, rot."

"Gross." She took their mother's favorite red scarf, sheen and long and fringed, and tied it around the bottom of the dress, cinching it closed. It looked like blood trailing off the body.

An hour earlier, sitting around Gem's bed, telling her not to be worried, they'd picked their way through the enchilada casserole Nancy had dropped off. Between bites, Luce checked on Gem's fluids and food, her mind still churning from her conversation with Juan, trying to make a plan for what would come next. Roo was dramatically recounting a *National Geographic* article he'd read, but Luce had stopped listening because—were those bruises on Gem's face? A sickly green, like pictures she'd seen of a tornado sky, spreading across her neck? It didn't make any sense—nobody would have hurt Gem. Luce leaned in closer to her—musty breath, crusts of sleep flecking her eyelashes—and then Roo had announced, loudly, that he knew how to talk to their mother. He was pointing to the dirty, crinkled *National Geographic*. And he'd torn out of Gem's room.

"Double-knot the scarf so her guts don't fall out," Roo said, tightening it again. Though it was early evening, the house's air felt stagnant and hot, no windows open in the living room, most of them throughout the house painted shut. Luce fanned her face with her hand, everything stagnant, nothing moving, and glanced out to the driveway again. A fly buzzed past her ear, and she looked around, sure she'd find the mass somewhere, but there were none. Roo reached up and laced his fingers through her other hand. "Goose," he said, tugging her hand. "The people in the magazine wait until the moon and stars are right to bury the body."

They looked at their mother's dress, now stuffed full. "Are you sure it's not too weird to do this without an actual body?" Luce said. "I mean, she's not dead, so it doesn't really make sense."

"It doesn't matter," Roo said, hopping from foot to foot. "It's a way to talk to her spirit. As long as the mummy is here with us, she will hear us." Luce arched her eyebrows, skeptical. "If it's true in Indonesia," Roo said, "why wouldn't it be true here? We need to find a way to talk to her. Because what if she's hurt?" His voice was muffled, but she could see his thin eyebrows scrunched up in worry. "What if she's scared?"

Luce set down the skirt she was folding. "Is she ever scared?"

He didn't answer, hid his mouth behind his arm.

"Hey," she said, pinching his freckled elbow. "Is she?" she asked, and did not let his face see her own mind ripping through all the terror of what could be.

"We should call the cops."

"Roo," Luce said, straightening. "That's so extreme. We don't need the cops. She's dealing with this guy somewhere else, but she's very capable of handling whatever is going on. She wouldn't be stupid enough to leave the Red Grove with him."

"I know."

"Do you know?" she asked. He nodded.

But *should* they call the cops? She'd been wondering too. Cops had special tools. They could find her car, maybe. Send out her description to diners and gas stations in the county. But every time she allowed herself to follow this path, what came next was all wrong—big, sweaty uniformed men on the doorstep, eyeing them all weird, scribbling notes that they weren't allowed to read, and deciding—she'd read enough sad stories in the news—that because they were both minors, Luce would be sent to some seemingly cookie-cutter family that really had a serial killer for a dad, and Roo would be sent to a different one, probably with a pedophile uncle, and Gem, well that was the part that kept her from even entertaining it as a real possibility. The cops would think they were sending Gem somewhere safer, to some low-income state-funded hospital full of people smashing their heads into the wall and yelling about Russian conspiracies, where they'd strap her to a bed in a windowless room. And she'd survive there one, maybe two days. No one would believe what had been plain to see for all those who had watched Gem stabilize, even improve, once she'd arrived in the Red Grove. She was alive because she was plugged in to something here.

And now her scared brother's brain was firing in all directions at once, calling the cops, building a mummy. "Maybe this isn't a good idea—" Luce started, but Roo cut her off.

"Please," he said. There was a pinch of real sadness around his eyes.

"It feels weird," Luce said.

"We don't even know what she does in there," he said, widening his eyes toward the office. "So who cares? First we gotta make this fake rotting corpse. That's the first step. And then we have to feed it and stuff, and give it offerings." Roo crouched down to the open magazine, scanning the article. "Like milk. And flowers. Fruit. Whiskey."

"And then supposedly we'll be able to talk to her and find out what's going on?"

"Exactamundo," he said.

It was a bad idea. Breaking into the office was a breach of trust, but this—messing with stuff Gloria held sacred—this was serious. But Luce hadn't seen Roo this excited or hopeful since Gloria left, and she wanted to prolong it. "Stuff these," she said, handing Roo two long socks and a roll of toilet paper.

"I know some mamas go buy milk and never come home," Roo said, unspooling a wad and reaching down to the bottom of the fabric. "But ours wouldn't." *Of course she would*, Luce didn't say.

"I want to talk to her," Roo said.

"I know." She ran her thumb along his knuckles. He was just a little kid. The phone rang then. Roo sprinted into the kitchen, but Luce yelled at him not to pick up. She took a deep breath. Heart thumping.

It was Una. Asking whether their mother was home. Whether they'd heard from the calling man. Una had tried calling the phone company to ask for the man's phone number, she said, but they could not give out private information.

Goddamn, Luce should have thought of that right away. If she had been thinking straight when they returned from seeing the lions, she could have used *69 and called the man back. But so many calls had come in and gone out since then—it was too late.

Una continued: the only way the phone company would give them the information was if there was an associated police report number. Also, and here Una's voice shifted a little bit higher, an indication, Luce knew, of something stressing her out, and for a moment Luce wished she was at Heartwood to rub Una's shoulders. Una said she'd been hearing talk. She paused a moment. "There are people who want to call in outside authorities. I'm sure they're saying it to you. But you know what they're like, my girl. I love you, and will respect your choices, but do you want to get them involved? Or should we focus our efforts here, within the Red Grove, with those we trust?"

Luce didn't hesitate. "Let's keep it with us," she said, knowing she was saying the right thing. Because focusing the efforts of her own people *was* the missing piece.

"I think you're right," Una said. "We'll find her, together." Luce heard the sound of pots and pans in the background, clanging. "Your wild mother. You know the other possibility that I've been thinking about? That maybe she's off on a beautiful adventure somewhere. I can picture it, actually—can't you? It's like she's on the back of a motorcycle somewhere, driving down a jungle road, and there are parrots in the trees all around—can't you picture her doing something like that?"

Luce didn't answer. I haven't been an easy daughter, she thought, too quiet, too dark, too many of the things her mother didn't like, she could admit that. She was the kind of daughter a mother could decide to leave for jungle parrots.

What she wanted was to ask Una about the list of names she found, hers included, and find out if Juan's hunch was right—but something cautioned her. Maybe it wasn't something she was supposed to see, it was in her mother's office, after all, and her mother and Una had a lot of issues. She didn't want Una thinking she was on her mother's side. She kept her mouth shut.

"You know sometimes we have to let people do what they need to do to become their full selves," Una said. "No woman is just who she is as a mother."

"Uh-huh," Luce said. It was true, she knew it was, but—would she really have left again, after all these years? If it were only Luce here, sure. But not leaving Roo behind, not without Gem.

"Tell me if you change your mind. If you are going to do anything else."

"I will."

"I'm planning a gathering so that we can get organized. Your mama is not alone. And, Luce—" And here Una paused a moment, cleared her throat. "I don't want you taking all the blame. Your note, the way you handled the man when he came to make peace—it's not all your fault. It was a mistake, yes, well a few mistakes, but you cannot take this all on. Okay? Good. See you soon, honey."

The line went dead. Luce was surprised to find her arm trembling. Una thought it was all her fault.

"Mama!" Roo yelled from the living room. Luce dropped the phone, hardly breathing, and raced into the living room. There was only Roo.

"There she is," he sang, looking down. He was on the couch, skinny legs folded into two triangles, and there, balanced on his lap, was a cantaloupe. He was leaning over it, a tube of their mother's lipstick in his hand. He pressed it to the skin of the melon.

"You shit," she said. "You can't say that. I thought she was here."

He looked up, surprised. "She is here," he said. "I heard her."

"Stop it, Roo, that's—"

"She's almost here, I mean," he said, nodding back down toward the melon. "I heard her voice, really quiet and far away, but it was her. She said, *knock knock*—"

"Stop it." A fucking knock-knock joke. Deep breath, Luce. She felt an itch on her neck, a fly, but no—nothing there. She would not tell him about the flies, the list, about her conversation with Una— how it was her fault. She would do what she needed to do to be in charge. Steady.

"Can you bring her to the office?" Roo asked, nodding to the mummy's body. The house flushed warm. Luce scooped up the mummy and carried her past the woven fabric from Guatemala pinned on the wall, past the cluster of melted-down candles and their frozen wax lakes on top of the piano, past a cup sitting on top of the coffee table that, with a jolt, made her stop.

"Is this your cup?" Luce asked.

"No," he said, an eyeliner cap between his teeth.

It was a small mug, faded, with painted rabbits playing games at a picnic, chipped on the bottom of the handle. Inside was an inch of coffee, the milk having gathered in a strange gray pool. The edge of this cup, its lip, had held her mother's lip so recently. A day ago, maybe two. And might there still be her spit on its edge, the feel of her dry kiss on their foreheads when they were sick. But more than that, Luce thought she could almost see her body making an indent in the couch, behind the cup. Was there a weight there? Of course not. A ghost was just grief taking form.

There is no such thing as coincidence, Gloria often said. Coincidence is communication. It always means something. Luce forced her eyes away from the indentation.

The office door creaked open as she approached. A little cold air from inside traveled up Luce's neck, made her shiver. She shook it off and stepped across the office threshold for the second time in two days. She set the headless mummy in Gloria's velvet chair. On one side was the phone plugged into nothing, on the other, the table full of silent, stilled equipment. In front of the mummy she placed the rabbit-painted cup with coffee, swirls of old milk.

Roo shuffled in, gazing down at the melon cradled in his arms. It was lumpy, a little overripe and soft, with a greenish hue beneath the scales of the skin. On the melon's face were two shakily drawn almond eyes, the left bigger than the right, with dense black irises drawn in eyeliner. There was a nose drawn like an upside-down 7, and two pencil-line eyebrows that arched into surprise. Her mouth was drawn in lipstick, a smile with two notches leading up from the top center lip. Their mother's mummy face was pocked with the crosshatched dried worms of cantaloupe rind. It was ugly. Monstrous. Luce glanced at Roo, expecting him to be laughing, but he was doe-eyed, grinning at the melon head with a look he'd give their mom when he was littler, wearing his top hat and magician's suit as she taught him how to escape from Siberian handcuffs, as she sewed him a mermaid tail, his wet eyes glowing up at her, a fawning jack-o'-lantern.

"I didn't even know I could draw," he said, his voice almost a whisper. "But she's perfect." Luce looked at the melon. The features were lopsided, out of proportion. Just the outlines of what they really were. "I can't believe it came out like that," he said.

"Like what, exactly?" she said slowly. She waited for him to bust up laughing, all of this a big joke.

"Just—it's her."

Luce looked back again at the melon, blurred her eyes, and for one smeared second the melon shifted, tightened—Roo was right—it looked *exactly* like their mom. It *was* their mom. Her pointed cheekbones, her mossy, twinkling eyes, her mouth grimacing in pain—

Luce blinked, and the melon was back with its disfigured face. A trick of the eye, surely, desire made physical. She blinked at the mummy again, willing it to change, but it didn't.

They propped the melon-head mummy up tall on Gloria's chair. The head was heavy, so to keep it on top of the mummy, they punched down the neck of the dress to make a kind of nest on which the melon head could balance. "We have to do an opening-of-the-mouth ceremony," Roo said. "To get her spirit in here. To talk to us."

"She's not a real mummy, Roo."

"Do you want this to work?"

He was looking at Luce with the wide-eyed exasperation she'd seen so many times. "Fine," she said. Moose pushed the unlatched door open with his head and then walked in, tongue lolling.

"Perfecto," Roo said, grabbing Moose around the belly and hoisting him up so his arms and legs stuck straight out. "A priest is supposed to be wearing a jackal-headed mask, but I'll hold Moose here instead. You're the priest, Moosey."

Moose licked his maw, yawned. "This is ridiculous," Luce said.

"Take something important and touch it to her mouth. Hurry. He's heavy."

Luce hesitated—it was one thing to help her brother make this little effigy, but now they were in the territory of ceremony, and even though nothing would happen from this little game, it still felt like walking up to the lip of a ledge they should not visit.

"Please, Goose. Please. You have to run the tip along her lips," he said.

Fine. She would keep playing his game while she formulated her own plan. She remembered the carved bone she'd found and grabbed it from her room, held it to the crudely drawn mouth.

"It will make her senses return, if they're lost," Roo said. "So she can hear and see and speak." Moose squirmed in Roo's arms, arcing his body to one side and then the other. Luce moved swiftly, rubbing the bone along the melon's lips, feeling ridiculous, sure that this would not open a portal into some world they hadn't tapped, yet for a moment, ridiculously, impossibly hopeful that it would. She imagined it: the flesh parting, the orange of the cantaloupe's insides visible as the rubbery lips split to whisper the secret about where she'd gone, how she'd be right back, how much she missed them.

Luce brought the bone away from the melon. They held perfectly still, staring at the face. Holding their breath. Luce's heart was all thrum. She thought of sleepovers when she was young, up late in the darkened bathrooms with the other girls, all of them holding hands and chanting into the mirror *Bloody Tamsen, Bloody Tamsen*—how much she did, and did not, want the ghost to appear. She slid her hand into Roo's—hot, sticky.

The house held its breath. Maybe it wouldn't happen all at once, maybe it was already happening right under their eyes, the kind of gradual atom-by-atom change, like that of a girl learning to survive in the world, becoming a woman without knowing when she became one.

They waited. And then Luce let out a little laugh. "It's a cantaloupe," she said.

Roo released his breath into a big sigh, slumping his head to the side in the most dramatic performance of disappointment.

"Roo, it wasn't going to actually—"

But then there was a loud pounding on the front door. The boom echoed into the house, bounced off wood and spiderwebs, and cracked open the silence they'd been stalled inside. Moose barked and ran out of the office.

"Oh my god," Roo said, his face an exploding galaxy. "It's her."

"No it's not," Luce said, though her voice was unsteady.

Roo ran out the office door, Luce calling after him to wait, because whoever was at the door was not a person who should be here. Because what if they had just messed with something they shouldn't have, what if they'd summoned something? Nobody should be there. Nobody who would knock.

Roo had already opened the front door when Luce got there. He was staring out at the deck. There stood a woman in a sweat-stained baseball cap and tracksuit. She smiled, raised a hand as if waving from a train, then coughed. Her eyes shifted between the two of them, uncomfortable.

"Gloria?" the woman said into their open front door.

The mummy's face, which was her mother's face, the flies, the carved bone, the list of names, the trees—all the layers of the unexplained were unmoving bricks inside her. Luce wasn't getting anywhere with what she'd been doing, and so she tried something entirely new.

"Come inside," Luce said. "I'm Gloria."

From *The Red Grove: The Story of the Sisters*

Tamsen wanted to growl and yowl and tell the mountain lion the story of her life and tell the mountain lion that she was simply trying to help and tell the mountain lion that she, too, was wounded, was doing her best, which was a best that wasn't good enough when the time came, that she, too, had let die those she was supposed to protect.

The lion roared. Tamsen raised her arms above her head, high, and started walking away from the baby, her eyes to the ground. She growled. She would make herself into a beast, enormous and frightening, too huge for the lion to charge.

A few steps, and the lion did not pounce. Was it possible that she'd escape without being killed? She kept her arms wide and her eyes down, though she could see the mother's ears pressed against her head. One more step, and she was almost far enough to have a bush and then a tree between her and the mother, one more step. The lion charged.

Tamsen closed her eyes and cringed and, suddenly back in the moment of finding her sisters in the snow, welcomed the bite.

The lion pinned Tamsen to the earth, teeth sinking into her arm. Pain exploded through her and the iron-dirt stench of old blood and musk and the heat of this giant animal's body on hers. The pounding of Tamsen's heart like an anvil smashing her bones. Her blood on the lion's mouth. The eyes of the mountain lion two suns burning holes through her.

Tamsen waited for the teeth to plunge into her face, her neck. But something else pierced her instead—a force urging her to survive. She screamed. It was loud and deep and full-throated, and at the same moment, she gathered all her strength. She could feel the bone she'd been carving sticking out of her bag, and she grabbed it with her one free hand, pressed her palms against the lion's body, straightened her elbows and pushed, and the tip of the bone pressed into the lion's chest. It wasn't much, not compared with the lion's size, but it was enough to startle the lion. Tamsen pressed harder, pressed with every ounce of her sisters, and it did not pierce the lion but shifted her weight enough to let go of Tamsen's arm.

Tamsen scrambled out from beneath, her arm wet with blood that ran in dark drips down the carved bone. The lion would pounce again, and that would be it, the end; there was no way of letting the lion know how tenderly she'd imagined caring for her baby, there was no way to convince a wild thing that you wanted to neither harm nor tame it. Meet wildness with wildness, Tamsen knew, shifting onto her toes, and as the lion lunged again, Tamsen moved out of the way, screaming her own mad, wild roar, swiping toward the lion with the bone in her hand. She held her arms wide and kept on with her sound, a desperate animal unbound within her, a woman in danger.

The lion's ears pressed back against her skull, but she did not pounce. Tamsen grabbed a branch from the ground and rose, bringing her body to its full height. This startled the lion, who stepped back, surprised at her size. Tamsen brought the branch up above her head, holding it in two hands, making herself into a beast, keeping on with her wild cry, not the low-pitched man growl her father had taught her, but a high, cackly scream not unlike the mountain lion's own scream, a woman's sound. She kept on, the sound pouring from her throat, backing farther and farther away from the lion, farther down the hill, far enough that she could not see the panting, bloody-mouthed animal, and then, she ran.

And ran.

And made it to her cabin, blockaded the door, and fainted.

The bite on her arm festered. In the days that followed, she strayed from her cabin as little as possible, cleaning and then wrapping her wound. It ached and throbbed, swelled hot. The wound was sick, and it was making her sick. A fever rendered what she saw impossible to tell apart from what she imagined. Day passed into night and then day. She would not make it long.

On the third day, Tamsen, radiating pain, needed medicine and nourishment, and she stumbled from her shelter to the small garden with the very few plants she'd been able to sprout. She knew nothing about medicine, though, and wandered around the edges, hoping a plant would speak to her in some way or offer itself as a suggestion of healing, as so many plants did. But nothing came to her, nothing moved her, and she was soon too weak. She made it back to her shelter, knowing, like a spear in her ribs, that she would not survive. That her husband would come bursting in and she would be able to raise no defense.

There came a rasp at the door. Her breath left. She did not move. A pounding on the wood. Tamsen tried to hide her injured arm beneath a shawl for fear of appearing weak, but even her healthy arm shook with fever. Standing outside would be her husband, of course it would, or if not him then the mountain lion, and out of the mountain lion's bloody mouth would swim her sisters.

She peered out through a crack and was surprised to see a woman standing outside, all by herself. She was older than Tamsen by ten or fifteen years, her face creased with sun, her neck hunched forward, with a small hump at the top of her back even though it was clear she was trying to stand up very straight.

Passing gold miners would sometimes stop to talk to her, but they were always men, and she told them her husband or brothers would soon be back, that she had nothing there for them. Some of those men had sniffed her out, though, and despite her wishes, news spread. It wasn't long before someone else heard about Tamsen's homesteading in the valley.

"I heard you have a place here without a husband," the woman said as Tamsen cracked open the door. Usually this statement was hurled with contempt or menace.

"What do you want?" Tamsen asked. She was calculating how long it would take to reach the bone tucked into the back of her skirt, how much strength she had left. The room began to blur.

"My husband died," the woman said. She shifted the small bag she was carrying from one shoulder to the other. "His father is trying to claim me." She paused then, and Tamsen waited for her to go on, but she didn't. Tamsen squinted at the woman, her body growing faint around the edges—was she doubling? "I can sew. And cook," the woman said. Tamsen began closing the door on the stranger, afraid of whatever scheme she was trying to pull over, afraid of the ache from her blindingly hot arm and what it was doing to her vision, but the stranger put her foot out and the door did not shut.

"I know you're hurt," the woman said, quickly. "I watched you in your garden. I know you need help."

Tamsen tried to force the door closed—her weakness exposed—but the woman kept talking more quickly. "Here," she said, thrusting a handful of herbs toward Tamsen. The stalks became two and then four, the green went black, and then everything did.

Tamsen woke. Margaret was beside her, her fine-haired sister, humming a tune while she scraped the fat off the inside of a hide. Tamsen's arm was wrapped in cloth, and beneath that, she could feel the heat releasing from the wound, something on her skin cooling the fire. She closed her eyes again, that warm, good feeling, wondering what her sister would do with the fur, trade it or add it to the pelt she was sewing together. She drifted away again.

When she woke, it was not Margaret beside her, but someone else. The stranger, here inside her cabin. She sat up quickly, woozy, and the stranger approached slowly.

"I've put a poultice of garlic and echinacea on your wound," she said. "The infection was deep. I can't guarantee that the herbs will work, but it's a lot better chance than what you had going." The woman held a small bowl in which she was mashing something green and brown. Tamsen opened her mouth, but didn't know what to say, still feeling like she wanted to run, knowing she couldn't. Maybe this woman was poisoning her—but for what good? She didn't have anything here worth taking, and if the woman really wanted to hurt her, it would have made more sense to do it while Tamsen was out cold.

"What do you want?" Tamsen asked the stranger. Her voice was a thin, weak croak.

"Just to stay," the woman said. "How did you come to be here?"

"My sisters," Tamsen started to say, but she was too weak, the throb in her arm returning like the summer crickets when she was young, pulsing out in the night fields, washing over her body until whatever else was in there became less and less.

The woman set the bowl on the ground and nodded, knelt beside Tamsen. "My name is Ines," she said. "My husband's father owns a silver mine. I cannot bear children, and so my husband's father has decided that he will send me down to the camps at the mine, for the workers to do with as they please. Because I cannot have children, he believes no mark will be left on me. Do you understand?"

The pain cooled in Tamsen's arm once again, as if the heat were pulled out by the story this stranger was telling her. "Yes," she said, understanding, even inside the throb and shiver, that she was not the only woman who needed refuge.

15

June 27, 1997 • Gone One Day

THE WOMAN IN THE SWEATY BALLCAP was on the futon in the living room, waiting, Roo and Luce in the kitchen. Luce opened and closed cupboard doors, looking for—she didn't know, an impulsive movement busying her arms against the slowly creeping jitters. Through the window over the sink she could see the day pulsing with quivery heat and chirping crickets, and where was her mother? Luce needed a plan, but what she had was an outsider.

Roo rested his cheeks in his palms at the kitchen table, glancing back and forth between the living room and Luce. "You can't," he whispered at Luce, but she leaned down right against his ear.

"Trust me," she said. "I received a sign." And that lie, she knew, might be enough to make him play along. It wasn't *totally* untrue. They'd done something with the melon-head mummy—disrupted something. Maybe called this woman to their front door. Or she had shown up as an absolute coincidence. Either way, she was here, and Luce was her mother.

Luce slipped on one of Gloria's kimonos that she'd found draped over a chair and approached the woman slowly. She swung her hips, held her chin high, imitating the way her mother radiated through space. Because she could not find her mother, she would become her. She led the woman back into the office, and when they reached the threshold, they walked right in, like it was entirely natural to step from one room into the next. "Sit," Luce instructed, pointing to a foldout chair and sitting across from her. The lady was cracking her knuckles, but she stopped once she saw the mummy. She stared. Should Luce have hidden it? Its melon head tilted as if it had a question, lopsided eyes already smeared at one outer edge. Shit. Well, there wasn't anywhere in here to stuff it, and besides, if the mummy had somehow called the woman here, it should stay.

The TV was no longer playing the video of the twins. She willed it to flick back on with some kind of instruction, for something to flash, to beep, to open. Nothing.

"I wasn't sure I wanted to keep this appointment," the woman said. "Been debating, trying to get a sign. But nothing's changed since we talked on the phone a few weeks ago."

Luce sucked in her breath and waited. So her mother had booked this weeks ago, and they'd talked about—something. She ran through a list of things to say, her cheeks growing pinker as nothing seemed right. Everything she and Roo had done up until this point could have been so easily explained if their mother came home right then. But this? She imagined the volcanoes of her mother's eyes. Volcanoes? Yes. She imagined what she would say to her mother—*the lady was desperate. It was our duty to help.*

The woman cleared her throat. "It's my daughter. She—"

"Died," Luce filled in, trying to channel Gloria and the way she filled up the space around her like rain spilling into the grooves of a road.

"Uh—yeah, but I was gonna say she was the whole sunshine of my world."

"Sorry," Luce said, casting her eyes to the floor. "Please go on." She did not need to be Gloria. She needed to listen.

"I was an addict for a long time," the woman said. "Bad stuff. Then she came along, and it got me to change." She was speaking slowly, voice cracking, dipping, falling. She touched her fingertips together into a kind of pyramid on her lap, worked her jaw. "Not right away. There was some struggle. But it stuck, eventually. I got clean. She played the piano. A real whiz. And then she died."

"I'm very sorry," Luce said. The woman gnawed on the inside of her cheek. Luce remained quiet, though it seemed obvious that she needed to offer something, some words of wisdom, some insight into what had happened to the daughter, or to reassure the woman that the girl was okay, when the woman spoke again.

"Who is that supposed to be?" she asked, nodding over at the mummy. Luce tried to come up with something that didn't sound crazy, but before she could, the woman spoke again. "She's the same size as my daughter was. Exactly. Same height, same body shape even, weird as that is. And I think my daughter had those same shoes. Or something really close. My god. And her face—Jesus." She paused and stared at Luce, crossed and uncrossed her arms. "This looks exactly like her. I don't understand—it's like you knew her."

The woman was biting her cheek again, but this time the skin around her mouth was quivering, little tremors built entirely of restraint, the shaking of a muscle under maximum capacity. This was a moment of paths diverging. Luce swerved. "Follow me."

Gem's eyes were closed. Luce leaned low, pressed her ear against Gem's chest, listened to her lungs. Just faintly, she could hear a rattle inside, a thickness. She looked up at the woman, who was staring at Gem, and gave her as much as she could remember of the speech her mother had given the man who'd died. Luce held a small tape recorder, something she'd grabbed from her mother's desk on the way out. Fumbling through the dark.

"We know you travel in a higher frequency," Luce said into the air. "Speak, and Gem will enable us to hear you." She pressed the record button on the machine, and the little red light flashed, wheels inside the machine turning. The woman nodded quickly. She was buying in. Luce stared at Gem, willing her to open her eyes or hum, something, anything, but the room was silent. They held still like that for one minute, two. The old floorboards in the house groaned and for a moment, Luce imagined it as the sound of the mummy calling out in search of her mother, what a thought, and why had she believed that something in this room would happen when she did not have the gift—of course nothing happened.

She'd have to invent it. "Sometimes a question helps," Luce said, winging it, her panic growing. "Or telling your daughter something you want her to know."

The woman cleared her throat again, wiped at her eyes with the pad of her thumb. She told the air that she missed her daughter. She cleared her throat, and then, closing her eyes, said slowly, her voice a little more hoarse, as if speaking directly to her, "I miss you." She wanted to know that the girl was okay. She wanted to know if she— and here the woman heaved once before going on—if she could forgive her. They sat in silence, listening, the woman alternatively looking at Gem and then over at Luce while Luce, wearing her mother's face, nodded at her aunt as if she were in conversation. Finally, she clicked off the recorder.

"So?" the woman asked, crossing and uncrossing her legs. "Did you hear something? 'Cause I didn't."

"Yes," Luce said, fumbling. "Sort of. Her voice is very faint."

The woman sat still and quiet, and Luce groped for more. Of course this wasn't what her mother said, of course this wasn't what her mother believed. People left this room weeping, grateful, hugging Gloria at the door or pressing items from their purses into her hands, oranges, dollars, photographs, envelopes. She ran her hand along Gem's arm, feeling the rough, dry skin beneath her fingertips, and coming up with no other idea, she rewound and then pressed play for them to listen to the silence she'd recorded. She turned the volume as high as it would go, thinking that perhaps, somehow, impossibly, beneath the silence there would be something else, Gem's voice maybe, and if there was, oh god, if she could have been hearing Gem all along? But the only sound was low static.

"What is that?" the woman asked, grabbing Luce's arm like forceps. "Is that Laura?"

There was a spike of static. Luce plugged the recorder into speakers they used to play music for Gem, turned the volume high. The tape cracked again, much louder this time. Was it her mother beneath the recording they'd just done? Both Luce and the seeker leaned forward in their seats, straining toward the speakers. If you listened hard enough, Luce thought, maybe your brain would invent a voice speaking back to fill your ache, like a phantom limb.

"I gotta say, I was skeptical before I came," the woman said, staring at the recorder. "I watched a *20/20* special on how psychics make their tricks work. No offense, but most of you guys are con artists. Anyway, I'd heard that the recorder catches sound waves from radios or TVs, and that's what makes it work. But this, oh my god—" She paused to listen. Brought her head closer to the speaker.

Static crackled again, and then a higher note, like the hum of repelling magnets. It didn't sound like a voice, really, Luce thought. It was like the breaking of a voice between notes, a crackle. She leaned in close too, closing her eyes, squinting her face up to try to concentrate her attention as the woman, wet-eyed, asked her to rewind.

Luce played it again. The silence returned, loud, then a creak from somewhere in the house's bones, a bird's call, a faint dog bark, and then the static jumped. The speaker volume was way up.

"There!" yelled the woman, and oh my god, she was right. "Rewind right there." The sound on the recording had jumped, the static clinging and gathering, sound layered, and, yes, Luce could hear something different, something noisier, something like words. "She's answering my questions," the woman said. "I hear her voice. I heard it. She said . . . she said, *love you, Mommy.*"

Static, and then something else. Yes, Luce was sure of it. Something else.

"I hear her. Oh my god," she cried, the tears bigger now, the pads of her thumbs not keeping up. "Hi, baby, hi Lolo," she said. She reached her hands up into the air, arms wide. "I hear you, honey, and I'm right here. Mommy's right here."

There was nothing she could do—the arc of the woman's arms reaching out toward the idea of her child in the air all around them made Luce's bones ache with longing. There was no time for that. She pushed a smile onto her face so that this seeker, should she glance over, would know that she, too, was sharing in this experience, that everything in this room—bed, table full of medicines, flies buzzing against the window, the redwoods outside, Gem in the bed—all of them were experiencing the same extraordinary thing.

But the thing was, Luce wasn't. She had heard something. Just not those words. In the static, lifting out of the sound like mist from a creek, were very different words, words she hadn't thought about in a long time. She had not allowed herself to replay the entire memory in years—*the cow-skull woman . . . you, locked out on the balcony*—

Luce was startled when the woman stood up. She wasn't wiping away tears anymore, just letting them collect on her chin. Straightening her jacket, she reached into her pocket and handed Luce a hundred-dollar bill. And then, moving very quickly, she was gone.

Back to the night of the cow-skull woman, when you were locked out on the balcony—and so back she went.

16

1989

I T HAD BEEN A SUNDAY when Gloria came back. Luce was eight, and she and Gem had just gotten home from camping for a night not far from where they lived, where they'd slept in a small, musty tent in the middle of the ponderosa pine forest. They'd returned dirty, happy, tired, unpacking their extra Jiffy Pop and peanut butter, when there was a knock on the door. And there was Gloria. She unsettled Luce each time, this copy of her Gem but with longer hair, shinier clothes. This time, the first thing Luce saw, at eye level, was how her shirt was open in little slits between the buttons, revealing smiling mouths of skin. Gloria had a melon belly. They hadn't kept it a secret from Luce; she knew Gloria was her birth mother. But families are made not born, is what Gem always told her. Gloria visited on holidays, brought Luce new dresses or dolls or, one time when Luce was five, a crimping iron that Luce immediately used on the previous year's Barbie gift, singeing off all her hair.

But the way Gloria stood at the door this time was different. She had two big suitcases with her. And she was red-eyed. The sisters shooed Luce into her bedroom and whispered loudly on the other side of the door. Their voices thumped against the wooden door-frame, and though she could not hear any specifics, Luce went cold inside. Her mother was here to take her away.

In her room the shadows grew long. Luce picked briars from her socks, a pine needle from her hair. And when Gem and Gloria brought her out of her room and sat her down on the couch, Gloria handed her orange juice. It was in a wineglass, all wet, small beads of water river-ing down, and didn't she know that was the wrong kind of cup for her, didn't she know to wipe down the glass because Luce didn't like her fingers sticky?

"I'm back," Gloria said, kneeling beside Luce.

"No thank you," Luce said, setting the juice on the coffee table. She wiped her fingers on her shorts, pleased with herself for remem-bering to say *no thank you*, and looked up at her Gem for a wink, but Gem was watching Gloria. The smell of the orange juice was wrong, too sweet, the pulp floaty like maggots.

"This is good, Goose," Gem said, smiling and nodding. "You are going to have a little sister or brother, isn't that exciting?" But Luce wasn't an idiot. Gem's face did not look excited.

So it went that Gloria moved in with Gem and Luce, shifting their perfect duo into a trio, and then, five months later, with the arrival of Roo they became four. Gem helped with the baby, showing Gloria easy things like how to make the right kind of peanut butter and banana sandwich, and the moves in cat's cradle. And Gloria told Gem that she should venture out more, meet a guy, preferably one with a rich, handsome brother, most definitely not one living in his mother's basement and crying on their second date, which was the kind of broken bird Gem naturally orbited toward saving. Luce sat on the lip of the tub while her mother curled Gem's hair, Gem mak-ing grossed-out faces back to Luce in the mirror. Gem shyly asking Luce how she looked in one of Gloria's dresses the night she went out on a date.

And that's where her memory of what comes next gets filled with static.

It wasn't a Christmas party, because there were big bouquets of roses on the table, but Luce swore there had been tinsel around— something shiny and splintered that was still all over the floor the next morning, after the axis of the world had tilted.

"You have to come home, you have to come home, you have to come home," Luce, eight, had chanted into the phone. Gem had promised her brand-new boyfriend, Frank LaJoy, oh la la, that she would go somewhere with him that weekend and would not be at Gloria's party that night, and Luce knew she was not supposed to be mad. But Gloria would not play Chinese checkers with Luce like Gem would, or read books about turtles, and sometimes it made Luce a little sick to her stomach when Gloria hugged her. Besides, Roo was upstairs in his crib, and it was Luce's job to watch him. She needed Gem to make it fun.

"I can't tonight, Goose," Gem said, her words soft across the phone line. She heard a low voice murmur in the background.

"Please please please," Luce said, hearing her mother's first guests arrive at the door. She had on her new blue dress with a yellow bow, and she needed Gem to see it. "You have to come home, and don't bring Frank," she whispered, wet and loud.

"I would love to, you know that." There was a pause then, more muffled murmuring, as if Gem were covering the phone with her hand. "Look, no promises, but maybe Frank and I can leave tomorrow instead. I'll try to come. Okay? And if I come, you have to give me a foot massage."

"Eeewww," Luce said.

"Come on, Goosepen," she said. "If I can come, I'll even bring ice cream if you promise me a foot massage. My dogs are barking." She heard the voice again in the background, loud. He wasn't nice. Luce wanted Gem all for herself.

"That's gross," Luce said again, laughing. She tongued the empty gums where two top teeth were gone. "Roo will give you one."

Gem laughed. "Go have fun, Goose." She lowered her voice once more. "You have to try. Be nice to your mom. And your little brother. You promised me you'd try. Okay?"

The next hours were a blur of adults tottering around, the boring world of whatever they talked about. She remembers looking to the front door, waiting for Gem. Checking on the sleeping baby upstairs, his sweaty back, the way he crossed his ankles in his sleep. And the next thing she remembers is that it is late, and her mother tells her she must go to bed. But Gloria wanders off for a moment, called over by another party guest, and Luce slips out onto their small balcony through the sliding glass doors. Luce of the shadows, loose, unnoticed.

That's where it all changes. After she slips out into the darkness.

It is a clear night. The stars stretch across the sky like handfuls of sand. There are muffled bouts of laughter and the rumble of cars on a nearby road and voices coming from down the street, too. And then there's the sound of a click—a sound she knows so well—as someone flips the lock on the sliding glass door. Click. Someone pulls the curtain closed. They don't know she's out here. The click is the sound of being out on the balcony, alone.

There's no need to be afraid. She will look up at the stars until someone notices she's out here, and it will be a grand adventure, she thinks, and she will tell Gem all about it. She takes a few steps, but stops when she sees a woman standing on the farthest corner of the balcony. Her back is to Luce. She doesn't recognize this woman. She is even taller than her mother, and longer limbed, like some tree deep in a forest that people hike to see, like a tree glowing by some un-known light. She's wearing a long white jacket.

The woman turns to look at Luce. She is an elegant woman. Gi-ant. Luce squints toward the woman—and that's how she sees that her face isn't a face so much as a shadow. Bone and shadow. Where the woman's head should be is a skull.

The skull has giant purple shadow holes for eyes. A long snout that reaches far past where a human face should end. The jaw is open. Inside are wide, yellow, cracked teeth. A cow's skull.

The white jacket's hood is up over her hair. She beckons Luce to come over.

Luce feels a flush as warm pee runs down her legs. The air is no longer cold. The cow-skull woman is full of heat. She waves again for Luce to come over. Luce knows, somehow—*how?*—that she has no choice. She takes a step, then a few. The cow-skull woman is looking right at her. She nods her skull. Luce is doing the right thing. There is sweat running into Luce's eyes. She rubs it with her trembling fingers.

The cow-skull woman seems to be growing taller as Luce approaches, and there, circling her body, diving and spinning, are flies. Hundreds of them. She raises her hand out toward Luce, her fingers long and very thin with short, chewed nails, and she's beckoning. Luce knows she wants her over there faster, sooner, and there's something else Luce understands too, as the cow-skull woman's nods grow deeper and more urgent, as her hands are calling her over faster and with more pull. The cow-skull woman isn't just beckoning to bring her closer, she needs something from her. Or is trying to give her something. Her arms are wildly circling, *come closer, come closer.* She's beckoning her away from something else. Something behind her.

It's that realization, suddenly, that whatever is behind her is worse than what is in front, that paralyzes her. There's this one last moment of her breath, fast, crazy, and then what is there to do? Luce buckles her knees and drops sideways to the ground. She falls with a thud onto the concrete balcony.

She will sleep, right at the feet of this cow-skull woman. Gem will lift her up, arms beneath her armpits. She will be here with ice cream and then hold Luce's limp body, and Luce will whimper this terrible nightmare into Gem's ear while Gem rubs her back.

Luce squeezes her eyes shut and counts one, two, three, four. She is counting, tensed, her head aching from where it hit, her dress cold with pee, waiting for the thing behind her to pounce. When she gets to ten, she squints one eye open. It is dark. She is on the balcony.

She can hear no music playing inside, no voices. She looks behind her, in front, but there is nobody else outside. There is not a cow-skull shadow where the elegant woman had been. She is alone.

She picks herself up off the ground. Her head is aching and her party dress is dirty. She wants to cry, feeling her chest getting fizzy, but then she stops.

Luce peeks over the edge of the balcony. Is the woman down there? There are a few lights in the parking lot, but she cannot see everything. She will not cry. But there is nothing. Dead leaves and the neighbor's trash and starlight shining on the known world.

But then a flash of brightness catches her eye. She looks up, and there. The elegant woman. Luce can only see the bottom of her white jacket as she scales the wall. She is halfway bent, disappearing. She is climbing into the window upstairs. Into Roo's bedroom.

Luce begins yelling then, pounding on the glass door. She tries to open it again, but it's still locked. Her breath makes warm, wet ghosts on the glass. The elegant woman is inside her baby brother's room and it is her job to protect him and she is stuck here, she is on the balcony, she is pounding and yelling, and that's when her mother appears at the door, clicks it open.

Luce tears past her, up the stairs, the longest stairs in the world, the walls closing in around her, and she is soaked with pee and moving too slow. Finally, she makes it into Roo's room. He is alone. There is no cow-skull woman in his room. He is asleep. In his crib. His sweaty blond head. And that's when she hears her mother downstairs. She is making a sound Luce has never heard before. Luce walks slowly back down the stairs and into the kitchen, one foot, then the other, toe and then heel, sneaking, she realizes, softly and slowly. Tinsel scattered across the floors like shards of glass. The sound from the kitchen is all animal. Something hoarse and deep from inside a body. Gulp. Choke. Luce knows what she will see. Her mother, at the table, with a cow skull where her head should be.

She takes the last step into the kitchen. There is a Before and After for this moment. She is holding her breath.

There, at the table, is her mother. Just her mother, with her regular head.

Luce takes careful steps forward, arms out, but stops. She lowers her arms. Something is off. There's a smell in the air. The sound her mother is making. Her mouth. The shape of it.

"There's been an incident," Gloria says, though her voice is static. Without breath. There are shadows on the wall that look like ghosts. Now Gem needs to slide out and wrap her arms around Luce and Gloria, and they will find themselves as a perfect sandwich of love.

But Gloria's mouth is open. It is open into a big, long *O*, a wail, a scream. Her mother says, "Gem is hurt." Luce cinches her arms around herself. Gem is hurt. "No—fuck it," her mother says, her voice full of mucus and grit. "I'm not going to lie. It was not an *incident*, or an *accident*. He beat the shit out of her," Gloria says, her voice breaking, and Luce starts telling a story to herself to keep out the words her mother is saying. *Once upon a time, there was a princess of bones.* Her mother is still talking, "He used a wrench, hands around the neck," and Luce thinks of the princess with the *whole kingdom to rule and nothing to help her but a cave full of bones.* Gloria is saying "Caused a brain bleed." Luce imagines the blood traveling up over the mountains, through blizzards, into the cave of bones. *She was in*

*her cave when suddenly a mountain lion wandered in and wanted the
cave for himself.*

Gloria wipes her face with both hands, the black and blue trails of
makeup that look like rivers smear all across her face like a painting,
and Luce can see, even beneath the makeup, the flaming pink rings
of her eyes. It scares her, all of it. Something confusing, something
huge is building inside her chest. "I want ice cream," she says. "Gem
was bringing it for me. Where is she?"

Gloria's face is wet all over and her shoulders are moving like
someone is shaking her from behind. Luce doesn't understand, but
also she does. "I want Gem, not you," she says. She brings her fist
down on her mother's back. Nothing happens. Her mother's shoulders keep shaking, and so she keeps hitting.

"Stop it," Gloria whispers, suddenly sitting up. She stands up,
raging, arms swinging wide as she gathers her keys, her purse, she is
wiping her face with the palms of her hands. "If you hadn't demanded
she come to the party, they never would have had that fight. This
never would have happened." She looks Luce right in the eyes.

Luce's body is gone. It doesn't belong to her anymore.

Gloria stands. She steadies herself against the sink and then
spins, kicking out as hard as she can, and her foot smashes into the
wooden cupboards with a horrible click and the cupboard breaks into
splinters and so do her mother's bones inside her big toe. There is
screaming.

In the silence inside the scream, in the breath, a fly. Buzzing
around the sink. Landing on a dirty plate. Rubbing its hands together, back and forth, back and forth.

She thought that night was the worst part. That nothing would ever
be as terrible as the cow-skull woman, as terrifying as her mother
undone.

But they hadn't even gotten to Gem yet.

To her most important person, head cracked open and staring all the way to Jupiter, never to return.

The worst part hadn't even started yet.

Luce was still here, inside the memory that was really just the on-ramp to sorrow, driving it over and over again.

17

1989

GEM HAD BEEN IN THE HOSPITAL two weeks, the first week fully unconscious, the second, awake, eyes open, but not meeting anyone's gaze. Unresponsive to voices, stimulation. *Aphasia*, the word was—no ability to communicate, no ability to understand. That's what the doctors said at least, but Gloria wasn't convinced. It wasn't possible that Gloria was still moving through the world, hearing birds and drinking coffee and scratching her arm if her sister wasn't—it would be like a body dancing without its head.

So she tried to find her wherever she was and bring her back. She started with the barroom trick, when they used to finish each other's sentences as kids. They hadn't done it in years. Focused her mind, asked where she was. Nothing. Thought, What I need to heal is—but there was no response. So Gloria had shown up at the hospital with a pad of paper and crayons. She pinched Gem's fingers around the mauve, moved her arm across the page so that faint purplish streaks appeared on the white, stripes of bruise. Gloria took her hand away, ready for Gem to take it up on her own. To confirm that the person she was pretty fucking sure had done this to her was in fact the person who had. But the crayon fell to the bed, Gem's hand limp and open.

Next came a typewriter Gloria heaved onto the bed, hoping Gem could find the keys, and later a set of pre-written sentences on flash cards Gem could point to, an alphabet she could indicate by blinking. Nothing worked. Gloria did not give up. She got more creative, shifting from the land of language into something else. She slid into the hospital bed beside her sister one night. Stiff sheets, the smell of antiseptic. Their faces, which for so long had been nearly identical, were growing further apart—Gem's bruised, swollen on one side, sticky from a line of dried pus. And yet, Gloria thought, perhaps she could still pull off the trick they used to play on their mother, where one pretended to be the other. Perhaps Gloria could find a way to take Gem's place here. She had to, because there was just one of them who was wholly good, just one of them who knew how to raise a child, just one of them who deserved, more than the other, to stay alive.

In those hospital months, Luce sat rigid beside her baby brother as he slept in his car seat, or she jiggled him on her lap if he cried, giving him a bottle. She overheard the nurses tell Gloria that kids bounce back quickly, they're so adaptable, they probably don't even really understand what's happening.

She understood.

It used to be that the worst thing she could imagine was her mother taking her away from Gem. But now she knew. There were always worse things that could come.

It was in the hospital lobby, on a take-a-book, leave-a-book shelf, that she found her first biography. It was about the man who stashed killing kits all over the country to murder women he stalked. She hid the book at first—Gem would have freaked out if she caught her reading something like that—but her mother didn't even notice. The words were dense and the book was long, but every time she found herself getting bored or scared, she looked over at Gem. The stories in this book were worse. Luce was taking action. She was acquiring a whole world of information that her mother didn't even know, true knowledge of the world that made what had happened to Gem not so extraordinary at all.

She watched her mother in the hospital, weeping, pleading, pacing. She heard her cuss and yell and chase a doctor down the hallway. She did not crouch down to where Luce sat to explain what was happening, to hug her, to see if she was okay. So Luce fed Roo his bottle. Shook a toy for him to paw. She remembered coming into the hospital room one day, dusk turning the corners into shadow, and her mother in the chair beside her sister's bed, head rolled back, moving her lips very quickly. Luce had never been to church, but she knew, from people who protested on the streets, that this was some kind of prayer. "I can't do this by myself," Gloria whispered to her sister. "I don't know how to keep you safe and help you heal and take care of these kids. Help. Tell me what to do."

"Gloria?" Luce asked quietly from the doorway.

"Sshh," Gloria said. "I'm trying to find her voice." She rocked forward then, knocking over a stack of magazines she'd brought in from the waiting room. One clattered by her foot and landed with the pages open. Gloria picked it up. The pages were stained and faded, but the image was unmistakable. Seven bald women, standing in front of an estuary. The redwood witches, who lived in a place where no woman could be harmed.

"You bitch," Gloria said, laughing as she picked up the magazine. Gem's hand, close to Gloria's face on the bed, clenched. Gloria grabbed it, asked her to squeeze if she could hear, kissed it. Nothing happened. Asked Gem if this was what she wanted for them, if this was where they needed to go. She set Gem's hand on the magazine, and still, nothing happened. Luce, tucked in the shadows of the doorway, watched all this unfold and understood only some of what she was seeing.

Gloria stared down at Gem's palm, studied it. Stared for a long time, willing communication. A nurse came by right then, scootching past Luce, and saw what Gloria was doing. "Oh, you're a palm reader?" she said to Gloria. "I've been dying to try it. Will you do mine? How much does it cost?"

And that was it, a fault line opening in their lives. The impetus that would move them to the Red Grove. The beginning of Gloria's business. It was that simple. Accidental. Gloria, in need of money, said yes to the nurse, and yes to the nurse's friends who wanted appointments, and yes to everyone else as the business grew. At first, after one of these sessions, Gloria would lean down to her sister, snorting, chuckling, say, Can you believe people are falling for this crap? It was easy enough to invent what to say to someone, what someone needed to hear. Making money had never been simple, until it suddenly was.

But something started to change once they moved to the Red Grove. Gloria noticed it only when she did a reading with her sister in the room. Sounds rose. As if she were backstage, listening to the cacophony of audience chatter before the curtain raised. Dozens of indistinguishable voices. She listened and listened and could not hear individual voices, but she listened on. And then, eventually, rising like an instrument readying for its solo, one voice grew a little louder.

18

June 28, 1997 • Gone Two Days

MORNING. Fog thinned itself into a skin of old milk. Luce lay on the couch, forearm covering her eyes, the other arm draped onto Moose's body on the floor, rubbing his belly. Each time she stopped, he lifted his head to look at her, tongue hanging out the side, so she'd start again. Her eyes stung, dry and raw. Spinning through the memory of the cow-skull woman, doubting she'd actually heard the voice in Gem's room say it, but she had, hadn't she, she had, and then she'd remembered, or dreamed it, that whole impossible night, the memory creeping through her, and it was morning again. And in her head—thick cobwebs, glue slowing everything down.

The house hushed. There was the low *grr* of the old refrigerator, the pipes gurgling, the beams creaking beneath the weight of their living. The scratch of a squirrel's claws on the roof. And then there was another sound, something farther away. A kind of clicking, like the sound of a sliding glass door locking shut.

It was not close by—how could she hear it? She stood up, pacing the room, called Moose over, and he came, good boy, his ears swiveling as he trotted. He heard it too.

Luce opened the front door. It was louder. Be rational. A bird, maybe, warning a predator. That was possible, probable, though the sound felt eerily human, and no longer unfamiliar. She'd heard it before. A human mouth's click. She could feel her heart quickening. Bravery wasn't complicated—it meant just doing the thing, she reminded herself, following the sound outside and toward the hills.

It was early enough that fog obscured everything beyond the first crowd of trees. *Click*. A cowboy's click for the horse to giddyap. Moose trotted out ahead, his nose low to the ground as he swerved with each smell he caught. Luce followed the trail behind her house that led through the redwoods and eventually up into the wild, dead hills—no, dead-*grass* hills, she corrected herself. Each step gave a little. Layers of dead needles beneath, dirt, stones, worms, and deeper, through time's flattening, carapaces, dried blood, crushed bones, everything that had lived and died right in this slice of earth. What should she make of all that history ever-present beneath and around her, she wondered, but the sound clicked again, louder than it was inside the house.

She left the redwoods, climbing out of the fog and into the brown grass. The sides of the trail were rimmed with hip-high thistles, dried cottony flowers on top and dark brown leaves sagging against the stalk all the way down, yielding to collapse. Tall dead things, Luce thought. Oh, dramatic. Good lord. Don't try to make this mean anything.

All at once, Moose was sprinting full speed off into the woods. A deer probably, which he would never catch. She watched him dart below bushes, leap over a fallen log, and disappear into the brush. And then the click came, loud. It was close. Something cold inside her sweatshirt, taking small, freezing nips at her backbone, so cold it almost felt as if it would transform her into something else, maybe one of the thistles she saw all around, and she was suddenly afraid all the way down her legs, thinking these stalks were other walkers, trapped.

Click.

Nonsense. She forced a step up the path. This was not her mother, clicking with Gem, faces pressed close. *Click.* Nobody around.

Luce was a quarter mile from home, marching up the hillside's spine. Not too much farther to the smash shack, and who would be there, wailing on the rocks. She remembered a story one of the women in the Red Grove had told when Luce was young: two illicit lovers trying to make love up in the hills had gone a little too far past the boundary, and the spurned husband, who'd learned of their plans ahead of time, was hiding behind a rock with a gun, and—we all know that story. And she thought about the man who called, standing out on their deck, maybe he was in the shadows somewhere, maybe he'd come for her—

She didn't yet see the low stone wall or the tree trunks ringed in red that indicated the boundary, though it was true that the wall wasn't completed all the way, had gaps, or even places where there'd once been wall but it had since fallen to rubble, or birds had pecked off the tree's thread—you could see them sometimes, a jay or a hawk flying past, a long red thread, like intestines, trailing from its mouth. From this trail the wall was particularly hard to spot. Sometimes the boundary between safe and unsafe was invisible.

The clicks had stopped. She came upon one of those rare patches of bright yellow daffodils, so startlingly vibrant against the drought of early summer. How did they survive? The click had stopped her here. She stepped off the path, scrambling up the steep hillside until she was beside them. If she turned around, she could see past the tops of trees and across the whole valley to the mounded hills on the other side, bare, too. But she did not turn around again. Her eyes were on the daffodils, yellow skulls. She took a few steps farther into their patch, crushing one beneath her foot, and then a few steps farther still. There was something in the ground, between the flowers. Dug-up grass, clods turned over and packed back down.

As if an animal—a mountain lion—had been digging for something right here. She backed away from the yellow skull flowers, wishing each step was a year back in time so that in ten steps she could be scooped up in Gem's arms, and then, beneath her foot, something hard.

It was not a rock. There was a glint of light against metal. It was packed into the hardened ground like it'd been there a long time. Her fingernails filled with dirt as she scratched it out. Old silver, tarnished, rusted. She picked it up. In her hand was a locket the size of a cherry, flat, dirty. She tried to pry the locket open, but it wouldn't budge. Rusted shut. Caked. What was so familiar about this?

She turned the locket over in her hand—yes. She knew this locket. When they first moved into the Red Grove, to this house at the top of the hill, she'd found it, coiled and rusty, on her bedroom floor. It was the necklace she'd slipped into Gem's hand in those early months, when she was still sure she'd die. When she wanted to infuse an object with her Gem so that she might always have her.

She hadn't even remembered losing it, but here it was, up on the ridge, beneath the dirt. She slipped it into her pocket, but then there it was again—*click*. She didn't wait to find out what came next.

She ran, nearly tumbling down the slope, back to the path. A cold whip against her neck, foolish, she knew, foolish to be afraid of what was surely the sound of squirrels cracking nuts between their teeth, the fog condensing into droplets and finding a puddle below. She ran faster. How could a sound follow her?

It was right beside her.

It was almost inside her ear.

She ran faster, but now she could hear another sound. Somewhere behind her, leaves were crunching. She knew, she knew, as if her mother's ice fingers had tiptoed all the way up to her throat, that she was being chased.

Click.

Luce ran, jumping over sticks, between rocks that would snap an ankle. Back down the dirt path, gone the winking daffodils, the tucked-in bones, gone the loose, hot rocks. A branch behind her snapped. She ran, not tripping, don't trip, running over rocks, around bends, the sharp, tall dead grasses scraping at her calves. Run. Don't look, can't, just run and run. And then all at once, almost laughing out loud, she thought, *Moose.* Of course.

She slowed her sprint to a jog, sighed out the breath she'd been gulping, her whole body loosening its muscled grip. Of course. Dog. She was about to turn around to greet him when something caught her eye up ahead. A rustle of leaves, a flash. She was at a slow jog, peering up ahead. Out of the bush, sprinting toward her, was Moose.

He was up ahead. And so what was the sound behind?

She could not look.

Back to a full sprint then, and she was nearly to the house, Moose barreling closer. Her chest was burning, lungs ready to explode. And then she was at the house, up the steps two at a time, Moose right at her heels, across the deck to the door, did not look back. She stood on the inside of the door. Waited for the click. She listened so hard, she heard tingles inside her ears, her breath still shooting out hot from her lungs. There would be a knock. A big, heavy pound on the door. There would be claws against the grain. Something wanting in. She would hear it, and the ice would be back, and she knew, she *knew*, that at that moment this foundational belief she'd held on to, that she was safe from what she wanted to be safe from, would be gone.

She waited. She listened. She heard only Moose's ragged breath, and her own.

And then she had a terrible thought. Why was she only listening for the sound outside the door? She turned slowly and faced the rest of the house. What was different?

Nothing.

Nothing, because nothing had been out there, nothing chasing her, nothing clicking. It was not a sound from her mother's mouth, speaking a language she didn't know. It was not her mother, clicking her onward toward—what?—what.

The kitchen floors were cold beneath her, creaking. Moose lapped at his water bowl.

"Roo," she called, but he didn't answer. She walked into the living room, not there, bathroom, nope, and then Gem's room. Gem was in bed, eyes open. But no Roo. His room was empty. What if whatever had made those clicks had come for him?

She walked into the hallway that led to the office. The door was cracked. Framed by the wall and the wood was a slice of the office, Roo standing inside. Luce could see that the windows were open, dust motes shimmering gold in the sun breaking through fog, and Roo seemed to glow a little, too. A breeze blew through the room, billowed the thin fuchsia sari with golden flowers tied above the windows out into the room unevenly, beside where Roo stood, so that there appeared to be a boy inside them, another boy, a little phantom body pressing against the cloth from the wall, though once the gust quelled, the boy who wasn't there was gone.

All the light in the room seemed to point to Roo. He stood perfectly still. There was something about his posture. His spine was straight and his legs, ivory toothpicks, freckled in great orange blotches, were locked, but the objects in the room seemed to be quivering, and Luce had the sense that they were readying to raise themselves into the air, join a galaxy of swirling objects.

He jerked. The objects stilled.

Luce could see that his arm was bent and, as he nodded his head to the side, he held something in his hand. It was the office phone. The one that sat with no cords, plugged into nothing.

Luce held very still. Goose bumps on the back of her neck.

"I can't hear you very well," Roo said, his voice cracking halfway through. His back was to Luce. "Can you say that again?" With his hand still holding the phone up to his ear, Roo heard a floorboard groan beneath Luce's foot and half turned his face to where she was. Were his eyes different? Was there some sort of milky skin across them, dulling the blue? He turned away from her again. She could see the pointy tips of his shoulder bones beneath his T-shirt, wings that never grew.

"Give me the phone," Luce whispered to Roo's back. He cocked his head away from her, pressing his ear harder into the receiver. He started to say something, but stopped. Nodded instead.

"Roo," Luce hissed, more aggressive than she'd meant, but he didn't move. She lurched forward then, grabbing the phone out of his hand and spinning in one motion, pressing the phone to her ear. *She* was the one with the special relationship to the Red Grove, he was a little kid, she should be the one to hear whatever was coming through. Shoulders crunched against her neck, she could not even imagine what she was about to hear. "Hello?" she said into the line. Tried to listen past the whooping throb of blood in her ears. The phone was heavy. A weight she hadn't noticed before. Maybe there was something else inside it. She waited for it to make a sound.

But the only sounds she could hear were crickets out the open window. A rumble in her stomach. She counted to ten. Squeezed her eyes shut so she could concentrate solely on her ears. When she turned back to Roo, he was blinking up at her with a small, hopeful smile, eyebrows raised.

"You shit," Luce said.

He squinted then, his smile gone. "What?"

"Roo. You're an asshole."

His freckles blended into an orange mass beneath his reddening cheeks. "Didn't you hear her?"

"Shut up."

"You didn't?" he said, his forehead creased and older than he was, concerned.

"What are you talking about?"

"Didn't you?"

"There was nobody on the line, Roo. The phone isn't even plugged in. It's a dead phone."

"It's not *just* a dead phone," he said. He started hopping from foot to foot, his excitement growing. "That's what I thought too, at first. But it's even more special than that. It can also talk to non-dead people."

"Stop it!" Luce yelled. The sound startled them both.

"I was talking to someone," Roo said. He'd stopped hopping, brought his voice lower and quieter. "I couldn't figure out who it was for a long time. The voice was hard to hear, and it kept breaking up, like that one time we got a call from the person in France. There was lots of static. But then I could hear. It was a faraway voice."

"Whose voice?"

"Hers."

"Fuck, who, Roo?"

"Well, I'm not exactly sure. It was hard to tell. But I think maybe—" He stopped, held still. All at once, Roo sprinted across the office and turned into the hallway. Luce followed, also moving fast, and watched him round the corner into Gem's room.

Because, what if it was Gem?

She would have woken up and called the phone. She would be smiling, yawning. She would blink, and when her eyelids opened again, she would reach a hand out to Luce, brushing her cheek. She'd say, *You found me.*

Roo stood beside Gem's bed. She did not have her eyes open. She was not blinking, did not extend an arm off the bed, and as Luce stepped closer, she saw that Gem's hands were more clawed than ever. The fingers were stiff and bent in on themselves. Her skin— pale with a chalky hue from so many years in bed, unmoving, out of the sun—was a different color. There were patches of purple with greens melting in, a gray around her face, a layer of storm clouds growing across her skin, and what did it mean? Gem's hand was cold. Luce squeezed it, her fingers leaving a white thumbprint that slowly filled itself back in with gray. Luce's heart kicked up again.

"What is buried must be uncovered," Roo said. "That's what the voice told me."

"What does that mean?" Luce asked, pressing her ear close to Gem's nose. Her breath was loud, ragged.

"I don't know."

"Roo," Luce said, keeping her eyes on Gem's chest to watch how slowly it expanded. It was her job to find stillness and calm she didn't have and offer it to him. "I know you miss Mom. And I know this is really scary. She'll come back."

"I think it's a puzzle," he said, close to Gem's face on the other side, but not touching her. "What is buried must be uncovered. Like a secret—that's the kind of thing that gets buried, right?" He was pulling one of his earlobes, something he'd done as a littler boy. Luce studied him carefully—he was inventing a voice, must be, and where had he even heard that line, so formal sounding? But, okay, taking it seriously for a minute, because enough strange things had been happening—what had been buried was the locket. It felt cold inside her pocket. She'd uncovered it. Same with that carved bone she'd found a few days back, before the altered axis of their lives. What answers were they supposed to provide? Perhaps if she could pry the locket open—she pulled it out, jimmied her thumbnail in, but it would not budge. She couldn't remember it ever having opened.

Light that had traveled through the maze of trees outside came into the room, not bright, but hazy and summer yellow, one beam landing on Roo's small, thumping heart. "I'll call back," Roo said, turning toward the office again.

"No," Luce said, squeezing his shoulder. She tapped his chin so he was looking right up at her. "Do not play with that again."

"I wasn't playing," he said, pushing her hand off. "You're jealous 'cause you don't know how to use it. Mom did. I do. Gem would. But not you. I should get to be the one in the office. Mom doesn't want you." Before she had time to respond, he ran down the hallway to his bedroom and slammed the door.

She didn't go after him. He was right.

She remembered back to a day when they'd been in the hospital visiting Gem, waiting to see if she'd live or die. Luce, eight, in a fold-out chair against the wall, bouncing baby Roo on her lap and staring at Gem. Willing her to wake up, promising whoever or whatever was listening in her mind that she'd spend the rest of her life, all of it, being good; they'd studied Gandhi in school, so that's what she promised. I'll be Gandhi forever, I'll be helpful and nice, if only you will wake Gem up.

But she didn't wake up. And then she still didn't wake up. Luce sat in her foldout chair, arms wrapped around the baby when he needed it but mostly around herself. What she needed was someone else's arms around her, and thinking this, she looked in front of her, at her mother's back, stooped beside Gem. Her mother was awake. Maybe if she got her mother to love her, it would travel through and wake up Gem. So she came up with a plan.

She said she had to pee, but instead of turning into the hallway bathroom, she kept walking into the elevator and through the lobby and right out the hospital's sliding glass doors and through the parking lot and along a small paved path that plopped her into the forest. Up above, the needles let little squints of light come through. The world suddenly smelled like dirt and water and wonderful, and even a faint stink from something rotting smelled wonderful too. She stayed there a long time, thinking, deliciously, about how worried her mother would be about where she'd gone. How big a hug she'd get. How much love it would shoot into her, jolting Gem right awake. When she couldn't stand it any longer, she returned.

She turned the corner into the room, holding back her smile.

Gloria was rocking Roo with one arm, kissing his small hot head. The other arm was stretched out across the hospital bed, holding Gem's hand.

Where have you been? her mother asked, but didn't reach out for her. Didn't pull her in close. Gem was still gone, and her mother's arms already held the things she found most precious. There was no space for anyone else.

From *The Red Grove: The Story of the Sisters*

It was a week before Tamsen was out of bed, but the stranger, Ines, had tended to the bite each day and, with instruction, fished the stream, taken care of the garden, gathered plants, pulled water from the creek. Within a week, the infection had subsided and Tamsen had regained much of her strength. The wound was still mending, though, and sometimes, in her dreams, the strangest thing would happen—she would hear a kind of mountain lion's scream coming from the sever in her skin.

One day, a few weeks after Ines arrived, Tamsen was down at the base of the valley, checking traps, when a passing traveler rode by. He was small, and he stopped just past where Tamsen worked to water his horse in the creek. The traveler told Tamsen that railroad construction was booming north and south of this little valley, but the railroad men had found this terrain impossible to build upon and so were taking another path clear around these hills to connect the big city on the bay south of the valley to the mountains full of gold farther north.

"Why, then, are there more horses traveling these treacherous paths?" Tamsen asked, nodding to his horse, who had waded into the creek.

Tamsen had no claim to the land, didn't actually know who owned it, but she appreciated that few people came through because of the difficulty of passage.

He shifted, leaned in closer to her, and spoke quietly. "You ever heard of Hank Monk?" Tamsen nodded. She didn't get much news up around here, but she'd heard another traveler mention Hank Monk. He was a stagecoach driver, best one in California, and the fiercest, too. Story went, a rattlesnake startled the horse he was watering, and the horse, standing beside Hank Monk, had kicked him right in the eye. It was gone, an empty flap of skin that he'd show little kids if they got in his way, though he mostly kept it covered with a black piece of cloth. Hank Monk knew all the mountain passes and game trails, and he drove his stagecoach fast and wild through whichever path would most quickly get him and his passengers to their destination, standing up with one hand on the reins and the other pointed backward to shoot away approaching danger. He was feared and respected. Bandits couldn't catch him, ghosts couldn't spook him.

"He's starting running his stagecoach here," the stranger said. He'd finished watering his horse and had mounted again, ready to take off. There had been more activity down in the base of the valley. Up the hill, Tamsen's cabin wasn't in the direct path of the increasing horse traffic, but she relied on fishing and hunting at the base of the valley, where the creeks were widest and the salmon spawned and she had the clearest open shot for deer. "I'd watch out if I were you," the man said. "Only good thing about Hank Monk being close is that mostly the Indians steer clear. He has some kind of agreement with them—you haven't seen any around these parts, have you?"

Tamsen shook her head. She didn't know anything about them beyond the tales her husband and his brothers told before they'd headed west. "Well, that's something to celebrate at least. But keep your watch. There are no good stories about what happens to a woman alone when Hank Monk comes along." She tucked this information away, straightened her spine, and went to work on the squirrel she'd trapped.

Fawns grew into deer, grasses died and lay down on the dirt, protecting spring's new shoots, and some time later, another woman appeared, a young widow who had lost her husband in a stagecoach accident. Whispers had spread in her town about where Ines had found shelter. This woman brought three small children along.

Tamsen refused. No space, she said, believing that more people here would attract more attention, make it more likely that her husband would find her. But she would not tell them the story of why she feared him and so told them no story at all, and the woman and her children stayed.

They built a shelter right alongside Tamsen's house, using one of the exterior walls as a new interior wall for an adjoining cabin, rooms blossoming into rooms. The children learned quickly how to trap small animals and weed the garden, and Tamsen did not like to admit how she felt hearing their light, laughing voices outside, little bells chiming in the wind. Their mother, however, did not laugh. She was a serious woman, and Tamsen often caught her staring down the hillside into the valley below, tensed.

The next woman who showed up hadn't lost a husband at all, because she'd obstinately refused to marry. Her mother had died in childbirth, and the idea of being split into two dead halves tormented her dreams. She showed up fleeing the marriage her family was arranging, could recite every line from the Bible and then tell you which ones she thought were worth paying attention to, and had the loudest laugh anyone had ever heard, a hee-haw donkey bray that sent all the other women and children laughing when she laughed, and so she did it often, and easily.

One night by the fire, once the children were asleep, the woman whose husband had been a stagecoach driver told them a story. On his last trip, they'd come under attack, and only one person, a teenage boy, had survived to tell the tale. The attacker, the boy told the police, had a black eye patch and black lips. Tamsen knew right away: Hank Monk. She tightened her shawl around her shoulders, asking the great red trees to keep them hidden.

And in this way the band of women grew. Women, sneaking away, in scandal or secrecy, alone or with children, leaving the world where their lives were directed by men and arriving at the red grove. They lived quietly up in the hills, adding on to the original shelter with new, small rooms, hunting, growing crops, fishing, tanning hides, sewing clothes, and gathering what they could. The winters were mild and the crops grew with diverted stream water and the creeks flowed with salmon. It was not hard to survive. That was the strangest thing. It felt as if something in this valley and upon these hillsides were blessing them with good fortune and abundance, which, for all those gathered, was foreign.

Late at night, Tamsen paced the cabin, as silent as a cat. What she wanted was sound sleep and to trust the shadows, to prowl the darkness and not think about her husband or the other husbands these women had fled, out there somewhere. Probably her own husband had not survived, had not made it back to where he'd left his brothers and their wives. Probably he would not be looking for her, this wife he'd left for dead. Certainly he wouldn't, she had to tell herself, and then tell herself again, peering out into the darkness.

There were eight people living together among the red groves with Tamsen Nightingale, and then there were twelve, then seventeen. The redwood forest provided easy hiding from wandering travelers and protected the women from weather. The longer they lived among the giant red trees, the more they came to know of the trees' particular uses, sometimes through the trials of the women there who knew plants and could discern a potential quality from smell or taste or growth pattern, and sometimes through the wisdom they gathered from those who'd had exchanges with the people who lived here before them. Fresh needles were steeped in warm water to treat earaches or to purify the blood of the sick. Gummy sap mixed with water would deliver a stimulating tonic for those with malaise.

Tamsen walked the slopes and valley, watching Ines teach a newcomer how to harvest the new pliable sprouts growing from the burls of

dead redwoods and weave them into baskets. Children nearby were collecting sloughed-off chunks of bark, thick and soft, and others were pulling strips of new bark from some of the trees—never too much from a
single tree or it could open it to infection. They marveled at the red spires,
how fire had entered the grove once and cleared out the dead and dry
underbrush, but the giant trees had remained intact, had, in fact, shot up
a new crop of young trees just afterward, as if the fire itself had enabled
new life. And they marveled that insects didn't eat away the bark, sicken-
ing the tree, or that no mold or mildew seemed to take hold despite the
dampness, all of it a miracle of fortitude and longevity that they would
both use and emulate.

Back at the cabin, other women stuffed the bark on the inside of the
walls for insulation against the chill of fog and occasional winter frost,
one holding a piece while another secured it, swatting at one another
playfully, sweating on the warm days, singing when the mood struck,
engaged with a kind of purpose, not just because of the work, for they
had all been working their whole lives in some form or another, but because it was suddenly true that the work of their hands was their shelter,
their food, their lives. And other women were out gathering plants for
food and medicine, or mending torn clothes, baking bread, whittling
wood into utensils, tools—women working in pairs or small groups as
gossip or instruction or the stories of their lives drew them closer. And in
making their lives together, a greater sense of safety germinated, not
only from the product of their industry but because of the women they
were growing to trust.

One day, Tamsen looked down at her hands and noticed new spots,
scars, knobs. It had been only a handful of years since she'd arrived—
five, or was it seven—and she was not yet an old woman, but she had been
working hard, and she realized, with surprise, that this was where she
would live out her life. Here, in this red grove, with these women whose
clenched jaws loosened the longer they lived out here, who startled less
easily, who spread their knees wider when they sat and let out the waists
of their dresses.

Ines liked to work outside, in the soil, expanding the area Tamsen had created for plants. The same plant could be both cure or poison, aphrodisiac or repellent. It depended upon the dose, upon the recipient, upon what was done to the plant before it entered the body of the receiver. As she worked, her silver locket glinted in the sun. Tamsen had never asked to see what was inside, and Ines had never offered.

Tamsen took long walks, sometimes for days at a time, deeper into the woods and beyond that to the rolling hills and, occasionally, even farther out toward the steep coast where the ocean broke against rocks in bright white explosions. Out there, on one of the thin stretches of land alongside the water, an amalgamation of birds gathered, birds that Tamsen had never seen before, big seabirds and tiny, delicate things and birds with iridescent stripes beneath their wings and a bird with feathers so blue it made the ocean look dull. She spooked them off their resting place and gathered the feathers they'd left behind, tucking them into her satchel alongside the herbs she pulled on these walks, learning year by year what was what, planting shoots into the garden they'd expanded and had come to reply upon.

Ines and Tamsen spent hours together in the garden, comparing what they knew about the properties of various plants and animal parts, cultivating nettles and nasturtium, violet and verbena, opening the gall bladders of snared hares and possums for their healing liquids, gathering the oil from glands in a skunk's back for liniment. But as much as they learned together, there were still times when what troubled Tamsen was beyond what Ines knew to help her heal.

Tamsen was not always inside the cabin once night came. If everyone fell silent at once, though, they could hear her somewhere outside, a distant yowl. "They're called mountain screamers where I'm from," one of the women said. "I always heard cougar," another said. "Or puma. Catamount." "Why so many names for the same creature?" Ines asked, and another of the women said that there were some animals you couldn't know well enough to name. On one of these nights—when the women, who both loved and feared Tamsen's wildness, whispered to one another that she might be out hunting with the lions, and then, in even lower, quieter whispers, that perhaps she *was* part lion—Ines told the gathered women a story.

Back in her mother's village, Ines began, "There was once a time when the men all beat their wives and the sons beat their sisters, and so mothers wished to have no sons. This was an area known for the biggest mountain lions in the world, giants who stalked the hillsides at night and could take down any man trying to hunt them, which they did, and beat them, since the men thought they could conquer all. In this town lived a family with three sons. One morning, the family woke and realized the oldest son had gone missing. Villagers searched and searched, but could not find the boy. They decided to hike the hill, between the thick trees, to the house where the witch lived, to see if she knew anything about the boy. She did not, she said, but the villagers didn't believe her, and they tortured her by piercing her ears with hot metal. The following morning, the second son was missing. The villagers searched, but could not find the boy, and once again returned to the witch. Like the last time, she said she knew nothing about the boy, but the villagers didn't believe her, seeking more information by slicing off one baby toe and then the next, one pinky finger and then the other. That night, not willing to risk his youngest son, the father and the villagers set a trap to catch the witch. They built a door that would slam shut and lock once anyone entered the child's room. In the darkest hours of the night they heard the trap slam shut, and they rushed into the room. The youngest son was gone. But in the room was the largest mountain lion anyone in the village had ever seen. She had pierced holes in her ears and only four toes on each of her massive paws. Filled with terror, the villagers parted, and the mountain lion walked out, licking her maw. From that day forward, men were too scared to want sons lest the witch eat them, and so they began to wish for daughters, and the daughters listened and arrived joyfully, filling the village with peace."

"Are you saying that Tamsen Nightingale is one of those witches?" asked one of the children.

"It's only a story," Ines said, braiding the hair of one of the other women, who was half-draped across her lap. But the children and women paid extra attention to mountain lion tracks, to Tamsen's absences and sorrows, feeling for her both reverence and terror, whispering to one another that they were quite sure they saw, inside her mouth, the point of one very long, very sharp tooth.

19

1989

How did you ever identify happiness? Even though the Red Grove offered assistance of all kinds—babysitting, food, subsidized lodging for a while, a shared closet where you could find most things you'd need—Gloria was not interested in relying on handouts. Never be in debt, she knew. So she set up her business quickly. Una had made it clear that they wanted few outsiders coming into the Red Grove; there were no gates or guards, so obviously people occasionally came through, but most of the community lived off of small, twisted roads in the woods and hillsides, far from the main road, which had no signs alerting a passer-through that they were anywhere at all, no stores or cafés advertising to outsiders, nothing to stop for, and that was how they liked it. So when Gloria began inviting outsiders into her home as part of her business, it was one of her and Una's many points of contention. How would Gloria maintain her business, for which she used her tools—namely, her sister as conduit—if she could not have seekers come into her home? It was a time of great need for Gloria and her family, and like the ever-adapting redwood trees around them, Una said that the community would adapt in this one special case, for a short time, until they could come up with a better solution. But Gloria would need to make it clear to the seekers that her special abilities were not a ubiquitous gift in the community, they were unique to Gloria. It was the reason, Una said, that they'd been moved to this house at the top of the hill, deep within the Red Grove; the house in the belly of the community, down many winding roads, through redwoods, up a big golden hill, where they would be entirely safe, entirely cared for. The Red Grove would do its protective work.

But the short time stretched, as time does, and Gloria kept seekers coming to the house even as Roo chewed solids, began to walk, lost a tooth, even as Luce fell in love with dolphins, fell out of love with dolphins, became the guide through the darkness, even as it became clear that Gem seemed to be holding still in this everdreaming state and didn't need the kind of full-time attention they'd first thought. Together, they found the rhythm of this life, and it became, as it does, normal.

Did normal mean happiness? In those first years of living in the Red Grove, Gloria wouldn't have said that she was happy. There was always hardship. There were her two small children to care for, flus, colds, rampant head lice, the crusted gunk of pink eye to scrape, a rogue strain of whooping cough because of the few anti-vaccination families, and yes, there were more hands helping her as Red Grovers stopped by, but they were not the hands she most wanted, they were not Gem's. There was money stress when her business was new and then periodically when seekers dried up for a while, there was laundry and dishes, there was the wave that occasionally overtook her, even though both her parents had been long dead, of orphanhood, that fundamental loneliness that came mostly, she knew, from her sister's absence. Well, not *absence* absence. That was the hardest part.

So there was all that, which was decidedly not happiness, yet there was something else, too. It started the day after they arrived.

The first visitor. Her name was Terry, she said, talking nonstop from the time Gloria answered the door to when Gloria finally ushered her out nearly an hour later. She'd been in the Red Grove three years, and she had four boys, who were grown and gone, and here was the tomato pie they loved so much, warm at 375 degrees for forty-five minutes, and how was Gloria feeling, it was a lot for most new women to take in and get adjusted to, took some time to sleep soundly for most, but now, Terry said, she slept like an old dog, not a baby, what a funny expression sleeping like a baby is, you've had babies so you know, they thrash and wake and stick one arm straight up, not good sleepers, no sireee, but if you've had an old dog, you get it, always sleepy, a sunny spot is nice, but any spot will do, just not afraid of a thing anymore.

The next person didn't knock at all, left a basket of jams and pickled veggies on the doorstep, and the next was a nurse, there because she'd heard there was someone who might need medical attention. She went right to where Gem lay and began checking her vitals, adjusting her posture in bed, talking to Gem with the assumption that she was still present inside, which was not something many of the nurses in the hospital had done. And Gloria thought this too, couldn't stop herself—maybe there *was* something about this place that could help heal her sister. Sure, the doctors had said there wasn't any chance of recovery, but there were also stories of miracles, weren't there, it was possible. And this was a place that traded in making the impossible possible.

And shortly thereafter was Una herself, there, she said, to watch the kids for a little while so Gloria could get settled in, unpack, or take a bath—or follow in the footsteps of many newcomers and find the Red Grove's boundary line, walk its low stone perimeter, run her hands along the red-yarn trees so that she could know, could feel, her own safety, and her proximity to the edge.

Baby Roo sat in his little bouncy chair and kicked his legs in joy, smiling at all the new people and babbling until they came close and let him gnaw on their fingers or made goofy faces until he cackled and clapped.

Luce mostly stayed in her bedroom, peeking out from the door-frame when a new person barged in. Gloria didn't blame her. The girl had been pulled from school and moved somewhere new, where strangers showed up on the doorstep in a constant rotation. When Luce did come out of her room, it was to creep into Gem's room, where Gloria would find her pressed against the wall, staring at the woman who had raised her. It would have broken Gloria's heart, if she had let it. She was getting to know this quiet, secretive daughter of hers. She needed to spend some quality solo time with Luce, to bond with her, learn about her, and she would, one day, once she had time and Roo was a little more independent and Gem was more set-tled, she would find the time soon.

It was a lot for Gloria to have all these people showing up at her house, too, right at first. She flinched when another fist knocked on the door. She jammed the first delivery of baked goods to the back of a cupboard where they'd never be seen again, not trusting that they were safe to eat. But the people kept coming. A bouquet of wildflow-ers. A bundle of turnips, still warm with soil. My god, Gloria had a lot on her plate, they said, and of course they would help her make it work however they could.

And they did. She relented, tasting the dilly beans someone brought by. The third time Una and the nurse came, Gloria let them stay with her sister and kids for an hour while she said she would go run errands, but instead she accepted the invitation of the neighbor, Juan, and showed up at his cabin to learn about mountain lions—there was an abundant population in the surrounding hills, she was told—but she quickly pulled him into bed to show him something else. She wanted to be sure that people fucked here. That a man could fuck. And boy, yeah, he could.

And so life unspooled and settled for them in the Red Grove. Seekers, children, sister, community dinners, raccoons in the garbage cans, rattlesnakes sunning on the rocks. And the place. The Red Grove itself. She'd been so hesitant, but it didn't take long before she felt it. She did not fear for her sister here. She didn't worry about Luce, let her daughter spend long, dark hours outside with her friends, catching herself before she spoke each time her impulse was to give Luce the don't-get-raped talk she'd been relentlessly given.

And so in the mornings, when she stepped out onto the deck and the fog made her shiver and she was wrapped in the chilled, gauzy cloak of these majestic trees, my god, who can even believe how enormous they are, how beautiful, the roughness of the red bark and their hush, she never thought she'd be one to fall in love with something as ridiculous as a tree—a tree!—but here she was, staring out at the trees whose tops she couldn't begin to see, touching them because the fog touched them both, feeling almost up in the sky herself, inside a cloud, as if she were a bird or maybe even a star. Inside, still tucked in their beds, were her wild boy and her quiet girl and her sister, her heart.

She would not have called it happiness; it felt like the on-ramp to the possibility of happiness. Like she might see it around some bend, not too distant. She'd never been as close to it. What she didn't realize until much later was that she was already there, in that moment. She was as close as anyone ever got; wrapped in morning fog on the deck, beside the trees she loved; her people safe, tucked in their beds; the cool blue wash running across her insides that knew, finally, she was starting to do something right.

20

June 28, 1997 • Gone Two Days

ONCE, WHEN LUCE WAS TWELVE, she stumbled upon a book in the library on Japanese cuisine and pored over it day and night. The pages were faded, but she studied how to slice fish across the grain for sashimi, the ideal springy texture for perfectly cooked udon. She'd never had Japanese food, didn't even know anyone who had, but something about the precision of the instructions, the presentation, the order, was enthralling. And then one day when she came home from school, there, on the kitchen counter, was a small chunk of fish, a packet of seaweed, a bag of rice. She hadn't asked her mother for it. She hadn't even talked to her about the book. It was just there, and then there was her mother, flinging a hand towel over her shoulder, pulling a knife from the drawer. Should we try hand rolls first? her mother had asked, and Luce had to bite the insides of her lips to keep from bursting right there with joy.

This was the thing she had never let herself remember. For all the time she spent trying to not care about her mother's betrayals, her returns, the fucked-up thing was that she did.

She cared.

She could hold on to that truth for only a few seconds before it was too heavy. She swiped at her face, got back to work.

Luce checked in on Roo—he was hunched over a piece of paper, drawing, ignoring her because he was mad at her about the phone thing. Fine. That couldn't be helped. He had to be asked three times if he was hungry before he lifted his head to respond. Of course he was hungry, he said, but he was focused at the moment on fulfilling another of the tasks he'd heard over the phone. That piqued her interest. She was going to ask more questions but decided against it— let him have his thing, if his thing was making him feel better. And then she heard a big, wet, rattling cough come from down the hall. She tore into Gem's room, laid her ear above Gem's mouth. She held Gem's thick-boned wrist, bony beneath such papery skin, and felt her pulse. It was slow. She needed to clear what was in her lungs.

Of course, one day, Gem would die. Death was natural, and there was something strange about people who resisted nature. She'd be released. And Luce knew that's what she was supposed to be whispering into Gem's ears right then, affirmations that she could let go, that they would be okay. But those sounds wouldn't come. It wasn't true. With her thumb stroking the soft inside of Gem's wrist, Luce leaned close to her ear and whispered, "Stay, stay, stay."

Maybe it was time to give in and call the police, call the hospital, let the outsiders come in and find Gloria and take these problems away from her. But every time she let her mind follow that fantasy, it slammed into the same wall: they'd all be separated. She wouldn't be allowed to care for Roo on her own, or for Gem. It was out of the question.

What should she do? What was there to do? The few Red Grovers who'd stopped by to drop off food or check on them said they were searching for Gloria too, so how could it be that nothing— *nothing*—had been figured out?

Gem's stomach was warm and soft beneath Luce's face. "Please," she whispered into the sheet, grabbing Gem's hand and placing it on top of her own hair. "Please, please, please, help." Gem's hand slid off, thumping back onto the mattress.

The woman on the phone was asking for Gloria. Luce said she wasn't home. She was about to hang up and move along, but something buzzed inside her, a sweep of bark along her chest. She reached, absently, to the dirty locket inside her shirt, still shut. Instead of ending the call, she asked if she could give a message to her mother. The woman on the phone sighed, a little frustrated, Luce thought, and said she'd like to reschedule their meeting, since Gloria hadn't shown up for the last one. And it hit her. Luce knew this voice.

It was the voice she followed closely, as it was breaking the story about the serial killer who was targeting young female prostitutes. It was the voice that broke the story of the teenage sex ring, that talked through rescue efforts in front of the fire. A voice she had trusted, that she blared on the TV at the community center, gathered around the flickering screen shoulder to shoulder with other kids in her class or friends hanging out after school, whoever happened to stop by when one of her stories came on.

"Ruby Wells?" Luce said, more meekly than she'd planned, because sure, it was possible she was wrong. The woman paused a moment on the other end of the line, startled—it had been a weird presumption. Then she said, "Yes, this is Ruby Wells."

Luce, flushed, thinking quickly, asked where and when she and Gloria were supposed to meet—her mother is forgetful, she said, often needs her help to remember things like this. "Thursday," Ruby told her, a little skeptically. "At Gribbons Park in Fairfax."

Thursday. The day her mother hadn't come home.

"I'll have her call back to reschedule," Luce said, flying in the dark, and then, taking a wild shot, "And I assume it's about the same thing as last time, but so I keep her in the loop, any updates she should know about?"

"Who did you say this was?" Ruby asked, and Luce wasn't surprised. Of course she wasn't going to give Luce all the intel. She was as pro as they come. Luce couldn't come up with a lie that seemed credible, and so she hoped the truth could work.

"Her daughter."

"Oh, hello there." Luce heard the rustling of some papers. "Luce, right? How old are you?"

"Yes, Luce," she said, knowing that if she admitted to being a minor, this call would be over. "I'm eighteen."

"Mmhm," Ruby said, the sound of her pen scribbling in the background. "Do you mind if I ask you a few questions?" Luce did not. In fact, she was sure this was going to get right to the bottom of things.

"You were there when Richard Dalton had a heart attack?" This was not what Luce was expecting, but she said yes, she had been. "Have you been contacted by his son, Bobby?" Luce's throat went dry. She thought about his face when she'd smashed his fingers in the door. The dinosaur umbrella he left behind. Bobby. So this was the calling man's name. The likeliest person to know where her mother was.

She'd had no contact with him, she said, her face going red with the lie. Should she be lying? If anyone was capable of tracking her mother down, it would be Ruby fucking Wells.

The fear scraped tight inside. Getting an outsider involved, a journalist, even esteemed, truth-telling Ruby Wells, would piss off a lot of people in the Red Grove, but surely they would understand—her mother was gone, she was gone!, and nobody seemed to be all that worried, and she needed someone who was extremely worried, a professional worrier. She was about to say more when another problem reared up: Luce and Roo were minors, alone and caring for a sick adult they'd surely try to force out of the Red Grove—no, no, it could not happen.

She knew nothing more, Luce said, and took down Ruby's information, promised her mother would call back soon.

Bobby Dalton.

Here, finally, was the next step: Luce would track down Bobby Dalton. She knew his name, and that Ruby Wells was interested in him. She knew that her mother had plans to meet with Ruby Wells— why? To give an interview about Richard Dalton's heart attack? That didn't make sense. What other information did she have that was worth the time of a reporter who would otherwise be cracking open cases that flushed out the worst kinds of men—rapists, traffickers, murderers? Ruby Wells did not deal in piddling trivialities. Learning what her mother had to offer might unlock the door to where she was.

Luce pulled out a container of rabbit stew from the fridge and dumped it into a pot. Juan had dropped by with it—he hadn't seen her mother's car anywhere in the Red Grove, surprise surprise. She flicked a lighter and lit the stove. There was the nub of a joint on the counter and she lit that too, pulling the smoke in.

She didn't need Ruby Wells because she could *be* Ruby Wells. She'd probably read as many books on predators as Ruby had. She exhaled slowly, coughing once. She could do this. Look for the obvious clues. The fact that they hadn't heard from Bobby Dalton since her mother had been gone was a pretty damn obvious clue. Ruby Wells might say something like, *much more than a coincidence.* In any kind of case, if an angry young man is involved, he is, statistically speaking, responsible. Do not skip over the connections right in front of your nose.

Heart pounding, she dialed directory assistance, asked for the address and phone number of Bobby Dalton. "City and state, please?" the operator asked. Luce stammered that she didn't know, could they try without that? They could not, the operator said. So Luce named a few nearby towns—Fairfax, San Anselmo, Inverness—but nothing came up. There had to be a way. She tried another town, the big city, and then another, but the operator said, "Sorry, no Bobby Daltons."

"Bob Dalton?" she said. Or, dammit, what was that short for, Robert? But no.

Luce hung up. She would not panic, she would not.

She lit the joint again, closed her eyes. What would Ruby do? She tried to conjure her mother's face, picture it somewhere and let it guide her, and it appeared in her mind but was quickly overtaken by shadow, purple lumps growing up around the eyes, blood on the forehead, tucked into a hospital bed, and then Luce is a little thing, Gloria and Gem the same, both of them fucked by the world, no.

No.

Not anymore. Not again. She remembered then: there was a phone book in the office at Heartwood. There she could find his name alphabetically—didn't need the city—and call every single Bobby Dalton until it was her very own mother who answered the phone, kidnapped, held hostage but unharmed, and so grateful for Luce, needing Luce to speed right over to slash the jugular of this psychopath, phew, amen, no more lives to ruin, his blood spurting across every millimeter of his shitty house, hallelujah, adios.

From *The Red Grove: The Story of the Sisters*

It was one of the children who first spotted the outsider.

There was a man, a stranger, hiking up a game trail through the woods, noisy as he passed between trees and brush. The child had been playing on a high rock that overlooked the hillside below and had sprinted back to the cabin to alert the women that someone was on the way. A man, thick but not tall, climbing the steep dirt path through the giant redwoods, a man who looked to have a black patch covering one eye.

By the time Tamsen came out to the rock, instructing the nearby women and children to stay in the cabin for safety, he was gone. But there was a clear trail of his pathway through the trees, with broken twigs and trampled brush, not the way the women and children moved through the forest here. Tamsen spotted dragonflies and honeybees, but the man had disappeared. This was not good. She was terrified of what his arrival might mean. She was quite sure the man was Hank Monk, and she'd encountered too many men who turned vicious and feral around women, especially, she thought, when that hive of women were operating perfectly without them.

"I have a problem," the man said, suddenly emerging from the forest, though still twenty feet from the cabin. As the children had described, he wore an eye patch. His lips were black and his teeth were black and the sun had left deep creases all across his face. He shifted from foot to foot, seemingly uncomfortable—perhaps all part of his act, Tamsen thought, notorious as he was. If he moved fast, he could probably take out everyone there before they could do anything to stop him.

Tamsen glanced over to Ines, out in the garden, and nodded. They weren't wholly unprepared.

"I need your help," he said, twisting the hat in his hands. He moved his gaze down from Tamsen to the ground, almost embarrassed, a strange gesture that didn't square with the rumors of Hank Monk she'd been hearing for years. "I mean you no harm," he said, and then something behind him caught her attention, something in the trees. She tensed, ready to see more of his men surrounding them. But the figure that emerged from the trees was small, wasn't a man at all. It was a child. Hank Monk followed Tamsen's gaze and turned to see the child, who shrank back halfway into the trees.

"Is that child with you?" Tamsen asked. She could see a half-moon of its face peeking out from behind a tree.

"It's part of the reason I came," Hank Monk said, then raised his voice. "Though I told the child to stay in the goddamned wagon." The child ducked all the way behind the tree.

Just then, from behind a tree on the other side, there was a blur of movement as Ines leapt out from hiding with a tincture-soaked cloth—a potent mixture she'd been perfecting for just such an occasion—jumped on Hank Monk's back, and smothered his face. Hank Monk threw elbows, landing blows in Ines's sides, but she held strong, clutched her feet even tighter around his waist. Tamsen took off, sprinting to where the child crouched behind the tree, lest the child run back to tell Hank Monk's men that he'd been ambushed. The child was not practiced in navigating the redwood forest and soon tripped, and Tamsen threw the child over her shoulder like an animal. The child flailed, but Tamsen held on tightly.

When she reached the small clearing in front of the cabin, she saw that Hank Monk had fallen to the ground. His eyes were closed. Ines, breathing hard, was tying his feet together. She'd called another woman out from the cabin, and the two of them began to drag Hank Monk, one pulling each arm, to a nearby tree to tie him up.

Tamsen swung the child off her shoulder and held their arms tightly. Though the child wore boy's clothes, trousers and a buttoned shirt, they had long hair tucked beneath a hat, like a girl, and a slim, delicate face. The child was no longer kicking and screaming, but instead cried with a quiet, private sorrow that looked to Tamsen like the face her sister Minnie made one year when she accidentally dropped a newly hatched chick into the pigpen, where it had been immediately trampled.

"Child," Tamsen said softly. "I won't hurt you." The child kept crying, but opened their eyes to Tamsen. "You're safe here. I couldn't have you running off. Who were you going to run to? How many men does Hank Monk have down below?"

The child shook their head, but only said, "My name is Mary."

"Okay, sshhh. Catch your breath, Mary. Breathe." Tamsen turned her attention back to Hank Monk. The women dragged him along the ground, and as they did, his shirt rose along his back.

Pointing to the cloth wound tight around his ribs, one of the women said he might be injured. Maybe that was the reason for his deference, Ines said, instructing them to work quickly—the herb was only potent for a few minutes of unconsciousness, and they needed to get him tied up tight. But as they dragged him, his shirt continued pulling up until everyone was transfixed. Beneath his shirt, winding around his ribs and chest, was a cloth that stretched from below his armpits to the base of his ribs, and beneath the cloth, it was plain to see, were breasts.

Tamsen looked to the child to see if she, too, was surprised by this information. But the child just wiped tears with the back of her hand, took a big breath, and looked up at Tamsen.

"Is my mama gonna be okay?" she asked.

Tamsen blinked back her surprise and put a reassuring hand on the child's shoulder. She told her that her mama would be fine, that she wanted to know, quickly, what she and her mama were doing there? The child wiped a string of snot from her upper lip and sighed, said that they'd heard there were ladies up here who could help them. "Down in the wagon is my aunt Rabbit. She's in trouble with somebody. She's about to blow, is what my mama says."

Ines had finished tying Hank Monk's arms back behind the tree, legs bound as well. Tamsen caught her eye and raised an eyebrow, wondering if this was necessary, but Ines double-knotted the ties, to be sure. Hank Monk began blinking awake.

Someone had brought the child a hunk of bread, which seemed to revive her. "Usually I don't see my mama, and I'm not allowed to call her that. I live with Mrs. Perkins, on Bryant Avenue. But I'm riding with her today and we're fighting bandits. Or, I think we will be anyways."

"Bastards," Hank Monk muttered as he woke all the way up, pulling at his arms and legs.

"I'm sorry we had to do this," Tamsen said, walking closer to where Hank Monk lay on the ground. "But we have to keep ourselves safe. Is what your child told us true, about who is down in your wagon?"

"Mary," Hank Monk bellowed out toward the child. "I told you to stay quiet." Then, turning to face Tamsen: "I'm not sure what she told you, but I will tell you what is true. My sister is down below, and she needs a place to stay hidden for a while. She is with child, and it is coming soon. I tried to come here peacefully, but that didn't work out." He strained against the ties.

"And you know what else," Mary said, her mouth muffled, full of bread. "I have a little dog named Sister. And you know what else? Even though it's only allowed for men, my mama voted in the election." She smiled wide while chewing, stuffing a piece of fallen bread back into her mouth.

"Shut your mouth, Mary," Hank Monk said.

Tamsen asked whether it was true. Hank Monk turned away and spat, but beneath the pucker Tamsen saw a flash of smile.

"Well I'll be damned," Ines said. "A woman voted."

"Why do you live as a man?" Tamsen asked, signaling for someone in the cabin to bring out a cup of water.

Hank Monk snorted. "You think I could run the best stagecoach line in all of California if anyone thought I was a woman?"

"Only I know," Mary said. "I'm the best secret-keeper in the West. And you have to be, too. Otherwise Mama will slit open your belly and feed you to crows, is what she says."

"I understand," Tamsen said before Hank Monk could comment.

"You searched me, clearly," said Hank Monk. "You know I carry no weapons. Please help my sister. Help with the baby, and then keep her a while out of harm's way."

"We have no room—" Ines started to say, but Tamsen lifted her arm and cut her off.

"We will help your sister," she said, a plan unspooling in her mind as if her own sisters' voices were in there whispering, as if the voices of the giant red trees were directing what she said. "And in return, you'll help us. I know you drive through our valley. As you do, lead any threats away from us. Don't let anyone set up camp on our hillside, don't tell anyone we're here. And those you can't lead away, you will get rid of. You will not let anyone do us harm. You will not tell any men who ask where we shelter. Only for that promise can we promise to keep your sister safe."

Ines waved Tamsen aside, worried. She said that getting into any sort of trade with violent folks was a bad deal, risky, foolish. But Hank Monk interrupted before Ines had a chance to go on. "I don't think I can make that promise."

"Yes, you can," Tamsen said, growing more sure by the moment, the voices inside louder and louder. "You will. This is the trade. We will keep this as a place of refuge, but we will not be soft in our rest. We will fight, if we must. Can we trust you to uphold this?"

Hank Monk dropped his chin to his chest, worked his jaw back and forth. "For the safety and care of my sister Rabbit and her companion, who has accompanied her on this journey."

Tamsen nodded. "And the baby."

Ines started to speak, agitated by how much Tamsen was agreeing to take on in this trade with a stranger, but Tamsen reached out to Ines, squeezing her hand. "I know you are worried, and for good reason, sister. But I want you to imagine something. What could this place become if we weren't afraid? If we never had to fear again? We are going to create and protect peace for our sisters."

"But with blood?" Ines asked.

"With whatever it takes," Tamsen replied. Tamsen and Ines held each other's eyes, but Ines frowned, worried still. "We'll mark the boundary, so you know exactly at which point someone is too close," Tamsen said to Hank Monk.

"It's a tragic thing, isn't it," Hank Monk said as Ines released the ropes. "It's women who keep other women safe. Men do it only for their own wives or daughters, because they consider them property. But only women look out for other women, at whatever cost."

21

IN RED GROVE ELEMENTARY, the young children sat on beanbags, learning their world. A redwood doesn't grow to be the tallest tree on earth alone, the teacher would say. Their roots reach down only six to twelve feet while their bodies reach up three hundred feet into the sky. So, little ones, how does a redwood grow so enormous, without deep roots?

It's because their roots spread shallow and wide, the children would say together.

How wide? the teacher would ask.

One hundred feet wide, the children would say, stretching their arms as wide as they'd go.

And does the tree stand up all on its own? the teacher would ask.

A redwood tree cannot survive without its grove, the children would say, their voices overlapping and singsongy. The roots intertwine with other roots and share their food and pass along the news, they would say, their voices twisting and rising together, their small fingers interlacing with the fingers of nearby children.

A redwood tree cannot survive without its grove. The childhood incantation looped in Luce's head, off-key, too loud even as she tried to stop thinking it.

Just as Luce was readying to head to Heartwood's office, where she was pretty sure that phone book lived, Boog stopped by. She was afluster, as usual, a bag full of newly jarred lotions and salves clinking as she walked, breezing past Roo and Luce to put two jars of strawberry jam into the cupboard. She'd been calling the theaters in Sacramento where Gloria used to perform, she said, in case they'd heard from her. No news yet. But—and here she hugged Roo in a sort of twirl that had them all marching down the hall toward Gem, still talking back over her shoulder—she and Una and others had decided to pull the community together to focus and coordinate efforts. They should come to Heartwood that afternoon.

"I'm staying to pamper Gem a minute," Boog said, pulling back the sheet covering Gem's leg and starting to massage her. "Go get some rest, Goose."

Standing in the entryway, Luce let her head fall against the door-frame. Boog began singing the old ballads she loved, humming when she forgot the words, pressing into Gem's muscles to keep the blood moving. Luce felt so tired all of a sudden. She wanted to talk to Boog, always did. As one of the people who, like Una, had been here longest, Boog was full of good stories. She had moved here when she was Luce's age. It had been her father. The whole of her childhood. And so as soon as she realized she could leave home, she did, not just Tuscaloosa but the whole of Alabama and then the entire South, making her way to the Red Grove and never looking back. She missed the South, she was fond of saying, only in her mouth. And so she made biscuits and corn casserole and fried green tomatoes, and there was no wondering whether you thought it was good when you tried it; she'd cut you out of her life if you didn't like her okra. Luce didn't much care for the okra and was smart enough to keep quiet about it. Now she wished she had the energy to say more, but the search for her mother was wearing her thin. So she just stood there, resting her head on the wood, watching Boog watch Gem, seeing Boog use the knuckle of her pinkie finger to wipe a tear from time to time—for Gem, maybe, for the lyrics to the old songs, perhaps, for her missing mother, because she, too, was embedded in the network of this forest. Boog felt the absence with the same ache, and her softness rippled into Luce, too, allowing in some breath because finally, with Boog here to help, with the community gathering in just a little while, someone would have some answers, someone would make an actionable, concrete plan.

Roo skidded his bike to a halt in front of Luce. They were on their way to Heartwood, and Luce was sure, she could feel it, that her mother would soon be found. A little flustered, sure, but unharmed. A redwood cannot survive without its grove. But Roo hopped off his bike, telling her to stop. He needed to follow another instruction from his phone call, he told her, pulling from his backpack a piece of paper on which he'd drawn a face, really much more an approximation of her mummy face than anything else. Across the top, he'd written LOST MOM.

Luce stifled a laugh—for the impossibility of anyone recognizing Gloria from his ridiculous line drawing, but also because who here in the Red Grove wouldn't already know she was gone? But he blinked up at Luce with his big, wet eyes and she saw how much he wanted to help, like he was canvasing the neighborhood for his lost dog, and so they taped up a few signs along their route.

Luce knew that Heartwood would be buzzing with people. It was one of the beautiful things—the way the whole community gathered, as they did twice a week to share meals, though this time with the concentrated attention turned to finally figuring out how to find her mom. And sure, there'd probably also be food, the kitchen was open anytime they gathered, plus anytime anyone needed it. Part of being safe was not being hungry, Una would say, and oh, it would be so very welcome to see Una. What Luce wanted was to lay all this down upon her, let Una take over, go to sleep by herself in her own bed, and wake up to things returned to normal.

Luce walked into Heartwood's crowded industrial kitchen. Already the air was rich with spices and sweat, steam fogging up the corners of the windows, voices overlapping one another. There were six or seven women in there, Una in the center at a frying pan, the others chopping and stirring, one counting out plates, one squeezing lemons, one leaning on the countertop and telling a loud, animated story directed toward whoever made eye contact. There was music beneath the voices, and beneath that, further still, the familiarity of this moment, all these bodies gathered in this kitchen, the sway of their hair as they turned on the faucet, their fingers as they clutched a knife, how they gripped one another's shoulders or forearms to make a point, their voices of concern, the high, wild, cackling laugh, the low bray, the sorrow in one of their tearful voices, the shriek of delight, this tight and fierce and loyal camaraderie.

"Goose-baby," one of the women called, and they all turned to look at her. Nancy moved toward her first, and the others quickly followed, arms outstretched or lips puckered in coos, one with a ladle dripping from her hand, and they engulfed her in their arms. They squeezed tight. "I'm so sorry, honey," someone said, and "You poor thing," and "Any word from your mom?" and "Oh let me squeeze you" and "Oh I'm so glad you're here, I was about to bring over lasagna, and we're getting organized with a plan, don't you even worry." Luce did not mean to be happy, but she felt a twinge of it accidentally, possible only because of her duress, and so she loved it a little bit, her hardship, this pure, focused attention.

Something on the stove boiled over and broke the hug, and the women hustled back to their tasks. Una lingered a moment, and Luce, sucking in a big breath, asked if she could speak to her privately. She wanted to ask Una about the list of names she'd found in her mother's office, about the locket she found in the dirt, cold now beneath her T-shirt, about using the phone book in the office.

"Of course, my girl," Una said, and grabbed Luce's chin, patted her cheek. "We're gonna meet soon to figure out our plan, then eat, and then you and I can chat. Too much to do right now." She gestured at all the bodies moving quickly around the cooking space and turned back to the stove, where Boog sidled up beside her. They exchanged a quick glance, and then something appeared above them for a blink—dark, moving, shadowed, yes, a mass of flies. Luce blinked again quickly, something wrong with her eyes. Una wouldn't tolerate a swarm of flies in the kitchen. When she looked again, Luce saw no flies, though beneath the chattering voices, was there a faint buzzing? She tried to concentrate on the sound—the same as the buzzing at her house? Was she losing her mind?—but was distracted by Una's voice. "But the grove holds strong," Una was saying, stirring the soup and nodding her head as if in agreement with herself.

When Luce walked out onto the deck, heads swiveled to take her in. She'd never been on the receiving end of these looks before, the ones people gave struggling newcomers, faces that said, *We are sorry for you, for all you've been through.* They were afraid for her.

They were worried.

All her people's crinkled brows, their frowns, it all cinched the fear inside her own body in a way nothing else had—she realized she'd been relying on everyone else's casual response to her missing mother as proof that nothing so bad could *really* be happening. But now? The burn of all this pity and worry was smoking out her insides, and she also felt a wash of embarrassment—why hadn't she been doing more on her own?

But there was no room for her to flip out. That was a thing a stereotypical teenager would do right at this moment, and she was not that, would not be that. Women in danger only ever escaped their predators by keeping a cool head, coming up with a plan. She needed to get a grip. Her job in the Red Grove was to help guide the women away from fear, and that should not be different today, just because it was harder for her. Every single moment could be located on a scale from easy to hard. She called to mind Gem's swollen purple face, those first weeks when they did not know if she would live or die—*that* was hard. That's what was really hard. This? This was still just a question.

She made her way to a picnic table on the deck, people coming over to hug her or say hello, and she thanked them for being there, saying she felt sure they'd figure something out. Across the deck, Juan sipped from his tin cup and waved her over. "I keep driving the roads of the Red Grove, but I still haven't seen your mom's car, Goose," he said. She hadn't expected anything different. "How you hanging in, kiddo?" Luce shrugged. Juan lifted an arm, unsure where to put it, lowered it down, then lifted it again and patted her back. So awkward, Juan. "It's all right to be worried. I'm worried too," he said, and again it felt good to hear it out loud, even though the recognition of it also felt worse, scarier. He picked a piece of lint off a hot tamale retrieved from his pocket and offered it to her. It made her laugh, the gross stick of it still coated in grime. "I thought more about that list of names you showed me," he said. "I was right. It's kids who stayed for some time here, in Heartwood. And I've got another one to add that's not on the list. Samantha, the new girl. She stayed here too. Her mom wanted her here, under the Red Grove's protection, as soon as possible, so she was alone here for the first two weeks while her mom finished her old job and packed them up to move. So she might be a good person to talk to, just see if anything strange happened while she was here." Luce wanted to ask Juan more, but the crowd was all turning to face front.

Una climbed up on her bench. They were gathered, she began, to concentrate and organize community efforts in locating their beloved

Gloria. Luce felt her cheeks redden under all the eyes on her. Una repeated the basic information they knew: Gloria had last been seen at the gathering of the lions. She'd been having a conflict with the son of the seeker who'd recently died.

Luce was about to add that they knew the calling man's name—she'd spoken to Ruby Wells, who knew about what was going on—but she caught herself. The guidelines were clear. No reporters. No outside attention, which might compromise the vulnerable women here. She could not repeat that her mother had been on the verge of meeting with a reporter. She did not want to be associated with that. Plus, she thought, it might make them less eager to find her, to help. Luce would have to move forward with this piece of information—Bobby Dalton—on her own.

They organized a phone tree, a food drop-off schedule for Luce and Roo. They divided into groups: a team to search the hills, another to get in touch with all known past acquaintances outside the Red Grove, another to figure out as much as they could about the calling man. Someone would call all the hospitals. Another all the jails. Nobody mentioned the police.

There were plans. Plans! The feeling of order they created was such a relief, even as all the unsettling things that had been happening seemed to shimmer just out of Luce's line of sight, with a buzz that told her—*how?*—that they couldn't be ignored. But she'd try. They had concrete plans. Plans were what made things happen.

Una called attention again. "It is in times of crisis that we must rely most heartily on our community and our strength, on each other. For that reason, I've asked Katie, who has been with us two months, if she'd be willing to participate in a reenactment today to energize us."

This was news to Luce—she was always willing to help guide a reenactment, of course, this was part of her training and practice, and she was always up for it—except for right now. Now? Wasn't the point here to focus on her own mother, to take action? But still—what could she say? She heard a few low murmurs, though she couldn't tell whether they were enthusiasm for a reenactment or, like her, for the unwelcome surprise. She nodded at Una, did her best to look encouraging—she could do this—but Una wasn't fooled. Una said that she was giving Luce a break, that for today only, she herself would narrate. A relief, at least, though also unsettling to have her job pulled out from beneath her.

Una went on. "Katie has directed today's reenactment to focus on a particularly challenging day in court and then move backward to an incident," Una said. Two people stepped up in front of the group, a man in khaki work pants and a black T-shirt, and Boog, wearing ripped jeans and a hoodie. A prickle on Luce's neck grew; she did not want to see this story right now, none of these stories. Boog sat down on a bench, said, to the assembled group, that for the first part of the reenactment, she'd be playing Katie. The man—Luce didn't remember his name—said he was playing an attorney, and towered over Boog as Katie. She pantomimed being sworn into court.

"Now ma'am," the man said, "I understand that you say you were very hurt by Mr. Conway, and I'm sorry to hear it. Can you please show the court the photographic evidence of your injuries?"

Boog, playing Katie, pretended to hand something over. "They're hard to see," she said.

"Hmm," the man said. He mimicked flipping through photographs. "Major injuries, as you call them, but they are hard to see?"

Luce glanced over at Katie, who stood in the front row of the crowd half-covering her eyes with her hands. Someone stood beside her, with her arm around Katie's shoulders, another squeezed her arm from behind. A sick twist in Luce's gut, imagining her mother as Katie, thinking of all the terrible things that might have happened to her, and what was everyone doing here in the past?

Boog, as Katie, said, "My boyfriend ruptured my spleen. I had two broken ribs. I was internally bleeding."

Though it was dusk, a few dust motes caught some unknown light and orbited slowly between the reenactors. How did they look so

peaceful? How did they stay aloft? "We make our sentencing decla-
rations based on photographic evidence of injuries, ma'am—it allows
for an unbiased look at hard evidence. You understand, it takes away
the 'he said, she said' mess of all this. And so I was glad to see only
minor abrasions in your photographs. A little bruising, yes. But everything looked pretty minor."

"I was hospitalized. I couldn't—"

"Ma'am, we're going to refer you to a social worker and provide you
with a telephone number to call should things get out of hand between
you two again. We recommend calling before arguments escalate."

"How would I be able to know ahead of time?" Boog, as Katie,
asked. Luce glanced around, and, strangely, people kept meeting her
eyes, though they immediately looked away. Like they didn't want to
be caught looking. Something felt hot at her neck. A little tight.

"That is the kind of emotional progress we hope the two of you
can accomplish if you work together in counseling. Your Honor, are
you ready to make a declaration?"

Una stood up on the bench, said, "Ninety days jail."

Katie burst out, "Such bullshit! If my injuries had been easier to
see, his sentence would have been so much longer. It would have
given me time to think and come up with a plan for how to leave, or
get a job, and save up enough money to rent us someplace else."

"You're right, Katie, dear," Una said. "And it is your turn to say
what you need to say. To do what you need to do." Katie stood up
shakily. Sometimes, here, Luce would reach a hand out to the woman
to help guide her into the role-playing. Somatic experiencing, it was
called, where Katie would take over the role that Boog had been
playing, finally playing herself, and this transition into it was the
hardest part. But today Luce kept her arms by her side, tried to concentrate on Katie's story, though all she could think about was her
mom. When would they be talking about Gloria?

Katie sat down beside Boog and looked up at the man. "I will not
be hurt by you anymore," she said.

Movement blurred in the edge of Luce's vision, but she didn't look. She willed herself to stare at Katie, to anticipate the even harder moment that would come next, where the violence would be emulated. She did not want to see a mass of flies, a cow skull, wanted to hear no clicks. She wanted plans and order, she wanted this goddamned reenactment to wrap up and for them to get on with what they were doing to find her mother. But the movement continued, and in it there was a flash of blond, and so she looked. Between the trunks of the darkening trees on the far side of the crowd, Roo slipped into the forest.

Katie was changing her narrative, they were moving back to an incident, and Luce knew how important it was to bear witness to this, but Roo—where was he going? She slipped through the crowd, smiling at those who looked at her with concern—nothing wrong, no problem here—walking back behind the gathered group to the darkening forest where Roo had disappeared.

Luce caught sight of him up ahead. He was running. She ducked and wove between trunks and over ferns, following him. He finally stopped, clutching his heart. "I'm not sad," Roo said when she reached him. "I'm on a mission." Roo, my kangaroo, you hop my heart to the moon, Gloria would say to him when he was sad. Roo would try not to smile when she said that, but it never worked.

"It's okay to feel sad," she said, reaching to pull him to her, but he threw his shoulder to get her hand off. "It'll be okay—" she started, but she stopped as his eyes widened into orbs.

"I knew it," he said, staring past Luce into the trees beyond. A strange sensation rose in Luce's throat, something scratchy, ticklish, something that felt like it needed to be coughed out. Little things scraping her skin on the inside. Like there were flies in her throat, yes, and the idea made her start coughing, gagging, and she bent over, closing her eyes, hacking, and then there was a fly buzzing around her head. Oh god. Had she coughed it out?

Roo pushed past her, walking farther into the trees. She straightened, swallowed down the scratch and panic in her throat, and went after him. "Here," he said, pointing to the ground. In front of them was the spot where, a week earlier, a large patch of invasive bamboo had been removed, but now the hole was filled with dirt. On top of the dirt were the small redwood saplings community members had been growing to replenish the forest. It was strange, though, that they had already been planted. Normally the saplings would be bigger before they'd go in the ground.

"What is buried must be uncovered," Roo said.

"I don't think that was, like, literal, Roo," Luce said. He crouched down, began digging in the dirt with both hands like a frantic little dog. Luce called his name to stop, said for him to be super careful, that they couldn't disturb the newly planted trees. He kept on, and then, with a gasp, stopped. Said he felt something. He grabbed the edge with two fingers, said he was going to pull it out, and yanked, tumbling back onto his butt. In his hand would be the skeletal fingers of her mother's corpse. But he held no bones. It was a stick. The bright mycorrhizal filaments dangled from the stick, they'd been dislodged from the underground network, but it was still just a stick.

"Oh," he said, letting out a little sigh.

"It's okay, buddy," she said, pulling him to his feet and brushing the dirt off his shorts. "We'll figure it out." She leaned in to hug him, but he slid out from her grasp and ran back toward Heartwood, shouting that he was going to find a shovel to dig more holes, and fine, let him feel like he was helping.

Luce walked slowly back through the redwoods, letting her fingertips brush against the rough bark, breathing in the deep, wet green smell of the forest. What's buried must be uncovered. Roo had heard something on the phone plugged into nothing, but she could not figure out what it was that would help them find Gloria. Perhaps the buried thing was the plan of the calling man, Bobby, and she needed to get to the telephone book and call him. Why hadn't anyone gone and knocked on his goddamned door? If she had some more time with Una, focused time, they could come up with a plan together.

She paused, still in the trees but close enough to Heartwood that she could see the reenactors fighting each other. These were her people, and fuck, she knew reenactments were important, but not like *important* important on the scale of a missing person. They were not actually doing any real thing to figure out where her mother was, not enough, not jumping into action with a solid plan, and for the first time, she had a moment where it felt as if she were seeing all of them from the outside—middle-aged hippies role-playing, acting, as if somehow it would help them in the real world.

Luce took a step backward and then a few more. This was who she was, slipping into the shadows of the tallest trees on earth, pressing up against the bark. She was a watcher, a hider, a shadow, and it was time for her to stop being anything else. She slipped her shoes off, walked silently along the forest floor, snaking between the trees, stepping along the paths she knew well.

She slid through the grove to Heartwood's far door, an emergency exit whose alarm had been broken for years. It was nearly dark. Nobody saw her. She knew where the spare key was hidden beneath a rock, and she slipped inside. The edges of sound made it in here, the trill notes of a few voices that carried, but this wing of Heartwood was hushed. She turned on no lights, stepping quietly down a hallway into one of the additions that had been built over the years. Past a window seat stuffed full of books and paperwork, alongside a filing cabinet. Finally, to the place she wanted. Heartwood's office.

There weren't many Bobby, or Robert, Daltons in the phone book, that was a bit of luck at least. Beside each one was a phone number and address. She imagined herself getting into a car, knuckles hard, tight angles around the steering wheel, fire pouring from her nose, driving through the redwoods and up and over the hill that enclosed the valley, passing the borderline with its rock wall, with the trees ringed in red yarn, her fingernails chiseling themselves into needles, until she finally reached his house. She'd show up on his doorstep like he'd shown up on hers, but she'd be sharp and aflame, terrifying, and he'd snivel and grovel and apologize, and her mother would be— where? Injured and left for dead in his backyard? Living with him to provide a continual channel to his father as a kind of atonement? His new lover? All the possibilities were ridiculous, and yet it had to be something, because two days, and she was still gone.

She'd start small. Picked up the phone and began dialing. The first number didn't go through, but the second rang. A man picked up after a few rings, youngish, gruff. "Hello," he said, and she saw his face out on her deck. It was her guy. She had not thought about what to say to this man, though, and she was usually a very considered person, a person who did not talk without having thought about what she'd say ahead of time. She was not brave. She did not think he'd actually pick up or that she'd call the right number. She hung up.

She scribbled the address on a sheet of paper, grabbed Una's keys off the desk, and traced her steps out into the parking lot, taking care to stay out of sight of everyone gathered for the meal on the other side of the building. By the time she arrived at his house, she'd know what to do. To say. She climbed into the car, slid the key into the ignition, but didn't turn it. She should turn the car on. Now was the time to do it. A bundle of dried herbs wrapped in string on the dash was coated in dust, so too a hawk feather, a thistle. Do it now. She held the key between her thumb and pointer finger, felt her palms growing hot and damp, her throat tightening. Turn the key now, fill your head with fire, confront the man, she demanded of herself, but nothing. So what that she didn't have her license, she could drive well enough anyway. Just do it. The evening sun dipped lower, swallows dove for bugs. She did not turn the key. Because doing those things meant leaving the Red Grove. Like flipping her upside down, protective shell gone, soft underbelly exposed. It was too dangerous out there. I am a coward, she thought.

She tucked her hair behind her ears, tucked it again. Bravery meant being afraid and doing the thing anyway. She swallowed. But fear is also a protector. She slid the key out of the ignition, wiped her sweaty palms on her shorts. Back inside. Chicken. She heard the office phone ringing down the hall, regular life trilling on, and then voices coming, so she ducked into the bathroom until they were gone. A peal of laughter from out on the deck. She would not leave, could not. Coward. A swell of panic—who is she right now, how is she so incapable? This is life, and she is failing at it.

When the hallway was clear, she slid back into the office, shut the door. Just a minute here, to think. What was her problem, she thought this was hard? On the scale of things that were horrible? This was nothing. She needed a moment alone to think through what to do next, but the office phone rang again. She didn't let herself pause; she picked up.

"Finally she picks up, damn. I recognized the number," the voice said. Oh dear god. It was him. She didn't speak. "Thought maybe you were calling to give me something else and then changed your mind. Well, don't change your mind, I'm open." He laughed, open-throated.

It was Bobby Dalton, and he recognized the number. This number. And someone calling from this number gave him something. Luce's head swirled.

"Hello?" he said. "Don't tell me you're scared off now."

She could not be afraid. This was it. "Where's Gloria," she said. Her voice was not a mountain lion's.

"Who is this?" he said.

And because, once again, she could not figure out a convincing lie that would also get her the information she needed, she said, "This is Luce, her daughter. Is my mom there? You tell me or I'll call the police."

He let out a laugh then, the trail of sound getting a little quieter as he moved his face away from the phone. "This girl," he said to someone else in the room, or maybe himself, "thinking your mom is here. Ha. That's too funny."

"So where is she?"

"Your mom? I don't know anything about her," he said. "It was that other lady came through and worked everything out."

A buckeye in Luce's throat. Slowly. "What lady?"

"Hell if I know. She came a couple days ago, said she was there on behalf of the Red Grove, something formal like that. Repaid my dad's money plus a little something, and told me to leave you all alone. I wasn't gonna be paid off like that, especially after what you did, but hell, she was generous, and the autopsy on my pops showed he had a real blockage in an artery, so." There was a galaxy in Luce's head, trying to connect all the fragments. Someone had gone to him to stop him from calling. To keep him quiet. "Look, if you're not offering anything else, I gotta go, little girl. Don't call over here again and re-piss me off," he said.

"One last thing," she said, "please. The lady who came. What did she look like?"

"Like any other one of you hippie queers who live out there," he said. "You all look the same to me." He gulped something down. "All your fucking necklaces." He cleared something in his throat, spat, and hung up.

All your necklaces. There was only one person in the Red Grove who could be described that way.

So Una had gone and found him, somehow, convinced him to leave them alone—to protect them, she was sure, to keep Luce from being afraid. A couple days ago, he'd said. All that was wonderful, it was good, wasn't it, and Luce was grateful. She was grateful, and there was a growing buzz in her head, in the room around her, because she was grateful except for one thing.

Just yesterday, Una had asked if Luce was afraid of the calling man. She hadn't told Luce she'd paid him off, convinced him to leave them alone. It was like Una wanted Luce to be afraid.

She looked out the window. The towering redwoods all around. A mountain lion up in the hills, protecting her babies. It was all the same as it had been earlier today, yesterday, yet it looked different. Una hadn't been totally honest. No, god—revise. Bobby Dalton had nothing to do with her missing mother. So, say it. Una had lied.

22

BACK OUTSIDE, into the trees along the road. Luce ran her fingers along the sharp redwood needles. They were bigger down here, larger leaves for more surface area to absorb the dappled light that made it through the thick branches. Up top, where they had full sun, the needles were small and fine. It was all adaptive. Everything natural shifts to survive.

It was full dark now, but there was a faint glow coming from down the road—Gramms. Maybe Luce could hide out with her for a little bit while she straightened out her head and decided what to do.

In Gramms's house, a baseball game was on the TV, the sound turned low, and the radio was on low too, familiar voices hushed and yammering. Gramms was in her tan, plush armchair, her heavy white tennis shoes clomping on the ground as she shifted. She gestured to the other armchair beside her and handed Luce a bowl of peanuts, her eyes never leaving the game.

"I like your mother. She's a tough cookie, that girl."

She could see the corner of Gramms's mouth flick into a smile, fragments of peanut shell caught in her spittle.

"You know she'd kill you if she heard you call her a girl instead of a woman," Luce said, cracking a peanut.

Gramms laughed, wet and thick. "I know. I've been saying it out loud since she's been gone because I'm hoping it'll make her mad enough to come on back and slap me." She winked over at Luce. Not the worst strategy. "Watch this one." She cupped her hands around her mouth, turned her head to the ceiling, and hollered, "Come on back, you ugly witch!" Luce couldn't help smiling.

Once, years before, Luce had asked her mother whether they were some kind of witches, which she'd learned from a library book was a thing people hated and feared. *Witches* is just a word people came up with as an excuse to kill strong women, Gloria had said.

What people? Who kills witches? Luce asked.

Historically, everyone.

Why?

Because they were afraid of female strength.

Does anyone still do it?

Ha, Gloria had laughed. It's sneakier now. Cops. The government. They arrest strong women who are helping other women. You know our herb patch? Luce nodded. It was a small bed within their larger garden, herbs spilling over the edges and regular collections by Gloria or Una, or sometimes other women who stopped by. Luce knew only a few of the plants in there. Mullein, red clover, peppermint, yarrow.

It's an abortifacient garden.

I know, Luce said.

But that's not what we'd ever call it to other people, Gloria said. You know not to use that word, right? Again, Luce nodded. And you know not to say what it's for—you can't say the word *abortion* or *birth control*. Or anything about it being a place to let women help themselves, decide when to have babies.

I know. So what.

So that's the whole point. That's the thing about witches. It scares people to think about women taking control of their own lives.

Gramms hocked a loogie and spit it into a cup beside her, then cracked another nut.

"That man who was threatening my mom," Luce said. Gramms nodded, tilted her recliner back a little. "I just talked to him. Turns out Una convinced him to leave us alone. Paid him to leave us alone."

"That was nice of her."

"No, no, listen. She didn't tell me. She's been saying he's the person we should be worried about."

Gramms winced, changing position in her chair as her arm unfurled, and she squeezed Luce's hand. "Now why would knuckleheaded Una do a thing like that?" Gramms asked.

"I was hoping you could tell me."

Her hand was rough, with salt and flecks of peanut shells stuck to her palm as she continued to squeeze Luce's hand, considering. The baseball crowd let out a quiet, triumphant roar. "I sure don't know," Gramms said quietly. She gathered another handful of nuts, nodding at the TV as she spoke, though to Luce her eyes seemed unfocused. "Una cares deeply about the Red Grove, and all the people in it. She feels responsible for all of us, you know. But I will tell you that sometimes her choices are a goddamned mystery to me."

Luce threw her head back against the headrest, looked up at the ceiling. Spiderwebs in the corners, water stains from long-ago leaks. There must be a reason Una had chosen not to tell her—some other information about her mother's whereabouts that was still secret, something Una was working on behind the scenes and would tell Luce about as soon as she could. She had to tamp down the queasiness, it was the only way forward. Living among the trees meant trusting the network, even if it was so deep you couldn't see it.

"Well, I'm thoroughly bent out of shape," Gramms said, "and I can't figure why all this is happening. I want to help you, Goose, and

I want to dump a bucket of sheep's feet on Una's head so they can kick some sense into her. I wonder how much you know about the history of the Red Grove."

"I don't want a history lesson, Gramms."

"I thought you wanted information about your mother," she said, snapping a peanut shell in two.

"I know the history," Luce said, her voice tentative. Newcomers often asked questions while they walked in the dark, and she prided herself on being a thorough repository of Red Grove lore.

Gramms threw nuts into her mouth, worked her jaw, lips parted. "There's a difference between history and story," she said.

"I know that."

"Good. So did your mother. She wasn't afraid to differentiate the two. And I believe she started to figure out that the history might, uh, differ from some of the stories."

Luce gnawed her lip, considering, but it didn't seem right. If there was more to the Tamsen Nightingale story, they'd know about it.

"Now I swear to God I don't know where she is, but I will tell you this much. She wasn't all in on the Red Grove. That's no news. She didn't like the stories people told here, about what the Red Grove should become, about what it had been in the past, about you."

"Me?"

"Those big plans everyone has for you, missy," Gramms said. "It's no secret you're probably the one Una will train to take over." The way Gramms said it didn't fill Luce with the kind of bashful pride she'd felt the few times someone had mentioned it before. "I do know that your mama has been worried for you—that sometimes being here can make people a little bit, how do I say it, too focused on what's scary about the world out there."

"It's scary because it's accurate," Luce said quickly, and she sounded defensive, she knew, but she couldn't help it. "Did you know that for Native American women, four out of five experience violence? And that they are murdered at ten times the national average?"

"You're not wrong, Goose."

"So not talking about it doesn't make it go away. It makes us part of the problem. There's honestly no gray area here."

"Kid, you want to know what I'll remember best from my whole life? The last thing I'll think about when I die? It was one night when I was a young woman and thought I was in love, doesn't matter with who. We were in San Francisco. After dinner, we started walking, and she pulled a bottle of rum from her jacket, and we kept walking all through the city, sipping that bottle and laughing our heads off, talking, and it got later and later, and we kept walking, we went through every neighborhood in the whole goddamned city, drunk and hysterical and kissing—we walked the entire night. It wasn't very safe, and certainly something could have happened, but it didn't. That's the thing. Usually it doesn't. The world is big and fun. There was risk in it, and the risk was part of what made it feel so good." She coughed, wet and meaty. "Goose, I think you're gonna want to understand what about this place is history and what is a story. I think it'll help you find your mama." There was worry across her forehead, her thin eyebrows. Tenderness there, too.

"How?" Luce said, twisting a peanut in her fingers until it snapped open, sharp against her skin. "It sounds like you're not telling me something."

"I wish to hell I knew where your mother was," Gramms said. "But I have a bad feeling that it's gonna have to be you who figures it out."

"You mean because I'm her daughter?" Luce asked.

Gramms raised her eyebrows at her. "No, no. That's bullshit. Bloodlines are a story that keeps the powerful people in charge. Screw bloodlines. It's cronyism. We don't pick who we're born to." A man in a bird costume, standing on top of a dugout, was using a wing to spank himself. Gramms split open another shell. Hoots of laughter drifted out from the radio.

"I thought you were going to tell me I had her gifts."

"Of course not."

"So you don't think I have her gifts?"

"How should I know?"

Luce gnawed on the outside of a peanut, taking in the salt and chewing the stringy tendrils of shells. Of all the people she'd ever met, Gramms seemed the least impressed by her mother. She loved her, teased her, winked at her even, but somehow didn't seem to fall for the spell she cast on so many others.

"Goose, there are a lot of kinds of inheritance," she said. "Decide what you want to inherit from your mother and take it. And then leave the rest behind."

What did she want to inherit from her mother? She'd spent so much of her life trying to figure out what of her came from Gloria and what came from Gem, but mostly the Gloria parts just felt like the bad parts. The parts she'd chosen to leave behind.

Luce was five, her hand tight around her mother's hand. They were getting off a packed train in the city. It was unusual that she was with her mom. Nearly all her young memories were with Gem, sturdy and safe Gem, slicing her apples, gluing googly eyes onto a toilet paper roll to make a snake.

But in this memory, Luce, hip-high, supposed to have a special day with her mother, had the sudden, choking fear that they were about to get separated. She was sure the train doors would close on their hands and she would be swept away from her in this sea of other huge bodies. She squeezed her mother's hand as hard as she could, a terror spiking through her body like a fever. Her mother looked down at her sharply, but then started moving them toward the door. Excuse me, she heard her mother say to the world of strangers above, Luce's fingers clawing into her mother's hand, squeezing, nearly quivering with force, clenching her teeth together for added strength to channel into the bond, *red rover red rover*, shaking, kids on the playground unable to run through their clenched hands, send *Luce-the-goose right over,* imagining herself unable to break their hands, Luce's hands squeezing tighter than they ever had, tethered.

When they reached the train's door, Luce gave one final squeeze to her mother's hand as hard as she possibly could.

Ow, Gloria said, her mouth twisting around the words. It wasn't a face Luce had seen before. The expression terrified her, pinging one nerve and then another, an eel of fear through her body that made her grip her mother's hand even tighter, and just as quickly, her mother, pained, tried to fling off her hand. But Luce was clinging too tightly for it to drop easily. Gloria had to work for it. She stilled their forward momentum and shook her wrist. She flung it.

They were disconnected.

And, separated, Gloria stepped off the train. Luce froze, mashed against ten thousand giants and suffocating beneath their rolls of fat. A person slid into the space where her mother had been. Loud bells chimed. The doors began to shut.

Her mother was leaving her behind.

Warm liquid ran down her leg, a giant's elbow smashed into her forehead. Nobody saw her there, nobody noticed the little shadow girl, all alone, lost in the woods, locked out on the balcony in the night, the end.

But then, for whatever reason, the train's sealed doors pulled apart. A bell rang from somewhere high. And there, suddenly, was Gloria lurching in past the doors, her big hands grabbing Luce by the shoulder and pulling her toward the door. Luce bounced between the purses and scratchy coats and got a jolt of elbow in the back of her head, but none of it mattered. Gloria had pulled her off the train.

Luce pressed her face against her mother's body, that warm animal smell, that softness in the middle of her giantess. She turned her face to the side to smell her mother's arm, pressed her lips against it, kissed, and then bit down.

Her teeth clamped. Not gently. She braced her neck, readied for her mother to push her forehead and get her off, to hook her fingers in Luce's mouth and, like a caught fish, toss. But after the initial flinch, her mother didn't move. Luce bit down harder. Her eyes and nose were leaking. Still, her mother did not move. The train doors closed, and she heard the rumble of the big cars as they began sliding into their future. People jostled around them, a rushing river, but they remained. Luce's teeth stayed sunk. She ground down with her front teeth, and Gloria started but didn't move, and finally Luce couldn't breathe for all the tears and snot blocking her nose. She unclamped. Two deep crescent moons ran along Gloria's arm.

Okay then, Gloria said, looking down at Luce. Her eyes were wet, too. A mother and daughter can only be connected for so long. It was true of mountain lions. Once the cubs were grown enough, two years old, enough to fend for themselves, the mother started to get annoyed with them. There was conflict. And then one day the mother leaves, and they never see each other again.

The man-bird was dancing with a woman in the front row, rubbing his tail feathers up and down her legs. Gramms clicked the TV off. There were peanut shell flakes all around her mouth, wet on her tongue as she spoke. "I'm going to try to help you figure out what the shit is going on. I'm slow as a turtle but mean as a snake when I need to be. But listen: you need to go to bed." Luce started to protest—too much to do—but Gramms cut her off. "No ifs, ands, or buts. Go home and go to sleep. Things'll make more sense in the morning. I'm old, so you have to do what I say. Meanwhile, do you have a cigarette?"

From *The Red Grove: The Story of the Sisters*

The hill was steep and the moaning sonorous as the women helped Rabbit climb to the cabin, resting against the enormous trunks of redwoods when the labor pains came. Rabbit, red-faced, cheeks burning, and her companion were ushered inside, given water to drink and seats upon which to rest. Her companion hadn't stopped talking, narrating their journey to this valley, how Hank Monk had whispered to them about this hidden place where women could be safe, how they knew they had no choice.

Wild blackberries that grew in the forest clearings hung heavy with fruit, and the children took Hank Monk's daughter out to gather the berries while the women rested. Ines brought Rabbit a steaming mug, fragments of herbs floating on the surface, and as she straightened to drink, her enormous belly pressed against the fabric of her cloak. "You undertook a long journey for someone in such delicate condition," Ines said from beside the fire.

"Didn't have a choice, did we?" Rabbit's companion said. "We heard there are women here with some special powers." She widened her eyes, nodding.

"We have no midwives here," Tamsen said.

"I want you to get rid of it," Rabbit said. It was the first time she'd spoken. There was a directness in her tone so unlike her companion, shadows under her eyes and a waxiness coating her cheeks and forehead. None of the women responded right away, but each of them eyed the belly, much too far to take it back, and imagined what she might want them to do after the baby arrived, an act none of them were willing to undertake. Would they be the ones who would take this unwanted baby, did they have it in them, could these women who'd fled to this place have enough inside them yet to withstand the heft of that new weight?

As afternoon turned into night, the forest rose up, hollering along-side Rabbit's hollering and moaning. The coyotes cried, one set of yips awakening the next in a chorus that circled the cabin, as if they could smell the precipice of life and death inside and yearned for it. The women had clean blankets on the bed, they boiled water, lit candles. Between contractions, Rabbit, wide-eyed with terror, was walking up and back the length of the room, a woman supporting her on each side.

She stopped when she was right in front of Tamsen, gripping Tamsen's forearms with a strength Tamsen had felt only in the maw of the mountain lion, and said, "Someone is coming." A pain caused her to double over again, hands on knees, moaning and shaking. The women helped her to the bed. Tamsen swallowed the strange bile rising in her throat; surely she was talking about the baby, that's who was coming, that's what she'd meant.

Rabbit's labors continued through the night, women coaxing her on with words of love or strength or wisdom, Rabbit's moans and tears and cries filling the cabin as the moon rose and stars shone, as the night animals prowled and their prey fled, as coyotes howled very close.

Just before the sun rose, Rabbit, exhausted and covered in sweat, sat up, blinking around the room at the gathered women. Something else was in her face, a ferocious clench of her jaw that alarmed Tamsen, but she looked over to Ines, who was nodding at Rabbit, yes, that was good, she was almost there. Rabbit beckoned Tamsen over again, clutched at her clothes, and pulled her face in close, sour, iron, wild. "He will come back," Rabbit said, barely audible though their faces were nearly pressed together. "He is looking for you."

"Who will?" Tamsen asked, matching Rabbit's hush, that acid rising again. "The man who did this to you? He won't find you here."

"He is still searching for you," Rabbit said, her pupils huge and locked. A wild panic rose in Tamsen's gut, her throat, but she could not let it show—there was no way Rabbit could know about her husband and his brothers from so long ago. She had not let anyone in on the steady fear that her husband was hunting her; she would not start.

Rabbit yelled out, her fingers digging into Tamsen's shoulders. And then, bringing her mouth close to Tamsen's ear again, she whispered that she was hearing things here, things she'd never heard. Whispering from the trees.

"Watch for him," she said, and then put a hand on her belly. "I didn't mean it. Don't get rid of her." And like tufts of steam rising from a kettle, Tamsen saw her sisters Margaret and Minnie, the outlines of their faces and bodies, as if they were hovering in the room, both curled in on themselves like sleeping cats.

The women said the baby would soon be there. Back on the bed, Rabbit pushed and screamed and pushed and wept and bore down, as taut as a bowstring, sweating, and hours passed, blood, shit, water, and then, finally, she was with them. A baby girl.

Tamsen cut her cord and was wiping the baby off when Ines shouted. Another baby's head had crowned. Rabbit swore and cried and pleaded, and that baby came fast, a new slippery creature in Ines's hands. Another girl. Rabbit lay flat on her back, breathing shallow and fast, no longer screaming. There was blood everywhere.

Tamsen and Ines held the slippery bodies, careful not to drop them, and each of them, too, had tears in their eyes, holding this kind of unexpected miracle. It was their doubleness that astonished Tamsen, their identicalness, the way they came into the world with a sister already in tow, each whole in and of themselves and also more by their proximity to each other.

They brought the babies to Rabbit, but her eyes were closed. They nudged her to wake, to hold the new babies, but she didn't budge. They'd wait, give her a moment to rest. The babies were small and pink and squished, and Tamsen couldn't imagine how creatures so tiny survived in the world.

Rabbit was still bleeding. They tried to wake her so they could clean her, help her, but she would not wake. She would not wake. Though her cheeks had a flush from exertion, the rest of her face was pale. Her companion crouched beside her, squeezing Rabbit's hand, stroking her forehead. But Rabbit was somewhere else.

Another woman who still had milk took the babies. Tamsen could no longer hear the coyotes outside, but she was sure there were animals close by, animals looking for blood. Hank Monk fell to his knees when he saw his sister, and though he would later deny it, his eye filled with tears.

While the women were busy holding the babies, tending to Rabbit, working to stop the bleeding, mixing roots and plants with shaking hands, Tamsen slipped out the door with a bundle wrapped in her arms. Dawn had broken, and the new day's light was thin beneath the fog that settled on these trees, tallest she'd ever seen. She climbed farther up the hill, toward the cave where she'd encountered the mountain lion and cubs. Once she was near, she unwrapped the bundle in her arms. Inside was the bloody placenta. She tossed it in the direction of the lions. An offering for the hunger of wild things.

Rabbit did not wake later that morning, or in the afternoon. The blood had soaked many blankets, and the color of her skin became closer to the color of fog. She did not wake in the evening. The babies, squirming grubs, slept and cried and ate from the breasts of the woman who'd taken them.

Through the following night, Hank Monk sat vigil in the corner of the room while the women checked on Rabbit, wet her dry lips with water, placed crushed herbs on her body to wake her organs, to promote circulation. But Ines did not know where to put the herbs to stop a bleeding that came from deep inside. Nobody knew how to help.

Tamsen slipped outside in the deepest part of the night, searching for flashes of eyes, remembering Minnie and Margaret as babies. She could not recall their scent, not exactly, but she remembered the spastic kick of their fat legs, the gummed smiles. She imagined her sisters, their bones out here in the wild, and she imagined them, too, as who they were before they died, bodies whole and strong, flying in the sky with their long dresses whipping behind them. She imagined them, and then it was as if they were right there, above Tamsen; there they were.

That night, Rabbit died. It was no surprise.

When light cracked through the dark sky the next morning, Ines awoke and saw Tamsen sitting in a chair by the door, her dark silhouette against the just-lightening sky. "Hank Monk left," Tamsen said, and Ines nodded, yawning. "And has left us his daughter to help with the babies."

"That wasn't part of the bargain," Ines said, sitting straight up.

Tamsen handed Ines a note from Hank Monk. "*If my girl and these babies have to grow up as women in this world, they should be your kind of women.*"

"What will we do with the babies?" Ines asked.

"They are our daughters," Tamsen said. "Margaret and Minnie."

"But we don't know what kind of people they really come from," Ines said.

"Bloodlines only matter to men because they don't make life," Tamsen said. "They do not matter to us. The babies will choose what they want to inherit."

The rains came that winter, and then the drought arrived with the summer, a fall of great abundance, the winter of toads, spring's fern, summer, winter, summer. Tamsen could feel the shifting pressure systems in her knuckles and knees, the passing years in her back, but still she had the strength of the forest.

Tamsen Nightingale knew that Hank Monk would keep his promise and threaten or mislead or hurt any herd of men who would encroach upon the women's refuge. They wrapped the occasional tree along the boundary of the valley with yarn they'd dyed red with their own blood, a signal to Hank Monk that all within the boundary should remain protected. There were a few among them who could fight if the situation arose, but most of the women's strengths were elsewhere, growing plants or cooking or teaching or understanding animals or hunting or tending to injuries and illness or listening or telling stories or building shelters or mending traps or offering extra love to the brokenhearted or envisioning the longevity of their refuge.

The twins, Margaret and Minnie, slept across each other's bodies at night, their limbs forming branches that crossed and curved around each other, and as they grew, it did not become easier to distinguish them. They would often shuffle out of bed together very early in the morning and come to stand beside Tamsen, who was the first awake. They would tell her, one at a time, of the dreams they'd had the night before, always identical. The stories rose the hair on Tamsen's arms as she listened quietly, nodding, building the fire or kneading bread.

"I was in a cave full of rabbits," one would say.

"Little baby pink rabbits, no hair yet," the other would say.

"And my head was hurting, and I needed to go find my sissy."

"I needed to search in the snow for my sissy," the other would say, and Tamsen would pat their heads, sit them down with bread, and try not to be flooded by fear but instead by wonder. "And then a man came here, and he was looking for you," one said. Tamsen listened, and the air grew sharp and prickled. She did not tell this story to the other women, wondering if, perhaps, the girls were having a regular dream, the kind most children dreamed, and also knowing that they weren't.

One of the women had brought with her a fiddle, which she played some evenings, and she was soon joined by another woman who could play the flute. Some nights the women built a fire outside and listened to the music and the children danced themselves tired, then slept against each other or the closest woman. And then one night the musicians played outside without the light of a fire, using the moonlight to help guide their hands, and this time instead of just the children being roused by the sounds, it was the women whose bodies started moving, two at first, and then pulling others out of the cabin or off their seats on the ground to join, the darkness seeming to cover shyness or apprehension, an erasure for the excuse of talent or knowing the steps or rhythm, opening instead into more and more bodies moving together to the strings and wind, and the treetops hundreds of feet overhead swaying too, owls calling and bats swooping, and the glimpse of teeth or a darkened open mouth in a smile as a face whirled by, the women dancing alone or with one another, spinning and dipping, leading, and two of them she'd seen linger when their hands brushed, pressing closer and closer, the children gripping one another and flinging each other into the darkness, a kind of hysteria born of their mothers' play. Even Tamsen was smiling, clapping along, grabbed eventually by Ines, who twisted and spun, both of them stomping and shuffling, an energy coursing through them. Tamsen, watching the rest of them move through the darkness, thought she'd never seen so much joy in her life, and then, revising that, thought that maybe she'd never felt so much, either.

23

1986

ONCE, GLORIA DECIDED to pick five-year-old Luce up from her sister's and take her out for a special date in the city nearby. It would just be the two of them, a whole day alone, window-shopping and nibbling on pastries and strolling through toy stores, maybe even giggling together at this high tea she'd heard a coworker talk about, where you sit on velvet chairs and are served cucumber sandwiches by people who call you miss and ma'am, like queens, the kind of day her daughter would remember for a long time, forever maybe, and when people asked her later what her mother had been like, she'd fill with crackling love and tell the story of this day. Gloria hadn't been around as much as she'd have liked, as much as she'd wanted. When she agreed to Gem's offer to raise Luce, she said that she'd be very involved as well, she'd be over most nights, take her on weekends, it would be more like coparenting. But auditions were mostly at night, and between rehearsals for the plays she was in, dates, her job, she was just so busy, and then it wasn't long before she knew that her biggest shimmering dream of stardom could only have a real shot from LA—where she'd intended to go from the beginning—and LA wasn't all that far from where Gem and Luce lived in Sacramento, six hours maybe, so they'd still see each other a lot. This was a thing she had to do.

But it was hard to get back up north. Couldn't get people to cover her shifts at the restaurant. Always a big audition she might get. She'd really planned on being with Luce so much more. When she let herself think about it, she felt as if there were some kind of worm inside her heart, chewing it, and so she didn't let herself think about it very much.

Now she was back for the weekend, and they would have this whole perfect day together. One day wouldn't make up for everything completely, she wasn't an idiot, but if it was perfect enough, it could do a lot.

From the beginning, something felt strange. Luce morphed from overly excited to sulky and distant, something her sister had said she might do, a sensitive little thing, her daughter, and Gloria had said it was no problem. Of course it wasn't. Her daughter sulked sometimes probably because she missed her mother, and Gloria was sorry about that, she truly was, but a woman is more than just a mother and she had so much else to do. Anyway, spending the day with her own mother would whisk Luce right out of anything else she had going on. But the little girl was stubborn. Quiet, despite how many times Gloria tried to start a conversation. Picked at the bear claw, uninterested, didn't want to gaze at the window displays, said she didn't like the taste of tea. Turned inward, like a private little whirl of dust. It was exhausting. Still, they carried on until early evening, finally finishing up their day together, taking the train back out of the city to where Gem had agreed to pick them up. It was rush hour, thousands of bodies hustling and jostling all around them. Gloria was holding her tight, making sure she stayed close—it wasn't easy to keep her safe in a big city after a long day—and Luce had squeezed her hand hard, surprising it could be that hard from such a little thing, but it was, and it hurt, like really hurt, and Gloria had no idea, none at all, why on earth her daughter would want to hurt her, and then, even more surprising, as Gloria held tight to keep her daughter close, ready to step off the train, her daughter let go of her hand. She let go. Gloria got off, and Luce stayed on the train. She would rather be lost in an unknown city than be with her mother a moment longer, Gloria thought, and thought again, unbelieving, feeling a physical pain inside her ribs she'd never felt before. Her daughter, this tiny, beautiful girl, did not want her.

The doors started to close. Gloria lunged back into the train, throwing her body between the closing doors, back pressing against one side, hands against the other, struggling, and then grabbing for the emergency cord. The doors sighed open. She shoved people aside, calling her girl's name. There Luce was, unmoving, afraid. Once she finally pulled her off the train, onto the platform, she hugged her tightly, too tightly maybe, pressing this small frame into hers, and said, down toward the top of her head, "Sorry, sorry, I'm so, so sorry." And she was. So sorry for a lot of things.

And then her daughter bit her.

Back at Gem's apartment that night, Gloria packed her suitcase while big-eyed Luce watched from across the room. The sun was setting, and Gem opened the sliding glass doors, sat herself on a bench on their small balcony. Luce followed her, sitting right beside her so their arms touched, legs dangling. Gloria on the other side of the glass, alone. The sun's final orange glow on the parking lot below, and Luce and Gem, side by side on the bench, not talking, just looking, a pigeon landing on the railing and then taking off, both of their heads turning to follow it as it disappeared. How did you ever find happiness? What was clear to Gloria was that Luce would not find it with her.

24

June 29, 1997 • Gone Three Days

LUCE WOKE UP BLINKING. Listened to the house. She hadn't planned on taking Gramms's advice about going to sleep, she'd planned on collecting Roo from Heartwood without interacting with anyone, getting home, checking on Gem, and then staying up all night putting the pieces together, plotting a course of action, and the last thing she remembered was lying on the floor, thinking, fuming, sure she'd never sleep again, and then.

Ferns unfurled in the early-morning fog. Purple morning glories opened their petals, wrapping a wooden stake in the garden. She listened to the house. Her mother was still gone.

And then she heard a small voice laughing from far off. Roo and Gem and I are in the house, she thought. Who is laughing?

She gripped the wall. A little voice was laughing. The little voice then—yes, she knew it. The small, tinkling laugh. It was *her* voice. When she was a child, laughing up into the wide-open smile of Gem, tickling her, Gem is here. And so am I, Luce thought. So am I, as a child.

"Gem," she called, pulling on her shorts, walking out of her bedroom. She could hear the sound of her own footsteps and the echo of those footsteps in conversation.

She stepped out into the hallway. "Gem?" she said. And that's when she saw the melon-headed mummy. The mummy had been in the office, and now the mummy was here, propped up on a chair beside the hallway table—she must've walked, or, no—what a crazy thing to think. She was facing the front door. Roo must have carried her into the hallway, though Luce was surprised that he could carry something so big. Someone rearranged us in the night, she thought.

Beside the mummy was a plate on which there looked to be a few pieces of dried mango and a glass of milk. The mummy's arms rested on her lap, legs crossed at the ankles, a posture Luce had seen her mother take when she was listening intently to someone talk, head a little cocked, too, like the mummy, a leftover kind of politeness, Luce thought, from Gloria's years out there, beyond the Red Grove, where a woman had to feign attention and interest as a matter of politeness, which was really a mode of survival. And what a strange thing, Luce thought, that the curve of a woman's lips or the cross of her ankles or the cock of her fine head, if it suggested interest, was enough to keep her safe, or not. But Luce caught herself—that binary of *out there* and *in here* was feeling a little fuzzy.

Luce shifted her gaze to where the mummy was looking, through the front door's window, where the trees had shadows beneath them. I will not be a person who is losing her mind, Luce thought. But she imagined herself as a balloon, her string billowing in the wind as she traveled farther and farther from home.

It was time to focus. She knew what she needed to do next, and she began moving toward the office, but then the laugh came again, her own laugh, a loose trill from far away, like a voice beside a hospital bed down the corridor. She could rescue that child. All those years as the terrified child beside Gem's swollen face, Luce hadn't thought this before—that she could rescue herself.

She began moving toward the voice, which was not laughing anymore, but deep in conversation in low, hurried whispers. What would happen when she pushed back the door to Gem's room and saw herself as a child, slumped in Gem's arms? There was a cold hand, no, breeze, on her back. She walked forward. The whispers were furious. She put one hand on the door to the room where Gem had spent years in everdream. Her palm was flat against the wood. She began to press, and there was a creak in the door and then a sharp cry of laugher coming from behind her.

She spun around. Behind her was the door to her mother's office. She went in fast.

Roo was sitting in the big velvet chair where the mummy had been. His legs were draped over one of the arms, right knee crossed over left, listening, paying attention, and in his hand, once again, was the telephone that was plugged into nothing.

He didn't glance at her. His gaze was fixed somewhere on the wall, and he was whispering, intensely, into the phone. It sounded like gibberish—like stage-whispering, fast and garbled, a string of sounds more than words. Luce reached out fast to take the phone from his hand and scold him, but he threw his shoulder into her, and though he was little, he almost knocked her backward.

He pressed the phone against his chest for a moment—"*I'm talking*," he hissed at her—and then put it back to his ear.

From a half-crouch on the other side of the room, Luce watched him. His concentration was complete, listening, nodding. And then another high laugh that took her breath because it was the wrong sound—it wasn't the sound that came out of his mouth when he laughed, it was *her* laugh. The sound he was making wasn't his own.

She couldn't move from the ground. Something was happening, and it was outside what she could understand, it was a light blinking on too far away for her to see. Roo was nodding into the phone then. "Okay," he said. "We'll learn the history."

Beneath the sound of his voice was another sound—a buzzing.

Luce swung her head around, looking for the cause, and this time, this time, she found it. A clump of flies was on top of her mother's desk. They were twitching, rubbing their legs, fifteen or twenty of them together.

Without thinking, she reached into her jean shorts pocket and pulled out the silver locket, turned it over in her hands. The metal against her skin felt alive, electric. She stared at the flies, felt the buzzing. Yes, she was waiting for another sound, for clicks.

In a blur of movement Roo dropped the phone and leapt from the velvet chair out toward the desk. The flies scattered. "Wait," Luce tried to yell, but the sound was a whimper.

"Here," he shouted, pounding his fists where the flies had been. Roo was in a flurry, picking things up from the desk and flinging them behind him, down onto the floor where Luce still crouched. Papers fluttered into the air, catching wing for a moment, her mother's handwriting across pages of seeker notes, grocery lists, a printout of the properties of various stones, old magazine articles on gardening, instructions for home birth, a copy of the LOST MOM flyer he'd made that he must've decided wasn't good enough.

She moved around Roo's flurry and reached for the folder she'd seen the last time she was in the office, where she'd found the list of names. Inside were newspaper articles, old, brittle, yellowed. Luce, still clutching the locket in one hand, unfolded the top article gently, carefully, not allowing it to snag. The frayed top of the paper read *San Francisco Herald*. Red Grove's closest big city. May 14, 1870.

MAN MISSING AFTER VISIT TO SECRET COVEN

On Tuesday, May 8, Mr. Arthur Nightingale, a good Christian and farmer, went in search of his wife, who had been missing for many years. Mr. Nightingale runs a farm with Mr. Roland Scully, and Mr. Scully attests that Mr. Nightingale never returned from his search. He was last seen leaving the farm, heading to the small settlement in the valley of the red grove after the Luber Farmlands.

Mr. Scully has called for a full investigation. After a trip out to the witches' purported homestead, the sheriff was not able to find any evidence of foul play and did not locate Mr. Nightingale, though he noted that there had been a major fire. Mr. Nightingale can be identified by his medium height and build, mustache, and birthmark on his left shoulder.

The locket's hinge dug into Luce's fingers where her grip had tightened as she read the article. I am supposed to figure something out, I can almost figure this out, Luce thought, though it felt like remembering the edges of a dream. If she concentrated hard enough, the edges would lose their blur.

She heard Gem's rattling cough from the other room. And then the edges sharpened. The locket in her hand was clicking, the clicking coming from up high, knowledge clicking things into place.

In the reenactment they performed of Tamsen Nightingale's story, Arthur Nightingale was long dead by the time Tamsen founded the Red Grove. He'd smashed her head, left her for dead, and then, with his brothers, eaten her sisters before dying himself, up in the Sierras. But this news article contradicted that story. Arthur had survived, though he had not seen Tamsen for years before coming to the Red Grove, and was never to be found.

Had Luce found this article a week earlier, she would have quickly assumed that the newspaper was involved in a scheme to discredit Tamsen Nightingale or harm the women of the Red Grove. But now? The world was shaded darker. What was history, and what was a story? The story they were telling in the Red Grove wasn't the truth.

Her mother had this article. Her mother had known. And her mother was going to hand over this secret to Ruby Wells.

A fly landed on her hand, another buzzed by her ear. Luce felt a shadow behind her. She clenched the locket in one hand, the papers in the other, squeezing so tight she could feel the bones of her fingers quivering. Between her fingers, the locket popped open, but she couldn't look at it. She knew the shape of the shadow behind her. What it felt like so close to her. Felt the hairs on her neck raise, as if it were the mother mountain lion come to feed, though she knew it was not. It was the elegant woman with the cow skull.

She wanted to scream, but could not make a sound, could feel only a buzzing filling her throat. She should turn and look at the shadow, she had to face it, face her. The shadow grew closer, hot, a fireball. She had to turn and look, but could not, and she squeezed her eyes shut instead.

"Luce," a voice said. It was Roo, calling her. She opened her eyes. He had knelt down beside her, reached out one tentative, sticky hand, and placed it on her knee. He was looking at her, worried. The shadow was gone. Her thumb was bleeding from the slice of the locket.

She looked down then, to the blood-smeared locket open in her palm. On one side, tucked into the frame, was a faded, dirty photograph. The face was hard to make out, but Luce brought the locket closer because somehow, impossibly, the face that seemed to be looking out at her from the locket was a face she knew. She brought it right up against her face. It didn't make sense. In the old locket there seemed to be a photograph of Roo.

"Is this yours?" she asked, "or Mom's?"

"Course not," he said, and she let a little air go, realizing that it was a trick of the light, maybe, her exhausted brain trying to tell stories. "The twins used to play with it."

"Mom and Gem?"

He sat up straighter, took his hand off her knee. "Duh, it's way older than that. Look at it. No, the first twins." She looked again. The little face was Roo. Faded, imprecise, but Roo. She closed the locket and slid the chain over her head.

"It's me in there because they knew we'd have this moment," Roo said. He sounded a hundred years old. "And you'd need to believe me in order for us to unbury what was covered."

The room tilted, a click somewhere close by. "They knew that you wouldn't be a good listener. That's why they talk to me. I listen. You have to learn how to listen."

"Roo, this is so important. Who was on the phone?"

He was looking at her sleepily, dreamily, and then he shook his head. "Did you know it isn't just all the plant roots that are connected in the dirt? That it's all the animals and bugs and people in the Red Grove too? Even the dead ones."

It happened all at once, everything between her and the dirt—chair and rug and wooden floor and concrete foundation—disappearing. She was part of the system of webs, the threads merging and reaching in every direction, tan and green and pink and brown, tingling in her fingers, and she understood she was being passed nutrients and water and then also, if she could just listen, yes, voices, so many faint voices all speaking at the same time. She lost the barrier of her skin, her whole body plugged in and prickling and swollen with revelation. All the voices were here, all the stories, all of it surrounding her for one second, two, and then it was gone.

Back inside her skin, the fibers of her T-shirt. The profound loneliness of being a separate thing.

She thought she knew what it meant to live here, but she suddenly felt that she knew nothing. Roo's picture in the locket, the history and story, what was buried must be uncovered, the roots and threads underground that connected—*how was it possible?*—everything. Everyone. "Something beneath the dreamer," Roo said, and that stopped her cold.

"Dreamer, Roo? You heard *beneath the dreamer*?" He closed his eyes, yawned, shrugged.

She tore out of the office and into Gem's room. Gem, the ever-dreamer. Finally, one thing that made sense. She crouched down and looked beneath the bed, but there was nothing. Scratched wooden floor that needed cleaning. Plastic wrappers from medical tubes and an empty vial. This had seemed so right. Beneath the dreamer. She sat down on the chair, defeated, and reached her arm over to Gem, who, gray-faced, labored breathing, oh god, shifted slightly beneath Luce's hand, rustling the fitted sheet. Luce brought her eye down to where the sheet was sliding off, and there, tucked between the mattress and frame, was a pad of paper. Luce jimmied it out. On the first page, in her mother's handwriting, it read:

The Red Grove: The Story of the Sisters
so that we may always remember and never repeat.

She flipped through the pages. It was completely full. On the very last page, her mother had written:

As told by Gem Shelley

From *The Red Grove: The Story of the Sisters
so that we may always remember and never repeat.*

Tamsen and Ines and the women and children sheltered in the great red grove, hidden from below through the dense trees, with nothing but the empty, wild hills above, protected by Hank Monk, close to fish, to game. New rooms adjoined the original cabin, their walls plastered when the materials could be afforded, roofs woven and patched. In the shadows of the giant red spires, the women did not fear being discovered. All, except for Tamsen.

One day a new woman arrived, with cuts on her cheek and a split lip. They took her in, as they had the women before her. But late that night, as the forest's nighttime hunters scurried back to their dens, there was a rattling at the door. The rattling turned into a pounding, one hard fist against the wood. The women rose from their sleep, some shaking, some taut with anger, and gathered together as the pounding continued. A man's voice, shouting to be let in.

Tamsen told the women to hush, not to listen. That she needed to think.

He slammed his fist against the window. Their home was sacred and needed protecting, and one of the women said that they would not turn out this newest arrival, shivering among them, even though she said she did not recognize this man's voice. They believed, of course they did, that the man was there for her. Without discussing it, the women arranged their bodies into concentric rings around the new arrival.

Tamsen knew the voice. She ran through everything that had happened on the mountains during their crossing, coming away only with rage for what her husband and his brothers had done. She felt no guilt, and so tried to swallow the worry that rose from the warnings the twins had given her.

The man shouted from outside. He thrashed the woodpile. He threw rocks against the windows, ripping through the greased paper coverings. His voice infected the cabin. "Tamsen Nightingale," he was calling. "You have been found. Come outside and face what you have done."

A few of the women, confused, were looking to Tamsen. She knew something else was needed here, something bigger and deeper than what they were doing to scare him away. Drawing deeply from each of the moments when she'd been hurt, or the most afraid, from whatever it was that kept this land dangerous, she opened her mouth. What emerged was not quite human. She screamed, high and throaty, but inside that scream was also a kind of roar, the sound of the earth cracking open, of two sails being torn in half—it was the sound she'd learned from the mountain lion.

She peered out through the hole in the window covering into the darkness. Even after all these years she recognized his silhouette in the darkness, the stoop of his neck, the thick trunks of his legs. Her husband. Stilled and silent, he'd stopped throwing rocks, and so Tamsen let out the roar again. Let him think they had a beast in here, a lion, yes, let him find fear.

She listened again, heard his footsteps moving away from the house. Tamsen turned back to her sisters, though she could only make out their dark shapes. Someone whispered, "Perhaps he's given up," but that's when they smelled the first of the smoke.

Outside, flames grew from the rows of their garden. Arthur was burning the crops. Fire crackled quickly through the corn and beans and tomatoes.

Tamsen Nightingale looked around to the faces of the women and children. They had come to her for respite. They were not her blood sisters, but they were as close as she would find, Ines her co-mother to these sisters, Emilia's trembling shoulders, Vee's braying laugh, Florence, Mary, Spoony and Jorgette and Speck and the twins, Minnie and Margaret, now four and clutching each other in the corner, more and more women, and none of them would've been safe if they'd stayed where they'd come from.

Tamsen flung open the door, revealing the flames as they spread quickly across the dry grass, grew toward the massive, towering trees at the edge of the clearing. She ran out toward her husband. The women did, too. It hadn't taken much time in the red grove for them to understand. The circular patterns in which the trees grew, the roots wound round one another, the interlaced network of fine filaments in the dirt, pulsing, sparking just past the corner of your eye, with stories they were sure they could almost hear of how to keep each other alive, it all made one truth self-evident: there would be no burning of this grove.

The women knew what to do. They'd been talking about this, practicing this. They knew what was worth protecting.

Tamsen came to face her husband, the women flanking her on each side, surrounding the man. "Just as I have not known peace since our crossing," she said, "you will never know peace again."

He began to shout at the women, saying, "You would not stand beside this witch if you knew what she has done," and Tamsen, for a moment, faltered. Would these sisters understand what she'd done? Was it a just act? The fires he'd started glowed behind him, crackling closer to their cabin, their trees, and then the women began to move toward the man. They did not ask what Tamsen had done. In their pockets were herbs, teeth, seeds. In their hands were knives and bricks. They pummeled the man by the haze of fire and on into the darkness.

But Ines, on the edge of the women, in the light of the flames, screamed for them to stop. It appeared that her heart was aflame, the fire's reflection sparking in her silver locket. "Do not harm this man," Ines yelled. "You cannot, or we will be no better than him."

But the women did not stop. Tamsen was amazed—it was as if the collective anger of all that had come before washed through them in a tidal swell.

"Stop it!" Ines screamed, trying to peel away one of the women's arms as it punched at Arthur. "This is not who we are!" A limb knocked Ines down. Arthur was in the center, kicking and flailing, but the women had many hands and feet to do their work on him.

From the ground, Ines screamed that they could not live with this kind of sin, that she herself was going to run right to the sheriff, but the women knew what they needed to protect, and what that was worth. They kept on. Ines clawed at Tamsen, begging her to make it stop. Tamsen turned slowly to face the pleading Ines, appearing twice as big as she usually was, her teeth looking longer, pointed, the fire reflecting in her eyes as it grew bigger around them, as the women's words grew louder. Arthur's blood pooled on the ground, fists and rocks and feet and sticks, and then his body was limp.

Ines finally understood that this thing could not be stopped. It was too late. She scrambled away from the women, running into the hills. Tamsen ran after her. The fire at their back grew, but did not chase them, and as they went higher into the hills, the light grew dimmer and dimmer until it was just the black wilderness. Ines stumbled, her foot catching on a root. She went down to the ground, but Tamsen was not close enough to grab her before she righted herself and kept moving. Tamsen tripped, twisting her ankle, but on she ran too. Their breath was heavy and dry. The trees didn't interfere. The owls stayed high on their branches. The women ran and ran, sisters chasing and being chased.

Farther up, near the edge of the tree line, was a redwood that the women sometimes visited because of its extraordinary wound, bigger than any other they'd yet found, capacious enough for a dozen children to hide inside. Though Tamsen was a little way back, she could tell that Ines was headed to the wound. What a fool.

Tamsen came slowly.

Ines was inside the tree, in the dark, pressed all the way back against the farthest wall. Around her, the charred interior was smooth, oiled by humans and animals rubbing themselves against the wood, like touching the sac around the beating heart of the world.

"This isn't right," Ines said, knees up by her chest, rocking. "I can't stand for it. I thought you were different, that we could be different here, but I see that you are no better than my husband's father."

Tamsen heard Ines's words clearly: Ines was no longer one of them. She would go right to the sheriff and tell them about what they were doing to Arthur, about all these women and their animals and spells, about who was living out here and who had run from where they should have been. She would betray them.

Tamsen crawled toward Ines. Inside the wound it was even darker than the night outside, and Tamsen's silhouette was a pure black monster against the gray light of the world.

"Save me," Ines said, her hand grasping at the tree. "Help me," she whimpered to the bark. Which is exactly what Tamsen had been learning to do for these years, practicing as each new woman joined them in this red grove, helping them find a kind of sanctuary.

"You have to accept," Tamsen said to her cowering friend, "that there are sacrifices necessary to keep all the women safe."

"You are murderers," Ines sobbed, clawing at the tree. No, not murderers, Tamsen thought. "It's unnatural," Ines yelled.

"Nature is filled with violence," Tamsen said with a calm that chilled even her own arms.

"But we are better than that. We have to be better," Ines said, pleading. But Tamsen shook her head. They were not better than nature. They were not worse, either.

Protectors. That's what they were.

Tamsen had never told everyone here that it would be entirely safe. She'd tried to make it so, to build this place alongside her sisters so that their safety was primary, but nothing guaranteed it. All she had was what she could do with her hands. She looked at her friend's beautiful hair, remembered the first days when Ines arrived, how she'd laid a tiny buttercup, the size of a bee, on Tamsen's healing arm. She drew a breath and, unlike the last time, was sorry for what had to come next.

From where it had been tucked into her dress, Tamsen pulled out the carved bone, a mountain lion etched into the center. She clenched it tightly in her fist and did not think she could do what she needed to do as Ines prayed for mercy. She hesitated, but did not let the tears blur her eyesight, took a breath, thought of her sisters, and cracked down hard on Ines's skull. Just one swing of Tamsen's arm. That was all.

Tamsen sat with Ines's body a long time. Though she did not weep as she had for her sisters, as she had when she was a younger woman, she sat in the shadow of the redwood, laid her hand across her friend's heart, and thought about how in sync they'd been until the very end—until they weren't. And she thought that soon, any minute, she would begin the slow, dark trudge down the hill toward the blaze, to her sisters, who would be working to put it out, who had turned, like her, so naturally toward eliminating anything—anyone—who threatened their safety, and she understood that this would be the terrible trade of this place.

Before the women went to work rebuilding their shelter or planting new crops or rounding up the spooked animals, before any of that, they climbed the hill. The sun was just up. Six women carried a man's shrouded body. When they reached a spot toward the top of the hills, near the mouth of the cave, you would soon be able to hear the cracking of bones and the slurp of blood as the mountain lions feasted. You could almost hear them licking their maws, preparing.

And then the women and children turned and walked toward the redwoods. As they walked, the children gathered wildflowers. One woman sang a slow, low song. The sound of her voice, the sound of the steps of the women and children carrying themselves up the hill, shoes on dirt, bare feet on dirt, the swish of the grasses against skirts and pants, the singing of the birds in the high branches, the creak of insects calling for mates— all of it gathered together and carried them up the hill, to the tree line, where the last big redwood stood with its gaping wound. It was empty.

Ines had decided to leave them, Tamsen told the rest of the women. It broke her heart, but the women here were free, and Ines had chosen her own future. Nobody need worry that she would tell anyone about what had been done. Ines had promised. And the women nodded and asked no further questions, perhaps because they knew, Tamsen thought, perhaps because they believed it was better not to know.

What Tamsen noticed in the wound each time she visited was something strange—a haze appearing around where Ines's body had been. A hum. A buzz. It was a mass of flies, forming almost a sheath around the wound, like a glow.

And she knew, having dragged her sweet friend's body farther into the wildness, that she would feed the animals and that eventually, her bones would find peace with the sacrifice made to keep the rest of the sisters and children safe.

After some years, the silver locket, which had fallen off inside the tree's wound, brought itself to the soil's surface, clicking open and closed until the twins, Margaret and Minnie, found it one day and slipped it on. They were young when Ines left, did not remember that the locket belonged to her. What they loved was the photo inside, a little face neither of the twins knew, but they practiced whispering secrets into the locket, the dreams they had of the cave and the hairless rabbits and the mountain covered in snow, of a creature that would come with nothing but a skull for a head. And then, one day, the locket fell while they were helping with chores in the cabin and was lost.

As the years passed, the sisters buried within themselves the night of Arthur Nightingale. Though they remembered what had been required, they decided that the story they would tell their children would be gentler. A story about the trees of the red grove and the community of women growing in their shade. And how, below these red trees and inside the red mist, their lives could be entirely safe—that it was, in fact, a miracle, some kind of magic, that in this valley alone, no woman could be harmed, can you even imagine, the kind of thing so amazing it was almost myth.

As told by Gem Shelley

25

June 29, 1997 • Gone Three Days

Luce could almost see how the pieces fit, where the borders aligned. Just a few edges that didn't quite meet. And this biggest piece of all: the story of the sisters was different from the story she had always been taught, and her mother had transcribed the story from Gem. Which meant Gem knew this story—how? Because she had one foot here, one foot with the dead of the Red Grove? Luce could hear Gloria's voice saying it, as if she were right here, whispering about the holiest of states, an everdream, for the ability to let the pulsing network of roots belowground communicate to both places at once.

The locket, still in her hand. Ines's locket.

Ines, a woman murdered in the Red Grove. Luce let that sentence play in her head once, twice, and then tucked it away. She was not quite ready to let it grow. How could she even be sure that it was real, was true? This is just the scribblings of a madwoman, someone might say—but even thinking that, she knew. She felt it. Flies in the gut, the sureness of the cow-skull woman, the roots and fungi knitting everything together around her, beneath her, holding them up right this moment, sparking in response to her question, yes, yes.

Slowly, shakily, Luce returned to the office. Roo was lying on the floor, his legs splayed, arms out in a T, as if talking on the phone had zapped all the energy out of him. Luce nudged him with her toe. "You okay?" He shrugged. "Did you already know what this says?" Luce asked, holding up the papers. He nodded, eyes closed. "You knew because someone on the phone told you?" He nodded again. "Who?" He put his thumb in his mouth, began to suck. She could see the tiny cage of his chest rising and falling. Maybe it was a trick of the light, but he seemed to have shadows under his eyes, like he was suddenly old, exhausted. She laid her own body down on the floor beside him. Closed her eyes.

She was holding her mind at the surface of thinking, like the water skeeters so delicately standing on top of the water in the creek; one more second there, where the world's foundational truths remained intact: north is north, sun is hot, the Red Grove is divinely protected.

She imagined her mother in here, in the velvet chair, these pages in hand. Gloria had always been skeptical of the Red Grove, apparently for no reason. Turned out she had reason. This was the real story of the Red Grove: Tamsen Nightingale and the women had condoned violence. Enacted it. Not just to outsiders to keep themselves safe, but to each other. A woman had been killed on this land. By one of their own.

All the women here in the Red Grove, believing they were safe. There was no magic.

If her mother knew this, and was going to tell someone, the danger was not from an outsider. Bobby Dalton was happy enough with his payoff. The danger was right here.

"Roo, I need you to stay." He opened his mouth to protest, but she held up a hand. "It's the most important job, buddy. Please. You gotta stay here with Gem. And Moose."

"Bullshit," Roo said, thumb still deep in his mouth.

"I need to know you're safe."

"Wherever you're going, I want to come," Roo said, his cheek pressed to the rug, looking at Luce.

"You have that special connection, right? What if the phone rings again and you find out something important?" He considered this, blinking at her, and then nodded just a little bit and stuck his plastic stegosaur's tail into his mouth.

"I'm scared," Roo said. She wished she had the strength to lie to him, tell him there was no reason to be, no problem, or to be a person who he trusted would make everything okay. But he had probably started putting all these little pieces together, like she'd been doing. She noticed, just barely, a shiver in his body that didn't stop. She folded him into her. His little bird-wing arms, his shelf of hair—had she told him to wash it lately? Had she combed it? There was an oak leaf matted in the back, so no, she hadn't. She rested her cheek on top of his head.

"Don't worry," she whispered, squeezing him tighter. "I've got a plan." She pulled him away so she could look him in the eyes. His little chin was puckered, quivering. "I need your help, though, okay?" Two huge drops ran down his cheeks, but he nodded. A little clear snot trail leaked from his nose. He didn't wipe it.

"What's the next step?" he said.

"Secret," she whispered, and then raised her eyebrows and winked. Roo nodded again, squeezing his eyes shut for a moment, nodding some more. Luce kissed the top of his stinky head, brambled, knotted.

She would walk out onto the deck. She would move on to what was required next. It was the movement she'd practiced over and over when she first learned about what to do in case she encountered a mountain lion up in the hills. Become your biggest self, a monster. It doesn't matter who you really are, deep inside. It doesn't matter how small you feel, how chipped away. Pick up sticks and hold them on top of your head as if the beast you are won't stop growing.

———

She kept her bike off the main road, following the trail beside the creek and through the trees. Damp and molding leaves in the trickle of water, dried, crushed stalks and crumbling dirt along the banks. The shimmer of mica in the smoothed creek rocks, insisting that every living thing had something precious inside, and didn't they, wasn't that the whole point? Around her neck was the locket, and tucked into her back pocket was the carved bone.

Luce knocked on the door of one of the trailers used for transitional housing. It was near the creek that had flooded twice the last winter and pulled the weight of the trailer a little farther down each time, now half sunk into the ground. The curtained window beside the door rustled as a sliver of a face peered out, then disappeared. Muffled voices inside, a light turning on. Finally Luce heard a lock turn and the door click open, and out slid Sam, pulling the door shut behind her. She had a loose, thin flannel shirt that she pulled tight around her chest.

"Sorry to bust in on you like this," Luce said. She started to lean toward Sam to give her a hug, but Sam flinched. "I'll make it quick. You stayed in Heartwood's apartment when you first got here, right?" Sam nodded. "I know this is a weird question, but did my mom come talk to you while you were there?"

Sam cocked her head, wiped her nose. Said she'd only met her mom at the reenactments, briefly. Luce pressed on. "I don't really know how to ask this, but was there anything, like, weird that happened in the apartment in Heartwood? Anything unusual?"

Sam glanced back to the trailer's window, and Luce followed her gaze. The curtain moved back into place—Sam's mom was watching them. "No," Sam said. "It was chill."

Luce hooked her arm through Sam's elbow, an echo of a movement of her mother's—where are you, whose elbow are you hooking?—and guided Sam away from the trailer, deeper into the trees. They stepped over a small gathering of mushrooms, gooey and browning. Luce spoke quietly, in a rush. "Please, anything you can tell me about your time there would be helpful. I can't totally explain why yet, but I think it might help me figure out where my mom is." Sam glanced back again to the trailer, unhooked her arm from Luce's, and stretched.

"Ever heard of zombie wasps?" Sam asked. Luce played along, said she hadn't. "They sting a cockroach twice, first to half paralyze it and then in this really special part of its brain that gets rid of natural flee-ing instincts. So it no longer wants to escape. Then the wasp uses the roach's antenna like a leash and pulls it into a hole it's dug for a den. The wasp lays its eggs in the den, and when they hatch, they eat the cockroach, who is still alive, from the inside. And then they crawl out and begin that whole nightmare process again."

"What the—"

"I know, it's repulsive and amazing. Like real-life biological mind control."

"I'm not sure what that has to do with—"

"Hear me out for a second," Sam said, leading them even a little deeper into the trees. "I know you really love Una, and I can see she's a good person. She's trying to be a good person. But I think she might be a little bit like those wasps. Everyone here follows what she says because they're so relieved to be safe. And, like, being safe is a big deal, don't get me wrong. But it's like they forget to see that they might be in another den. Not a terrible den, but a den. Nothing weird happened while I was in the apartment—she's not, like, a pedophile or something, before you ask. But there was this one thing. Some inspector or something came out while I was there. I heard them talking in the office. What they were saying didn't really make sense. Una told her she had another one, and yes, she was blessed to have so many, and yes, the transition was going okay, a little bumpy of course. I had no idea what they were talking about, and honestly, I wasn't even paying attention at first, but after a few minutes I heard them coming, so I went back to the apartment and Una brought the inspector by to see me. She didn't say much, just hi, how's the transition, and I told her it was fine. Once they left, I peeked my head out into the hallway again and heard something that, at the time, I wrote off. But maybe it means something. The inspector said, not all foster kids get so lucky."

"Wait—as if *you* were a foster kid?"

"I guess? I don't know. My mom said to go along with whatever Una said, because she was doing us such a big favor to let us stay here for free and give us food and stuff until my mom can find a new job. I don't know how it all works, but I had a friend at my old school who was a foster kid, and she always talked about how her foster parents did it for the money."

Edges of the puzzle felt like they were close to clicking together. If the list of names were all kids who had stayed in Heartwood's apartment, had they all been claimed as foster children? For the money? Luce wouldn't believe it. Una devoted all her time, every second of it, to the Red Grove. She was not the kind of person who would be stealing money for herself—though it turned out that Luce didn't know Una as well as she thought, and then, revising that, she maybe didn't know her at all.

Sam glanced back at the trailer, scratched at her arm with her fingernail. Luce asked why she was worried about her mom hearing them. Sam tightened her ponytail, wrapped her flannel a little tighter. Then, in a low whisper, "She wants to be sure I don't get involved in anything that might possibly get us kicked out. We've got nowhere else. So—leave me out of it. Okay?" Luce nodded. Then, Sam's regular voice again, "Sorry, I gotta go. See you soon, okay?" She turned and walked away. Luce heard the trailer door lock behind her.

Back on her bike, whizzing toward Heartwood. As she came closer, her legs slowed until she wasn't pedaling at all. She jumped off her bike and walked it, staying in the cover of trees. Panic rising. She couldn't just go there. She needed a plan. She required a strategy, she—something hit her shoulder. She held still. Listening. Again, something bouncing against her elbow. She looked down, and a few shelled peanuts lay in the dirt. She spun in the direction they'd come from, and another was barreling right past her face. She squinted her eyes then, toward the dark, small window that opened into Gramms's bathroom, and one more peanut came flying out through the open crack, coming right at her chest.

"Bingo!" she heard Gramms yell. Luce batted the peanut away and saw Gramms's hand extended out the small crack in the window, beckoning her.

"I can't right now," Luce called out, still making her way toward Heartwood.

But Gramms's hand kept waving, and so Luce, unsure whether Gramms had heard her at all, set down her bike and walked to the high, rectangular window. Gramms's hand disappeared inside. It was dim in her little apartment, and once Luce was close to the window, she could smell the familiar must and smoke and then, appearing in the six-inch opening, the cherry ember of a lit cigarette.

"Can I stop by later?" Luce asked into the open window, impatient. "I'm in kind of a hurry—" but Gramms cut her off. She pushed her face to the opening, which was not quite as wide as the width of her head, her face taking up the entire space, teeth dark and yellow, skin folded and dry.

"Goose, listen," Gramms said. "I was out for a cruise in the cart earlier and saw one of the Lost Mom flyers on a telephone poll. I'm guessing that's Roo's handiwork, good little penguin. Anyway, there was something written on it at the bottom. I don't know whose handwriting it is, and I have no idea if this is true, but it said 'Gloria's car was at Heartwood while everyone was watching the mountain lion cubs.'"

Luce's limbs felt warm and elastic. Watching the mountain lion cubs had been the last time she'd seen Gloria.

"I called your house but didn't want to tell this to Roo. Don't want to worry him any more than is needed. Goose, I don't know if it holds any water," Gramms said, something else in her voice, worry maybe. "But it's something." She brought her face back from the window's opening for a moment to drag on her cigarette.

"Gramms, are you standing on the toilet?" Luce asked.

"Let's gather an angry mob and storm Heartwood."

"Get off the toilet. You're going fall and hurt yourself."

"Oh, leave it be. I've got my good sneakers on." She took another drag and looked hard at Luce, one eye squinting. Luce trusted Gramms. She always had. "Whatever you're doing, I'm helping," Gramms said.

"Can I come in and use your phone?" Luce asked. "I have an idea."

"Of course."

"Also I'm going to help you get off your toilet."

"You little asshole. I love you. Get in here."

26

June 29, 1997 • Gone Three Days

THE EVENING WAS FALLING BLUE, the air chilling. Luce, in the shadows of the trees outside Heartwood, gnawing her thumb. It did not take much thought to know where and how to lean into the bark to remain unseen, unheard—this is what she has been practicing for years, as she led the women into the darkness, as she followed the women without being seen. This is what she was made for. She listened. She waited. She watched. She knew there were other creatures out here in the forest that she couldn't see, their eyes trained on her the way her eyes were trained on Una.

Una was walking in and out of Heartwood's back door onto the deck. She watered two tubs of flowers, geraniums that can't drink the air like the redwoods can. Once twilight had fallen enough that Una turned the lights on inside, Luce watched her putter around the kitchen. A fly circled, then landed on Luce's hand pressed against the redwood bark. "Hello," she whispered to it, feeling ridiculous, feeling insane, but saying it nonetheless. "Hello. I'm paying attention. I'm listening."

Finally Una wandered out of the kitchen, back into the hallway where she could no longer be seen, and so, Luce hoped, it was time. She made a run for the pay phone at the edge of Heartwood's playground. Black marker graffiti across the metal sides, gunk on the numbers, a faint stink on the receiver. There was one dim light near the phone that illuminated it, so she must accept the loss of darkness, this gamble. She dialed.

"I wanted to let you know the amazing news," Luce said as soon as Una picked up. She'd hoped Una was walking back through Heartwood into the office, and she had been right. "My mom came back. She's home."

Listening with every ounce of her concentration, Luce heard, yes, what she was listening for. The slightest moment of hesitation in Una's voice. "Oh, that's fabulous news," Una said. And that's it. Una was shocked. Or she didn't believe Luce. Because Una knew that Gloria was not home.

"We're so relieved," Luce said. "And she's fine. The calling man didn't hurt her, it was a big misunderstanding."

"Well," Una said. And again, Luce waited to see if Una would reveal the truth, tell Luce that she, in fact, had talked to the calling man herself, knew he had nothing to do with it. "Well," Una said again. "That is the best news I've heard in a long, long time. So where was she, exactly?"

"Oh shoot, gotta run," Luce said. "Just wanted to share the great news." And she clunked the phone back onto its holder. A moth dipped into her face, fled. Even up until this moment, even with everything she had learned, a sliver of Luce's heart held on to all the years she'd believed in Una's goodness. She'd given her this one last chance. And now the sliver was gone.

Luce must move quickly. She checked to make sure she couldn't see anyone and then backed into the dark cover of trees. What happened next is what she could have predicted the least.

She waited. She watched. There was no movement inside Heartwood, no new lights flicking on that she could see. Una was, as far as Luce could tell, still back in the office. Doing what? She waited five minutes, then ten. Maybe she needed to creep closer, to see if, somehow, she could peer past the blinds covering the office window to see inside, listen in—but then, there. Lights going off, on in a new room. Una was on the move.

Luce crept back farther into the trees, quickly, as Una walked with purpose out onto the deck. This was it, the moment. What her plan was hinging upon. Una moved quickly, and Luce stepped farther back, wanted to be completely unseeable in the darkness here, moving quickly, and then, oh no, oh shit. She was falling. Normally she was so careful, impossibly quiet, but she was nervous, she was trying to keep her eye on Una and she had not seen the dead branch behind her, which snapped under her weight and she was falling, hard, halfway into a rhododendron bush. It was not quiet.

Una, on the deck, froze. She had been walking quickly, but now she was still. She turned her head to look right at Luce, right at where she had made a careless mistake. Beyond careless. Idiotic. Devastating. Maybe ruining everything. From the ground, Luce lifted her head enough, carefully, to see Una, but not enough to create more noise. She did not sit up. There were branches and leaves and darkness between them, but Una was practiced in walking through the forest, too.

"Hello," Una called out. "Is anyone there?" Luce did not answer, her heart echoing through her ears and off the trees and hills and sky. Maybe Una would chalk the sound up to a deer, so plentiful out in these woods, a squirrel, some other brush creature. Why would it be anything else?

But then Una walked toward her. Down the steps of the deck, past the first big tree and then the next, into the edge of the forest. She moved slowly, with caution, an animal on alert. Una had lived among the trees of the Red Grove a long time, true, but she did not navigate the night as Luce did, and here, in this one way, Luce had the advantage. Still, Una stepped closer. This was Luce's only plan. She couldn't be found.

Una came closer again, and as she did, another feeling washed over Luce. She was cowering. She'd lied to Una with this phone call, she'd betrayed her with this deceit, she was afraid of Una seeing her because of the potential of Una's fury. But that was bullshit. Una was the liar.

A burning sensation on Luce's chest, the locket's metal suddenly so cold against her skin, scalding. Una was the liar, and the fact of that was its own fire. Una's steps were loud in the quiet dark, and Luce was close, splayed out on the ground. Una was looking right at her, and shitohshit the plan will not work. Una will deny, deny, deny, and will have the upper hand, she will tell the story she wants to tell. And so Luce squeezed her eyes. Wished for a fly, for the clicks, brought to mind the cow-skull woman, the face in the locket, the carved bone burning in her back pocket, all the underground filaments of root and fungi that connected Gem to this place, that connected all of them. She collected all of the forest's will and pleaded with it to remain hidden.

Una was ten feet from her, and Luce, only a fraction of her obscured by the bush she had fallen into, was looking right at her. Eye to eye. But she did not call Luce by name. Una's eyes kept moving, kept searching. She turned and stepped, noisily, back through the forest and then probably back up the steps of the deck, into Heartwood, where Luce would have to find a way to follow and listen, but that's not where Una went. Una walked to the far side of the deck and then down the steps to the path Luce had led the women on a few days back, through the old-growth forest.

Once Una had gone far enough that Luce was confident she wouldn't be heard, she untangled herself from the brush. She must keep her eyes on Una. It was her time to do what she knew how to do in the forest.

There was high wind swishing branches and an owl's call that sounded like an electric shaver. The trees creaked. How many animals were watching her even then, right then, as she walked through the trees adjacent to the path Una had taken, up through the grove of trees on the other side of Heartwood. How many layers of life and death had happened in each exact spot where she stepped—all stacked on top of one another, here and here and here.

She was walking toward something dark and heavy. She knew that, felt it more certainly with each step. Felt, too, that she was not ready for it. Closing her eyes, she leaned back against the scratchy heft of a redwood, a pause to catch her breath for one moment before she came into whatever truth she'd learn next. Did there ever come a moment when you were ready to learn the worst things? Let her palm rough the tree's ridges. Let her breathe in the cool waft of moist air, even in this drought.

A buzz made her open her eyes. There were two flies circling each other. Landing on her arm, her head. And then, as if she'd asked them a question, the flies darted away, following the path Una had taken into the grove.

The trail wasn't long, and Una was taking it fast. Something dark ahead. Good that Roo wasn't here. Whatever Luce would find there, whatever needed doing, it needed to be done alone. She'd started looking for her mother alone, and she would find her alone.

Deeper into the trees. Feet moving themselves along the dirt trail, tendrils of sword ferns brushing her ankles, azalea to the left, salmonberry growing low and wide on the shadow-dappled ground. She had so many of the pieces. Her mother was going to meet with Ruby Wells. She had materials that revised the history the Red Grove purported was true, as well as a list of names of kids who'd stayed in the apartment. And Una, who'd lied about talking to the calling man again and again. Luce could think like Ruby, cross-reference the encyclopedia of harm she'd been building in her mind all these years, and every time she did, she came back to what she'd learned in the dozens of books on serial killers and from Juan's science lessons on human aggression and all the stories the women had shared: it was men who enacted violence. It was not women, and it was not the person she thought she knew best of all. But she walked on because, of course, it was.

She walked past the fern and sorrel, and there she was. Una, bent low over the new redwood saplings that'd been planted in the small clearing where the bamboo had been ripped out. She was holding a watering can, releasing a gentle shower onto the thin plants. This had been Luce's plan: to panic Una into confusion, hope she made a mistake, that she slipped up and said something or went somewhere that would reveal the truth. And so here they were. But her mother was nowhere in sight. Only—as Roo had pointed out days ago—the redwood saplings on top of the newly filled-in dirt.

And the dirt was moving the smallest bit, a shimmering in the shape of the tendrils below.

What is buried must be uncovered. The hole, buried.

Una looked over, smiled tiredly, and did not seem surprised to see Luce. "Did I ever tell you about the ghost redwoods?" she asked. Luce didn't answer, didn't know where to begin. Tried to quiet the pounding in her ears. "They're extremely rare. It's a kind of albinism in the trees. One will sprout that is totally white, as white as milk, and without the chlorophyll that makes it green, it can't feed itself. A plant needs chlorophyll to convert sunlight to sugars, of course. So the ghost tree stays connected to the parent tree its whole life. Gets everything it needs from the parent. Remains a ghost."

Luce kept her hand on a trunk, steadying herself. She could not get the words out.

"I've never seen a ghost redwood, but I want to," Una said. "Imagine it—a redwood tree, pure white. Surviving only, *only*, because of its community." She shook out the last of the water from the can, set it down. "You're here, which means you've figured some things out. I'm glad, Goose. These have been a torturous few days. I want to promise you that I'm going to be completely honest."

"Why have you been lying?" Luce asked, wanting to sound like a lion, sounding, instead, like a scared little lamb.

Una's shoulders clenched and rose, her eyes blinking quickly. "I love Gloria, I always have. Even though we've had our differences, she's a sister."

"Did my mom tell you the real history of the Red Grove?"

Una set down the watering can, straightened up, and gestured at the trees around her. "I trust what I experience, not someone else's version of life in the Red Grove. My experience here has been one of pure safety and protection. Has yours?"

"That's not the question."

"But has it?"

"Of course it has." The twilight made Una's eyes flare, the dirt all around her blue-silver. It was time to go further; Luce needed answers. She took a big breath, steadied herself against a tree. Did not want to give away the devastation of her betrayal. "I know you've been claiming kids here—me—as your foster kids to get money, and—"

Una let out a burst of laughter. "That's what you think I'm up to? The foster system is way too complicated for that." Luce said that she'd found the list of names, that she knew it meant something, and Una cut her off. "Darling, you know these community meals you eat every week? The medical help we provide for those who arrive injured? The free housing until people get on their feet? The community closet—darling, how do you think we could afford anything without money coming in? I am not ashamed to tell you that I have an arrangement with someone who works for social services—I won't tell you who, but I'll tell you that you'd know her, she was out here for a while—and that we get a little bit of extra funding. Welfare, food stamps, that kind of thing. She signs off on it because she gets it, she just has to come out here from time to time. I wish to hell there was an easier way to support everyone who needs it, but I make the best of what I have. And what I have are a lot of people who need extra help."

Luce was startled. How quickly Una had admitted to this wrong-doing. "But it's lying."

"Oh, for fuck's sake, who cares," Una said, throwing up her hand. Her careful voice was gone. "The government is a bunch of corrupt rapists and abusers, and they cheat us all the time, so why not even it out a hair." Una picked up a trowel, knelt down to the dirt beside a plastic tray that held a few more redwood saplings, but she didn't yet dig. She held the trowel in front of her, the pointed tip darkened with mud.

"My mom knew you were cheating, though. She was going to turn you in."

"I don't know if she was or not." Una stabbed the trowel into the ground, began making a new hole.

"Bullshit. You knew. You had her come meet you at Heartwood so you could convince her to keep quiet. I know all that. But then what happened? Where did she go?"

Something in Una shifted, a rigidity in her spine softening as she dug. Luce thought this was the point at which Una should crumple completely with exhaustion, tearfully apologize, and hand over the address or phone number where her mother had been forced to hide out for a while. What she wanted to say over and over again, what she meant most of all, was *How could you?*

Una paused her digging and sat back on her heels. She set the trowel across her thighs. "Okay, my girl. I didn't want you to have to find out like this, and for that, I'm so sorry. But your mother was last seen with Bobby, the man who wouldn't stop calling." Luce froze, some childlike impulse still so desperately wanting to trust Una and believe this thing she was saying, as frightening as it was, because it was less frightening than the possibility that Una was lying to her. And there *were* countless stories of psychopaths passing lie detector tests, tricking the police because they did not possess the kind of empathy that jangled their nerves. Bobby sounded so relaxed on the phone, and if he was one of the true psychopaths, it might make sense.

But—and here she let go of that safe tether to what she'd believed—
Una had lied. Everything Luce learned kept pointing back to her.

A fury rose in her, molten. She reached into her back pocket and
pulled out the carved bone she'd found beneath her house, one of
Tamsen Nightingale's sisters' bones. The bone that had killed Ines, a
woman murdered right here in the Red Grove. That was the truth,
and she knew it in her own bones. She clenched it in her fist. Eyed
the trowel on Una's lap. Luce held the bone up at Una like a knife.

"You. Are. Lying. I know you called Bobby off. Paid him to leave
us alone. Tell me what happened," Luce said. Una was shaking her
head, but even from a distance Luce could see tears building in her
eyes. She needed something to convince Una that she was serious,
that she needed the truth. She spun, starting on the path back to
Heartwood. "I'm going to call 911. I will tell them what's happening.
The cops will come, fast. And then whatever it is you're hiding won't
be hidden anymore. That, and—" She didn't have to say more words,
gestured around her at the valley of the Red Grove, all the houses,
the gardens, the people.

Una was shaking her head, wiping at tears. "I'm so sorry," she
said, so quiet Luce could barely hear. She turned to look. "My girl,"
Una said, dropping to her knees, palms up in supplication. The trowel
had fallen away, into the shadows. There were two dark trails of
makeup pooling and riveting down her cheeks. "You're right. I am
lying."

27

June 26, 1997 • The Day Of

A MOUNTAIN LION would rip open the throat of anyone, any-thing at all, if it was trying to harm her babies. Gloria breathed in again, shakily, reassuring herself that she was doing right. Got into the car, started the ignition.

She could do this one thing, and even if her daughter didn't understand everything right now, she would come to understand it. The crowd of lion-watchers grew smaller in the rearview mirror. She was ready for her meeting with Ruby. Just one quick stop at Heartwood first, per Una's request. A final favor, Una had called it, before Gloria went to the reporter, because that's what she was up to, wasn't it? Una had her ways of finding things out, she said, and obviously Gloria could do whatever she thought was best for her and her family. Come to Heartwood, Una had said, while everyone is watching the lions. It'll give us a little bit of alone time to bury the hatchet, make our peace.

And, after all this time, yeah, Gloria would give Una a few minutes before everything here changed. The Red Grove *had* given their family a lot. She wasn't so stupid as to bring the transcribed story of Tamsen Nightingale or the list of kids Una used as false dependents. What was the point? Una had refused to have a conversation whenever Gloria tried over these last few weeks. But she wanted Una to know that she was doing this for everyone's sake, not just Luce's, even if she knew herself that it was mostly for Luce. She'd been practicing how she would explain it to Ruby Wells, so she could feel comfortable being quoted, and also to Una and other Red Grovers so they could fully understand her reasons.

Yes, there is something extraordinary about the Red Grove, she would say. *But it's not what most people think. It is not a magic spell cast by the first woman to create the community, not something emanating from these particular redwoods. No, what makes it extraordinary*—and here she would speak slowly, to make sure everyone really heard—*is that people here* choose *to protect and care for one another. The belief in safety creates safety. I'll say that again. The belief in safety creates safety. Plus, the action required to back that up. There's no magic. No curse. No protective shield. Violence against women has happened everywhere since the beginning of human time. In the Red Grove, too. But we've chosen to believe we can do better, and so we have.* And she'd tell the story of Arthur Nightingale and Ines and the first women.

It would break Luce's heart, but there were too many reasons to tell. To free her, for one.

It would stop the calling man's obsessive belief that this place had caused his father's death.

It would give the women the truth of their power, which was within them, their actions and tenderness, so much stronger than a myth.

When Gloria arrived at Heartwood, she saw Una's car in the parking lot, but no Una. She walked up the stairs to the main building, peeked into Heartwood's office, kitchen, back out across the deck, still rehearsing the speech. "Hello," she shouted, but there was no reply. A crow cawed from somewhere she couldn't see, amazing animals, crows, how they gather around their dead, she thought as she left through Heartwood's back door and called to Una out back. Una was always moving at a hundred miles an hour. Gloria had read debates about what exactly the crows are doing when they gather around the dead; whether they are participating in some kind of mourning ritual, which many intelligent animals are known to do, or whether they are gathering information about the dead, how they died, and how long ago, assessing potential danger.

Gloria called for Una again, no response. She walked off the back deck and down the path that led farther into the redwoods. Of course Una was making this conversation a dramatic exchange among the trees, she would probably have a soundtrack playing back there, something to try to make Gloria too guilty to talk to Ruby. Well screw that, she was ready, she wouldn't be swayed.

And then there was Una.

Una, standing in the small clearing where they'd dug away the bamboo meditation garden, near the gaping hole. A dried fern frond stuck to her white linen pants. She waved, beckoned Gloria closer.

The crow in the nearby trees cawed again, a sign of distress, it sounded like, or calling others to a funeral, and Gloria started to smile up toward it, but something was suddenly covering her face.

Blackness.

Nothing.

A slice of green as she opened her eyes then closed them again, her head pounding. Dark.

She opened her eyes.

Branches above. Needles blurred into clouds. And the taste of dust. Something in her mouth, something pulling. She remembered the crow, blinked, thought to cough, but could not; there was something in her mouth tight and choking. She should call for help, but could make no sound.

"Gloria," a voice said, Una's voice. "Please try to remain calm. I'm so sorry to do it this way, but I didn't feel like there was a choice."

Gloria tried to pull the thing out of her mouth, but her arms were bound, tied behind her back. It was time to clear her head enough to take stock of what the fuck was happening, and she did, she tried, her brain still tired and foggy. She was seated on an old camp chair. In addition to her wrists, her ankles were also tied tight, too tight, with big plastic zip ties. She could not get up. She could not scream.

"I know this seems awful, and I'm so sorry," Una said, crouching down in front of her, "but it is vital that you understand all that could be lost if a lie spreads about the Red Grove. You've forgotten how this place saved you and your sister and your children. You can't forget any longer." This cannot be happening, Gloria thought, pulling at her bound arms, biting at whatever was in her mouth. This is not the kind of thing that happens in real life, or, rather, this is not the kind of thing that women do to one another—yes, Tamsen had, but that was back then, things were different now.

She squinted at the ground. The redwood sorrel, which grows only in the shade, closes its four-petaled leaves if any sun touches it; they sunburn, the leaves, Gloria knows. They protect themselves perfectly.

There was movement in the trees a little farther back. Coming from between two massive trunks was someone else, someone in jeans and a big, dirty black jacket, and, most startlingly, something covering the face. She could not tell who it was. Over the head was a pillowcase, with two holes cut for eyes, and on top of that, a moon mask. She tried again, then, to kick her legs free of the ties, to shake her wrists loose, anything, but she was stuck. Una was still close, watching the person approach.

"You have not been willing to accept the full power of the reenactments in your own life," Una said. "And you need to. You need to understand what the women have been through."

The hooded figure was by her side. She felt them place their hand on her back. Whose hand, how soft, she could not tell. There was movement then in the trees once again, and she turned to look, saw another person approaching. She wanted to call out for help, but still could not. The new person stepped out from behind a massive trunk. Khaki work pants. Black T-shirt. She recognized the costume from previous reenactments. Underneath these clothes was someone she knew, someone she trusted, but here they were. Wearing a pillowcase over their head. Moon mask on top. Two black tunnels where the eyes should be.

She wanted to shout for them to let her go, that she was full of fucking compassion, that this insane little scare tactic would not change her mind about anything, or sure, fine, that it changed her mind about everything, whatever they wanted to hear to let her go. She has known Una to take things too far in the past, but this is so far over the line. Whoever's story they were going to reenact would obviously be one she had seen before, and what would be different now? She kicked against the restraints.

She could not wait, could not fucking wait, to get the materials to Ruby Wells. Up until now she'd felt bad about what a sea change this was going to be for Una, maybe even for some of the women here, but it was for the best. The truth was the only choice, she'd thought to herself again and again, watching Luce, her little palila bird, grow more and more extreme in her allegiance to this place, in how it choked the rest of what she might be able to do in her life in the wider world. She has thought this line again and again: I wish I had a choice, but if I want to save my daughter, I do not. She can think of no other way to break the enchantment this place has on Luce. No other way to give her daughter the gift of choosing her own life, her own destiny. And having Ruby Wells—Luce's own hero—break the story was the kindest, most credible way she could do it. The gentlest. We have got to want the best for our daughters, to give them the best, and finally, she was making a great sacrifice in order to do that.

Gloria stopped struggling, thinking all this. Her justice would be sweet. So let Una finish this ridiculous game.

And then one final person emerged from the woods. Someone smaller. Leaner. Someone who looked like a child. They also had a pillowcase over their face, which they were adjusting with their small white hand—whose hand, whose?—walking carefully over a fallen branch, moon mask on top, walking slowly toward the other hooded figures, and no, it could not be—the child was wearing a small blue dress with a yellow ribbon. A shiver up Gloria's spine.

Una asked the people in costumes if they were ready, and they nodded. She turned to Gloria. "My friend. Here's what happens next. You will be reminded of the horrors that unfold outside the boundary of the Red Grove. And what you'd be ruining by spreading lies to that journalist. How you will ruin your daughter's life, and all the work we've put into making her the next leader here. So you will participate in this reenactment, and understand, and then we'll reach an agreement. Again, I'm sorry, but this seemed to be the only way. Understand?"

The cloth in her mouth muffled her words, but still, as loud as she could, Gloria said, "Fuck. You."

"You'll be persuaded. I'm confident." Una smiled with a gentleness that Gloria had seen a thousand times, all soft grace and light. How could this person be all these things at once? The people in hoods stepped closer.

And then Una turned and began walking up the path, toward Heartwood. Gloria watched her go, calling after her, but she didn't turn. She was gone. So Una would not even be part of this thing she had set in motion. What a coward.

"Please, please, you have to come," the child in the blue dress said. She was holding her hand up to her ear as if on the phone. The reenactment had begun.

The person in the black jacket replied. "I don't think I can tonight, honey." It was a woman's voice. What she was saying raised the hair on the back of Gloria's neck. "We are supposed to leave for a trip tonight, Frank is all packed up," the black jacket said, and Gloria was getting a little seasick, no, this was not what she thought, it couldn't be. "But I'll try to be there. Kiss your mama and baby brother for me."

No fucking way was she doing this.

"I'm tired of your sister taking advantage of you," the third person said. "She abandoned Luce and made you raise her and do all the work."

The little blue dress with the yellow ribbon looked just like Luce's dress from when she was small. The dress she wore for three days straight, those first three days in the hospital with Gem.

Gloria kicked her legs against the chair.

"You don't know Gloria like I do," the black jacket said. "Don't talk about her like that."

"I'll say whatever I want," he said, and took a step closer to her. No. She would not watch this. She knew what was coming. The reenactments always turned to include the victim. The victim becomes an actor. To help take ownership of the story, the idea goes. To take power. To change the outcome. This is not her story, not really, but they will make her play her sister, she knows this. They will make her sit here, tied up, and feel the horror of what her sister went through on the last real day of her life, and no, she will not sit here for that. She thrashed with all her strength and heard one of the chair legs crack and got the cloth halfway out of her mouth and began to scream.

The two hooded adults ran over, and she kicked as hard as she could. She would free herself and get the fuck out of this nightmare she had been running from all these years. She kicked and swung all her bodyweight, and arms came toward her, grabbing at her, pushing at her, the little child screaming, and she was flailing and yelling despite the choker in her mouth and there were limbs all over, one trying to pull her forward, another pushing her back, she was wildly swinging and kicking and punching, and some voice was screaming at her to stop, calm down, but she could not, and she was unmoored from the earth and somehow—how?—tumbling backward. She was still tied to the chair. She was falling backward, and she was in the air.

The smell was wet earth. Worms. As soon as she was free-falling, she knew where she was. She'd helped dig it. The pit where there'd once been bamboo.

The traveling time was short, but something came clearly, perfectly, into Gloria's mind. A scent. The smell of her face pressed up against her infant daughter's neck. The softness of her baby skin on her nose and cheeks. The gurgle and coo, warm milk breath. A sweet smell, honeysuckle, earth.

28

June 29, 1997 • And Then

UNA MOVED TOWARD LUCE on her knees, opened her mouth, closed it quickly to swallow. "It was an accident."

Luce's body was weightless.

"A horrible, tragic accident," Una said, her hands meeting in prayer on her chest. There had been time and sense, and now there was none.

"Nobody meant for it to happen," Una said, weak and small. The bones in Luce's legs were gone, the blood, gone. What she needed was for her mother to enter this place and tell her what to do.

Luce reached her arm out toward Una, the bone clenched in the palm of her hand. "What happened?" Luce managed to say.

"She fell into the pit, honey," Una said, and through Luce's body a fire roared. It could not be true, she would not let it be true. Luce raised the bone higher into the air. She could protect this place with blood, too. One charge forward, one swing of the bone and she could crack Una's skull. She could do that. She would. Una, palms on the dirt, went on. "An accident, Luce, I swear to you. She fell. Broke her neck, I think. She didn't suffer."

Luce's shoulders were shaking, how long had they been doing that, where were her legs? "I don't believe you, why should I believe you?"

"I don't know," Una said. She wouldn't stop shaking her head. "You don't have much reason to, but this is the truth. I wasn't there, but this is what was told to me. She fell."

She fell.

Her mother had fallen into the hole.

Luce looked down to her feet, to the earth. The dirt. A tremor started in her chest, but she did not speak. Somehow this knowledge had already been at the edge of her mind. The dirt on her shoes, dirt from near her mother. She would not let herself think about her mother's hands against her cheeks, saying, softly, *you're mine.*

Her world had been uprooted, Una said, when she learned what happened. She wasn't there for it. Had heard screaming and run. Una started to reach out a hand toward Luce, but Luce ducked away.

"I should have told you right away. I'm so sorry, but I was afraid it would have been harmful to everyone. Because of what your mom had been planning. I don't even know what she was going to give Ruby, but she said that nobody would believe in the Red Grove any-more." A cricket began its high chirp nearby, grinding one leg against the other in a pulsating scream. Luce wasn't sure there was any breath in her body. Una went on. "It doesn't have to be the end. All the other people in our community can still live, can still thrive. What we have here is so much bigger than one person."

The hills contracted. Spun. Her mother was here, right here this whole time, under the earth. She was what was buried.

This dirt, already growing things. The saplings planted before they were ready. Planted a day after Luce had last seen her mother. Someone shoveling dirt over her body, somebody she knew covering her own mother in dirt. Carefully planting the saplings.

Una went on, her voice sounding so far away. She'd had to make a terrible choice once she learned of what happened. One option was to follow outsiders' corrupt legal system and call the cops, forever breaking the community. Because it would break the Red Grove, Una explained. The idea of the protection would be over. And they would have taken Gloria's beautiful body to some sterile, anonymous morgue. Nobody wanted that, Una explained.

And so the other option was to save this place. Give Gloria the ritual and respect she deserved. They purified the site with white sage. Scattered golden marigold petals into the earth. Luce covered her ears with her hands. Una was on her knees, in front of Luce, and though her words kept coming, she was wiping her cheeks with the palms of her hands, keeping the tears, coming fast, from falling to the dirt. Luce gripped the bone in her right hand, knuckles white and taut, shaking.

"Tell me I made the wrong choice," Una said. "Did I? God, I don't know." She gripped her head, pulling her hair. "You're going to face the biggest decision in your life, Luce, and I need you to think about it more carefully than you've ever thought about anything. On one side of the decision is outsiders and jail and the destruction of all the lives—every single one—of the people who live here. On the other side is love. Peace. Refuge for the women here and the women to come."

What Luce wanted was to climb into one of the redwood's wounds, curl around herself, and never be seen again. She struggled against the depths she wanted to fall into. She could not. And the mad, hot flame, buried, was what she needed to tend. She needed the flame to help her figure out what to do. The world had been one way, and now it was another.

"If it was really an accident," Luce said, tending the flame, "it would not have caused anyone to question the Red Grove. Accidents happen. You've said that so many times. It was not an accident."

"Does it really matter? Listen, I wept over her. There were all these flies that kept wanting to land on her, and we did our best to shoo them, we—"

But that was enough. Luce flung out her arm, the bone clenched in her fist, and slashed Una's jaw. The blood came fast. Una held her hands over the wound.

There was noise behind them then, up the path, a big animal crashing through the brush. Luce clenched, readied to flee, but then turned toward the familiar metallic clink. The sound of a tin cup clinking against a belt buckle.

"Luce," Juan yelled, getting close. "Luce, kiddo, you here?"

"I'm here," she said, Juan's appearance righting the world for a brief, beautiful moment before the new truth crashed in, crushing her chest.

"I came as fast as I could," he said, out of breath, wild-eyed. "You were right, on the phone. Boog went to your house, like you asked, to keep an eye on Roo. And so I kept my eye on the road for anyone else driving up, anything to be wary of. I thought you were, you know, overreacting. But Luce—god I'm sorry I didn't stop it—"

"What, who came?"

"Nobody came."

"That's good, Juan, that's—"

"No no, Luce, listen. When Boog drove away, she wasn't alone."

"What?"

"Roo was in the car," Juan said.

She could hardly hear for the thump of her heart in her ears. This was not right.

"I went straightaway to Boog's, as fast as I could, but they weren't there. I thought maybe they'd be here. But they're not. What's happening, Luce?"

Una, on the ground, held her face in her hand. Luce could see darker shadows of blood between her fingers.

"Oh god, Una, what happened?" Juan asked, but Luce shook her head at him. He held still, blinking, trying to put the pieces together.

From beneath her clutched hands, Una spoke. "It's my fault. Oh, god," she said. "I told Boog that you'd called to say your mother was home. She knew your mother had all those documents still at the house. I didn't think she'd do anything about any of it. But oh god."

"Where did Boog take Roo?" Juan asked, squinting at Una. Luce could not imagine explaining it all to him.

Una sat up straight, her hand still on her bleeding face. "Honestly, I don't know what she's doing. She was the one who told me about the accident. She—she was there." Luce sat up then too, the bone falling from her hand as she did.

"Roo's in danger," Luce said, the words blurring out of her mouth. She stood up and looked at Una, felt her rage cut down for a moment into pure pain, this person she loved, this person she thought loved her.

"Wait," Una said. "Katie is Boog's niece. I know Katie's husband is back in jail and she has an apartment not too far, maybe twenty minutes outside the Red Grove. In San Rafael. Maybe Boog went there? That's the only thing I can think of. It's the only place I can imagine Boog might have to go."

Luce stood, came to Una, and towered above her.

"I promise you, that is my best guess," Una said, wiping tears from her eyes.

"You swear on everything that this is not some trick?"

"I swear it. The address is written in the office. Under Katie's name. And Luce," Una said, but the words choked in her throat in a sob. "I'm so, so sorry. I never meant for this to happen."

The only thing Luce could do was keep going, and so she did. "Juan, you stay here with Una. Make sure she doesn't call anyone to warn them, make sure she doesn't try to run, okay?" Luce said.

"Goose, please tell me—" Juan tried, but Luce kept going.

"Give me your car keys," Luce said to Una.

"Let me come with you. I can reason with her, I can—"

But Luce wouldn't hear anymore. "Keys," she said.

"You are not going alone," Juan said, starting to come after Luce, but she spun to him, feeling herself grow taller, feeling suddenly steadied by the earth as if tendrils had reached up from the dirt, supporting her ankles.

"You both will do exactly as I have asked." The trees gusted above them, the worms turned in the earth below. "I know what comes next. I'm listening."

Up above, though it was night, when they were usually tucked away safe in a tree, crows circled between branches, coming in close to where a buzz grew louder and louder. As if they wanted to see what the danger was, how worried to be. Black feathers in the black night. And they stayed a long time, watching.

29

June 29, 1997

S AN RAFAEL WAS A FEW TOWNS OVER, but it might as well have been across the Pacific Ocean. Luce had never been outside the Red Grove alone. Her palm was damp as she slid the key in Una's car for the second time in the last few days, but this time, she did not stop to think. She turned the key. She did not want to press the gas pedal, but her brother was somewhere out there, the pad of his feet in his morning pajamas, and she could not stall, did not let herself think, just foot down and here we go.

She drove. The dark giants and their shadows passing on each side of the car illuminated a moment in the headlights before they returned to darkness. Swallow what was rising in the throat. Take a breath and swallow and keep the car pointed on the road, keep the foot on the gas.

At the crest of the hill leading out of the valley, she could see, on either side of the road, the low stone wall, trees on each side, their necks wrapped in red yarn. That was it right there, the border of the Red Grove just ahead of her, then just exactly to the sides, and then just behind. Her hands would not stop shaking on the wheel, the distance between her and what she thought she knew of the world growing and growing.

She swerved, slammed on the brakes and pulled off the road. Not much of a shoulder here on this narrow road that connected the valley up and then down the steep hillside to the next town below, no redwoods along this road, just the dry old earth, the whiskers and cobwebs of roots sticking out from the side of the hill where the cracked dirt had crumbled away. Her hands shaking, sick everywhere, she could not go, she would not, shaking, it was too much to know what had happened to her mother, she could not think of it, couldn't know it yet. There would be a time she could sit with it, but not now. She pressed her palms hard enough into her eyeballs that she saw confetti, until they ached.

She should turn the wheel to guide her back onto the road, press the gas. Do it. Now. Wiping the snot, thin and hot, falling from her chin. Stop being afraid, she could not be afraid, not right now. It didn't matter that she had no license, that wasn't what tethered her to what was behind her. She closed her eyes, let her neck loose and her forehead drop against the steering wheel. There was nobody else.

Eyes closed, forehead throbbing against the steering wheel. As if they were standing right in front of her, in the darkness, in front of the dry dirt, she saw her mother holding Roo on her hip. She wasn't saying anything, and neither was Roo, there was just the sound of his little footy pajamas smacking the floor in the mornings, *thwack*, *thwack*, the sound of the flies hitting their heads against the window, the sound of the sliding glass door shutting behind her, out on the balcony in the dark. And then, beside her mother, Gem, before her everdream, reaching one arm up and out toward her.

She lifted her head. Opened her eyes. Wiped them with the back of her hands, everything still shaking. On she went.

———

Luce pulled into an apartment complex, dull brown and three stories high. Double-checked the address she'd written down, lucky, so lucky, that this was along a main road she'd taken each time she left the community, one she knew how to find. Cigarette butts in the parking lot, flattened soda cups. She scanned the lot for Boog's car and didn't see it, but no matter. She had to go in. There were a few people here, outsiders locking their apartment doors as they left to go somewhere, someone sitting in their car with music on, windows down. Just because she was outside the Red Grove did not mean something terrible was necessarily going to happen, she told herself, and told herself again, shoulders clenched as she forced one foot in front of the other, past these people, right out here in the open, she had to go and so she did. The stairs smelled faintly of pee, and she took them two at a time, the blood thrumming in her neck, her ears. Apartment 312.

She reached the door. It was unlocked. Inside, then.

Silence. The shadow of Gloria and Gem and baby Roo flickered on again, then was gone. She was in a living room with an over-stuffed couch, old smell of cats, musty, everything in tans and beiges with coral flower accents, scanning quickly for signs of Boog, of Roo, but they were not here.

What was in here, near the door, was the melon-headed mummy. It was impossible. But here she was. The mummy, seated upright in a chair, staring at the front door. As if she were guarding it. Her lop-sided eyes, watchful. A jolt of adrenaline, seeing the mummy so far from their house, why here, what could be happening, and she started to walk over to touch it, see if it was real, but then she heard Roo's small, high voice, singing. *"Who's afraid of the big bad wolf, the big bad wolf, the big bad wolf."* His voice was muffled, coming from behind a closed door.

She turned the handle. Roo was sitting cross-legged on a bed, his legs scooted up beneath his body. His palms rested on his knees. He looked like a little Buddha, calm, tranquil, alarmingly so.

With her palm against the door, Luce pressed the wood, widening the angle of the room so she could see inside. Standing across from Roo was Boog, rocking, cracking the knuckles on each finger again and again.

"Goose," Roo said, looking relieved. "Boog took me on an adventure."

"Come here," Luce said, loud and fast, but Boog cut her off.

"Stay, Roo. Wait right there. Luce, Roo was about to tell me about an envelope with some special papers in it," she said. Her face was dry in patches, more than before, splotchy red. She looked Luce right in the eyes. "I am so, so very sorry. Luce, I need you to go back, slowly, into the other room. I'm going to stay in here with Roo." Luce squeezed her fingers into her palms—clammy, shaking.

"I'm not—" Luce started to say, but Boog cut her off.

"Roo," Boog said. "Sweetie. I was hoping we'd have a little more time here, just the two of us, to play. That's why I brought you all the way over here to Katie's house, because I was hoping for some more time before your sister was here too, to help you remember where those papers are, that's what I was hoping. But okay, since we're all here—"

"Sure," Roo said. He looked pleased, scooched his butt off the chair, and pulled a piece of paper from his back pocket. Luce watched, swallowing a knot. She had called him and told him to hide the folder. Surely he wouldn't be stupid enough to have hidden it in his pocket? Boog unfolded the paper, concentrated on what was in front of her. Roo looked up at Luce then. "I brought Mom along," he said. "I wouldn't come on this adventure with Boog until she let me bring Mom. Did you see her?"

"I sure did, Roo," Luce said, catching a glimpse of the paper over Boog's shoulder. It was one of Roo's drawings, a template for a robotic ball gown. Boog smiled, thin and fake, and set the paper down, pinching her temple. The fake smile faded from her mouth. "Other papers," she said, and this time her voice was less friendly. "This can all be over soon, easy, no problems. I need to be sure"—she swung her face back to where Luce stood, still frozen in the doorway—"you understand that we need to keep things as they are in the Red Grove. Too many people's lives are at stake. Our whole community. If you ruin this place, where will they go? What will happen to my Katie and her kids? Back here, where she is one wrong word away from being choked or punched or killed? No. Katie believes she's safe in the Red Grove and so she stays. Doesn't go back to him. Is looked after and supported. The women's belief that they are safe in the Red Grove makes them so. Do you get that?"

"We'll leave," Luce said, her voice low, barely a voice at all. She was staring at Boog, willing her to make eye contact and remember that they were kids, that she knew them, loved them. "Roo, come on. We'll go. We'll drive away, across the country, even. We won't tell anyone. You'll never see us again."

"Luce, honey," Boog said, and she, too, was crying, wiping tears from her face. "I am so, so sorry. I loved your mother, loved her fiercely. If she'd have cooperated with what we were helping her with, none of this would have happened. But we can still save it all together." Boog's face, turned half sideways to Luce, held a kind of demented, hopeful grin, as if somehow she thought Luce would agree to sweep her mother's death under the rug.

There was a sound just then, by the front door. One sound, and then many. It seemed impossible, yet that was the sound Luce heard—the clicks. There were clicks in the other room. And some kind of pressure change, her ears popping, and a warmer current of air blowing into the room. Boog turned back quickly to Luce and Roo. Luce couldn't believe the clicks had followed them here, outside the Red Grove, but here they were. "Who's here?" Boog asked. So she could hear the clicks too. She ran into the living room, and as Roo jumped up to follow, Luce grabbed his shirt to catch him, held him to her.

"Una?" Boog called. "Who's there?"

Luce looked wildly around the room for an out—she could toss Roo out the window and climb after. She pushed him toward it, away from the door, trying to keep quiet against the creak of wood beneath their feet. But then there was another click, so loud, so close, nearly inside Luce's head. She looked back into the other room, and Boog was reeling around too, spinning fast toward them, trying to find the source of the strange sound, human but disembodied, a language she didn't speak.

As Boog spun toward them, there was another motion. Boog's foot clattered against something, and the mummy—perched on a chair by the front door—was suddenly tumbling off its chair in front of where Boog spun. It looked, for a blurred, impossible second, like her mother, and then it—*she*—clattered into Boog.

Boog's hands, on reflex, moved up to protect her face as her body's momentum was moving toward the ground, off-balance already, panicked, her legs and arms twisted in with the mummy's. Boog was thrown backward onto the wooden floor. Her head smacked the ground with a huge, flat thud. She was still. Her face gaped open, her eyes, still open, blinking at Luce.

There was only one way out. The window was three stories high, so they had to make it to the front door, passing Boog. Every inch of Luce's body was pulsing, sweating. She grabbed Roo's hand, and they went, each step the loudest she'd ever taken, and with each one, she prepared to kick out wild if Boog sat up. She nodded at Roo to walk past Boog—there was a berth of about two feet he needed to pass to reach the door, but Boog could lurch up at any second, grab his ankle, anything.

Roo, whimpering, crept forward, almost next to Boog's face, but when they came close, the sounds changed. A squelch, as Roo's foot touched the sticky, wet floor. Surrounding Boog's head was blood.

Luce grabbed Roo's hand and ran out the front door. It didn't matter that she didn't know where to go to keep Roo safe right now, or ever, she just needed to get them out. They had to go fast. She ran down the steps and across the parking lot, holding him tight. Who could they trust? How many people had known about their mother and not told them?

The parking lot's lights cast yellow circles on the asphalt, a swarm of insects fluttering in and out of the beam of light. The person was still in their car, music blaring, as if life were the same as it had been fifteen minutes earlier, a day ago, a week. Luce kept on, close to the car, and then a man stepped out of the shadows, right in front of them. Luce screamed and clutched Roo tighter, jumping backward. Here it was; the next awful thing.

"Whoa whoa whoa," the man said, putting his hands up. "Take it easy. I didn't mean to scare you, sorry." She took a shaky breath, but it was too late, she was scared, terrified, flies buzzing around the lights, darkness hiding the danger, not her darkness in the grove, but the infinity of this open night. She ducked past him and into the car, locking the doors.

Do not wait, do not think, go. She tore out of the parking space, screeching to the edge of the lot where she needed to turn onto the road, but she froze. Where was it safe to go?

For the first time since she'd arrived in the Red Grove, she didn't know.

30

June 30, 1997

"HERE'S WHAT WILL HAPPEN," Luce said, standing on Heartwood's deck. Una was seated in front of her. Morning sun dulled by the wash of fog. Heartwood's deck was dark with damp.

Luce hadn't known where to go, but in the end, there was only one place she could think of. They'd gone home. Roo had slept on Gem's floor, one arm flung over Moose, both of them snoring gently while Luce sat up beside him. She did not want the runaway horse of her heart to slow, she would not loosen her grip on the bone. Everything was different, but still, looking up, she wondered how it was that the moonlight on the ceiling cast the same pearl blue light it always had. She wondered about that, but choked back her mind when it wandered too far, letting the sharp edges of the carved bone in her palm bring her back. There was not much time until morning, when she'd need a plan.

Juan had slept on the couch. She'd told him she wasn't ready to talk yet, but she would be, soon. First, in the morning, she needed to see Una.

"You will leave," Luce said to Una. A woodpecker nearby, hammering in search of breakfast. Una spun a necklace bead as she sometimes did in meditation, but Luce would not be distracted. "Anyone else who was involved in this will leave. Anyone who knew. You'll make up some reason why you are leaving." Streaks of sunbeams through the fog, and Luce could not pause, couldn't go soft, forcing a hardness inside like the giant trees.

"I don't care what reason you give," Luce said, "but it'll have nothing to do with the integrity of the Red Grove. You'll go far away with Boog and the others, and you'll never come back for any reason. If you do this, and do it now, I won't send you to prison. Because you know that if you get sent to prison, and the truth about your secret comes out, nobody will believe it was an accident. I don't think I do. And this whole place will be ruined."

"You wouldn't do that to everyone here," Una said, letting the gemstones of her eyes sparkle, reaching a hand, tentatively, to squeeze Luce's hand. "These are your people."

Luce pulled her hand away. "Try me."

Una's face flashed surprise but quickly shifted. Pulled together in what looked to Luce as a kind of genuine despair. Her shoulders sank, neck softened. "Okay," she said, low and soft. Luce didn't believe her. Some kind of trick. But Una said it again. "Okay. You're right." She said she would take the necessary people with her. Those who knew. Those who were willing to carry the terrible burden of this secret for the greater good, those who—but Luce cut her off.

"Shut up," Luce said. "My mom—" but her voice broke and she couldn't say anything else and so clenched her jaw, bore down with her teeth.

Una took a breath, and then, her fingers clasping together, said she had lived as part of the Red Grove's ecosystem for so long that she wouldn't know how to live anywhere outside of this matrix.

Luce nodded; she didn't doubt that Una believed this.

"Everything I've done has been for the Red Grove. Keeping this from you was a terrible mistake, but surely you can find some softness, sweetheart. You can forgive me?"

"No," Luce said, and did not want to cry, did not realize it was happening until it was too late. Standing in front of her was the person she'd loved as a mother. Who she'd poured herself into, turning away from her own mother. It was too much, to bear that truth.

She wiped at her eyes, imagined a closet filled with severed heads. "No, never."

Luce walked the trail to the new redwood shoots. She passed the redwood wounds she knew so well. Smooth and black inside, cobwebbed. Past the redwoods, the sword fern, over the burrows of unseen things.

Luce had the documents, Una knew that. Luce had the documents, and the fact was she would decide what was best, what to do with them.

And then there was also the fact of her mother's body.

It was sometime deep in the middle of the night, and Luce had a fever. She was eight. Just after Gloria moved back in with Gem and Luce. Drums in Luce's brain, some subterranean world the fever kept her swirling around inside. She had woken around dawn, fever broken, light trickling into the window, feeling the first tether to the earth she'd felt in days. A flicker of movement caught her eye. On the floor, beside her bed, was Gem, in the place she always lay when Luce was very sick. A pillow beneath her head, small blanket across her body. She rolled over, and that's when Luce saw her belly. Huge, pressing beneath the blanket.

It wasn't Gem lying there, watching over her. It was her mother.

Hugely pregnant, on the ground, worried for her. Such a surprising, specific, warm washed over her when she saw who was there. The fact of her body.

Luce stood at the redwood saplings. A billow of wind blew the tiny trees so that they all bowed together, almost toward her.

A sound came from deep in her body. A howl.

She held Tamsen Nightingale's carved bone in her hand, the bone of one of her sisters. It was not heavy. She held it in her open palms, and it stretched from thumb to thumb. The bone and the mummy and the locket and the flies and the clicks, her constellation of aid. Her version of a gift. Not her mother's gift, not Roo's, but her own. The Red Grove had unburied it for her.

What she wanted was to swallow the dirt beneath her feet. One gulp of the earth covering her mother, and this woman who let go of her on a train but then grabbed her again would be inside her, this woman who left but then came back, she came back, she had not chosen to leave.

She put a fistful on her tongue. Iron. Bark. Roses.

How do you say goodbye to your mother?

She swallowed it down. There was nothing to do but swallow it down.

There was a photo of her mother onstage, tap dancing, jazz-fingered, lunging to the left, grinning like a slice of melon, a halo of giant felt flower petals surrounding her face. Always so, so bright, Gloria.

Luce might not ever know the whole story. The true story, the full story, of exactly what her mother had been trying to do. She may never know how things had gone so catastrophically wrong. There was one thing that felt simple and clear, and the truth of it cracked her in half. Gloria had done it for Luce.

Their foreheads skin to skin. The smell of roses. You're mine, her mother had said.

I did not understand it yet, Luce thought. She knew it, could say it now. Fingers rubbing the leftover dirt across her palm.

And you are mine.

Luce took one long breath. As she did, she heard the clicks, felt the shadow of a thing behind her, creeping closer. She held still, afraid to move. The shadow climbed her body as it approached, goose bumps on her legs, her stomach. The cold spreading across her neck. It was right there, right behind her. She knew that in place of a head, it would have a cow's skull. It smelled like sour grass, like plant matter decomposing, like warm dirt recycling leaves. Luce did not turn around. Every muscle was tensed, but she knew not to run. The creature was right behind her, two heads taller than she was. It was bending closer, she could smell it. She could feel the cold on her skin growing deeper as it leaned into her body.

Black shadows climbed the ground as it raised its arms. Still, she would not move, fixed to this place on earth like her mother was, like the bones of Tamsen's sisters, like Ines. The women of the Red Grove whose fates were echoes, all under the dirt.

The soft clicks carried on, closer together, more urgent, and then the arms came down upon Luce's shoulders. Gently, the hands, fingers long as forks, inched themselves across her shoulder blades, her sternum, walking like emaciated animals. She was being pulled closer to the body behind her. The bone still clutched in her fist, Luce did not resist. All those years ago, the fear she felt out on the deck alone at night with the elegant woman, the cow-skull head, felt a great distance away. Her back was against the creature. The arms were wrapped all the way around her, the clicks a crescendo coming through the air above and below and on all sides, and it felt so clear. This was an embrace.

Gem. She had the strongest sensation of Gem, and the decomposing plant smell shifted to pine and sweat and peppermint soap, Gem's smells, and her tenderness. She thought about what her mother had told her again and again, that she wouldn't be able to know, or sometimes recognize, the gifts in her life, and was the cow-skull woman one? Had she always been afraid of the wrong thing?

She clutched the bone and heard the world come back, crows shrieking farther up in the hills, the low hum of crickets in the dry fields. The fact of this body behind her, holding on.

"You can live here," she said to the cow-skull woman, to the clicks, the flies. "Please stay."

How do you say goodbye to your mother? You don't.

31

June 30, 1997

L UCE WENT HOME. Up the wooden steps, across the deck. Moose at the door, wagging his tail. Good boy. She moved slowly, knew what she was heading toward.

Down the hall, passing through the doorway but this time wanting all the smells of this life, urine and sweat and plastics and old tree branches decomposing. She pulled back the blanket, squeezed into bed with Gem. Arms wrapped around Gem's body. She pressed her nose to Gem's neck. Breathed in, held her breath. And when she exhaled, there, finally, she wept.

Gem's chest, beneath her arms, did not rise or fall. Her eyes were closed. The steady beat of her heart, which had thrummed on and on all these years with its magnificent, mysterious perseverance, was stilled.

A faint warmth remained in Gem's body. Luce held on and held on. Thought about when Gem taught her to build fairy traps out of old abalone shells and sticks when they camped by the beach. Gem's stinky breath in the morning, when Luce crawled into bed beside her and pressed their eyelashes together in a butterfly kiss. She held her and cried until she felt emptied out. It was a long time.

Roo came in and stood in the doorway, watching them, and then he understood. Juan peeked around the corner then, too, saw what was happening and started coming over, but Luce shook her head no, and he left them alone. Roo climbed in on the other side and put his arm around Gem and did not cry. Lay there, eyes staring at the ceiling, unblinking.

It was too much, she knew. It was too much for anyone, for kids, for Roo, but here they were. Luce reached her arm across the bed, around him, too. "Mom's not coming back either," he said.

"Roo—" Luce started, trying to find something to say to soften it, contradict it, because how did he know this? His hair was tangled again, and she ran her fingers through it. "She would if she could," Luce said.

"I know that," Roo said. "We're her favorite things."

Luce had wondered how long her aunt could survive without her mother as some kind of tether to the world of the living. She'd guessed it wouldn't be long, and she was right. Just long enough to guide them to what they needed to know.

Later, after they'd unwound themselves from Gem, Juan helped them fold her body in a clean cotton sheet. Light candles. They gathered flowers from the yard, roses and lavender and buttercup, a few sprigs of rosemary, and placed them along Gem's body. It didn't take much conversation for them to agree where she would go.

"Do you remember when we went to the beach, where there was an oil spill a long time ago, and the big lake that connected to the ocean?" Roo asked. Luce said yes, the estuary, where there had once been big hair logs to soak up the spill, and how did he remember that, he'd been a baby. Roo didn't answer her, just went on. It was afternoon, chilly and gray, and they'd shared a jar of dill pickles. "Mama and Gem and you and me." And they'd all buried each other in the sand and given each other sand mermaid tails and seaweed hair, did she remember? She did remember. Roo said, "It was all a great day, but that was my favorite part." What part, Luce wanted to know. "When we were all the same species."

By the next morning, Una was gone.

So were a big handful of other Red Grovers, eight or ten. It was more people than Una had said were involved, though Luce wasn't sure whether that was because Una had lied or had convinced a bigger group to leave so that Luce would never be positive exactly who knew. Maybe, even, there were people who did not think it was worthwhile to live in the Red Grove without Una.

There was still a lot that Roo didn't know. She wasn't sure if she'd ever tell him all of it. It seemed like there were some things better left in the dark. But he did know that their mother and Gem had both died, and that, in a few days, they would need to leave the Red Grove. He knew that a lot of other people were leaving, too, like Boog, first to a hospital to recover and then somewhere farther away, which he was happy about, the way she'd scared him on their adventure, but he didn't know why, not really, not the whole thing. It was a lot for a little kid to take in, and Luce watched him carefully. Told him that soon, as soon as things were a little calmer, they could get another pet. A cat or hamster or fish maybe? Anything he wanted. He nodded, rubbing Moose's belly, asking if Moose thought it was a good plan. Moose narrowed his eyes, rubbed his nose into the ground. Roo reported that Moose said yes, it was a very, very good plan.

———

The next morning, Juan helped them dig a hole right next to where the new redwood saplings had been planted, beside where their mother was buried. She told Juan. Had to. She would not spread it out through the Red Grove to ruin it for everyone, but she could not hold it alone.

Though she knew there were lots of people who would have liked to mourn Gem, Luce did not yet know who to trust, who she could talk to about the last few days. And so it was just Luce, Roo, Gramms, and Juan as they set Gem's shrouded body into the hole. They lowered her body into the ground, covered it in flowers and herbs, and sprinkled dirt onto the cloth, and right away the tiny threaded filaments began growing over her, into her. Receiving her. It wouldn't be long before nature began the work of returning Gem to earth, as her sister was returning beside her.

"Hi, Gem," Roo said, looking up into the trees. "Hi, Mama."

They filled the hole. Chose the new trees to go on top. Gramms asked if anyone wanted to say anything, and Luce did, she wanted to say everything. She needed to, but the muscles in her throat were too tired. She grabbed Roo's hand instead. They looked together at the dirt, at the very small redwood saplings planted over their mother, over their aunt. The trees would grow and grow for a hundred, maybe a thousand years. They would be indestructible.

Juan proposed that they sing "Amazing Grace," but nobody knew the words.

"*Who's afraid of the big bad wolf,*" Roo started humming and then singing, and Gramms chuckled, and Juan looked at them—weird?—but Luce joined him and then they all did.

Was it different now? Luce had been grieving Gem for eight years, since she'd been lost to her everdream. And in some ways she'd been grieving her mother her whole life. So was this different, now that they were dead? She kept wondering, telling herself that it wasn't, even though she felt a new kind of pinching, piercing inside. She thought of the story her mother had told her about the performer Mirin Dajo. Believing himself invulnerable, he pierced holes all the way through his body, sliding swords into the back and out the front. Some moments, when Luce felt the searing and pinching and piercing inside, she wanted to scream, *Help me! Help! I am having a heart attack!* But she didn't. She knew better. It was just her holes, pierced all the way through.

Gramms and Juan both said they wanted to stay with Luce and Roo, but she said no. Not yet. She needed some time to think, pacing the kitchen, cleaning, trying to figure out what came next. She was sure that Gramms and Juan were being nice for the moment, felt obligated to stick around, that before long they would leave.

Luce stared out at the trees, trying to figure out what to have them do. A figure appeared in the doorframe, thin-boned and snuffling, a slow-moving Roo wrapped in a blanket. He shuffled toward her. He'd been crying. Of course he had. His mother was dead. Hers too, but fucking hell, if she could feel triple the pain so that he would have none, she would. Wrapped up like this, his small, puffy face looked so gentle, so eager. He put one sweaty hand on Luce's knee. "How are you doing?" he asked. Heart the size of the ocean, her Roo.

She scooped him up onto her hip and carried him back into his bedroom, the floor scattered with toys and costumes. She set him down, and he spread the blanket out, lay belly-down on top of it, his face smooshed into the rug. She sat down beside him. He was wearing basketball shorts, no shirt, his hair scattershot in all directions. Moose trotted in and lay against Roo's other side. This was Gloria's act. In those rare quiet moments when she'd appear in the doorway as one or the other was getting ready for bed, or when they'd had fevers, in the two weeks they'd been laid out with whooping cough, there she'd be. Her weight on the side of the bed, tilting their small bodies toward her, scratching their backs.

Luce used her fingertips. Gently they brushed across the skin of his back, the fingers trailing with such lightness that it left a trail of goose bumps in its wake. Roo shivered, and she scratched a little harder, watching his breathing even out under her fingers, watching his scrunched frown soften into dream. And then, as Luce lay down beside him, he opened his eyes and nodded at her. "She's okay now," he said. "It's very peaceful in there."

32

July 1, 1997

G RAMMS WAS WORRIED. She told Luce so again and again. "So worried about you two," she said, zipping herself onto Luce as constantly as Luce would let her. Feeling sorry for us, Luce thought, giving us one last dose of pity before she started to disappear—not that Gramms had said as much, but Luce just didn't see any reason why she'd stick around.

But she wouldn't leave. Chain-smoking out on the deck when Luce locked her out. Twiddling her thumbs on the futon once Luce let her back in. She wouldn't intrude if they didn't want her to, Gramms said at first, and then she said, "Eh, fuck it, you can't get rid of me so quick." She asked what she could do for them. And Roo, gazing up at her with his tiny, sad puppy face, said, "Pizza."

She brought over an extra-large everything, hugged them, though it was hard to get a good grip on Roo while he jumped up and down, up and down, clapping and hollering. He picked up a piece and ate it straight down, tossing the crust back into the box. For the next piece, he ate it ingredient by ingredient, first olives and then the green peppers, sausage, onions, pepperoni, topping after topping, a piece at a time so he could build his own stack of ingredients inside, he said, until there was a thin triangle of pockmarked cheese, and then he chomped that down too.

Luce watched Roo, and she saw that Gramms did too, everyone checking to see if he was falling apart, to see what he needed, because how did you get a little kid through the death of his mother, of his aunt, the impending sea change of leaving everything he knew? That's what Luce was most worried about. She'd get to her own grief later. For now, she let him do whatever he wanted. She did not interrupt him when he sat on the velvet chair in the office, little legs sticking straight out, chatting quietly into the unconnected phone.

"I feel so sick," Roo said, picking up the fourth slice of pizza, impossible that it could even fit in his little body. Luce belched in response, her stomach lurching. The pepperoni was so beautiful, perfect circles of pink, like frisbees floating in a slippery orange sea.

Roo slid his hand into hers when they were done with the pizza, and even though his hand was covered in grease and tomato sauce, she let him. She smiled up at Gramms, wanting to make sure she saw that he was okay, that she could leave, but Gramms was looking right at her this time. The smallest little smile on her mouth, wiping a tear with her knuckle.

"Well, you monsters, what do you want next?" Gramms wanted to know. "Television? Vodka? Pop-Tarts?" Dear god how they wanted Pop-Tarts. Also the juice that was so beautifully bright and came in plastic milk jugs, sweet and perfect. And they would get frozen corn dogs. Hot dogs. Eggos. Lunchables. Pizza every day. "If I were president, I would outlaw brussels sprouts," Roo said. "They're disgusting."

"So nasty," Luce agreed.

When Roo went to the bathroom, Luce, in a rush, asked Gramms if she was sad that Una had moved away. They'd lived in the same place for so long, and didn't Una feel almost like Gramms's surrogate daughter after all that time, and did she think she'd eventually follow

Una? Gramms knew the whole story, but everyone else in the Red Grove knew this version: that Una and a handful of others had left on good terms, of their own volition, and that there'd be some good changes coming soon. And that Gloria was gone too, though thank goodness not because of that sketchy man who'd been sniffing around, no, she'd finally landed a role in a theater production, but it was overseas, so she'd be gone, but her family was going to stay.

It had been part of her agreement with Una. Keep the story stitched tight.

"Course I'm sad Una's gone," Gramms said. "She was a good leader, strong and wise. Except when she wasn't. But mostly she was." Luce nodded. Gramms lit a cigarette, and Luce told her about Una's fraud, claiming all those kids as in her care for the money. She thought Gramms would be outraged, but instead she laughed hard, slapping her knee. "That clever, sneaky bitch."

"So you're not mad at me that Una left?" Luce asked. It was a childish thing to ask, but she needed to hear it.

"No, you fool," Gramms said. "I love you little shits." She scraped at a piece of dried cheese on the cardboard, plopped it into her mouth as Roo came back into the room. "I'm not going anywhere, Luce," she said. And Luce would not let herself believe it entirely, but also— this was Gramms. And so she did, a little bit. "What I am is eager to see if you guys like Hawaiian flavor pizza next time. They put pineapple on there with the ham. Pineapple!"

Tangerine, Aya, and Sam showed up at Luce's door that afternoon to check on her, help pack, they said. They didn't know any details, only that Luce's mother was still gone, her aunt had died, and that, for some reason, she and Roo were leaving. They were subdued at first, saying that they were sorry and how much it sucked, blowing bubbles with their gum while staring side-eyed at Luce, who was suddenly more interesting based on her proximity to tragedy and her trajectory into the outside world, though they must have been warned against asking too much. Their eyes traveled around the house like they were searching for clues, but they did not ask about Gloria.

Luce couldn't think about what had happened to her mother. She would not allow herself to imagine the hands of people she had known her whole life being the last thing to touch her mother as she plunged into the earth. As she was pushed? Or as they failed to keep her from falling? She would likely not get to know that part. But what she did know was that the hands of people she'd known and loved had shoveled dirt on top of her mother's body. She could not let herself think about what it meant for so many people to know and then decide to keep this secret. Instead, she sorted through her mother's record collection. Decided which lipstick to keep.

They settled into the living room, this pack of girls, unfurling themselves on the couch, the floor, trailing their limbs over half-packed boxes and falling into normal overlapping conversation soon enough. Aya fiddled with a paper clip, straightening the tight bends and then folding it into a soft arc around her teeth. Pretend braces. The other girls did the same. They talked about nothing, about eternal love, about nipple hair, who had the most or least, about Peter Rosenthal's new Prince Albert piercing, about the star sapphire Tangerine wanted, about how Aya had been hooking up with a newcomer and thought they were falling in love. "That's called lust," Tangerine said, and Aya kicked her, smiling.

Luce knew that she and Roo couldn't stay in the Red Grove. They couldn't be in this place she knew to be false, where this horror had happened. She would rent them an apartment somewhere, with matching plates and mugs. Maybe she would even find a friend of her mother's from before their days in the Red Grove, someone who had known and loved Gem, too, and they would go live with her and her husband and their two children for a while, until Luce turned eighteen. And she would have nice kids who did karate and football, and there would be a spare room with bunk beds all ready for them, no problem at all, and a high school with a biology lab and dissection tools and a greenhouse for growing carnivorous plants.

Outside, roses baked in the midday midsummer sun. "I'm too hot," Sam said, and stripped down to her underwear. "I guess I'm getting used to it here," she said, laughing as she let her legs splay in frayed underwear, hints of dark hair feathering out from her inner thighs. "I've been riding one of the horses on the ranch, Prince Cassian, taking long rides up in the hills, by the freaky red-rimmed trees. He's a beauty, but he's giving me rashes." She was rubbing along the inside of her thigh. Aya stripped down too, to show off her weird butt tan lines, Tangerine told Sam to put lip gloss on the rash to stop the itch, their world rolling forward in familiar orbits, and how strange that was, and how right.

Luce could tell them the truth about the Red Grove, everything that had happened to her mom and the true history she'd learned from the transcribed documents. It would give them the gift of full knowledge.

She could, and she might. She thought about it, taping boxes, listening. The girls splayed and hunched and passed a joint, and maybe she should, she might, she wasn't sure, the girls squeezing Luce's hand when she passed nearby, planting star stickers beside her eyes when they glowed with tears.

33

July 2, 1997

T HEY HAD THEIR MOTHER'S CAR—it had been parked in a nearby town, hidden, Una had eventually explained—and were driving away from the Red Grove. Piled high in the back seat were trash bags full of clothes, blankets, a box with plates and forks, their record player. They'd grabbed all that they could from the house, knowing they were leaving a lot, too much. Knowing also that there was no way to carry everything forward, that the heaviness was too much to bear.

What they had was a car pointed northeast, toward Sacramento, driving in the slow lane because every now and then Luce fantasized about taking the next exit, finding a pay phone, and making a call that would send other cars, their lights flashing, barreling toward the community. She could do that. She could, still. Cops with their bull-horns out, ready to dig up her mother.

But then all the other women, all the other people of the community. It was thinking about where they would go.

The community had failed her and Roo, but it had not failed everyone.

———

She drove on, tapping the steering wheel with a nervous twitch. Roo licked a pink smear of Pop-Tart goo from his finger, one of the many supplies Gramms had wedged into the car as they'd packed. How would she raise him all by herself? How would she do it with all this ache? She would learn that the loss doesn't go away. It lives in you, with you, a snake around your throat, and—this is the secret nobody tells you—the coils don't let go. You just learn to live with your ghosts.

Moose's nose twitched out the window, taking in the new smells as the redwoods were behind them, the coastal fog disappearing into the rearview mirror as they drove higher into the foothills, past the spread of live oaks and a cluster of buzzards winging one another toward a deer carcass, past an empty high school, a shopping mall, and as the air grew drier and hotter against the car, Roo kept his eyes trained out the window, taking in the new shapes of the world.

They stayed in a Motel 6 in Sacramento while they looked for an apartment. The stink of bleach, old smoke, the plastic feel of the blanket. That's just a person, Luce would tell herself when they passed a man who looked at them a little too long, when someone hollered out a car window at her. She started to throw her middle finger in the air at the car, gut reaction, but caught herself before she'd gone all the way. Hell, what did she know about how those sorts of things were reacted to out here? This was the land of the statistics.

She'd taken her mom's shoebox of money from her closet, but even with that, matching dinnerware was stupidly expensive. Every apartment building they could afford had at least one skeezy-looking guy lurking nearby. The screens affixed to the windows were torn or easy to pop out if someone wanted to break in, and the sun, without the cover of trees, scalded their scalps. Still. "This could be nice," she told Roo as they toured apartments. "We could make it okay."

Roo didn't talk much, said, monotone, he liked each place the same amount, but where would he ride his bike? Or catch frogs? And did she really think Moosey would be okay out here? And how would they know what kind of pizza to order without Gramms, and didn't she think Juan would miss them?

Late at night, Roo shook her awake. She gasped, asked what was wrong, her heart racing, feeling around for the carved bone she kept beneath the pillow. Roo said, whispering, that it was too quiet. Luce listened. Roar of truck on the highway, car door slamming in the parking lot, TV murmurs from the room next door. This was the loudest place they'd ever lived, she told him.

"No, not like that," he said. "I can't hear things out here. I can't hear her."

They stayed six nights, then she drove them back.

Much later, Luce and Roo are crouched between their old wooden garden beds, overrun with weeds at the moment. Luce has not kept the plants watered, and so as they've wilted, the dry-loving filaree, foxtail, and mallow have sprouted up and grown fast, overtaking the tomatoes.

Neither Luce nor Roo is looking at the garden, though. They are staring down at the ground between them, where a small box turtle is hiding in its shell. Roo extends his hand toward the turtle's head. He is holding a slice of apple, making kissy sounds with his mouth.

Above them, their old deck creaks in the shadows of the redwood trees. They glance up, catch a wave from Gramms as she finishes her cigarette before she turns back into the house—she's promised meat loaf tonight, which they've only read about, a sort of compressed square of hamburger allegedly; they can't wait. And then there's the faintest click from the window above the garden, and Luce looks up. She can make out the silhouette of the mummy perched on a chair,

melon head long discarded and replaced with a soccer ball, a photograph taped on its surface: Gloria's and Gem's faces up close, cheek
to cheek, their eyes sparkling into the camera.

Under Luce's and Roo's feet, moles dig between the interwoven
blanket of roots, dead matter relaxes back into the earth. Juan, his
hands around his mouth, hollers up at Luce and Roo from the bottom of the cracked driveway. "I'm about to patch up my moon mask—
got kinda broken last time. Want me to patch up either of yours
before tonight?"

"Nah," Luce tells him—theirs are in good shape.

"Anyway, you may not need yours anymore, Goose," he says.
"Una didn't always wear one."

Luce shrugs. She hasn't decided how much to keep the same,
what to change.

Clouds passing overhead shadow her face. There is so much to
untangle. The mess of kids Una was claiming. What story to tell in
the reenactments. Who to tell the whole truth—

Juan waved, turned to walk back down the hill.

For tonight, she is going to try something new. She'd been practicing with a few of the kids. They'd focus the story on one regular
week in the life of the women, call it "The Story of the Sisters," Tamsen and Ines and the others working together to plant a garden, to
make peace with mountain lions—a story about how they built community. About the people doing the work of caring for one another.
She wouldn't dispel the protective myth—not yet, probably not
ever—but maybe she could redirect the wonder.

She isn't sure the people will like it, with so much less drama and
violence. But she'll try. They'll try it.

Una had left a note. In her absence, the next leader was to be Luce
Shelley.

And Luce, calling a community gathering right away, said that
her first and only announcement as leader was that they'd all vote to

elect a council to run this place. And, looking across at these faces, taking in who actually lived here, listening, yes, listening to the women she loved and also the men, not just to the stories of horror but also the stories of love, she said that while the council would remain majority women, they'd always have at least one man.

She has a small stack of catalogs on the kitchen table, their covers showing students smiling on wide lawns, laughing in the shade of big trees. There are three community colleges within driving distance. She will bring those catalogs to a meeting soon as well. That and the other list of ideas she's been compiling—Amish quilts, Mennonite furniture, the isolated group out in Utah who farm lavender. They could make a business. They could give, connect beyond the boundary. Be seen.

She had been trying to explain the whole thing to herself, to imagine how she might one day tell the story to someone else. But there was no clarifying moment of insight, no revelation that she'd been wrong to be afraid of the outside world. All that she knew about serial killers and rapists and human traffickers and pedophiles, all the suffering she'd heard women tell about their own lives at reenactments, all of it was still true. It was real. What had happened to Gem was real.

And what was also true was that out past the boundary of the Red Grove, there were college psychology courses—ha, she could probably use a few of those—and aquariums with real beluga whales and the salt flats of Utah and wild horses on some island in North Carolina and billions of people, and most of them—not all, but most—would not hurt you.

The turtle pokes his head halfway out the shell. Roo squeals. "Did you hear him?" Roo asks, looking up at Luce's face. She raises her eyebrows, strains an ear toward the turtle. Roo adds, "He said, 'I'm starving.'"

"Well, I guess we need more apples," she says, and he looks up at her, his grin as wide as a frog's. Above them, three flies buzz in slow, drowsy circles, and above that, a jay dives for a dragonfly, and farther up still, higher than the mats of moss in the canopy, on the highest point of the closest hill, a mountain lion swivels her ear toward them, listening, then walks on, yawning, toward the shadow ahead.

ACKNOWLEDGMENTS

I am immensely grateful to the vibrant community of writers, readers, and beloveds who have shaped and supported this book, and me, in every way. Writing can be lonely business. You all keep me just the right amount of weird.

Thank you to the following people who engaged with this novel through reading or conversation: Alex McWalters, Danilo John Thomas, Dara Ewing, Heather Newton, Jesse Delong, Jessica Jacobs, Jessica Richardson (x2!), Joe Sacksteder, Latria Graham, Mary Edith Burrell, Tom Cotsonas, the Flatiron Writers, the Accountability Workshop writers, who keep me on my toes, and, really, anyone I've talked to about writing in the last four years and said some version of "I definitely cannot write this novel," and you said some version of "I think you probably can."

Thank you to the institutions that supported my writing life during the creation of this book: the Virginia Center for the Creative Arts, the Sewanee Writers' Conference, Warren Wilson College, and Tin House's Next Book Residency.

Every book is in conversation with its predecessors; I am grateful to these authors especially: Shirley Jackson, Toni Morrison, Gabriel Tallent, Leni Zumas, Lauren Groff, Ross Gay, Li-Young Lee, Bessel van der Kolk, Jacqueline Rose, Suzanne Simard, and Mary Shelley.

Ellen Levine, agent I admire; Jenna Johnson, editor I adore, who trusted that I would find my way with this book: thank you, thank you. And thanks, too, to the wonderous team at FSG: Lianna Culp, Janine Barlow, Sara Wood—who designed the book's beautiful cover—and all the other hands behind the scenes who make our stories into books.

To the Hot Moms Writing Club, aka the Dog Pound, aka the Mothers of Destruction, Annie Hartnett, Clare Beams, and Rufi Thorpe: boundless gratitude and admiration; I am learning how to be a writer in the world from you. And Annie, especially, business wife who always has the best jokes—thank you.

For friendships that sustain me, for brilliance that dazzles: Devin Gribbons, Anna Welton, and AB Gorham. My tree's roots.

And my family, always: Davy, Sam, Dad, Nico, and my mom, Teresa, who is no longer alive and yet is alive in every single sentence I write.

Thank you to Jeremy, whose love and support make this all possible. And to Leela, whose arrival has made everything new again. And to coffee, for helping us survive Leela's arrival.

And finally, thank you to the women who told me about how they thought their lives might be different if they were never afraid. I wish it for you.

A Note About the Author

Tessa Fontaine is the author of *The Electric Woman: A Memoir in Death-Defying Acts*, which was named a *New York Times Book Review* Editors' Choice and a best book of the year by *Southern Living*, *Refinery29*, and the *New York Post*. Her writing can be found in *Outside*, *Glamour*, *Agni*, and *The Believer*. She has been a sideshow performer, shoe saleswoman, and professor, and she taught for years in jails and prisons. She cofounded and runs the Accountability Workshops with the writer Annie Hartnett. Raised among the redwoods of Northern California, she now lives in Asheville, North Carolina, with her husband, daughter, goofy dog, and sassy cat.